Praise for *War Torn*

"As the former Berlin bureau chief for *U.S. News & World Report*, Marks knows the political geography of post–Cold War Europe intimately. What's surprising is that he's just as adept at mapping out the emotional topography of living, breathing beings. [A] reporter's ear for detail and [a] deft, nonlinear narrative." —*Entertainment Weekly*

"This complex, beautifully savage novel is well named, for every character in it is torn between past and present, between the promise of an adoptive country and the pull of a ruined homeland. Former *U.S. News* Berlin bureau chief Marks posits that the collapse of communism ('the greatest hangover of the twentieth century') in 1989 was but a prelude to yet another European apocalypse . . . and illustrates his thesis in harrowing fashion. Marks's rendering of the period pulls no punches . . . and every principle is wrenched between flickering and insubstantial poles. Like a latter-day Herman Wouk or Irwin Shaw, he writes with unabashed romanticism and passionate intensity." —*Publishers Weekly*

"Marks's five years as Berlin correspondent for *U.S. News & World Report* come across undeniably in the tone of international news correspondence that permeates his prose. Marks obviously enjoys the increased literary real estate offered by the novel format, and delivers generous passages of poetic description." —*Rocky Mountain News*

"Marks . . . has written a heartfelt and engrossing narrative that reads like a thriller but carries a great deal more significance. He's excellent at both the heartrending details of individual human tragedy and the larger considerations of what it takes to tear a city apart—and make it whole again. Writing about war can be tricky—is one exploiting human suffering?—but Marks instead illuminates. And he earns the note of hope at the end. Highly recommended." —*Library Journal*

Praise for *The Wall*
A *New York Times* Notable Book

"Places the reader in the vortex of the Cold War endgame in Eastern Europe . . . The story is captivating and reminds us that although each side of the Cold War was guided by strategy, it was still a time of individual choices: to defect, to hold one's ground, to believe in one side or the other, to be ideologically agnostic. *The Wall* entertains while effectively exploring such choices buoyed by the drama of history."

—*The New York Times Book Review*

"Marks handles his involved story line with assurance. His success in conveying the deeper truths beneath the headlines results in an intelligent, memorable, and thoroughly engaging debut."

—*Publishers Weekly* (starred review)

"Insightful . . . gripping . . . [Marks] manages to capture perfectly the heady mixture of hope and fear surrounding the collapse of the East German government in 1989." —*Chicago Tribune*

"[Marks has] a reporter's eye for detail and . . . a true novelist's flair. *The Wall* is superior entertainment, and the work of a resourceful and intelligent writer who uses his experience of these events to comment on the fate of post-Soviet Europe, and the hold its troubled past still has upon an uncertain future." —*Pittsburgh Tribune-Review*

WAR TORN

JOHN MARKS

RIVERHEAD BOOKS

New York

Riverhead Books
Published by The Berkley Publishing Group
A division of Penguin Group (USA) Inc.
375 Hudson Street
New York, New York 10014

Copyright © 2003 by John Marks
Book design by Amanda Dewey
Cover design by Ben Gibson

First Riverhead hardcover edition: November 2003
First Riverhead trade paperback edition: October 2004
Riverhead trade paperback ISBN: 1-59448-036-2

The Library of Congress has catalogued the Riverhead hardcover
edition as follows:

Marks, John, date.
War torn / John Marks.
p.   cm.
ISBN 1-57322-254-2 (alk. paper)
1. Journalists—Fiction.   2. Former Yugoslav republics—
Fiction.   3. Americans—Foreign countries—Fiction.   I. Title.
PS3563.A66655W37   2003   2003055110
813'.54—dc21

Printed in the United States of America

10 9 8 7 6 5 4 3 2 1

FOR JOE

Accordingly, since things are changeable and can never be at rest, what man in his right mind will deny that the wise man ought, as I have said, to depart from them to that city which stays at rest and abides to all eternity? This is the City of God, the heavenly Jerusalem, for which the children of God sigh while they are set in this land of sojourn, oppressed by the turmoil of the things of time as if they were oppressed by the Babylonian captivity. For inasmuch as there are two cities—the one of time, the other of eternity; the one of the earth, earthly, the other of heaven, heavenly; the one of the devil, the other of Christ—ecclesiastical writers have declared that the former is Babylon, the latter Jerusalem.

OTTO OF FREISING

Lord of the Two Easts
Lord of the Two Wests
Oh which of your Lord's bounties will you and you deny?

THE KORAN

BOOK I

UNIFICATION

ONE

STEPPING OUT of his apartment building, pausing an instant to listen for the thick metal doors to click—and lock—behind him, Arthur Cape caught a blast of rain in the face. The storm was far worse than he'd imagined. He wiped his eyes with gloved hands. He bent over to stretch the hems of his blue jeans down to the ankles of his ostrich-skin cowboy boots.

A few yards from his door, a chestnut tree had fallen into the street. Blue lights flashed atop police cars. Maintenance crews swarmed. In front of Arthur, in the street, buffeted by wind, stood a heavy man with a pale, round face. The face looked familiar and strange at the same time, the features of someone Arthur had known but could no longer name. The man stared at him, and for a moment Arthur froze.

The stranger squeezed between two small cars, one French, one German, parked at right angles to the curb. His hair hung to his shoulders, concealing everything but the inner gleams of two dark eyes, a cavernous nose, and thick, parted lips. He raised a white chop of hand in greeting. Arthur felt the glimmer of familiarity between them, the unmistakable surge of a connection. But he couldn't nail it down, and this sensation frightened him for reasons that he didn't quite understand. He felt an urge to run.

No one else seemed to notice the man. People on the street, on their way to the warmth of the Portuguese café at the corner of Apostel-Paulus-Strasse and Akkazien-Strasse, either kept their heads down against the storm or stole a glance at the smashed chestnut. The crews broke out chain saws, and the cops blocked the end of Apostel-Paulus with cones. Drivers leaned on horns. The tree had thrashed down onto a row of recycling bins and scared the hell out of a heroin junkie, but otherwise its demise hadn't harmed a soul. Arthur looked at it for a second. When he glanced back, the stranger between the cars had gone.

H E H U R R I E D L E F T down Apostel-Paulus-Strasse. Anna's apartment lay six blocks away, but it would seem like a mile in this weather. Air howled, rattling jalousies, hoisting trash cans. It was an hour before midnight, and western Berlin lay under a cyclonic siege.

Arthur peered over his shoulder, thinking to catch another glimpse of the face. It could have been one of the Bosnians from the ground floor of his building. They had moved into the room he was passing at that very moment, the studio to his left, formerly a copy shop, three adults and two children, from Banja Luka. One of them was an older man, but he could not be described as overweight or unkempt. Of course, the flash of police lights, the blur of storm, might have distorted his vision. That was possible.

Arthur paused a moment, listening. Rain sheeted onto the pavement. Voices receded. He had a sense of isolation, as if curtains had closed around him. Then he experienced a certainty. Someone close to him had died. A gust of wind stung his eyes, and he snapped the collar of his coat up, regretting that he had worn his boots. They were already soaked.

As a journalist, Arthur worked more by intuition than observation; certain phenomena haunted him, and he pursued them until they coalesced into stories. Hampton, his senior colleague, called it "copy conjuring." Arthur did not like this term. It made him feel like a fraud. But he understood what Hampton meant. He was sensitive to invisible strands. The stranger in the street had news for him. Such messengers were called revenants; it was wartime in Europe, and revenants were walking the land.

H E   T U R N E D into Merseburgerstrasse, boot heels skidding across black, wet exposed brick. He shouldn't have worn the boots, but when he wore them, Anna called him her *grosse Texaner,* and he liked it. Apartment buildings rose six stories on either side of him, like the walls of an arroyo.

It was cold, but he thought warm thoughts. Anna would be wearing her little black party dress, and she would have been dancing for hours, perspiring, drinking goblets of sangria. She would look sexy as hell. She would smell like sex itself. She would want to go into the closet. The party would last till dawn.

He spun around. An old woman trailed him with a dachshund. Her eyes widened in fear.

"Was ist denn los?" she asked Arthur with palpable anxiety.

"Nichts," replied Arthur, shaking his head in dismay, apologizing. *"Tut mir Leid."*

She hurried her animal away. But Arthur lingered, peering back down Merseburger toward his own street. He saw a figure there, where the Apostel-Paulus-Strasse flowed past his line of vision, the shape of a big round man limned by the intermittent flashing of police lights. The women in Arthur's family had inklings when people died, but Arthur never had before. He thought of war again. Not so long ago, war had been here, too, in this street. One could still find bullet holes in the walls. Bones must still lie beneath the concrete under his feet, a thousand restless ghosts for every inch of Berlin. But no, he saw, it was nothing. The shape of the man became a series of shapes, clumps of people moving, like Arthur, against the rain and darkness.

T HE WAR IN the Balkans upset Arthur. Maybe it was that he had never been so close to a war before. Vietnam had been on television until he was thirteen or fourteen. His uncle had flown a chopper there, but the war had never been real. Or maybe it was that he felt guilty and ashamed that he had not been sent to cover the fighting in the Balkans, the biggest story in Europe, or that he had not put up more of a fight for the job. Maybe it was the children who lived on the ground floor of his apartment building and had lost their mother. The super in the building, a Bosnian who had lived in Berlin for many years, had told him that the mother had been murdered before their eyes. The children were becoming beggars.

Tears welled into his eyes. It was Marta. For an instant, he felt blind on the street. He fought back by telling himself that he would get very drunk on sangria. He would dance. His woman would do a flamenco to her favorite song, a one-hit wonder by Maxine Nightingale. After drinking, dancing, and maybe fucking, he would sit on the floor and listen to the war correspondents. Eric Hampton would be there. His colleague Hampton had left Sarajevo at the beginning of the week and promised to be in Berlin for the party. He never missed Anna's Halloweens, unparalleled opportunities to network and schmooze, though Hampton wouldn't have put it quite that way. Arthur loved to listen to Hampton. He covered war zones with aplomb and rage, as if thirty years of being escorted down ministerial halls had made him immune to bullets but not to their effects. He took Bosnia as his cause. He called for the return of Margaret Thatcher and invoked the Spanish Civil War. He talked about the two cities, an idea borrowed from Saint Augustine, applied to everything; the city of God, the city of man; *la cité réel, la cité ideal;* city of facts, city of fictions; and on and on, divided, burning cities running through every aspect of his thought.

Arthur turned into Wartburgstrasse and stood at Anna's door. He stared up at the façade and was struck by overwhelming sorrow. The façade had been annihilated in the Second World War and replaced by a sheet of poured gray concrete, dead lines from the top of the building to the street, interrupted at intervals by balconies. He started to ring the buzzer but hesitated. The feeling of dark presence would not go away. It was Marta, a voice kept telling him. Something had happened to Marta. How could he go to a Halloween party?

Lots of American expats threw Halloween parties, but Anna, a German, had a reputation for throwing the very best that the city of Berlin had ever seen. She knew everyone who mattered. As a press flack for the city's cultural ministry, she had lots of government contacts. So the bureaucrats came. As a lapsed performance artist, she had countless artistic and intellectual friends who worked on hundreds of different, well-funded projects: cabaret singers, memoirists, unpublished metaphysical philosophers, avant-garde composers, adherents of fluxus and situationism, constructivists, minimalists, lots of video and Internet pioneers, though no conventional painters or sculptors, never any of these.

Also in attendance would be the two strands of her father's side of the family, members of the local German aristocracy and civil servants of the former East Germany, two mutually hostile groups from different branches of the von Hakenberg line, torn asunder by population relocations at the end of the Second World War and rejoined uneasily by German Unification. Anna's cousin Günther, a former East German interpreter and self-confessed paid informant for the government security apparatus, was her particular favorite. For the last three years, he had helped her make her celebrated pumpkin pies.

Through Anna's mother came a fair number of boozy, chain-smoking, hard-living filmmakers of the 1960s generation, men who

had had romantic ties of one kind or another with Fran von Hakenberg, who had come to Berlin in 1961, married and divorced Nikolai
von Hakenberg, slept with a lot of cinematographers, then died of
lung cancer before Anna turned five.

Finally, there were the journalists. As a gorgeous twenty-eight-
year-old brunette who spoke perfect English as well as German,
Anna had been the most popular interpreter and fixer for the English-
language press during the months of revolution and upheaval in
1989, when the Berlin Wall fell and the world changed. Every news
organization in the world had come to the city and set up shop.
Arthur himself had been part of that vast rolling wave. Hundreds of
hacks had stayed, though most of them now spent their time down
south, covering the Bosnian War, unlike Arthur, who followed the
fighting from a distance but had never received an assignment from
his magazine to go there and had never asked for one. His colleague
Hampton owned that story, and Arthur respected deeply the lines of
authority within the camps of *Sense* magazine. Also, he was afraid of
dying. Journalists had been killed down there.

Anna had thrown open the French doors of her balcony, the only
way to cool off the rooms, packed to overload with hundreds of
people, and Arthur could hear the spirit of the party. He could hear
people talking about Belgrade, Auschwitz, and New York. Drumbeats
pounded the background like a cannon. He could hear Russians.

History engulfed Berlin. This is what Arthur felt. History engulfed
the city—in every conversation and every street name, in each café,
in every bland wall. Marta had left him in this place, where he didn't
belong. Thanks to her, he had never been able to leave the city.
Thanks to her, he had drifted to Anna, the substitute, the ersatz, the
child of East and West. Before that division, her Nazi grandfather had
shaken Field Marshal Hermann Göring's hand; and before that, the
family name dated back seven centuries, into the world of knights
and nobility. There was a ruined castle in Saxony. What a bore for
Anna! But it secretly thrilled Arthur. Anna slid through history like

an eel through dark waters. Arthur was a child of Dallas, Texas, a place not much older than the first radio; the oldest thing in Dallas, Texas, was a log cabin, and it was a fake.

Arthur pressed the door buzzer and waited. He rang again. No one heard him.

"Goddammit!" he shouted up at the balcony. "Will someone please let me in?"

THE DOOR TO the apartment hung open. Dragon breath steamed out, smelling of cigarettes. Arthur tried to push inside, but masked, reeling human beings barred his way. He gently pressed the crowd, trying to dislodge it, but nothing gave. Conversations would not break up. A photojournalist in a ponytail described how his car, his flak jacket, and his blood supply had been taken from him at gunpoint outside Velika Kladusa. His entire fucking blood supply! And the prick didn't even bother to ask the type! There was heated discussion of a new Italian restaurant in Kreuzberg. Delicious homemade orechiette, superb Florentine ice cream, but the wine list! Jesus Christ! And then the cost of a square meter of living space, the lousiness of dentists, the inconvenience of shopping hours, the nastiness of Berliners, the laziness of eastern Germans, the arrogance of western Germans, the violence of Russians, the dumbness of Americans. Arthur recognized an Eric von Stroheim in drag, monocled and lipsticked. He saw Hamlet in leotards and leopard-skin vest, an architect designing public toilets in the French classical style, Hans something, who cackled at Marlene Dietrich in authentic fishnet hose and bowler. Beyond them, two British diplomats affiliated with the Leipzig mission bickered about the flaws in the European Exchange Rate Mechanism.

At last, Arthur said, "Excuse me," and for no particular reason, a way opened. He embarked on a systematic room-to-room search for his girlfriend. One long corridor ran the length of Anna's place. Two wide, high-ceilinged bedrooms fed off the right. The kitchen, the bathroom, and a last extra-large bedroom branched to the left. Anna's bedroom, to the immediate right, had been converted into a dance floor. He peeked in. Jack-o'-lanterns glimmered against windowsills. Candlelit candy corn and Fritos, courtesy of someone's American PX card, glowed in golden bowls. Between the tables, in the middle of the room, citizens of the unified city of Berlin swayed and roamed to a Germanic hip-hop dirge blasting out of Japanese speakers.

A babe bounced into his vision. She wore a flouncy black party dress and a witch's peaked hat. Her eyes shone with moist rims. She closed in on him, her skin reeking of nutmeg and sangria.

"I came as fast as I could," he began.

"My Texan!" Anna threw herself into his arms, and he understood that she wasn't wearing underwear. They kissed. She looked into his eyes. "You okay?"

"Please tell me they haven't played Maxine Nightingale yet."

"Three times!"

"I'm sorry I'm so late. The Heidegger story."

Her eyes sparkled. "*Egal.* You wore your boots. That's all that counts."

They kissed again, and the gloom of the street started to lift. He needed sangria. She got out of his arms and led him by the hand through the hordes to the bathtub, heaped with bottles of *sekt*, sangria, and beer, stuck like ships in the ice. Arthur heard his nickname, "Look at that! The Aryan decided to show." Arthur stood six foot two, with big shoulders, blond hair, and blue eyes, so Anna's artistic friends had taken to calling him her Aryan, which pissed him off but made it impossible for him to respond. If he so much as glowered, her German friends said, "Beware the master race!"

They drank sangria together and kissed some more against the bathroom wall. "I want to take you into my closet right now," she whispered into his ear. "You look cowboy good."

But Arthur wasn't quite there yet. He had the urge, in the midst of the revelry and heat, to tell her about his apparition. She bit his shoulder hard.

"I saw something," he stammered. She took his hand and put it between her legs. "I think I saw, like, a ghost."

"It's Halloween. Of course you did."

"No."

"Into the coats and sweaters, " she said. "You need a fuck."

Arthur dropped his cup of sangria into the tub of ice and allowed himself to be tugged into the corridor and toward the back of the apartment, where her closet lay. He glanced back over his shoulder and felt sick to his stomach. Anna's hand slipped out of his fingers.

The man was overweight and red-faced, his mouth and chest heaving as he leaned against one wall. The trip up five floors of steps seemed to have devastated him. His long black hair cascaded down one side of his face, concealing everything but the wide-holed nose, the parted lips, the dark familiar eyes. He wore a black leather jacket, a size too small, over a florid white Italian shirt, as well as a pair of offensively tight black leather pants. Within his jacket, clearly visible in a shoulder holster, was a nine-millimeter pistol.

Arthur shoved his way toward the back of the apartment. He came to the end of the corridor, Anna's closet. He could hide in there. Had she gone inside? Where the hell was she?

To Arthur's right lay her office, a sparsely furnished room with an Art Deco desk and two sets of wire shelves. Storm wind bumped against the open French doors. Here was the civilized corner of the party. People held wine in cups and chatted in the glare of halogen lights.

To Arthur's left, the darkness deepened in the last of the bedrooms, the space where the performance artists staged their events. An Austrian dropped her kimono and began to play the banjo in the candlelit gloom. Her body had been fashioned in the school of Egon Schiele, sharp curvings of bone, adamantine breasts, a musculature suggesting anguish and extremity. Arthur recognized the Nietzschean tattoo, the words, *Gotzen umwerfen*—"overthrow the Gods"—inscribed in black Gothic lettering on the delta fanning out from her vagina; Anna had dragged him to her show at the Bar Jeder Vernunft several times, and the Austrian—Gisele was her name—had explained to the audience that the line had been lifted from Nietzsche's *Ecce Homo,* a work written beyond the wings of sanity, in that twilight period before the philosopher collapsed on a street in Turin. Anna had told Arthur that Gisele had moved to Bulgaria and taken up with an arms dealer. But here she was again, stone naked in a haze of folk music. Her nipples gleamed like silver bullets. She drew a crowd, young German lesbians and aged American photojournalists clapping in time. She sang in accented English, "Takes a worried man to sing a worried song," while a scene from a low-budget Spanish horror film looped on the television set beneath her chair; Knights Templar hacked at a nude girl on a rack.

The song ended, and the Austrian looked right into Arthur's eyes.

"Someone's following you," she said.

Arthur staggered backwards into the corridor, and Anna tackled him. She caught him around the neck and kissed him hard. She pressed him into her closet and pulled the door shut behind them. She unbuttoned his trousers with an urgency that thrilled and worried him.

"Did you see the guy with the gun?" He wanted a very short pause, a breath, to obtain serious information.

"He's in costume!" she rasped.

She raised her arms, and he lifted her dress over her head and hoisted her high. The door banged open. She gave a moan of disintegrating pleasure, a wildly horny woman feeling suddenly and catastrophically ill. She lurched back into the sweaters. Arthur stood a moment, her calves in his hands, erect in the darkness, wondering what to do. Outside, in the hall, dim lights shone, hundreds of eyes, gleaming yellow, forest creatures peering at his lover's bare legs, his

Aryan tumescence. He was a satyr. There was applause. He slammed the door shut. His lover had passed out.

H E M A D E A B E D of sweaters for Anna and covered her in coats and mufflers. He cracked the closet door and waited until the crowd outside had found other entertainments. Then he crept into the room of conversations and set his back against a wall. His head dropped into his hands. This was wrong. Worlds were colliding. War had come to the party, in the form of a ghost, a specter. He could not stop thinking of Marta, but he was aroused by Anna and afraid for his life. It's too much, he thought; one more element and my mind will explode. It will ignite like a grenade. He felt sick again. He felt exhausted. Anna wouldn't miss him if he left now. He should slither off between the legs of the revelers, a snake on his belly, and make for the front door. He heard a familiar voice, speaking familiar words.

"A question," Eric Hampton was saying. "What divides the Europe where we're standing from the Europe that is burning? Berlin from Bosnia?"

"Guns," answered an American woman.

"There are guns in Berlin, too."

"Not really."

"Not now, you mean."

She laughed. "But that's everything."

"It's nothing. Fifty years. And fifty years is nothing in the life of the race."

The storm banged at the open French doors. Folk music played in the room across the corridor. Dance beats thumped in the dimness beyond.

"It seems to me that you're being precocious," she said.

"That's because you're an American," Hampton replied with superiority, "and I'm a European. We don't see time the same way."

"You work for an American magazine, I'll remind you."

"That's true. I love Americans. But it doesn't change the fact."

She laughed. "Oh no? Are you telling me that when you report the Bosnian story that you don't take into account little niceties like chronology? Is that it?"

"No such thing. But I do remind my readers—and my editors, for that matter—that this is a continent only just recovering from horror. That was yesterday, and on the morning after, with one good night's rest, we wake up and find the horror again, flickering in a dusty corner, true, but alive. Very much alive."

This sobered the dialogue. "I see your point, but it's still a bit esoteric, and it doesn't change my thoughts on intervention. I simply don't agree with you. We cannot drop bombs on Belgrade. That might bring about exactly the crisis that you fear. Besides, history or no, this whole thing looks to me like a street fight in a bad neighborhood."

Arthur could almost see a mordant smile crossing Hampton's lips. It was the just the sort of remark he longed for. "It could be your neighborhood tomorrow. It wasn't long ago and could be again. In every city on this earth, there is a second city, its mirror, waiting to be born, my dear. Even in your Los Angeles, in New York, there is another metropolis deep inside, and it looks nothing like the one in the postcards. Nothing at all. I can assure you."

She sighed. "You make it sound so inevitable, Eric, like time itself. But it's not, is it?" She paused, but her temper was up. Hampton had a talent for infuriating people. "I know what's going on here. You miss the Cold War." Arthur could almost see the woman's blazing eyes. "You really miss it, don't you?"

"I miss its vast application."

The words had a wounded sound. Arthur drew the coat tighter around his body.

"Just explain that to me," she demanded.

"Between 1948 and 1989, the world had a shape. Elegant. Like an egg. You could see it and write about it, even if it was an illusion. You could act on it as if it were a principle. And do you know, at the same time, I'm just now realizing—"

"What, Eric? And then I have to pee."

"There was always this bloody shadow, this Bosnia, the antithesis of shape, the chaos on the waters. A horrifying thought. But that's my point. The entire world is waiting to turn inside out. A whole civilization of ruptured cities. To stop it, we must do the paradoxical. We must bomb Belgrade and stop the infection at the source. My fellow Englishmen may not approve. War has made us reticent about the virtuous uses of ordnance. But as an American, I expect you to show some fortitude. We must send an unequivocal message. Bomb the Serbs. Suppress the dark."

"Too late," said a third voice, interrupting the conversation. "Dark is motherfucking here."

"Jesus!" cried the woman. "That's a real gun!"

Arthur leapt up, knocking over a halogen lamp. A guy next to him regurgitated beer. People dropped to the floor or pitched back against the walls. The room went silent. In the middle of it, a fat man in a black leather jacket balanced on one hand a paper plate containing a wedge of pumpkin pie. In the other hand, he held a nine-millimeter pistol aimed at Eric Hampton's head.

"You want to bomb a Serb?" cried the man, his arm trembling, his breath coming with labor. "I am Serb."

Hampton gave him a withering look.

"How about it?" The man's voice was lowering. "Not so easy to say bomb with a motherfucking gun in your face."

Arthur's mind popped like a flashbulb. He knew the identity of his ghost. "George!" he cried. "George Markovic!"

"Bro," replied the voice of the revenant. Arthur had not seen him in three years.

"George Markovic," he whispered in happy shock, and then he caught himself. "Please put away the gun."

"Cheers, Arthur," Hampton said, disapproving. "You know this chap?"

"I actually do, Eric."

George turned his head toward Arthur and chuckled. A wave of gastric odor hit Arthur's senses: roast meat, nicotine, schnapps. Hampton pivoted toward Arthur, and George's trigger hand snapped up.

"George, please," said Arthur. "I'm sorry that I didn't recognize you."

"I am fat and unwell. That's why. It's a blue age. Subterranean homesick blue."

Guests inched toward the corridor, the avant-garde of fear. George had introduced Arthur to Marta. Afterward, he had disappeared like a sprite into the earth. There could be only one reason for his reappearance. Arthur had known. His mind had recognized George in the street and had made the connection to Marta.

"She's dead, isn't she?"

George and Hampton were glaring at each other. George spat on the floor.

"Please," said Arthur, "just put the goddamn thing away."

George dropped the pie.

"Very funny," said Arthur. "Now the gun."

George's eyes narrowed to slits. He clicked the safety and holstered the pistol. Putting a hand to his mouth, he gave a shuddering cough. He was really ill, Arthur saw.

"Don't know what it is," he said. "Maybe change in the weather. My appetite is going, too."

Hampton regarded the two of them, Arthur and George, with perplexity. He seemed to be attempting to stretch a line of logic between the two men but without success. For the moment, Arthur didn't try to explain. How could he? He threw his arms around George, and George kissed him twice on both cheeks, and once right on the mouth. The kiss shocked Arthur with the force of revelation.

"I thought you were a ghost," he said. "That's the honest truth."

"Yes. In the street. I scared shit out of you. That's why I backed off a little."

"I'm sorry."

"No," said George, patting Arthur on the cheek. "I am sorry. Believe me. I am in sad shape. But you are too, bro. Jesus Christ."

George stood back from Arthur and marveled. "My fucking God. We are not for the Bolshoi, I think. Maybe mud wrestling."

Arthur slapped his belly and pointed back in his friend's face. In a police lineup, he could not have identified George Markovic. The skin of George's face was damp and pale, his hair glistening in curls around his cheeks; in the storm, Berlin had become a river, and he'd washed up in it like a corpse. He must be near two hundred fifty pounds. He had nothing of the common crook's trade left in him. He was no longer a small-time smuggler, Arthur thought. He didn't have the body for it. George looked into his eyes for a time, too, shaking his head.

"Is she, George?" Arthur asked him again.

George cocked his head at Hampton. "I say nothing in front of this Serb-hating cunt."

Guests had begun to stampede. Arthur could hear them running into one another in the corridor, making for the front door, shouting for police. Poor Anna, he thought. She had missed the outstanding moment in what would become her most legendary party. Hampton hadn't moved. Now he got into George's face.

"Just so you know, I despise the coward who pulls a gun on an unarmed man," he said. "And I despise governments that murder their own people in cold blood."

Arthur shot a glance at the journalist who had been sparring with Hampton, and she took Hampton by the shoulder, urging him out of the room. George gave the sigh of a man whose performance has ended poorly.

"You're not a nationalist, are you, George?" Arthur asked.

"I am nothing, just businessman. But I don't like this arrogant prick who is talking about bombing my people. And I have too much alcohol in my head. That's a real problem."

There was a moment of awkward silence. Then George pointed at the wedge of pie on the floor. "What is that stuff?"

"Pumpkin pie."

George made a face. "Tastes like baby food," he said.

Arthur suggested that he take a seat in the room's one chair, a spindly Deco object, and went to shut the French doors against the storm. George stopped him with a wave.

"Keep them open." He settled into the chair with a damning crack. "This won't take long."

"How did you find me?" Arthur asked, returning to the middle of the room.

George looked at him as if he had asked a stupid question. "You live in same place as before. Right next to travel agency where she worked. Wasn't hard. Believe me. War criminals who owe me money—they are hard to track."

"What about Marta, George?"

George put up a hand. He outlined his situation. Interpol had picked up his trail in Hamburg, thanks to a compromised business partner, and he had had to catch a plane to Budapest, where he had a legitimate import-export business. But there was one last errand, which had been assigned him at the last minute, and he was honor-bound to complete it.

"What errand?"

George reached into a pocket of the black jacket and produced a powder blue envelope. Arthur took the envelope, and George fixed an eye on him. "The letter is everything I know," he said, raising a finger.

The corridor creaked. George got up from the chair, walked to the room's entrance, and peeked into the hallway. It seemed to be empty. There was no door, but he took Anna's metal bookshelves, laden with art catalogues, and placed them in the frame. This seemed to make him feel more secure.

On the envelope, at the bottom left-hand corner, Arthur read a telephone number in black ink. George squeezed Arthur's shoulder and smiled at him, a frank generous smile.

"My phone number in Budapest."

Arthur nodded. "I haven't heard from her in three years."

"And still you haven't. This letter is from her sister. Dubravka."

"Hallo?" called an officious German voice. It sounded as if it could be coming from the stairwell. *"Alles in Ordnung, Freunde?"*

"Is she still married?"

George became irritated.

"Give me back fucking letter."

"I'm sorry."

"One thing is important only. If she stays in that city, she dies. Maybe she's dead now. But it's bullshit question to ask is she married. Her sister is refugee in Metkovic. She is the most important fact. You know her, Arthur, I am sure. Dubravka is the name."

"I remember Dubravka. The great beauty."

"Freunde?" called the German voice again, coming from the far end of the corridor, no more than twenty feet from the door to their room. Cops, said the expression on George's face, no doubt about it.

George pulled his nine-millimeter from the holster, plucked a bright orange Halloween napkin off the floor, and wiped down the gun.

"You could give yourself up," Arthur suggested, in retreat.

"And you could get under the table. Just a thought."

He was pointing at Anna's work desk, which barred the entrance to the balcony so that no drunken guest could wander out and fall. Arthur got under it. George produced a small bottle of schnapps from a coat pocket and drained it. He took a moment to perform what looked like calisthenics, trying to touch the tips of his shoes with his fingers. With the weapon in one hand, the empty bottle in the other, he could almost do it. At last, he flicked the bottle aside and put the gun on the carpet. He winked at Arthur and crossed himself. The apartment was audibly filling with law enforcement. Arthur could hear the scratch of walkie-talkies beyond the bookshelves. George closed his eyes and appeared to count. Wind pulsed through the French doors on either side of Arthur. George opened his eyes. He made a ferocious pair of fists and charged at the table. He sprang. The table groaned for its life, as he landed with a crash on top. He seemed to take one more breath, above Arthur, then he bounded again, through the French doors, over the balcony, into the storm.

The bookshelves collapsed. Men in green uniforms descended on the room.

TWO

I N SEPTEMBER OF 1990, two weeks before the Unification of the two Germanys, Arthur Cape landed in Berlin, Germany—in East Berlin, to be exact, in the country of East Germany, which had fourteen more sunsets to go. It was an auspicious moment for Arthur. As soon as the Interflug Tupolew from New Delhi thumped down, Arthur ceased to be a freelancer, and a long, difficult period of his life ended. In that instant, he became a staff reporter for *Sense* magazine, circulation 2.5 million, third-largest newsweekly in the United States of America. It was more than just a matter of title. He had benefits, a corporate credit card, and stature. Other correspondents in India, hearing the news, bought him drinks.

On his way across the tarmac, Arthur began to imagine in detail the room reserved for him at the Grand Kempinski in West Berlin. He envisioned the contents of the minibar as described by a fellow super-stringer out of Bombay, the Toblerone candy bars, dark and milk chocolate, the vacuum-packed cans of salted peanuts, the French wine, the Finnish vodka, the three different kinds of mineral water, luxuries that he had rarely if ever seen during his years as a business magazine contributor on the Indian subcontinent. He imagined the vastness of the bathtub, the depth and breadth of selections on the room's satellite television set, the pay channels featuring, in particular, a couple of horror movies that he had read about in the *International Herald Tribune* but had never had a chance to see. He anticipated treated air and Czechoslovak porn.

A stranger in a mauve suit and a blue tie intruded on the panorama.

"Arthur Cape?"

He acknowledged the name.

"Come with me, please."

"Sure," said Arthur, feeling generous toward everyone and everything, even this man, whose hair resembled a dandelion. The man put his hands in his pockets, leaned a shoulder against a door in an otherwise seamless metal wall, and gestured for Arthur to enter.

"What's this about?" Arthur asked.

"You're a journalist?"

"That's right."

"Which publication, please?" the man asked.

"Sense."

"Don't know it," the man said.

Arthur took a deep breath. That was to be expected. Unlike *Time* and *Newsweek, Sense* did not have an international edition.

"But accredited journalists are always welcome."

"Thank you."

He was an accredited journalist. *Sense* had made him its Central Europe correspondent. He would focus on business reporting, which had been his specialty in South Asia. He also had a mandate, when time permitted, to write features on politics and society. But only in Germany, his chief of correspondents had said, at least for the moment. Everything else belonged to the senior European correspondent, Eric Hampton.

"Your first time in Germany?" the man from airport security wanted to know.

"I was a student here once."

"And you are how old, if I may ask?" the bureaucrat inquired, pulling keys from a pocket.

"I just turned thirty. Why have you singled me out?"

"You had some trouble in the Delhi airport, I believe."

Arthur shrugged. He had. It was true. The number of Pakistani stamps in the passport had triggered a response.

The airport official opened a door with his key. He walked two or three steps ahead down a chlorine-scalded, gray-tiled corridor. His dandelion fluff of hair caught an otherwise imperceptible breeze. They made a right turn in the corridor and reached a door labeled *Zoll*. The man unlocked a second door and stepped aside for him. It took Arthur a moment to grasp what he was seeing. At the far end of a table, a naked man folded chubby arms across his chest. He seemed cheerfully bored. A swivel of black hair covered the top half of his head, a scrap of five-day growth the bottom half. He reminded Arthur, in his appearance, and his loose, amiable posture, of a certain kind of slacker that he had known in a former life in northern New Mexico, not exactly criminal but not at all a good citizen.

Beside the naked man, seated at the table, sat a customs agent in a gray uniform. He was running his fingers through the clothing: a pair of black socks, a pair of stonewashed blue jeans, a black concert T-shirt, and scarlet underwear. On the table, lumped beside unfamiliar plastic sacks, lay Arthur's duffel bags.

The door to the room banged behind Arthur, and he got a cold feeling inside. This would happen to him now. The dandelion had blown away.

UNTIL HIS TWENTIETH birthday, Arthur Cape had crossed only one international border in his life, across the Rio Grande to the city of Juarez in Mexico, where he had spent five full days around a hotel swimming pool, eating banana splits and cheese enchiladas. He could no longer remember if he had needed a passport for that journey. What he recalled was the sense that the rest of the world could not be reached by crossing the Rio Grande. There would have to be another way. That border contained a purgatory, in the form of a tourist hotel, and one could never get out of it.

He received his first passport at the age of nineteen, and it was the beginning of an addiction. He went to Germany as a student, and on that trip he must have hit twenty borders, from the Soviet Union down to Israel, a backpacker's year. He still had that passport somewhere, buried in a drawer in his parents' home in Dallas, a document gnarled by the dozens of stamps impressed on it. As an American, he'd had his share of problems. The East Bloc countries hadn't liked the look of him. The Canadians always had it better. But once over those borders, hopping from one country to the next, he became disdainful of a world without them. The meaningless frontiers between the states back home in the U.S. came to seem like flaws.

After a stint in New Mexico, which had been the closest thing to a foreign country, he had gone to India, and for the first time, the borders turned violent on him. He tried to get into China over roads in Ladakh and almost got himself shot. On the Indian border with Pakistan, he had been detained by Kashmiri freedom fighters. They had called him a spy and beaten him up, but he'd bribed his way out of a worse fate. Pakistan into Afghanistan had been a complete failure of nerve. Maybe that's why he hadn't loved India, as so many of his colleagues had. The exotic face of the world had gone ugly in India. International borders had ceased to be glamorous rivers between fabulous territories. They had become lines of blood and wire, separating deserts and armies. Arthur had fallen out of love with the world in India, and this trip west, he had been forced to admit, was a retreat back to more familiar terrain. He needed a breather. A retreat didn't mean a defeat. And in Europe, frontiers closed to him under Communism had opened wide. Whole new countries had begun to proliferate. Yet here he was, stuck at the entry to the continent.

"Unfathomable swinery," the customs agent grumbled to himself in German. The creases in his face, the sconces beneath his eyes, the webs upholding his chin, expressed a terrible foreknowledge—total defeat slung in nets of age. He would be out of a job before long.

He pushed the clothes of the naked man to the far end of the table and urged him to get dressed. Next, he addressed Arthur, requesting a passport. His nose dripped snuff onto the page displaying Arthur's photograph. I won't disrobe, thought Arthur. I won't begin my first real job with a strip search. Fuck that.

"Sprechen Sie deutsch?" the East German asked.

Arthur nodded yes. He spoke German.

"Sind Sie Deutscher?"

Arthur shook his head no. He was not German. His face could have been German: blue eyes, blond hair, round chin. But Arthur's father's people were Poles from Gdynia named Caplawitz or Caplericz or Caplerovicz. No one knew for sure. They had shortened the name in America to Cape. Arthur's mother's people were Creek Indian, Irish, and maybe a Jew back there somewhere.

The customs officer asked where Arthur had learned his German, and Arthur explained that he had spent a student year abroad in the West German university city of Marburg but had been out of practice for more than a decade. The East German looked up, at last, and studied Arthur with heavy, red-sprigged eyes. He was troubled by something. He indicated a chair on his side of the table, and said, *"Bitte."*

Arthur sat, and the conversation proceeded in German.

"Your business in India."

"Journalist."

"What kind?"

"Print."

Arthur produced a freelancer's card. The new ones would be waiting for him at the Grand Kempinski.

The East German didn't ask Arthur to take off his clothes, thank

God. He slipped the business card into the passport, placed the passport on the table, and unzipped each of the three duffel bags. He thumbed through the pages of Arthur's books, turned the pockets of his pants inside out, snicked with a pocket knife through one or two seams, repeated the shaving cream and cassette recorder experiments of his Indian counterparts, then caught sight of the brown paper sack that had been stuffed, with a furtive quality, in a far corner of the smallest duffel bag.

He opened the mouth of the sack. Inside, he found a duty-free Cadbury raisin-and-nut candy bar, a pack of King's Flake cigarettes, several loose betel nuts, and a clump of foil. He sighed from the depths of his chest and pried apart the foil's crumpled edges. He stuck his nose down into white powder.

He gave Arthur an inquiring look.

"I've never seen that before in my life."

It was not really true. There had been a party in Delhi to send him off, and the narcotic had appeared as a farewell present. Arthur had handed it back. He wanted it out of his apartment, in fact, but the giver had been insulted. Arthur's bags had been in his bedroom, mostly packed, and this person had done him the disservice, without telling him, of adding these last few ounces to the weight.

The room became tense. Arthur began to feel dark forces at work. At heart, like his sister, he was a superstitious man, and when bad luck mounted, he dismissed the idea of luck all together. His knee-jerk belief in demonic hegemony welled up inside. He should never have been detained in Delhi and never stopped in Berlin. There was no good reason. And why had this man been so thorough? And why had the friend in Delhi insisted on giving him the stash? Arthur hardly did drugs at all. Now his career would be destroyed. He would be lucky to get home.

The official demanded his wallet. He counted Indian rupees and examined photographs and receipts. The search for more evidence became intense. The East German frowned with deepening conviction. And then, suddenly, he produced the last item in the wallet, and Arthur did not believe, at first, what he was seeing.

Even the other man in the room took notice. He squinted in the room's sallow light, then barked out a laugh. Annoyed, the customs official ordered him to turn his chair around and face the wall. He held a cross in the palm of his hand.

ARTHUR NO LONGER BELIEVED in Jesus Christ. Unlike his sister Philippa, a devout Episcopalian, he had given up on religion. He had seen the tomb of Christ in Kashmir, and the last of the scales had fallen from his eyes. In Kashmir, the people believed that Christ had escaped Palestine and wandered eastward to the court of a famous Himalayan ruler, where he had died in honor and safety. Stories fought with other stories. What seemed colossal turned out to be someone else's noonday shadow. And in Kashmir, if not long before, that's what Christ had become for Arthur, beyond the multitude of memorized Bible verses, beyond the real love for a spirit with whom he'd once had daily conversations, beyond the fear of a living Satan. Christ had become a shadow at noon.

But Philippa still believed, and fiercely, and five or six years ago, at the end of Arthur's stay in New Mexico, she had given him the cross. At the time, Arthur had almost been offended. He told her that he didn't believe in Jesus anymore, which she already knew, and that he certainly didn't believe that God would protect him, but, he'd said, if it would make her feel better, if it meant something to her, he would carry the gift, and without thinking about it, he had.

Philippa had called it a pocket cross. It was not for wearing around the neck, not for public display, but more like a note to oneself, a tiny totem of divine agony and redemption within a plastic sheath. Behind the cross, three times as long, lay a yellow slip of paper explaining that the object had been made with the wood of genuine Lebanese cedars. The cross was not meant to be used as a talisman, according to the script, but was a reminder that the one who bore it had a relationship with Christ, and that this relationship had a personal significance.

The East German folded his hands and spoke to Arthur gently for the first time.

"I am a Christian, too," he said in German.

His eyes shone a new, moist blue. Veins had burst in his nose. Hair sprouted from his ears.

"I kept that a secret for two decades. To this day, not one of my colleagues here, men and women I have known for most of my adult life, knows that I am a devout follower of our Lord."

Arthur shook his head. He could not believe what he was hearing. He was astonished. The customs official touched the cross with the tip of one finger, as he might caress the nose of an infant.

"My faith survived the last batch of thugs," he said, "and it will survive this batch."

The customs official poked a finger at the makeshift tray of narcotic. "Where did you get this shit?"

"New Delhi. Someone at a farewell party put that in my bag. I swear it."

The customs official grunted. The room softened, as if light had entered through a hidden window. He returned the cross to Arthur, repacked the duffel bags, and zipped them up. Rising from the table, he crumpled the foil containing the white powder and disappeared through the rear door of the room. The man facing the wall glanced over his shoulder, and Arthur exchanged a questioning glance with him. What the hell would happen now? Things had taken an extraordinary turn. Arthur felt a sudden bond with this soul, who looked sympathetic enough, but who also had the furtive appearance of a man getting away with murder. Together, they sat on more than just a border. This way station meant something. The customs official reappeared in an official cap with a dark blue bill. He pointed at Arthur's bags. "Take them."

The other man had a gleam of hope in his eyes.

"You as well," said the official.

He led them back out into the corridor, through a pair of heavy steel doors, and out of the terminal to a line at a taxi stand. The air on the pavement smelled of curried sausages and exhaust. A plane skidded down. The morning edged toward noon.

The official offered Arthur his hand, and he spoke, his voice quavering. "I would look on this hour as a decisive one. You were not meant to pass here, but you have. Nothing that happens after this can be an accident."

Arthur took the man's hand and bent his head. "Thank you for your kindness," he said.

The official lifted a finger in admonishment.

"It had nothing to do with kindness. The Lord has His finger on you."

He tipped his hat and hurried back into the dark concrete of the terminal. A searing sense of wonder hit Arthur. He believed that the man must be right. Something was about to happen. Until that moment, he had seen his move from East to West as a professional and personal matter, but his sister's cross had revealed another reality to him. It was not the reality of Christ. It was the fact of a great destiny. Arthur had come to Europe for a reason. He covered his tired eyes with his palms. When he opened his eyes again, the world seemed different. The northern European sun shone stark as lightning. Distant planes cut like vast black crows through the sky. This border was different from any he had ever crossed, except maybe the first, the one into Mexico. This, too, was a first, in its way, a border of meaning, where crosses succeeded and passports failed.

A hand squeezed his shoulder. It was the man who had been stripsearched. He was shaking his head in sympathy. In English, at last, he offered his condolences.

"I'm sorry, bro," he said. "That guy just stole your heroin."

He introduced himself as George Markovic.

THREE

A TAXI HONKED UP, and George knew the driver. The driver winked. His name was Marko. Arthur shook Marko's hand, too, and saw that he had bright silver in his eyelashes, an angelic quality.

The cab behind Marko gave a maddened honk. George scrambled for the front seat. Arthur tossed his bags into the back.

"Where to, *gnädiger Herr?*" asked Marko.

"Grand Kempinski."

"You never get a room there!" cried George.

"I bet he already has one!" snapped Marko.

George changed the subject and told Marko what had happened in customs. Marko let out a shriek. "That *Ossi* really stole your stuff?"

"I don't know if he stole it," replied Arthur in his dream state, "and I never will. I don't care. His motive is nothing to me."

"Suit yourself," said George. He assured Marko that the *Ossi* had come up with that ridiculous act about God and made off with enough Afghan narcotic to buy himself a new house in Spandau. Arthur paid little attention. He was gulping down the air, his ecstatic feeling turning to drowsiness.

George changed the subject. "I am just coming from Belgrade," he said, "where I have seen the most beautiful women in Europe."

Marko rolled his eyes in the rearview mirror. George explained that East Berlin customs knew him well and usually took his money with professionalism and pleasure, but this guy was a last-minute replacement and hadn't known to skip over the crude details.

"You'd never seen him before?"

George shook his head. "*Niemals.* You're American?"

Arthur nodded. "And where are you from?" Arthur asked.

"Serbs from Yugoslavia," said Marko.

"Yugoslavs," corrected George.

Marko made a hooking gesture with his hand, a mark of seasoned irritation. "He is a traitor to his people," said Marko. "And I am not."

Then he pointed out the window at a construction site. "The Berlin Wall," he said.

On either side of the car, bulldozers moved sections of earth. Forklifts spun in opposing directions, wheeling slabs of plain white concrete. Arthur rolled down his window. At first, he thought that Marko must be mistaken; it couldn't be the Berlin Wall. The slabs looked too thin, and they weren't the same color as the stretches of the wall that he had seen in photographs and on television. They could have been materials at any construction site in the world. The cab slowed behind a stalled truck. In the distance, Arthur saw an abandoned guard tower. It was a day of wonders. Marko must be right. This indifferent stuff must be the remains of the Wall.

"What will they do with it?" he asked.

George's eyes appeared to count granules in the slabs closest to the car. "Smash it. Sell it. Make money."

THE GRAND KEMPINSKI sat on the corner of the elegant West Berlin shopping boulevard known as the Kudamm. The entrance lay down Meineckestrasse. Arthur paid Marko, and shook hands with George, who gave him a last skeptical glance.

"You won't get a room now," he predicted. "Wait and see."

A bellhop opened the door of the cab and snatched Arthur away from the two Yugoslavs, as if to protect him. A gleaming brass cart appeared. Arthur's luggage trundled through glass doors, across a lobby of fresh white roses to a front desk mobbed by people with light blue credit cards. The bellhop received his tip.

Arthur handed over his passport, and the reservations clerk informed him that a change had been made at the last minute by the travel office at *Sense* magazine. His room had been given to Eric Hampton. Arthur gazed at the proud young woman in disbelief. He wanted to laugh.

"Just give me another room then."

The reservations clerk thumped a ledger onto the mahogany counter. "Nothing available until after the third of October. See for yourself."

She flicked through pages and showed him names. She informed him that it wasn't just the Grand Kempinski. The world had cracked open. The Unification of Germany had set loose floods of humanity. People were streaming into Berlin, the future capital of the country, as if to see Jesus.

Arthur demanded a phone and called his chief of correspondents at home in New York, though it was past midnight. Gavin Morsch had given him the number in case of emergency.

"I'm sorry to call so late, Gavin."

"What is it, Arthur?"

"My hotel room?"

"Hold on." The chief of correspondents could be heard rising from bed, crossing the carpeted floor in his socks, shutting a door, and turning on a water tap. He lowered his voice and, at the same time, stressed each of his words, as if he believed someone was wiretapping the line, as if he wanted to be recorded as clearly as possible by his eavesdroppers.

"It was felt," Morsch said, speaking to his secret listeners in an exculpatory passive voice, "that Eric Hampton—a twenty-year veteran—deserved a valediction, and it was agreed that the Unification of the two Germanys—should be—that valediction, as it tied together so many of the strands of his career. After this, he takes residence in London and becomes your distant overlord. It was discussed that our man in India had been tasked to do our Unification coverage, that tickets had been bought, and rooms had been booked, but it was eventually felt—by *everyone*—that two more weeks of paid downtime would not make a—pardon my bluntness—goddamn bit of difference to our man in Berlin, and might, in fact, be greatly, if not profoundly, appreciated by him. Were we wrong?"

Arthur swallowed. He should not have complained. It was bad form. "I was just concerned about getting a room."

Morsch sounded exasperated. "A man who has taken a stolen camel into a Pakistani security zone will somehow find a bed in West Berlin. I feel sure."

Morsch hung up. Arthur was not meant to stay at the Grand Kempinski. George had foreseen it. The Lord has His finger on you, the customs official had told him. A gentle force tugged him back into the street and placed him on the curb beside his bags. He heard a loud, leaping car honk. George sprang out of the cab, which idled in front of the synagogue across the street from the Kempinski, and started to cross in front of oncoming traffic.

"This is fated," said George.

Arthur felt the same truth welling up in him. He couldn't fight it. These men might be criminals, but they had been sent to him. The bags dropped to the sidewalk, and George collected them.

"You saved me from the East Germans," he said. "Now I will save you from the West Germans."

. . .

THE SUN MOVED to midmorning, and shadows shrank. Arthur's eyes opened and closed in the backseat. His contact lenses had dried out and were giving him pain. Fate seemed in a lull.

"Are there homeless shelters?" he asked. "I'd take a homeless shelter, at this point."

They inquired at modest family hotels on the edges of the Grünewald. These were modestly priced and obviously clean, but none were available. They tried inner-city hotels where famous authors had gone to die; then Scandinavian cubes with Helmut Newton nudes on the walls; then ex-Communist megaliths on Alexanderplatz, where the lobby smelled like gasoline and the clientele seemed to fear the staff; same-sex pensions, despotic youth hostels, rooms for let in phoneless apartments in East Berlin, hidden spas in the woods at the western end of town. Arthur offered to pay twice and three times the going rate of any domicile. But no one had room.

At last, George snapped his fingers. "My cousin!"

She ran a travel business in town. She didn't like him and had never strictly acknowledged him as a relative. But she was, generally speaking, a decent person and had nice looks for a working woman; nice legs.

Marko hadn't said much during the search. Now he shook his head. "No."

"It's Apostel-Paulus-Strasse," George ordered him. "Just drive."

They parked among low apartment buildings, beside a church with a pale green steeple, rising amid willows and chestnuts. Marko rolled down the windows, and a pleasing hum descended—cricket, bee, and fly. Morning light shimmered off the exposed blue bricks of the street. Café windows were shining. Beside the church, Muslim women in creamy white hoods and long black gowns sat on the brink of a sandbox in a playground and fed bread crumbs to birds. Everything seemed sweet and sleepy. A rill of water sparkled in the gutter in front of the car, and just beyond the dashboard window, at a café table, two bare-legged women poured honey on golden rolls. They licked their fingers and laughed. This is the place, thought Arthur.

"I'm not participating." Marko lit a cigarette and adjusted the seat back into a reclining position. "No way, no chance."

George scolded him.

Marko turned in his seat and gave a sigh. "Is this what you want, friend?"

"If you don't mind."

Marko shrugged and flipped the butt of his cigarette out the window. He popped the trunk. Arthur tried to get his bags, but the men insisted. George pointed to a window three stories above the café, and his brow furrowed. Then he had a moment of crisis. He couldn't remember his cousin's name. Farida Muquadimovic? Or was it Osmanovic? Suada Osmanovic? Her husband had a name like that.

"Marta," said Marko with a chuckle, lighting another cigarette. "Her name is Marta Mehmedovic."

THE TWO MEN hoisted the duffels up three flights of stairs, staggering and cursing until they came to a sign for the Adria Travel Agency. The words appeared in bold-faced black letters on a rectangle of brass-rimmed brown plastic. George didn't bother to knock. He let Arthur's bags fall with a boom on the landing and shoved open the door, which slammed back against an inside wall of the travel agency. A woman sprang from the chair behind her desk. She looked mythological, like a tree nymph, her hair a pale green, the color of the church steeple, her skin gleaming pale white, tinged with the shade of her hair. Her lips glittered a moist emerald.

George charged at the woman's desk. "My cousin, please?"

"*Ach!*" the woman cried in German. "*Du!*"

Marko heard this word as an alarm and tore back down the flight of stairs. George raised a fist after him.

"I'm calling the police!" the woman cried, lifting the receiver of her phone.

George strode forward and smashed his fist down on the desk, scattering papers. The woman dropped the receiver. Arthur started to feel alarmed. George began to shout his cousin's name. The girl ran away, through a rear door of the office. A recorded voice spoke incoherently and distantly from the receiver on the floor.

Arthur lifted his bags and headed for the stairwell. "It was worth a try," he said.

Behind him, a door banged open, and heels clacked on the hardwood floor. They had authority. Arthur hesitated. He turned in curiosity, and he beheld Marta. It had to be Marta. Her violet eyes burned. Her hair swung in a golden ponytail. In her fist lay a bright green apple.

"My God," said Arthur. He took a step forward. George lurched backward, tumbling down the stairwell.

She cocked back one brown bare arm. Arthur found himself alone, facing her across the room. Their eyes met, and he understood that this exact thing, about to happen, had been meant to happen. This was the beginning of his real life.

"Fucking drug dealer!" she shouted.

He raised his right hand, his lips parting to speak. The apple burst between them.

FOUR

MARTA'S DAY HAD BEGUN, in the darkness before dawn, with a riddle. She didn't own a dog, but there was one in her bed.

"What have you done?" she moaned to her husband.

Tino waved to her with a steel-bristled brush, then went back to styling his hair. He was wearing his *passeggiata* jacket, his favorite piece of clothing, tan suede, though the sun hadn't risen.

"What is going on?" she called. "Are you leaving me?"

He put down the brush and plucked something up in his arms, a thing small and animate, desperately struggling. My son, Marta thought. He's taking Pino away. You alone we worship, she thought, to you alone we pray for help. She threw off the covers, got out of bed, and headed for her son's room. She fell to her knees beside Pino, who was sound asleep, curled up like a bumblebee. She stuck her face in his black hair and inhaled. She had been having another of those nightmares in which her son toddled along the edge of a body of water, sometimes the Neretva River, sometimes the canal outside the apartment. He refused to listen to her; he went to the water's edge; he went in. Marta had the dreams a lot. They woke her from deep sleep and drove her into Pino's room, where he was always okay, dear boy, unlike his father, who was trying to sneak out of the house on his business trip.

She returned to their bedroom. Her husband dropped the dog onto the bed, and it navigated the folds in the blankets. It was a puppy. Everything was normal. Everything was fine, except for the dog.

A flannel robe hung on the back of her mother's antique paravent. Marta reached for the robe and wrapped herself. Her husband reached into the sheets.

"Mama will love you," he whispered into one of the puppy's languid ears.

Marta turned on the bedside lamp. "Can I have a glass of water, please," she said.

He went into the kitchen, and she studied the dog for a minute. This breed, she thought, is not supposed to have a stub tail. She had seen pointer puppies from time to time in the neighborhood, and their tails made curlicues. This little creature had been clipped. A little girl, she saw. That was good. Male dogs made terrible pets. Fur like a chocolate sheen covered the puppy's head. Her flanks glowed a luminous white in the halogen light. Her ears glistened as if damp, and her eyes were dark sparks. She was beautiful. Tino returned with the water.

"She's mutilated," Marta said.

"It's an American practice, according to Dubravka's boyfriend."

"What does he know?"

"He breeds them."

"That criminal breeds dogs for the American market? For God's sake, Tino. Please."

"Marta—"

"I don't want it. Not if it comes from Branko."

Marta crossed her arms and gave him a look that he could not misunderstand. This gift had nothing to do with her need for a pet. He knew it; she knew it. He was no dog lover. He certainly didn't hunt. His mother had never allowed animals in the house, as far as Marta knew.

This was about their son. Pino's first words had come at eleven months, and they had been in his parents' native tongue, which was Bosnian. The first word had been *voda*, for water; the second *pero*, feather, the third *patka*, duck—he adored the ducks that swam in the Landwehrkanal and treasured the bright red duck feather that his mother had sterilized, dyed, and given to him on his second birthday. But on a Sunday, three weeks ago, on a walk along the canal, a new creature had caught Pino's eye. Tino had stopped at his favorite café for a Turkish coffee, and Pino had seen a terrier pass. There had been plenty of dogs before. Neighbors loved to walk their dogs along the canal in the evenings. But this one struck Pino somehow, and he cried out, *"Hoon!"* He meant the German word for dog, which was *Hund.*

Tino spoke this word to Marta in a despondent voice, seated at their kitchen table before a glass of loza and a plate of kajmak cheese, as if food and drink from his native country might help him overcome the evil. Where had Pino learned this word? Who spoke German with him? Was it German kids? There was a long pause. Had Marta taught him the word? Surely she hadn't.

She was filled with a secret delight. Since that day, three weeks ago, even more German had emerged—in particular, *feder*, for feather, and *ente*, for duck. Pino had begun to act as if he didn't know the Bosnian words for dog or feather anymore, though Marta was sure that he did. He still said *mama* and *tata* for mama and daddy, but Tino heard these words with new anxiety; at any moment, they might be lost.

"We are leaving this country," he had said at the end of the bottle of loza.

. . .

GERMAN WORDS SOUNDED like a death knell to Tino, the death of a hope that he had cherished, without really knowing it, above everything else. They signaled the obliteration of a dream home rising like a sunlit palace between rock, sea, and river, collapsing before his eyes into the stable darkness of a modern European childhood in which the only things that counted were American movies and hamburgers, things that Tino himself had consumed with endless hunger from the day of his arrival in West Berlin.

He saw the beginning of his wife's ultimate triumph. The German word for dog had come upon him in the form of a surprise attack. It had never occurred to him that his son would speak German. Tino had expected to have a grace period of years before these matters became urgent.

But on every corner, in every café, in each and every park, *hoooon,* like the howl of a ghost. And then came *kaetzchen,* for kitty cat. His wife had launched her linguistic Barbarossa, and Tino could not look at her ever again in the same way. She felt it. To him, she had become the enemy. And the dog was his counterattack.

He gentled the animal into her arms. Marta poked her nose down into the wiggling furry mass and received a lick on her chin.

"Claudia is her name," her husband said.

Marta gave him a look.

The young Claudia Cardinale was Tino's ideal woman, but Marta looked nothing at all like that human cannoli with heaving bosom, thick brunette tresses, and whore's eyes. If Claudia Cardinale was his ideal, Marta had often said to him, she didn't know why on earth he would want to spend the rest of his life with her opposite, the anti-Cardinale, a blonde with a definite Germanic streak, a child of Austrians and Hungarians. Marta looked more like Monica Vitti, but Tino didn't care for Monica Vitti. She was too intellectual for his tastes.

Tino lingered at the foot of the bed, studying himself in the mirror. "Branko says it's not really humane to keep a hunting dog in a big city like this," he said, "and I think he's right."

Marta put the dog down. Tino checked inside his coat for plane tickets. He glanced at his watch and left the room. Marta followed him down the corridor, past the boy's room, into the kitchen, where he saw her coming and glanced at his watch again. The sun rose through the windows of the washroom, which overlooked the court-yard. Dubravka, her sister, who was staying with them, had stepped quietly into the bathroom.

Marta pointed at her husband. "I'm telling you now. We're not moving back to Mostar."

Tino wore a bland expression. It was too late to talk about it. He had a flight.

"Why did we come here in the first place, Tino?"

"Because you like Germans—"

She pointed back at Pino's room. "So *he* will have everything. The very best schools, the very best clothes—so he will have the *passport.*"

Tino shrugged.

"But if you want to go back to Mostar, have your *fufa,* run your fa-ther's business, make half as much money as I make at the travel agency, be my guest. Pino and I are staying."

Tino went for his luggage. It never failed. She brought up his other women, and he went into full retreat, staggering like a defeated army toward the sea. She could not identify the *fufa* by name, but Dubravka had given her enough details.

Tino held a bag in each hand. His face was crumbling. "My son is no German," he said.

"You want him to be one more citizen of an ex-Communist coun-try? Another beggar? So he can be stopped at the borders of his own country and treated like a criminal every time he wants to go home? So he can pay a hundred marks just to bring a toaster back to his grandmother?"

Tino's reserve burst at last. "Fucking cunt smoke, all this!"

He did not attempt to lower his voice. He wanted the boy to wake up, and Dubravka to hear. That way, he could make his escape.

"My country," he shouted, "has the most beautiful coast in Europe! Seventy thousand visitors last year alone! One hundred and twenty thousand beds!"

He sounded like a Yugoslav government brochure. She shook her head at these numbers. They meant nothing if the right people didn't come, and the right people never would.

"*Ma* Tino. Please. A lost cause"

Pino called from his bed, "Mama."

"Germany is his home," said Marta.

Tino lifted the hand holding the carry-on and glanced again at his Cartier, of which he was justifiably proud (she had bought it for him). Bravo, she said to herself. She had kept him from running away.

"You're deluded," he said, shaking his head. "German nationality is a matter of blood."

She yawned in his face.

"How many people do we know who have citizenship, Marta? How many non-Germans? No one. Because their blood isn't German. It takes fifteen years to get citizenship, and even then, no fucking guarantees. So I tell you. Pino will become a German criminal before he becomes a German citizen."

A car outside began to honk.

She stepped between Tino and the front door. "I wrote the Interior Ministry," she said.

She gave him a grim smile. He put down the luggage, laid his hands on the back of a kitchen chair, and hung his head. He blew out a sigh and listened.

"I'm German," she said. "So none of those rules apply to me."

"You're not German."

"My mother was Austro-Hungarian. And so am I. Pino's blood is German. Only yours is not."

"What the hell did you tell the German government about us?"

"As soon as the Yugoslav state security archives open, I will have documented proof that my mother was the daughter of Swabians. I urged the Interior Ministry to send me information on how to proceed."

Tino studied her face for a while. If he had loved her more, he might have put his fingers on her cheek. She sensed it. A memory of love passed across his face. But his feelings, which had once been young and strong, were dying.

"Here's the German connection," he finally said. "Your mother's parents were lined up against a wall by Germans. They were executed by Germans. They were tossed into a limestone pit by Germans. Be sure and put that in the letter. You might actually have a chance at citizenship."

He went into his son's bedroom and kissed Pino goodbye. The noises of the Berlin street rose through the windows of their apartment. Outside, another new day had come in the great city. Tino slid past Marta and into the echoing hallway. She slammed the door behind him.

FIVE

MARTA'S SISTER EMERGED from the bathroom in a cloud of steam and soap, a cigarette in her mouth. She wrapped her hair in a dark blue towel, fished a lighter from a drawer beside the refrigerator, and put the flame to her mouth. Marta waved smoke away from her face. Dubravka smiled, rewrapping her tresses one more time.

Her hair had river magnificence, brown and rich and violent, plunging past her shoulderblades to the swing of her behind, flowing without morality or fear around the oval of her soft, creamy face. Marta had always been a little envious of that hair, which now disappeared into a blue towel. Blue was Dubravka's color; the color of her eyes, of the river cutting through the rocks of her home.

She flipped through the pages of a movie magazine. When she finally reached the last page, she caught Marta's stare.

"I'm thinking of going to the movies today," she said.

Pino rushed out of his room, burbling in his father's tongue about the puppy. *Slatka stene, Mami!*

"Keep it?" The puppy bobbled behind, as if to second the request. "Keep it, please, please, please? *Molim, molim, molim.*"

The dyed red duck feather danced at the back of Pino's head. He tumbled into her lap.

"My Mohican," she whispered.

Dubravka sipped at a cup of Nescafé and plucked a green apple from the basket on the kitchen table. She grabbed for Pino, who threw his arms around her and gave her a kiss before he squirmed away, tripping over the puppy, knocking the apple out of her hand, and then chasing it along the shining tiles of the floor. The puppy wiggled on its back, ears splayed against the floor.

"Keep the puppy! Keep it! Keep it!"

And not one single *Hund,* thought Marta ruefully. Maybe he would forget the German as quickly as he had learned it. Dubravka retrieved her apple. She stuck it into her mouth and bit.

"You heard the argument, didn't you?" Marta asked her sister. "You think I'm wrong?"

Dubravka seemed surprised by the question, but she lowered the apple and answered. "You're hardly ever wrong."

Marta had always found it difficult to ask others for advice, particularly when it came to personal matters, and especially when the person in question was her sister, whom she had scolded countless times over the years for her reckless decisions and taste in men. But this was *notfall*—a state of emergency.

"I mean it. Do you think I'm wrong to want to raise my son in Germany?"

Dubravka's big blue eyes blinked. "I see the advantages of this country, of course. The passport. Everything."

Marta felt herself chastised. "But you still agree with Tino."

Dubravka took another bite of the apple.

"I didn't say that. If I were you, I would stay here, and even more, I would—" Her words trailed off.

"Say it."

"You'll be mad."

Marta waited.

"For me, it's important to be with a man who isn't scared of me. Who worships me a little, you know, but doesn't take my shit. That's very important to me—"

"Branko *hits* you!"

Dubravka finished the apple. She wrapped the core in a napkin, because Marta had told her to do so before she threw a finished piece of fruit into the trash. She gave her sister a dull stare of resistance.

"My marriage has problems, yes," said Marta, "but I'm not sleeping with a man who sells drugs and guns, who is a sadist—"

"On the other hand, he doesn't fuck around behind my back. He pays for my trips to Germany, and he buys me delicious meals and nice clothes and tells me that he wants to marry me and have a house full of kids one day."

Marta had made the mistake of asking. One should never ask family for advice on questions of marriage or money. One must trust instinct, and Marta would, and *basta*. She tuned the radio to a local Yugoslav station and listened to the news, which was, as usual, miserable. She pursued Pino, who, at two, had just comprehended, along with German language, the joys of climbing. Using a chair, he had attained the counter.

"Leave him," said her sister. "Go do your yoga."

Marta gave Pino ten kisses, up and down his cheeks, until he pushed her away, giggling, crying, "No more!"

Dubravka had a lovely way with Pino. She seemed to understand his mind. She got down on the floor with him and entered his games with the gusto of another child. She makes it look easy, thought Marta, who stayed at the door a few more seconds. She wished that Dubravka would get married to a decent sort and have her own kids, but her sister never would. Dubravka appeared to like kids. She mentioned the prospect of home and a family from time to time. But she lived her life for other things. A great love? A great adventure? Branko? That ugly, dangerous man? Who knew? With the passing of years, Marta feared for her sister more and more. She dreaded the

day, coming soon, when her visit would end, and she would return
home to Mostar.

"Give him a bun with Nutella. It's all that he'll eat for breakfast
now."

"Go."

"No candy."

"Go!"

M ARTA FOUND HER place in the apartment's one quiet corner,
a wedge of carpet between the paravent and the wall in her
bedroom. She began to do her breathing exercises. Dubravka misun-
derstood the practice. It wasn't yoga. Marta wished that she'd had
time to learn that discipline. She crossed her legs and closed her eyes.
She exhaled and inhaled, in too much of a hurry, she thought, with
too much agitation. She considered the four elements of her body—
fire, water, earth, and air—and then concentrated on each of them
inside her body, and then on each of them in the world, her own der-
ivation of the Ayurvedic practice, learned from her teacher, Frau
Regina Schnarf, at the Schöneberg Community College. The class
had culminated in a single discovery. One could become semideliri-
ous by breathing out first, then breathing deeply in. Tino and Dubravka
assumed that she must be seeking enlightenment or inner peace. But
Marta, in her own discreet way, was escaping into the ether. For a
few seconds, she was leaving this world. Beneath the bed, the puppy
observed.

Marta showered. She whipped her hair into a ponytail and selected
a black bra that had been hanging to dry from the curtain rod. She
ate a slice of dry toast and checked the contents of the refrigerator
while Dubravka fought with the necessary ruthlessness to get the
naked two-year-old with the red feather sticking out of his hair into
clothes. He was such a little Mohican. What would he be at sixteen?
An Apache! Marta laughed.

In the kitchen, Dubravka peeled off her aquamarine dessous and plucked a sleeveless blue V-neck blouse from the slush pile beside her cot. A bruise faded on the thin collarbone above her left breast. Marta tried not to stare at the bruise and didn't ask. What would be the point? Her sister didn't welcome questions about her personal life, and she had other problems anyway. Just before or after this act of violence, she had lost her job at the photo shop in Medjugorje, and her father had kicked her out of his home for a few weeks. He had prevailed upon Marta to take Dubravka and straighten her out, and Marta had been happy to have her sister. That shit Branko, feeling guilty, had bankrolled the journey, but when she returned to Mostar, fresh and clean, he would hit her again.

"He's so strong," Dubravka said, grinning at the boy, who squeezed her fingers. He prattled in his father's language about the ducks in the Landwehrkanal. Then he blurted the word for duck in German, as if rediscovering language—and ducks—all over again.

"Enten, Mami!"

Marta and Dubravka looked at each other and burst out laughing.

Marta picked him up and gave him more kisses on his ripe, brown cheeks. He had his father's lovely olive coloring.

"So you're going to the movies today?" she asked her sister. "After the babysitter comes?"

"Or buying shoes."

"On the Kudamm?"

Dubravka grimaced. "Walter-Schreiber-Platz."

"Branko gave you money? I mean, I could give you some."

Dubravka didn't answer. She took Pino and finished buttoning his smart red sweater, something relatively new from KaDeWe, something French, a playful black scrawl of a bunny rabbit on the pocket. Looking at him in this sweater made Marta very happy. The puppy rolled yapping at their feet. What it wanted, Marta did not know.

"Can you look after that thing, too?" Marta asked.

"After her?"

"After her, I mean?"

Marta snatched the last green apple from the basket on the kitchen table, gave final hugs and kisses to sister and son, and hurried out the door.

S HE CLATTERED in heels along the Landwehrkanal, missing the bus to work by seconds. The ducks in the canal seemed hopeful. They seemed to recognize her as the mother of Pino, the boy who showered them with bread.

Her boss, Herr Dieterle, liked to appear at the travel agency between the hours of nine and ten, just ahead of the day's first customers. He liked to find the fax machine humming. He took serious pleasure in the sight of the floppy paperback train and ferry schedules spread wide in Marta's hands. The telephone receiver must be cupped against the side of her head. The smell of chamomile and fresh flowers must waft down to him as he lumbered his one hundred kilos up the stairwell. These sensations made him feel as if he owned a real business.

Dieterle made promises. He promised a new computer, a larger staff, and a more comfortable office on the ground floor of a better building. But he never delivered, and never would, she thought, catching the next bus, finding her usual seat right behind the back door of the number 83 from Kreuzberg. He wouldn't deliver until his competitors had computers, and by that time, she'd be working for one of them. She'd *be* one of them. Out the window of the bus, on the bike path beside the street, a girl with her hair in black ribbons sailed through the morning on her bike. She looked young and free; head dancing up, life flashing, as Marta had been when Tino first wooed her on the old bridge over the Neretva.

She unlatched her calfskin ledger, a gift from her mother, and thumbed through ruled pages to that day's date. A ledger entry from the previous day caught her eye. Bookings to Korcula, Dubrovnik,

Rijeka, and Split had been disastrously confused. It wasn't her fault. Marta had prepared the itinerary down to the finest details, as if she herself were planning to go on these trips. She had arranged for the cheapest fares, and the most *authentic* places to stay, at the customers' request. She had booked a charter boat, day trips to Mostar and the Bay of Kotor, but her Yugoslav colleagues had botched it, sending one large group to the island of Brac by accident and booking the couples into the wrong kinds of hotels, into the big awful state-run places instead of the smaller family-run *alberghi* and *pensioni*. Her compatriots expressed no regret for their mistakes. If anything, they were defiant. Fuck the Germans!

Mistakes would eat away the business; that's what she always told Herr Dieterle when he walked into the agency and disingenuously expressed shock and dismay that she came to work so early.

"Do you ever see your child, Frau Mehmedovic?" he asked her at least once a month. Swallowing her anger, which could be quite pronounced, she told him that she spent lots of time with her child, but she had another one, a very demanding one, which was his travel agency, and if she didn't keep watch like an anxious mother, the elf king would grab it, just as in the song.

She climbed out of the bus. Sunlight fizzed in the trees. Burnishing leaves skittered along the ground. In the playground beside the Apostel Paulus Church a group of women watched their children. They were Muslims, garbed head to toe, and they always gave her a pang. She hurried across the exposed bricks of Apostel-Paulus-Strasse, then slowed down, enjoying the scents of the late summer morning, a far-off trace of woodsmoke, a hint of cold rain, the salt reek of frying potatoes. Jalousies rattled up. The butcher Duben wiped the inside of his display window.

"Frau Mehmedovic," he said.

"Herr Duben."

The butcher liked to instruct her in the proper method for cooking wild boar and corn-fed hen. These were German hunters' methods,

tried and true. He considered his meat to be exemplary. He shot
many of the animals himself in East Prussia, or so he had told her
more than once.

Whenever he used that expression, East Prussia, Marta inserted the
correction: "Poland."

Tino did not like wild game or wild fowl, she had repeatedly informed the butcher. He liked mutton. When pressed, he would eat
British beef. She herself was Ayurvedic and a vegetarian.

"I have a question, Herr Duben, about our new dog."

"Bitte sehr."

"A German pointer."

"A *hunting* dog."

"Exactly right. A hunting dog."

"Your husband, Frau Mehmedovic, is a hunter? I had no idea. He
must come with me sometime to the Masurian Lakes."

Marta grinned at the thought of her husband in Poland with a gun,
tracking wild boar in his Cartier watch and suede jacket, sharing a
homemade schnapps in a frigid hunting lodge with Herr Duben, who
gazed at her tenderly, his perfect beard trimmed to bristle points
from ear to ear.

"What does one feed a hunting dog, Herr Duben?"

He thought about it a moment.

"No chicken bones, of course. They could be fatal. Swine bones in
milk might do. But this is a young dog?"

She jangled up her keys. "Very young."

"Then I like veal in milk."

She told him that she wouldn't waste veal on a dog, and he gave
her a polite expression of dismay. She thanked him. He followed her,
as if he had something else to say. She unlocked the heavy metal door
to her building, but had to hand him the ledger and purse to get it
open. He took these things with visible pleasure.

"I was listening to the radio this morning." He lingered in the
vestibule of her building, holding the door open for her, handing her

the ledger and purse. "And they were speaking about your homeland."

He didn't mean any harm, she told herself.

"They say the most fantastic things down there, but they don't
mean it, I suspect. They like to talk that way, don't they, very—
very—theatrical? That talk of Constantinople and Turkish invasions?
In your homeland?"

Her homeland? She had lived in West Germany for a quarter of her
entire life, three years as a child, five as an adult. She'd given birth to
a child here. Hadn't she spoken good German with Herr Duben?
Weren't they good neighbors in a fine street? A bell in his shop jingled, and he excused himself with a slight bow of his upper body. She
saw him glance back just once in mortification. Frustration had made
her blush, and he had seen it. He knew, and she was sorry. She collapsed for a moment against the wall of the vestibule and held a hand
over her eyes.

GABY LÖWE, her assistant, came at a quarter after nine, very late,
looking more fragile and poisoned than usual. Her skin was becoming greener than the hair on her head. Marta did not admonish
the girl. Gaby might lead a questionable life, but she had a good work
ethic and never made excuses. Marta left her alone. Daughter of a
provincial city in a totalitarian state, she reviled nosiness even more
than she respected authority.

By ten, Gaby had begun to sob. Marta placed a cup of chamomile
tea on the desk. The girl was trying to find cigarettes in the bottom of
a shopping bag woven from spiderwebs and old newspapers. She had
no luck. With each attempt, she brought up more detritus—toothless
blue comb, pill bottle, shriveled lemon rind. Tears streamed out of
her eyes.

"Stop a moment," Marta advised. "Take a long good breath, the
way I showed you."

Gaby found a cigarette. Kohl, applied without art, streamed down her cheeks. She couldn't keep her lips on the smoke. Marta pulled up a chair.

"What's this about?"

The girl reminded her in so many ways of Dubravka. She was twenty. She should be in university, of course, but would never go. She didn't like teachers or books, had absolutely no love of culture or beautiful things, which surprised Marta, because she had smart eyes, and her work attested to a quick mind. Marta had told the girl many times that if she washed the ugly green dye out of her hair, and let the natural blond come through, and if she ate a little something, she would be lovely, and could have her pick of men, which was true, as far as it went; Gaby did not care for the kind of men that Marta considered eligible. Like Dubravka, she had a taste for the lost, the doomed, and the vicious.

"Real estate companies." Gaby wiped the back of her hand across the point of her nose. "The building is sold to some Munich conglomerate. We have to get out." She gave a faint smile of embarrassment, which touched Marta. "Udo is too sick, you know, for a fight. He needs peace and quiet."

"What will you do, then?"

Gaby shrugged. "Move."

Marta crossed her arms. "The men in our lives often determine what kind of life we will lead, whether we will be happy or not, I'm afraid."

Gaby resisted. She scowled. "In your country, maybe. But in this country, in *my* country, we don't allow men to run our lives. If they *fuck* us up, we *kick* them out."

Marta rose from the chair, which, she had argued to Dieterle, needed reupholstering, plucked a large brown envelope off her desk, and headed for the employee rest area, a modified washroom from the days when the travel agency had been someone's home. Not even

ten o'clock, and the day had grown hostile. Such days came. One had
to bend to them or break.

In the rest area, Marta pulled the receipts from the envelope and
started to leaf through them. Here, too, she found bad news. International politics had begun to cause problems. Thanks to the Iraqi invasion of Kuwait, trips had been canceled. Commissions had been
lost. She plucked the green apple from her purse and took one of her
long breaths, absorbing the aroma of the object, letting its simplicity
and grace seep into her lungs. Food was God's medicine. The apple
had been intended for lunch, but she needed its sweetness to still her
anger. She put it to her lips.

Her door banged open, slamming back against the wall.

Marta reared up. "Fräulein Löwe—!"

Gaby pointed back toward the front office. Her skinny arm shook.
"George Markovic!" she screamed.

SIX

ARTHUR STAGGERED BACK against the wall. He wiped his nose with the back of his hand and held it to his left eye, which felt funny. Crimson and pale green blurred in his vision. George's cousin, this Marta, had hit him with superb precision.

He was bleeding. A contact lens had popped out of the eye. He could see only half of the world with clarity, and in the clear half, Marta dialed the telephone and asked for the police. That took nerve. He crouched and began searching for his lost lens, moving on all fours in concentric circles from the point of impact.

The police arrived and walked around him. They went straight to Marta, who immediately accused Arthur of peddling heroin. Strangely, even then Arthur did not feel the collapse of his illusions. Fate would intervene. If the police did their homework, they could trace Arthur all the way back to the East Berlin airport, to his customs official. And what would happen then? Would the memory of the cross linger? It would, thought Arthur. He didn't know why. He had landed in a field of total unpredictability. Berlin kept changing on him, one minute a friend, the next an enemy. But a new certainty lived in him. He couldn't shake it.

The three of them, the two women and Arthur, were taken in separate cars to the local precinct, a cramped station in a small house next to a park. Two of the police questioned the women, and two more handled Arthur, who sat in a corner of a crowded room, holding a tissue to his nose, reflecting that he would have to turn this situation around on his own. At last, after more than an hour of banal repetition, the men started to pay attention to the details of his story, and the truth became clear. They had the wrong man. The real criminal, George Markovic, had made his getaway.

"I admit that I have never seen this man before in my life," said Marta.

"Then why did you suppose he was a drug dealer?" the police inquired.

"I *presumed.*"

Arthur seized his opportunity. He pulled a pen and small notebook from the pocket of his coat and gave the man in charge of the investigation his freelancer's business card. As if he himself had arranged the meeting, with the purpose of doing a story about Berlin law enforcement on the eve of German Unification, he began to fire off questions. At first, the men in the precinct put up their hands and referred him to the Bundeskriminalamt in Wiesbaden. Before long, they were offering coffee and answering him with grins. How many of you will be working on October 3? What are your chief concerns? Are you worried about right-wing violence? Left-wing violence? Do you think Unification is a good thing? Will crime in Berlin become worse now?

He could feel Marta watching him in mortification. The matter turned into a lark. A holiday mood could be detected in the station. Police officers began asking for copies of the magazine containing the story. Would there be photographs? Arthur was taken aside. One of the women was a known anarchist, he was told. The other didn't happen to be German. Rates of domestic violence tended to be higher among Yugoslavs. Most Germans loved Americans and the American way of life.

Both Marko and George had records, it turned out, though George was by far the more accomplished criminal. Feeling generous, the officer in charge of the matter revealed some details of the record to Arthur. Convicted as a teenager on repeated charges of auto theft, George had spent two years in a juvenile detention center north of Frankfurt before escaping and embarking on a lifetime of gunrunning, drug peddling, shoplifting, and, on behalf of Albanian street gangs, shell-game organizing.

Arthur was released with hilarity. The police asked him where in Berlin he intended to stay, and he explained to them his bad luck at the Grand Kempinski, but they shrugged and assured him that he'd find something.

"Of course, he will," interjected Marta Mehmedovic. "I'm his travel agent now."

THE THREE OF THEM returned to the travel agency. The girl with green hair cursed her enemies, the fucking cops. She bounded up a flight of stairs and out of sight, as if eager to toss rocks at them from the roof of the building. Marta stayed at the bottom of the steps. She crossed her arms.

"I apologize," she said in firm English, brushing a strand of hair from her face, assessing him with her cautious, violet eyes. They were sad. The light of the day had made them seem bright, but the shadows in the stairwell gave them a bruised tinge. She obviously has a right to her grievance with George, thought Arthur, and he felt bad that she was apologizing.

"Not necessary," he said.

She gave him a hand up the stairs, though he didn't really need the assistance. They took slow steps, as if he had sprained an ankle. Her right arm hooked around his left elbow, and the landings rose to them in a mournful succession. Light lay thick and heavy in the stairwell, sunbeams hung in dust and kitchen smoke. They moved at a spectral pace, as if they were climbing steps to a different sky from the one outside. She had become yet one more guide across yet one more border.

Once upstairs, he asked for a desk and chair. "I have to write my story," he said.

Her eyes widened. "Not about me, please!"

He smiled. "About the police."

Her cheeks turned a lovely shade of pink, and he noticed the strap of a black bra pressing the skin of a pinkish-brown shoulder. She gave him a desk, and he wrote a five-hundred-word sketch of Precinct 32 in Schöneberg. He wrestled his black acoustic cups from one of the duffel bags. Marta watched him. When he set the acoustic cups on the desk, she asked, "What are those?"

Gaby was curious, too.

"They allow me to send my story through the computer, over the phone line to my office in New York."

He asked if he could use the phone, and both women nodded in unison. Their astonishment charmed him. There were no computers anywhere in the travel agency. In his Filofax, courtesy of Morsch, Arthur found a local Berlin number for his magazine's computer network. He dialed it and pressed the receiver hard down into the acoustic cups. The line picked up and shrieked. The two women grinned at each other.

"Is it sending?' one of them asked.

"Should be."

The confirmation came through. The story had landed. Now, thought Arthur, I can sleep.

M ARTA SAW HIM yawning.

"You're not going to refuse my help, are you?" Marta asked him. "Herr Cape?"

"My name is Arthur," he said. "What's yours?"

"Frau Mehmedovic," she said.

"Marta," said Gaby. "And I'm Gaby."

Then she said it herself: "Marta."

Arthur received a cup of orange juice, and Marta changed the subject. "You were in India?"

"I was."

"Did you ever see the caves of Ellora and Ajanta?"

She asked the question with a sense of longing, and he knew that she had never been.

"I saw Ellora. By myself except for the monkeys. You sound as if you know a lot about India."

She shook her head. "I'm just a travel agent."

Breezes brought the noises of afternoon. The church tower gave five chimes. A man hawked potatoes and eggs, crying the words for potatoes and eggs with great passion, and beneath the words rumbled what sounded like the wooden wheels of a wagon on a cobbled street. Arthur felt a drowsy dislocation. The city seemed to be deepening in his ears, revealing other versions of itself, more ancient Berlins, receding to a limitless depth. Marta brought chamomile tea and told Gaby to go for roses, in case the boss showed up. In the meantime, she had soaked a cloth in warm water.

"Lie down on the floor, if you like," she insisted. "You can use your duffel bag as a pillow."

Arthur complied, and she stretched the cloth across his forehead. Again, he noticed the black bra strap against her skin. She leaned over him, and he adjusted his head to put her body in the clear half of his vision until he could read the freckles on her chest and see the rise of her breasts beneath the rayon of a light blue shirt. He smelled soap on her skin and apple on her breath. He had not been this close to a female in six months.

She gave him a rueful look. "I am a decent person most of the time," she said.

"I'm sure."

She gave him a suspicious smile. "How do you know?"

"I have a sense about you."

Then she gasped. "Your contact lens! I almost forgot! I'm going to find it now."

Some time later, his cheek tickled. He opened his eyes, and she lowered the index finger of her right hand to his eye.

She whispered, "That's it?"

He looked at the tip of her index finger, which gleamed in the heavy light.

"It's very dirty," she said.

He took the lens from the tip of her finger. There was a long silence.

She leaned over him. "You put it in now," she said.

"No. I'm taking the other one out, and I'm putting them both away. So I can take a catnap."

"Would you like me to teach you a breathing exercise?" she asked. "It might help you to sleep."

"If you'd like."

She rolled her ponytail up into a bun. "I can't really do it in this skirt, but I will try."

She attempted to loosen the waist of her skirt and sit cross-legged on the floor beside his body, positioning herself, it seemed, for a yoga session. But there was a sudden rip of fabric, and she got back up.

"I will just tell you how," she said, taking a seat on a chair. "You have to exhale first, *then* inhale, but very slowly. You must release the poison in your body. It's an Indian practice. Ayurveda. You might know it from your journeys."

Arthur followed her instructions, exhaling first, then inhaling, bringing into his lungs the scent of her body, chamomile, apple, soap, and sweat. She did the long breath, too, her lips puckering as she blew out, her eyes narrowing to slits.

"Close your eyes," she said.

He did.

"Think of a place that you love. I think, for instance, of the *Kamenita Vrata.* It's in the city of Zagreb, where I used to go with my mother. It's a kind of church. We sat in the benches and watched the old women pray in the candle smoke, and we talked to each other or just rested. It is a good place for thinking. Maybe you can pick somewhere in India."

New Mexico, he thought, the old adobe house on the rim road above the Hondo Valley, the evening cicada hum, the pale gold sunlight on the mountainsides, remote peaks of Colorado at the horizon, red into violet as the sun fails beyond the gorge of the Rio Grande; aspens shivering, *acequia* burbling, wild dogs snarling beyond the lattias fence.

"Dobro," she said, dipping another rag into cool water, splaying it across his skull.

"What does that mean?"

"Means *good.* Means *fine.*"

"In what language?"

She looked down. "Serbo-Croatian. You shouldn't be talking. You'll ruin the effect."

He opened his eyes and stared into hers. They had a steady curiosity. She put a hand back through her hair, darkish blond and shiny, falling almost to his face. She came back to the subject of his job.

"You're moving to Germany now, because of all the changes?"

He nodded with difficulty.

"And you have a room at the Grand Kempinski, you said?"

"I thought I had one."

She was looking at Arthur with fond skepticism.

"I will find you something," she said, "Arthur Cape."

Arthur liked the sound of his name in her mouth, as if something good in the world had agreed to recognize him. She sat at her desk and began to make phone calls. He fell asleep.

. . .

WHEN HE WOKE, Marta was shutting windows. Crimson burned in the cracks of the sky. Arthur stretched his arms.

"Here is our situation," she said, as if they had been in business negotiations. She clasped her hands behind her back.

"I am not able to find a hotel room." She clasped her hands over the front of her skirt. "So."

"What if I paid you to let me stay here? In the office?"

"My *chef* Dieterle would never allow it."

"We won't tell him."

She gave a polite snap of her head. "There is only one real possibility," she said.

He sat up, rubbing his eyes, and waited.

"You stay in my apartment—until you find something else. Pay me thirty marks a night for lodging, and ten marks a meal for food, if you want."

The sun had gone. Dusk glowed on the floor. Arthur pondered. Was he ready for this?

"Okay?" she persisted.

"All right," he said. He offered his hand. "Marta," he said.

"Arthur," she said.

They shook on the deal.

SEVEN

ARTHUR WOKE PAST MIDNIGHT in the sitting room of the Mehmedovic family, his head brimming with an excess of travel, with faces and locations that he had seen in the coldness of transit. He lay in fresh-washed sheets on a cot and found that he couldn't sleep anymore. He concentrated on a point in the darkness ahead of him. He had a feeling that he had just missed something. An echo of shouts seemed to hover. Tiny noises multiplied. The second hand of a clock nattered. Cool air rippled, catching his cheek. There was a rhythm like breath. He could almost believe that another person shared the room with him. But this was not a dream. He was not aboard an airplane en route in the night, caught between Delhi and Berlin. He lay within the pale of a permanent settlement, surrounded by family. He switched on a reading lamp, and human faces jumped into the light.

They clustered on the walls of his room, among movie posters in Serbo-Croatian and German, nudes in oil and watercolor, Cubist, Fauvist, and Anatomical, a print of Rousseau's "The Origin of the World," a vagina like a continent of shadow above his head. But the photographs were the point of the room; they created a biography, and one face recurred time and again, every third picture or so, the face of a woman who bore a keen resemblance to his hostess.

This woman had unvarying features—thick, dark eyebrows, burning eyes, flared nostrils—but her costumes shifted constantly. In Tyrolean mountain kit, she grappled with Alpine dolomite. In Buffalo hide, hair dyed, she gazed at horizon smoke. She fired a bolt-action rifle as a partisan and crouched on a rice paddy in what appeared to be a surrealist production of Brecht's *The Good Man of Szechuan*. Her leading men were dressed as SS officers, French court fops, United States cavalry officers, and Sioux warriors. Vistas of the American West were everywhere.

Children packed the spaces between the publicity stills, every one of them with a version of this woman's face, and there, in fact, was Marta as an exact replica of her mother on the beach, the bikini more revealing, the hair shorter and less theatrical, but the legs just as sleek and long, the thick upper lip, the defiant nose, remarkable in their fidelity to the original.

He searched for more images of Marta and found her again, posed in a portrait beside a man whom he took to be her husband, proud possessor of wavy black hair, then again in sprawling group shots on a rock-strewn coast, or looking wistfully pleased in a simple sleeveless wedding dress, or glowering in what might have been a director's chair. In one picture, taken when she could not have been more than six or seven years old, she sat in the lap of an immense man with a familiar face. Arthur couldn't place him at first. He aimed the lamp beam at the wall and studied the features. Marta had a bright snowcap of blond hair and sun-browned legs. She was dressed in a simple summer frock and occupied the knee of one granitic leg. She had sad eyes then, too; so did the adult in the photograph.

"Shit," whispered Arthur to himself. "That's Orson Welles."

Something moved at the end of his cot. Was it a rat? His arm flailed out, knocking the lamp off the table, extinguishing its light. He froze in the darkness and understood what had happened. His own goddamn feet had unnerved him. He had been scared to death by a twitch of his ankles in the sheets. He picked up the lamp and worked his fingers in blindness around the base until he found the switch. He flicked back on. At the end of the cot, a small brown dog was staring at him.

A dark nose sniffed at his toes. It was a puppy no more than a few weeks old. Arthur reached for the dog, but she lowered her haunches, and a stain spread beneath the cot.

"Marta won't like that," said Arthur.

The dog raised a paw and pointed her nose at him. He saw no identification. She had no collar, no tag. Her eyelids fluttered. He stroked her belly, soft and white, and ran his fingers down her ears. He placed her back in the sheets where she had been. Arthur's stomach gave a groan, and her ears pricked up. He was famished. He hadn't eaten a real meal in almost a day. The dog looked at him in expectation.

ARTHUR THREW ON a T-shirt and jogging sweats and cracked the door. He tiptoed down the hall, floorboards creaking. Ahead of him, radio static hissed. Radiators tinkled. He entered the kitchen. Halfway across the room, back turned to him, sat Marta.

Her head rested on her shoulder. She seemed to be listening to a broadcast in a tongue that was vaguely Russian, reminiscent of broadcasts that he had heard on shortwave radios in Srinagar— Serbo-Croatian, of course. He stood there, watching her; he felt like one of the dead on a haunt. She might have been asleep.

The refrigerator next to him began to hum. He contemplated his options. She had urged him to treat the kitchen as his own personal pantry. But people said such things without meaning them, and she no doubt already regretted her generosity. He turned and walked a few feet back down the corridor. From a culinary standpoint, it was either a German or a Yugoslav home, meaning cold meats, potato salad, cheeses, jellies. There would be good bread. There might be chocolate. His mouth began to water. He could keep very quiet. He would return with the food to his room.

He knelt in front of the refrigerator and popped open the door. He saw a hunk of goat cheese wrapped in cellophane, a plate of cold roast lamb, a cup of Bulgarian yogurt, and a tomato. He reached for the goat cheese.

"Guten appetit." She got up and opened a cupboard. "Plates," she said. She pulled out a drawer. "Silverware."

She beckoned to a chair beside the table. Arthur slipped into the chair. She put a finger to her lips and pointed down a corridor. *Sleeping boy.* He nodded his head.

"Sorry," he whispered. "I was feeling peckish—"

"Don't be ridiculous." She wore a flannel robe, sashed at the waist, and he could see the reddish freckles on the triangle of skin between the lapels. "I'm sure my fight with Dubravka woke you up."

Marta took out the lamb, the yogurt, the tomato, plums, and a bowl of olives he hadn't seen.

"Would you like some chamomile tea?"

Arthur surrendered. At bedtime, she had offered chamomile, and he had declined. He had never liked the stuff. But she was determined to get it down his throat. Her faith in the beverage seemed to go beyond the medicinal qualities inherent in the herb. She seemed to believe in the very principle of chamomile, whatever that might be. She put on a kettle. On the radio, a chamber orchestra playing Bartók was interrupted by a news broadcast.

The teakettle started to shake. She placed a bright yellow mug in front of Arthur. As she did this, she shook her head and muttered words that he didn't understand.

"Everything okay?" he asked.

"Everything's going to hell," she said.

"Sorry to hear it."

"Everything's going to hell, and my husband wants to go back. He's going to force me to go back."

"Back?"

"To Yugoslavia."

She wanted him to ask another question. He was certain. "Does he have a job there?"

She looked away.

Arthur changed the subject. "There's a dog in my room," he said.

This raised her eyebrows.

"I like dogs," he added.

"Yes?" She interrogated him with a gaze. "Is that true?"

"I grew up with a mutt."

"What is a mutt?"

"No pedigree. But your dog looks like a very fine animal."

"Are you looking for a pet?"

He wanted to say yes, but what would he do with a puppy? She gave him a weary grin, appreciating his dilemma. She appeared to be ashamed of herself for asking. She narrowed one eye at him.

"You must be careful what you say."

She reached behind her head and pinned up her hair. She was less German in the shadows of the kitchen, darker, more Slavic, though Arthur hardly knew what the word meant beyond the clichés of James Bond movies and Cold War politics. She'd rubbed the makeup off her face, and he saw that her eyebrows did not seem quite as thick as those in the photographs. Her lashes looked even longer, descending lines of silk. She had a few reddish freckles on her cheeks and nose, and the mother's upper lip over a thin bottom one.

"You have been to Yugoslavia?"

"No."

She crossed her long legs, and he glimpsed a tan calf.

"We Yugoslavs fight one another. Sometimes we make babies, too. You never know." She leaned forward on the table, elbows apart, her head cocked toward the radio. "There is a place in a part of Yugoslavia called Knin, very ugly. No one ever wanted to live there. Rocks, train yards, an old castle, wild dogs. *Schluss.* This is not exaggeration."

Arthur ate the last bite of the lamb. Her eyes watched the meat disappear down his mouth.

"Now some men have barricaded Knin—"

"Barricaded?"

She thought that she had used the wrong English word. "Blocking the roads so no one can get in. You know?"

He nodded. The crazy men, she went on, seemed to think that they were going to be slaughtered. They seemed to be under the delusion that their neighbors were reincarnated versions of the Fascists of the Second World War. It was incomprehensible. The whole mess had to do with a symbol on a flag, and talk of secession, and many other things that Arthur had read about here and there in the *International Herald Tribune* but had not really examined.

"There will be a war," she said. "Though my husband doesn't think so."

She presented this fact as if it guaranteed the outbreak of hostilities. Arthur nodded, distracted by her reference to the husband, wondering if it meant that their conversation had gone far enough, that she now found his presence unwelcome.

"Could he possibly be right?"

Arthur knew a little about her country's history. The German invasion of Yugoslavia had resulted in two wars, one between the invaders and the natives, one between the natives, a civil war. Neither had begun until the Germans attacked. Both had been bloody and terrible, but the civil war had arguably been more catastrophic. Huge numbers of civilians had died.

For a moment, neither of them said a word. She did not appear to believe that her husband could be right. Arthur remembered his tea. He could not leave without drinking down his chamomile.

"I didn't see any pictures of Marko and George in my room," he said. She laughed. "You wouldn't."

"George isn't really your cousin?"

"A very complicated question."

He sipped the chamomile tea and found that it wasn't so bad.

"My mother is an actress, a fairly well-known actress, and she had many husbands, which is typical for actresses, I think. George comes to us through one of those husbands, even though he would argue that he is related by blood. He claims to be her last remaining blood relative."

"What happened to the others?"

"Others?"

"Her other blood relatives."

Marta put a finger to her throat and slid it across the skin. There was a long pause. Arthur thought it must be time to go back to his room, but he couldn't make himself.

"Is that Orson Welles in the picture with you?" he asked.

She nodded. "My mother became great friends with him after he came to Yugoslavia to make *The Battle of Neretva*. You know that movie? We called him Vracar. I think it means wizard in your language."

Marta blew on the hot water in her cup.

"Your mother was famous?"

Marta cleared her throat. Her chair had somehow moved an inch closer to Arthur's chair. "Here. In East Germany, I mean. She played the Indian girl in a lot of East German westerns. The Politburo gave her a dacha."

She told him the story of her mother. According to the official Yugoslav state biography, which was the only reliable guide, Vesna Bistritza had been reared an orphan in the Bosnian city of Mostar. When she was fifteen, she wandered into a high school production of Strindberg's *Miss Julie,* and after a casual reading, won the lead role. For a few years, she lived a normal life. She met and married Marta's father, Osman Lazic, a rising young star of the local Communist Party; he was an aspiring playwright, and a nonpracticing Muslim, descendant of generations of Ottoman civil servants. They had two children, Marta, a daughter, and Esad, a son, who drowned in the river Neretva when Marta was four.

"That's terrible," said Arthur.

"Long ago," said Marta, but she was staring at his plate again, resting her cup of tea against the side of her face.

He placed his hand on the table beside her hand. "So your mother left Mostar?"

"Yes," said Marta.

Her mother became frustrated with small-town life and small-town ways in Mostar, she told him, with the petty ambitions of minor party functionaries; she had an affair with an aeronautics engineer, a Croat who had renounced Catholicism for science. She divorced the lapsed Muslim and married the lapsed Catholic, who took her off to Tripoli and Moscow for a few years. In Moscow, she was cast in her first movie, and after that, there was no keeping her in the kitchen. Leaving behind yet another child, Marta's half-brother Mato, the son of the engineer, she ran home for a last tryst with Marta's father, and had one more baby with him, Marta's sister Dubravka, before taking up with the infamous Serbian composer Stepan Markovic, nicknamed Dushan. She gave Dushan a daughter, and Marta a half-sister, named Isadora, who turned out to be the last of her progeny that anyone knew about.

"George may be related to Dushan by marriage," Marta explained. "Personally, I don't believe he's related to me at all."

Arthur watched her face and drank his tea. He was getting to the bottom.

"Tell me about you," she said after a while.

"What would you like to know?"

"What's your ethnicity?'

It was not a word that he often heard in casual conversation. At first, he hesitated to answer.

"Mischling," he finally said, using a German term that appeared at the same moment in his mouth and head, an offensive word, really, used by the Nazis to describe peoples of mixed origins, particularly Jews who had German blood. That's how he'd heard his father once

describe himself to a family friend, and he'd never forgotten the exchange, a moment in passing that had meant nothing to his father, a rather thoughtless reply among millions, but indelible to Arthur. He sometimes believed that his entire foray into the German language grew out of the mystery of this stray answer to an indifferent question. The name of the family friend had been forgotten, along with the environing conversation, but the word had been hovering around in the back of Arthur's mind ever since; his origins were safely locked within it. If anything, he considered himself a Texan, but he didn't say this to Marta; Texan would not qualify as an ethnicity.

He tried to explain: "Pole—on my father's side. His name used to be Caplawitz, or something like that. On my mother's side, German, Irish, and through her mother, American Indian."

Arthur noticed an uptick in Marta's interest.

"You're a Mohican?" Marta asked.

The eagerness of her question took him by surprise. "Creek. They're a tribe in Oklahoma."

"Whenever I hear about the Indians of America," she said, "I think of Mohicans."

"And what about you?" He had a feeling that she had asked him in order to be asked herself.

"My mother is Austro-Hungarian. My father Ottoman. Bosnian-Turkish-Vlach-Gypsy-Circassian. My father is the son of Muslims, so I was raised theoretically a Muslim."

"*You* are a Muslim?" The idea thrilled and astonished him. It perplexed him, too.

"Why is that so hard to believe?"

He backtracked. "I just meant that Muslims in India don't—look much like you—they aren't blond—"

She sat in silence, thinking about something. She looked around the kitchen until her eyes lit on a thick, brown, leatherbound book. She took the book from the kitchen counter and thumbed to a blank page.

"You want to know a little more about me, Arthur?"

He was taken aback by the question, and by the pointed use of his name. He didn't know exactly what she meant. Hadn't he been listening for the last half hour?

"Please," he said.

A history lesson followed. Later, he would think of it as his very first history lesson. Before it, he had not understood the meaning of the word.

SHE RUMMAGED THROUGH her purse and came up with a tube of vermilion lipstick. She applied the lipstick to the ruled paper, sketching out a paramecium of land. She wrote a word in German within the confines of the paramecium: *Jugoslawien.* Yugoslavia.

"Okay?"

"Okay," Arthur said. He was being made to pay for his provincialism. There were millions of Muslims around the world. Of course they didn't all look like Kashmiris.

It was a very crude map. She put the lipstick back in her bag, and went to find a pencil.

"This thing," she indicated on her return, pointing with the pencil at the paramecium, "represents a state, with borders, and laws, and a flag. It does not—absolutely does not—represent a people, or a nation. It is not a piece of land. It is a *state.* You understand?"

He managed a studious expression.

"A very young state, younger than the United States of America. Since 1918 only. But in this very young state live peoples who have been on this land"—she made markings outside the vermilion lipstick blob of Yugoslavia to indicate mere territory—"for hundreds and hundreds of years. You understand? Young state. Old peoples."

"Jawohl."

Her pedantry had real charm. She began to write names. "Some peoples were there before the Romans." The word *Albanen* appeared, for Albanians. "Some came with the barbarian invasions that de-stroyed Rome." She wrote the word *Slawen,* for Slavs. "Peoples, peoples, peoples, pouring into this one little piece of land, this Balkan Penin-sula. You understand?"

Now she drew a much larger blob around the paramecium of Yu-goslavia, and this blob stretched down to the bottom of the sheet of paper, a peninsula beginning south of the Danube River, which was a squiggle, labeled as *Donau,* and ending with the southern tip of the Peloponnesus in Greece. She made dots for the islands of the Aegean.

"And now," she said, touching his hand, giving him a violent tremor, "it gets more complicated."

She pronounced "complicated" oddly, with the stress on the next-to-last syllable—compli-*CAT*-ed.

"The religions. First, *Christentum.*"

Christianity. She spoke this word with great force.

"Christentum," Arthur repeated, thinking of the cross that had helped him across the border. That cross, carried before armies, carved on tombs, stretching back into earlier times, before the crucifixion, now became even more marvelous than it had been in the hands of the customs official at the airport. Marta smelled like warm lotion. She drew an arrow between the word *Christentum* and the word *Slawen.*

"You know the Roman Emperor Diocletian? His palace in Spalato? No? He made East Rome and West Rome, and the Christian Church split along that line, which runs, by the way"—she drew a dark streak right through the middle of the lipstick Yugoslavia—"right through the middle of my country. Christianity and Rome became the same thing, you see. Rome splits and makes two halves. The reli-gion splits and makes two halves. East. West. Like that."

She wasn't just teaching Arthur the history of Yugoslavia. She was giving him the whole of Western civilization since the Roman Empire.

"Western side was Latin Christianity. Eastern side became Greek. The two sides stopped speaking the same language. Their liturgies were different. You know liturgies?"

Arthur listened in a state of growing trance to her voice, which was deep and warm, deeper than he would have expected from this slender woman, a voice that made him think of chocolate and plums. He began to eat one of the plums from the refrigerator. He ceased to pay attention in the strictest sense. The nape of Marta's neck had the smoothness of water. Her hair hung above the nape in slips and coils. The nape lay within reach of his hand, but one touch would have ended the lesson. He dropped the pit of the plum into the empty cup of tea and contemplated the nape of her neck like a man on the bank of a river, lost in ripples and eddies.

"Catholic Slavs," she said, suddenly looking at him, "and Orthodox Slavs. I mean to say, Latin Slavs and Greek Slavs, West Slavs and East Slavs, just as there were two Christian churches, Latin Church and Greek Church. And the Catholics, the West Slavs, became"— with speeding fingers, she wrote the word *Kroaten*—"Croats."

The heat of history emanated from her body. She was staring right into his eyes.

"And the Greek Church Slavs," she said, "the East Slavs, became—"

"Serbs."

"Yes."

Then Islam, the hordes of Mohammed sweeping up the Arabian Peninsula in the sixth century A.D., hurling back the armies of Byzantium, engulfing territory under the flag of the Crescent and Stars, carrying the message of Allah into North Africa, into Europe, up through Spain and France, taking Sicily, Syria, even the Holy City, Jerusalem. Her nose flared above her moist upper lip. She belonged to places that Arthur had never seen. And yet, he could not explain it, she called up a memory of home within him—not the home that he remembered from his childhood, but some other place, larger, less defined, but known to him since his childhood. He recalled a line from the frontispiece of one of his father's old leatherbound histories, a volume about the fall of Constantinople in 1453. *The spider weaves*

owl calls the watches in the towers of

to this place." Her pencil came
ed lipstick state of Yugoslavia. "On
e made an X at the bottom of the
ght the Christians in 1389 and wiped
father's ancestors became Muslims.

b invisible currents in the house. A
A child spoke unintelligible words in
sleep. Marta lowe____ _e to a whisper.

"After that battle, these peoples that I am telling you about lived under Ottoman Turks for five hundred years. Until 1918, and then—" She snapped her fingers. "Everything fell apart, and these peoples—peoples cast loose in the great world without a home—they formed this state with the name of 'Yugoslavia.'"

Arthur thought that the lecture must be at an end. His teacup had been drained, and he was ready to kiss her lips.

"Yugoslavia means Land of South Slavs," she said, beginning to read his intention, but undecided. "South Slavs are Yugoslavs. But who is a South Slav really? No one says to himself, I am South Slav. They say, I am Croat. I am Serb. I am Bosnian." She drew a swastika on the paramecium. "Germans invade. Hundreds of thousands die. First government of South Slavs is destroyed. Germans leave. Just like Turks, they run." She crossed out the swastika. "And then we have Tito and Communists. Tens of thousands die, and that is state of my youth. Why not? We try everything else. We try every religion. We try monarchy. We try Fascism and democracy. Everything fails. So why not Communism?" She drew a red star with the lipststick. "And, of course, in fifty years, Communism is kaput. This young state full of old peoples eats every government and spits it out." She seemed on the verge of tears. "So we will try once more the civil war."

He touched the nape of her neck. She withstood him, gazing a long time into the shadows of her kitchen. But she was trembling. Arthur touched her cheek. He was startled by the word that came out of his mouth.

"History," he said.

Another human being padded into the kitchen. Arthur sensed a presence a few inches from the table, gathering in the scene: the cheese rinds and bread crusts scattered around the plates, the emptied teacups, the two heads inclined over the leatherbound book, Arthur's fingers frozen on Marta's cheek. He looked up. A stunning female stood there. She drew strands of hair back from her face, as if emerging from a forest into a clearing. Her eyes, red from crying, glowed in wonder. The sister, thought Arthur, the sister Dubravka.

EIGHT

THE NEXT MORNING, Dubravka packed her bags, and Marta inquired on her behalf about train times. A train left for Vienna at 12:30 A.M., and from Vienna, her sister could catch an express to Zagreb.

In the meantime, Marta pondered her obligations to Arthur Cape. For a journalist, Arthur knew very little about how one got established in Berlin. He planned to work in Germany, but when the police had asked about his registration papers, he hadn't seemed to understand. In fact, she knew he didn't. If Marta didn't urge him to register, he wouldn't bother, and he'd get into trouble.

He hadn't given much thought to the residency permit either. In India, he had worked out his residency through some office that routinely accepted bribes, but here, she had told him, that wouldn't work. He had to go to an office called the Ausländeramt to get a residency permit if he intended to stay longer than three months in the country. Americans were not exempt. Despite victory in the Second World War, they couldn't just run free.

And then there was the matter of money. He had one hundred German marks to his name. Marta shook her head in disbelief that an

American journalist for a serious publication could show up with so little hard currency. The rest, he told her, was in American checks, and when she asked him what he expected to do with American checks in Berlin, he said that he expected to deposit them, and draw off his bank account. When she told him that it could take two months or longer for those checks to clear, he informed her that she was mistaken. The American banking system and the German banking system worked in tandem. He had lived in the country as a university student, and he knew. But he did not know. Those nine months as a student could actually hurt him. They might lead him to think things that simply weren't true.

So she must help. She must make up for the apple. That act, which he dismissed, troubled her conscience. She had been a bad Muslim. She had been angry about other matters, and this strapping blond American had walked into her office, and she had assaulted him. Though she knew as little about the Koran as it was possible to know and still be an adherent of the faith of Islam, she knew that peace mattered above all else.

She had compromised the business, too. Thank God no customers had witnessed the incident. If Herr Dieterle had seen her behavior, he would have been mortified. She would have been fired.

She knew that her insistence on obeying rules could be oppressive. Her husband and sister had told her so often enough. But this time she was right. She didn't want to go overboard or give the American the impression that she was trying to please him, and she certainly didn't want him to know that she was doing everything out of a sense of shame, but nevertheless she had to try to organize his life for him. She had to try to make his entry into Berlin a bit easier than it had been so far.

At the same time, she told herself, the gesture must not make her life more difficult. Unfortunately, it already had. She had offered Arthur a bed in her home, and her sister had implied with a single look that something untoward was happening; her sister, who had never shown the slightest impulse toward chastity or virtue, who asked old soothsayers and witches in Medjugorje to direct her love affairs, who carried around the bark of hawthorn trees and the bones of birds, who slept with none but the cruel, the sadistic, and the criminal.

Dubravka packed her bags while Arthur slept. It had been her idea to leave.

"You should thank me," she said to Marta.

"Why?"

Dubravka's lips parted, but she thought better of her reply and closed them again.

"Why do you have to go back now? Aren't you worried about the trouble?" Marta then asked. "Doesn't it concern you even a little?"

"You're the trouble I'm worried about, sister."

Dubravka went into the bedroom and returned with her one bag. Marta fought the impulse to explain herself. Dubravka could not understand. She was young and had nothing in her life to protect. She had no belief that could not be compromised, no loyalty that could not be turned. Except maybe for one, Marta thought.

"I know what people think of me," Dubravka had once said to her. "Poor orphan. But that's mistaken. You're the orphan. I have my home."

Dubravka's long hair swung in the morning light. She checked her purse a last time, making sure that she had everything.

"Want my advice?"

Marta wiped tears from her eyes. "No."

"You should fuck this guy."

"Thank you. I'm very grateful."

"I won't say a word to Tino."

Dubravka gave her a kiss on either cheek. Her high-heeled footsteps receded down the corridor. Dubravka never wore practical shoes. She didn't own a single pair. Marta put her hands over her eyes. Her husband had left her; now her sister, too. Her chest heaved. The American was still asleep.

. . .

AFTER A MORNING at work, Marta met Arthur in the park beside the Apostel Paulus Church. He had cleaned up and even shaved. He was still wearing a pair of dusty old cowboy boots and a flannel shirt, neither of which would make much of an impression on the German authorities, but otherwise he had vastly improved. In his own way, thought Marta, he was quite good-looking.

He volunteered to push the stroller. Pino's red feather trembled in the wind. "I like good candy," Pino told Arthur, though Arthur didn't understand a word.

First she made Arthur register at the Hauptstrasse police station near the travel agency. He gave her office as his address. After filling out the registration form, Arthur was handed a grayish slip of paper and told to go to the Ausländeramt in Moabit. Marta had known this visit was next, but the words made her heart sink anyway. The Ausländeramt was the office for foreigners, a grim place, and she hated it.

They emerged from the subway stop in Moabit onto the banks of a brown river making its way between smokestacks and trash bluffs. Marta didn't like this part of the city. She had bad memories of her first and only trip to the Ausländeramt, when she was treated like a sluttish invader. She had walked by herself before dawn in a neighborhood where water rats, derelicts, and prostitutes congregated.

They came to a long, rectangular building beneath a highway overpass. Men in kurtas, skullcaps, and dashikis, women in saris, veils, and hoods lined up in the heat of the afternoon for the process of national admittance. Marta discovered that she and Arthur had come too late. By one o'clock in the afternoon, the clerks of the Ausländeramt no longer accepted the applications of newcomers. They would have to come again—the next morning, around five A.M.

"Hungry?" asked Arthur.

They stopped for lunch at a Turkish street stall, where he ordered roast meat drowned in yogurt sauce, a Döner kebab. Before Marta could stop him, he gave some of the meat to Pino. Marta ordered vegetarian. It was a moral matter for her. And it was control. She did not have sway over governments, over the flow of currencies, or even over the comings and goings of her own husband, but she could determine what went into her mouth. Though her husband raged at her in restaurants when she tormented German waiters, though no one, not even her mother, sympathized with her position, she persisted. Meat was unnecessary. Meat was forced on people by states and business conglomerates. It was like oil.

"My family would rather have a Communist than a vegetarian in the family," said Arthur.

"I'm both," she said.

"You're a Communist?"

"My father is."

"Hitler was a vegetarian," he said.

She gave him a stern look. "What does that mean exactly?"

Arthur's face turned red.

"Are you saying that I am like Hitler because I am a vegetarian? Or that just because Hitler was a vegetarian, no one else should be?"

"It was just a comment."

"You think I am ridiculous for being a vegetarian."

His mouth began to grin. "Misguided."

"Why?"

"Cooked meat is one of the world's delights."

"I disagree."

"That's your good right," he said.

"It is," she said.

"But I guarantee you that if you ate the meat that I cooked, you would stop being a vegetarian."

"And I guarantee that you're wrong."

After lunch, they went to a bank on the Kudamm, an institution that handled international wire transfers. Marta used it in transactions for the travel agency, and the tellers knew her face. Arthur tickled

Pino with the red feather and did silly dances in the bank foyer, making the child giggle uncontrollably. Marta explained that she wanted to have a chat with Frau Miep, and after the chat, Frau Miep opened Arthur's bank account. He became liquid.

Outside the bank, he threw his arms around Marta. She proposed a coffee. They had time, and she was feeling the need of a warm drink. They took chairs at a café on the street near her office. Pino fell asleep in the stroller.

"You have a wife?" she asked him.

He seemed startled by the question. "No."

Marta had been thinking about it some, she had to admit, idly thinking about it. She didn't believe that he did have a wife, but he might have someone else, a girl back in India, someone at home. One never knew. But it really wasn't her business, and she wished that she could take back her question. Of course, he was unmarried. He didn't have a ring. He hadn't mentioned a wife once.

"I've been married for eight years," she said, and then, again, wished that she had said nothing at all, because her words gave him an opening to discuss what had happened the night before, an inappropriate moment that she would rather have forgotten. "Hard to believe for someone like you, I imagine."

She changed the subject. "Where is your family, Arthur?"

"Mostly in Texas." .

Marta grinned widely. "When I was a girl, it seemed to me sometimes that my mother lived in Texas, even though I'm pretty sure that she has never been there in her life. In her movies, she was always getting kidnapped by Texas Rangers or Texas ranchers or somebody like that, but I never met a real Texan before. You don't wear a cowboy hat?"

"Just the boots," he said, and he lifted them up for her to see. "Ostrich-skin. Justin Ropers."

Over her objection, he paid for their coffees and then bought a new fluorescent pink leash for the puppy.

"Now we must get you a place to stay," she said.

She led him to an apartment building next door to the café, right around the corner from the travel agency, a six-floor, prewar building that had been sandblasted, water-sealed, and repainted a historical yellow. The final step in his habilitation would be shelter. They walked up five flights of stairs, Arthur bearing the stroller in his arms.

"You remember my assistant Gaby?" Marta asked Arthur.

He did.

"This woman is Gaby's great-aunt. She loves Americans, and if you tell her that you work for a well-known American magazine, she will certainly accept you as a tenant."

Just then, the light in the stairwell went out. Marta reached across Arthur to press a button, and for an instant, in the darkness, the heat of his climbing body rose through her senses. Unlike her husband, he didn't wear cologne. She pressed the button. The light blinked back on.

"After the war, she worked as a governess in the home of a wealthy Jewish family in New York."

"During the workweek, you and I would be neighbors," Arthur said. "Wouldn't we?"

"It will be less than you'd pay for your own place. Real estate prices are very high now. And if you don't like it, you can always move."

They reached the door. Marta gave three firm raps and waited.

A few seconds elapsed. *"Ja?"* called a high-pitched voice at last. *"Wer ist da?"*

"Hello, it's Frau Mehmedovic, from Herr Dieterle's travel agency. Gaby's boss. May we speak a moment?"

Marta whispered in Arthur's ear. "She despises her niece. She probably thinks that I have come to make a complaint."

The door creaked open, and before them stood an ancient woman in a magenta dress patterned with black maple leaves. Necklaces of gilt and pearl drooped in great loops around her neck. Her hair suggested the elegance of the 1930s, precociously bouncy and trimmed to reveal the neck.

Marta indicated Arthur. "May I introduce Herr Arthur Cape?"

Arthur gave a stiff, odd bow.

"What is it? What do you want? It's my birthday, and my nephew is coming this instant to take me to the Kempinski."

"Lucky you," said Arthur.

"It's not *my* Kempinski, of course. My Kempinski is gone. But the champagne is still decent, and they serve a nice lobster bisque." Arthur helped the old woman into her coat, which pleased her. She regarded him with newfound interest. "You have manners."

"Thank you."

Marta felt an odd rush of pride.

"How old am I, would you guess?" the old woman then asked.

"Seventy."

She cackled. "I am ninety, young man."

"Nein."

Frau Herbst turned to Marta. "This isn't your husband, Frau——"

"Mehmedovic."

Frau Herbst gave Arthur a sideways glance. "*Nein, nein,* he's no Mehmedovic."

Frau Herbst extended an arm, and Arthur assisted her down the corridor to an elevator accessible only by key.

"I received a phone call last week from a piece of dreck who wanted a room," Frau Herbst related, as she managed, with trembling fingers, to press the button for the ground floor. "I said to him that I didn't like the way that he talked, that he sounded ill-mannered, and he said, 'What's the matter, you old bitch, you don't think I have the *bread?*'"

The old woman suddenly rounded on them. "This isn't one of *her* friends you've brought me, is it?" She regarded Arthur with possible distaste. The old woman obviously meant Gaby.

Marta took a scolding tone. "Certainly not. Herr Cape is a well-known American journalist. Isn't that right? He came to the agency seeking lodging."

Her nephew had not yet appeared, so they decided to take a table at the café on the street. Arthur pulled out chairs for both of them. Pino woke with a yowl of complaint. He was hungry and wanted out of the stroller.

"Jürgen drives a Porsche," Frau Herbst said.

The waiters were lazy, but Marta grabbed one and ordered bread, cheese, and apricot juice for her son. She looked at her watch and realized the time. She couldn't wait much longer, and she wanted an answer about the room from the old lady. She was resolved to finish the day on a successful note.

The old woman went on. "Russian women are good in bed, I hear."

Arthur looked across the table at Marta and winked. "I don't believe Frau Mehmedovic is Russian."

Marta glared back at him. She pretended not to have understood the comment, but she could feel her cheeks burning.

The horrifically rude old woman went on. "In the 1920s, I frequented gigolos. My husband never minded. All he cared about was baccarat."

Arthur asked Frau Herbst how much she wanted for a room.

"Verdammt," she cursed under her breath. "Doesn't that Porsche go fast enough for him?"

Just then, mercifully, a dark blue fish of a car finned up to the curb. A middle-aged man in a tuxedo stepped out of the driver's side and waved at the old woman. Arthur helped Frau Herbst to her feet. Her nephew took her by the arm and led her to the open door of the Porsche, but before he could get her legs tucked beneath the dash, she whispered in his ear, and he returned to them.

"Come by again," the nephew said. "And bring lots of cash. German marks are preferred."

NINE

APAINED SILENCE hung over the café table. In the midst of it, Pino gulped apricot juice, tore open rolls for inspection, and turned slices of Havarti cheese into grubby gray balls before popping them into his mouth.

Grinning at the spectacle, Arthur said, "She's a wretched old soul. Thanks for the introduction."

Marta laughed. "She's planning to seduce you."

"Was that your idea?"

She crossed her arms. "It's the least I could do."

"The very least."

The waitress brought the check, and they rose from their chairs. Arthur insisted on buying groceries. He offered to make dinner. In her experience, most men didn't cook. She reminded him that she was a vegetarian and very picky. "No meat," she warned.

They hurried to a grocery store, slipping through doors just minutes before closing time. He bought a small roasting chicken for himself, eggplants, onions, and tomatoes for ratatouille for her; he bought assorted cheeses, olives, and bread. On the way to the subway, he purchased two dark green bottles of Vernaccia di San Gimignano from a

Tuscan wine shop. She bought a bag of Turkish coffee beans for Bosnian coffee after dinner.

Marta had not been alone with another man in more than a decade, not since the age of seventeen, when she first met Tino Mehmedovic. Back then, her husband was a magician and made the other boys disappear—quite a feat, when she looked back. She'd loved his wavy hair, his instant charm upon everyone he met, even his silly Italian affectations. He swept her off her feet, no point in disputing it. Then he'd been her husband. Later, in the habit of a settled life, she had not sought the company of other men. She had not bothered even to think about them or look at them. But she was doing it now. Her pleasure came as a shock and a fright. Her stomach popped. They hurried to catch the subway. Once on board, Marta realized that they hadn't paid.

The trains ran on an honor system. Without a ticket, one could ride, but it was called black riding, *schwarzfahren,* an illegal act with a financial penalty. Marta had mixed feelings about black riding. She had once seen a fellow Yugoslav busted for the practice, and it had been a strange experience. She had been ashamed *for* the man and ashamed *of* him. Now she felt no shame at all. She was enjoying the sense of lightness in her arms, in her soul. She relished the delight of an insignificant crime.

Two stations down, men in royal blue uniforms stepped into the car. When the train rolled forward, they demanded tickets, and she was surprised at how little she minded. Arthur pleaded ignorance. After inspecting his passport, they let him off. But Marta had no excuse. Not even her son, talking in German about his new puppy, moved the hearts of the U-Bahn officials. With everyone watching, with several of the passengers staring in disdain, the men escorted man, woman, and boy off the train. She received a one-hundred-mark fine, which stung. Tino could never find out.

Pino started to whine. More rolls, more cheese, more apricot juice. *Mama.*

She picked him up. "That is the first time that I have ever been fined in this country. Do you believe it? In five years."

"Oops."

"Until now, I am a model citizen. Except, of course, for the fact that I am not a citizen."

"You want to be a citizen?" asked Arthur, without a trace of guile. He really didn't know.

"It would be a help," she replied.

B Y T H E T I M E they got home, the sun had melted in the western sky. Reflections of bar lights shimmered in the greasy waters of the Landwehrkanal. She fed Pino fried eggs, green beans, and apples. Afterward, Arthur kicked her out of the kitchen and started to work on his menu.

She bundled up her son and took the puppy for a stroll along the canal. Houseboats at the shore trembled and creaked. Rock music blared from a *kneipe* on the far bank, until its noise drowned in the clanking wail of a passing police siren. The puppy bumbled down an incline to the water's edge, yapping at ducks. Pino scrambled after. Marta caught him just on the edge of the stone embankment. The night cooled. What was she going to do about the American upstairs? When she returned to the apartment, the odor of garlic, salt, and fat rose to her nose. Arthur simmered the chicken in two pans.

The puppy tongued grease off the floor. Marta had to leave the kitchen, Arthur said. Pino could stay, but Pino didn't want to. Her son followed her into the sitting room. She must remember to call her mother in Tel Aviv. They hadn't spoken in weeks.

Marta switched on the television. There was nothing about Yugoslavia but lots on Germany. Fear in Berlin grew in advance of Unification. The whole world was watching. What if neo-Nazis marched? What if someone attacked a synagogue? What if this whole thing, merging East and West, had been a mistake? She smiled to herself.

Served the Germans right for thinking they could pull Unification off so easily. But they would.

Pino put his fingers, then his lips, on the television screen. She dragged him away and turned off the set. Arthur came to the door. The puppy tripped into the room. Arthur gave Marta a glass of wine and a plate of olives. They toasted Pino and drank.

"You would not like help?" Marta asked.

"No, thanks."

"How is the chicken?"

He gave a broad smile. His hands opened up as if to beckon her to the meal. "Delectable. Having second thoughts?"

The puppy licked her ankle. Pino took a bite of an olive. Marta drained her wine and asked for another glass.

"Dinner in minutes," Arthur said.

Pino threw his arms around the puppy, but she slipped away. The boy tumbled with a giggle to the floor. He did somersaults. He wasn't afraid. She had been a fearless child, too. She smelled his hair and became a little delirious with its perfume.

The phone rang, and Marta knew who it was. Usually, on trips, Tino made one call, invariably between ten and eleven on Friday or Saturday night.

This time he was drunk.

"You okay?" he shouted over a thumping dance beat. She could feel his hand gripping the receiver, as if he were squeezing her fingers. There was a pause. A woman spoke to him, telling him to come or dance or drink. Marta hung up. Arthur carried plates, silverware, and napkins into the room. He took the blanket off the cot and laid it across the floor.

"Picnic," he said.

They needed candles, he said. She told him where to find them, and he lit them and placed them on the mantel, out of reach of dog and baby. Pino wanted to see, so Arthur lifted him up and let him blow the flames out, not once but twice. Marta announced that it was time for Pino to say good night. The boy wailed in objection but wiped his eyes with his knuckles. He inspected his nose with his chubby fingers. *Nase,* Marta told her son: nose. She thought that she might start to cry, and knew that it was because she had been drinking too much.

Pino did not fight sleep. Marta hadn't even finished her first lullaby, the Sandman song, *auf deutsch,* when the boy curled his legs underneath him, shoved his bottom in the air, and went to sleep.

Arthur laid the crispy brown pieces of chicken on the plates, a breast and leg for each, and spooned out cloves of garlic. She was hungry. She devoured the chicken. In a few minutes, only bones remained, and she cracked those with her teeth.

"You're a vegetarian disgrace," he said.

She wiped her mouth. He opened the second bottle of wine, and she had that, too, and there was cheese, and dessert, *pflaumkuchen,* which she barely tasted. They pushed their plates back into a cove between tumbled books and played with the puppy for a while.

"What's her name?" Arthur asked.

"I haven't decided."

"She looks smart."

"My husband wants to name her after Claudia Cardinale."

"They both have brown hair," said Arthur.

"Do you know the actress Monica Vitti?" she asked him.

"Vaguely."

"Do you think I look like her?"

Their shoulders were touching. They had pulled off their shoes and socks, and their bare feet touched, too. He brushed strands of hair from her eyes. His fingers grazed her chin. It might have been hours later, it might have been minutes, she could never recall, that she found herself lying with him on the picnic blanket. She was staring up into his eyes, putting her fingers into his rich blond hair, kissing his lips, drinking him as if he were wine from the dark green bottles of Vernaccia di San Gimignano. And then she was naked, on top of his body, falling asleep in his arms.

TEN

H E HAD MADE A MISTAKE. Not a week in his new country, and he had already made a huge mistake. In the morning darkness, he gathered his things. He was not in his twenties anymore. She didn't hurry him in his packing. She urged him to explore every last corner of the room. She stripped the sheets off the cot.

He wanted to tell her that he had not intended matters to go so far, but he could not bring himself to lie. He had wanted everything. He hadn't once restrained himself or suggested that they leave the second bottle of wine for another night or asked Marta if she wanted to stop. On the contrary, he had removed her clothes with the urgency of a sapper defusing a bomb. When they woke, she acted as if the bomb had exploded. Right out of bed, she began to clean.

He hauled the packed bags into the kitchen, where Pino drank a cup of milk. Marta made his breakfast, spreading Nutella on a hard roll. She studied the bags with reddened eyes. Arthur thought that she might be on the verge of tears.

"I'll go," he said. "Frau Herbst has that room."

"No," she said, her eyes locked on his. "It won't work."

He almost spoke, but didn't. What won't work? Another thought rushed into his mind. This was not going to be simple. She had a plan. He couldn't guess what, but it wouldn't be a handshake and a farewell. She did not want him to leave, but he couldn't stay. In between lay a mystery. He nodded, and she nodded back.

She dressed quickly and led him out of the apartment. He didn't ask questions. He was in her hands. With dog and boy, they caught a bus. A few minutes later, on the far side of Tempelhof Airport, he caught sight of a vast round mass of blackened stone in the middle of an overgrown lot. It could have been a medieval fortress, though Berlin was a young city and didn't have many of those. The bus came to a stop.

"Our stop," said Marta.

At last, Arthur felt compelled to ask, "Where are we going? Not inside that thing?"

She almost smiled. "No, Arthur. We're not going inside that thing."

He helped her get the stroller out of the bus. "Where, then?"

"We're going on the other side of *das schwarze Ding*. That's what the kids around here call it. The Black Thing."

"What is it? "

Marta pushed the stroller on the pavement running beside the edifice.

"A Nazi creation. It's complicated."

Her words made Arthur feel strange, as if he had wandered out of the natural order of things, out of the universe of hard facts and dates, and into some fabulous other place, where time oozed in every direction. Through the yellowed leaves of plane trees, the Black Thing hulked, inscrutable, glowering, like an ancient meteor, spat at the earth. Another reality rose around him, a shadow of the first, but more dense, reminiscent of smoke from a burning ruin, enveloping the golden morning.

"Will you please tell me where you are taking me?" he asked Marta, who observed him in quiet. Pino seemed to feel the stillness between them. He looked from face to face.

"We're almost there," she said.

On the far side of the Black Thing, she jingled keys out of her pocket and inserted one into a lock in a gate. Beyond the gate lay a row of small cottages, each one as distinct as a house. They were a German specialty, Arthur knew, little garden houses, homes away from home in the big, loud city. Some of the cottages were made of wood, others of rough stone. Each cottage overlooked a miniature plot of land. Some people had planted masses of roses or raised tiny plum and apple orchards. Still others had designed bonsai gardens or built Bavarian beer tents. There were several different rows of cottages, separated by fence lines, arranged on lanes with quaint-sounding names. Marta led Arthur down a lane called Jasminpfad, the Jasmine Path, before stopping at a second gate and inserting a second key.

"This is my *Laube*," she said. "My bower."

Bower, thought Arthur. She had brought him to her *bower*. That was a word from a fairy tale. He thought that he must still be in bed, dreaming. Her bower was made of concrete and painted a dark, alpine green. It had a single, narrow door set precisely between a pair of small windows. Beyond the panes hung white lacy curtains of the kind Arthur had seen in every window in every home in Berlin. The bower had a lawn, about eight by twelve yards. On one side of the lawn grew a lush fruit-bloated plum tree. On the other was an un-kempt bed of roses and tomato plants. Grass grew high and wild. In the midst of the bedraggled roses stood a garden gnome, its once-bright paint fading away; the gnome hoisted a beer, and his green eyes twinkled. Above it all, heavy as a thundercloud, loomed the crum-bling black back of the Black Thing. Arthur stole a look at her, and she gave him a frank, warm stare. She wanted him to stay in her bower.

She helped him get the duffel bags inside the cottage. The dog lolled in the grass. Pino went for plums that had dropped in the grass. Marta shut the cottage door behind them. At Arthur's knees lay a low, cobwebbed cot.

"My bed," he said.

He turned around, and Marta kissed him hard, pressing him against the back wall of the cottage.

"Jesus," he whispered.

"This will have to do for a while," she whispered back. She beckoned him outside.

Arthur followed, but he stopped at the threshold of the door. "I'm lost," he said. "I need you to tell me what you're thinking."

"This will be our place," she told him. "No one will bother us here. That's what you want, isn't it?"

"Is it what you want?"

Marta didn't answer right away. She strapped Pino back into the stroller and leashed the dog.

Finally, when everything was ready to go, she said, "If you don't know the answer to your question already, I don't know what else I can say."

Her words made him feel stupid, but he didn't try to pretend. Maybe he wanted too much. Maybe she didn't know what she wanted. So he asked a different question. "What now?"

"Now you have some free time," she replied. "I have to think and run a few errands. But if you want to talk some more, we could meet. There is a place called Café unter den Linden. Three blocks east of the Brandenburg Gate. Taxi drivers know it." She handed him the keys to the two gates. "Can you be there by one o'clock?"

He nodded. He could. She took the Jasmine Path to the gate and turned to wave goodbye. Arthur waved back. She vanished into the shadow of the Black Thing.

HE PAID LITTLE attention as his taxi skimmed over the border between the East and West German states. He couldn't really tell where one frontier ended and another began. And he didn't care. The cabbie didn't know the exact address for Café unter den Linden, so Arthur paid and got out. He started to ask people in his rusty German for directions. Before long, he stood at the glass door, peeking in, trying to catch a glimpse of his woman. His Muslim woman, he thought, a little impressed with himself. Muslim girls had been off limits in India.

He opened the door to the café. There, in a corner of the room, sat Marta. She wore a cuffed, pink button-down shirt and blue jeans, and her hair curled in its ponytail down one of her shoulders. She watched his approach with interested caution. He comprehended that she was more beautiful than he realized.

"Hi," he said, feeling nervous. "Where's Pino?"

"With the babysitter."

Arthur sat. On either side were East Germans. He recognized them by their clothes—drab blues, demoralizing grays and mauves, and other colors that suggested mist, fog, and driving rain. The café lay technically in East Berlin, just a kilometer or so into the post-Communist side of the city, and had served ice cream to despondent Cold War tourists for ten or fifteen years. He was almost sure that he had been in this café on his junior-year class trip to East Berlin. Marta told him that it would soon close. Here and there, Arthur spotted Western tennis shoe brands.

"Now that I have slept with you," Marta said without smiling, "I would like to know who you are."

Arthur ordered a coffee and one of the red *himbeertorte* that he had seen in the case on his way to the table. Marta ordered the same.

"What do you want to know?" he began.

"Where were you born?"

"Austin, Texas. United States of America."

"When is your birthday?"

To save time, he handed his passport across the table. She had a look and handed it back.

"You grew up in Austin, Texas?"

"In Dallas, Texas."

"Do you remember the assassination of John F. Kennedy?"

"I was three years old at the time," he told her. "On my mama's lap in Post, Texas."

She stopped asking questions, and he started telling her everything. He had a father, a geologist for Shell, and a mother who was a *hausfrau,* a homemaker. He had been a talkative boy who liked to read and hated to hunt, unlike most of the men in his extended family. His grades in school had been uneven. On the day after his graduation from the University of Texas, without a job, in the year 1982, he drove five hundred miles from Austin, Texas, to Taos, New Mexico, blowing out the engine of an El Camino—that was a kind of car— and becoming stranded. He got a job as a river-rafting guide and found a room in a loosely structured artist's commune outside of the village of Arroyo Seco. In the evenings, he drank *cerveza* with lime at a place called Abe's Cantina and kept out of the conversations between gringo earthshippers, drug dealers, hippies, and everyone else who wanted to pick a fight or make a score. He put on dozens of pounds and became another person, the beloved, worthless, wide-bottomed water rat Artie, who made the tourists laugh with his self-deprecating wit.

"It was a good life, very comfortable, but I was meant for higher things."

"Do you believe that?"

Arthur paused before his answer. "I do. That's why I'm a journalist now."

"That's the higher thing you wanted to be?"

Arthur paused again. She wasn't making it sound like a higher thing. "I suppose it was."

"Do you believe in God?"

Her eyes probed him. Arthur didn't want to lie. "I'll have to answer that when I know you better," he said.

"Fair answer," Marta said. She had begun to smile. "I was meant for higher things, too. Go on. What happened next?"

Arthur met Rosa Salazar, daughter of a maker of adobe homes, what they called an *adobero,* and the descendant of Hispanic Land Grant settlers. Her people had come into New Mexico with the Spanish conquistadors in the sixteenth century, and Rosa was proud of it. At the time, she didn't seem to mind that Arthur couldn't trace his lineage much further back than Ellis Island. She was a journalist making a decent wage at the local newspaper. She encouraged Arthur to write, and he did. He wrote business pieces, which she avoided; she avoided, in particular, the articles about water rights in Arroyo Seco, where her family owned all the wells.

When her grandmother died, Rosa invited Arthur to move into the family's old homestead on the rim road above Arroyo Hondo. This caused a great scandal, but the two of them had quite a time, never discussing marriage or children or anything more serious than the coming weekend. Time eased Arthur's tensions with the Salazar family, and in the spring, he helped Rosa's brothers clear brush from their stretch of the local irrigation ditch, the *acequia.* The following winter, when the river-rafting companies shut down, he waited tables in one of the Salazar family restaurants in the ski valley.

During the spring of his second year in New Mexico, Arthur wrote a series of articles about water shortages in Arroyo Seco, implicating one of his lover's distant cousins in a corruption scandal. The cousin had to leave town. Rosa had an extreme reaction. She broke down and had to be hospitalized. When she got out, she had changed. She retreated into the bosom of her family. Arthur woke one night in their bed in the old adobe house, the sky out the window a span of black ice, and he said to himself with absolute clarity, "I don't belong here anymore."

"I don't understand," said Marta.

"Those articles somehow touched off an inner, hidden Rosa, someone that I didn't really know. Her ancestors woke in her blood. That's how she put it to me. And her ancestors wanted me the hell out of there."

Marta leaned toward him, her eyes glistening. "I have ancestors in my blood, too, and they never went to sleep. I am telling them to shut up right this minute."

Arthur stammered. "I wasn't trying to compare the situation——"

"I won't bend anymore. I refuse. No matter what the ancestors say."

Arthur accidentally knocked his silverware off the table, and Marta put a stern hand on one of his arms.

"Let's go for a walk," she said.

THE BERLIN SKY burned clear and blue. They walked down the Boulevard unter den Linden to the Brandenburg Gate.

"I don't feel guilty!" Arthur blurted out.

"Oh yes you do. I'm glad that you do. But please continue your story."

Confused, wary, a little thrilled, Arthur did. Back in New Mexico, with the help of the editor of his newspaper, he made contact with news organizations that needed correspondents in South Asia. India had begun to call to Arthur; Shiva, Gandhi, Satyajit Ray, the *lux orientale*. A week before he left Taos, Rosa became engaged to a Hispanic Land Grant scion whose family, like hers, had been in that part of the world since the coming of the conquistadors. Arthur was sad. He loved Arroyo Seco. He had loved to wake in the dawn and watch the view to the west rise pink-washed into the world, a view stretching to Colorado and beyond, into Utah, into the infinite West. He loved the crooked *lattias* fence that marked the Salazar eastern property line, and the soft, lush hush of mountain waters hurtling down the banks of the irrigation ditches. Even though it had never belonged to him, he thought of that old adobe home as one of his few fixed places on earth, a comfortable, welcoming chair, secure in the universe. But he had tried the West, and the West had failed him. Now he would go East.

"You travel wherever you want," Marta said. "India. Germany. It's unimaginable to me. Like you have wings. Like you're a bird."

"It's called a passport."

"Go on," she said.

In India, for the first time, Arthur made money and a name for himself. He lacked a pension plan and health benefits, but he had a serious byline, Arthur J. Cape, in business journals, in-flight magazines, and the travel section of the *New York Times*. He lived at the YMCA, traveling without rest on assignment. He wrote about the battle of the highly toxic soft drinks Pimco and Fancy-cola; about the miraculous neem tree, about attempts by multinational corporations to steal its bounties from poor farmers. He wrote about microbanks in the Bengali hinterlands; about accountant wallahs who slaved away for bandit lords in Madhya Pradesh; about the bartering habits of the hill tribes in Orissa, and crime and profit in the Bombay movie industry.

And then, in his triumph, the story that led directly to Berlin, he wrote about the houseboat economy on Lake Dal in the Kashmiri city of Srinagar, which had survived a three-year civil war. The story won an American Magazine Award, and within weeks, *Sense* offered him the full position in Berlin, under the oversight of Eric Hampton, the senior European editor, the man who had stolen his room at the Grand Kempinski.

Marta and Arthur paused under one of the three arches of the Brandenburg Gate—thick, dark stone asleep in the afternoon. The oaks in the Tierpark creaked in the wind.

"We're in the death strip now," Marta said.

Arthur nodded. He looked around, robbed of words. Until a year ago, concrete, wire, and armies had bordered the empty land south of them. People running across that land had been shot on sight. Arthur became acutely aware of the insignificance of his personal biography. In Marta's presence, he had begun to feel something new, hard to describe. Time seemed to be thickening. He could taste and smell it.

They left the Brandenburg Gate behind and walked across a waste of impacted mud and stray grass. Marta pointed at the grim brown square of the Reichstag, floating like a ship over the treetops to the northwest, and he smelled her. He tasted a memory in his mouth, the salt and garlic of her naked body, the perspiring recesses and corners. The Reichstag had burned in 1933. A Bulgarian artist had been trying for years to wrap the building in some kind of material. Marta described the last hours of the Second World War, Soviet soldiers scaling the sides of the skeletal mass, the hammer-and-sickle flag rising above the smoke to be snapped, in a famous image, by a photographer swinging like the Angel of Propaganda from a ledge. Arthur complimented her on the range of her knowledge.

"I'm a travel agent," she said.

They headed south onto the bare plain of Potsdamerplatz.

"Two cities," she said.

She pointed. Ahead of them, half a kilometer away, sat bland white apartment buildings, the edge of East Berlin. Just behind them marched the trees of a park, marking West Berlin. Between the apartment buildings and the trees was the place where they stood, an absence, Arthur thought, like the absence between the banks of a vanished river, like the arroyos running through northern New Mexico, spaces hollowed by waters long since gone to sky. Potsdamerplatz had once been the busiest square in Europe, the place where the rail lines of the continent converged, a mass of steel and tar, home to the great cafés and hotels of Europe. Arthur felt himself moved almost to tears by something huge and invisible. He gazed at a vast space in obscurity, two cities, light and dark, and between them a trench like a grave. One city lay behind him. The other sparkled ahead. Clouds raced from the horizons toward the center of the sky. The temperature dropped, and night rose.

. . .

MARTA AND ARTHUR relieved the babysitter. With blankets and stroller and a basket of food, they hurried down the canal to catch the bus. Across the black water, people groaned in unison. A soccer game flickered on a television set in a bar. They caught the bus and looked out the windows at the lights in the shops. Their picnic took place on the cottage lawn, in the dark beside the garden gnome; wine, cheese, olives, bread. They danced to German smash hits on a transistor radio. A breeze ruffled Pino's hair. The puppy whined beneath the plum tree. Arthur and Marta held hands and gazed at stars twinkling through clouds in the northern European sky.

ELEVEN

SIX DAYS LATER, on the Friday evening before German Unification, Marta and Arthur were strolling along the Landwehrkanal
with the dog and the boy when they heard a splash. Ducks scattered into the sky. Arthur looked down the embankment and saw a
pale boy recede into waters as black as night. He didn't think or pause.
He hurled himself. He landed headfirst into a shock of cold, his left
shoulder grazing stone on the way down. He clawed at the water, he
threw it back, but there was always more. He heard nothing and saw
nothing. In his mind were two words. God, please. His hands touched
an object solid but soft, and he threw out his arms, and grabbed hold,
and spun around. He thrust himself up. He broke the water, and there
was Marta, in the canal, too, head bobbing, mouth wide, gasping. Pino
spat up water. People gathered on the bank. Hands reached for them.
Towels were brought. Marta clutched her son close and wept and wept.

ARTHUR COULD NOT stop shaking. He returned to the cottage
for a fresh change of clothes and cleaned himself up. He couldn't
get warm. He kept seeing the pale shape of the boy dropping in

the blackness of the water. An hour passed, and another. He shook on the cot. Get up, a voice told him. Go to her. At last, he did. He stole a sunflower from a neighbor's cottage and bought a bottle of vino tinto in a Greek restaurant. When he stepped out of the taxi in Marta's neighborhood, his heart started to pound. The canal had smelled of rot and decay and malevolence. How many bodies lay at its bottom?

He gave a single knock on the door of the apartment before the door swung open and a man blasted out. He moved low and hard, throwing fists. Arthur tripped backward, the wine spinning from his fingers, the sunflower bursting. Marta yelled at the man to let go, and he did.

Tino, thought Arthur, one week early.

His assailant helped him off the ground. He looked different from what Arthur expected. In Arthur's imagination, based mostly on the photographs on the walls, Tino had possessed a boxer's lean, angry body. In fact, he carried himself like one of the lesser lifeguards of the world, with no chest at all, and a pair of skinny legs. His shoulders were brittle, and his arms overwrought by ten-pound weights. Dark hair sailed around his head. He was no fighter, but an annihilating will simmered in his eyes.

Marta retrieved the wine bottle. She spoke to her husband in a hushed voice that Arthur had not heard before, in Serbo-Croatian. Tino became glum. He rubbed his elbows and glanced at Arthur, who saw that Marta had told him a fifty percent truth. Arthur was the boarder whom she had mentioned. He was staying in the garden house. She had hit him with an apple. He had saved Pino's life. Tino said something in a soft, chastened voice. Marta translated.

"He thanks you from the bottom of the heart and says now that both husband and wife have attacked you, you should consider your-self an honorary member of the family."

Arthur tried to be lighthearted. They all did. In German, very difficult for him, Tino expressed regret. He was tired from his trip. He'd seen the sunflower and the wine and made the wrong assumptions. Tino's personality, like his body, did not correspond to Arthur's idea of him. He didn't seem like an arrogant swine. He seemed like one of the very ordinary human beings of the world, a man of simple tastes, simple ambitions; too much hairspray, too much cologne, but no harm in that. Before long, the two men were drinking loza, chewing on slices of sausage and Tino's mother's homemade flatbread. They talked as if they had become friends. Pino rambled around his father's chair, obviously delighted. He had been bathed and coddled and kissed. The canal seemed to have vanished from his memory. The boy made fish faces at Arthur, buried his hands in the puppy's silky ears and said *hoooooon.* And then he pointed at the table and said *ein tisch?* A table? Arthur saw a moment of distress on Tino's face, but it vanished when Marta came to the table.

After one more round of lavish kisses, Marta took the boy to bed. Sleep wasn't a little death. Sleep was a gift. No one had ever explained this to Arthur. His sister might have said it was God's gift. His hands were shaking again. Tino saw, but acted as if he didn't. He found a basket somewhere in the depths of the apartment, packed it with sausage, cheese, dark chocolate, and a spare bottle of the loza brought from home. He asked Arthur, in his own language, and in bits and pieces of German, to forgive him again for his irrational behavior. Marta didn't look at her husband, and she hardly gave Arthur a glance. Instead, she set about cleaning the dinner table, brushing away crumbs of bread.

The evening came to an end. Tino gave Arthur another hug. "Thank you," he said in English, in a voice trembling with emotion. Marta patted Tino on the back and told him that she had called a taxi and would show Arthur to the door of the building. She walked Arthur down the stairs, and on the way, whispering, she explained to him that Dubravka's sudden appearance back in Mostar had made

Tino suspicious, and he had come home a few days earlier than expected. He remained uneasy, she told Arthur, but she had told him nothing.

"What can I possibly say to you?" she sighed at last, crossing her arms, ignoring the cool brace of wind outside. "I owe you everything."

"I don't want that," he said, his eyes growing wet. "I want you."

She looked in his eyes. "But you see my circumstance."

She was conscious of people watching them, and he understood that she would prefer a quick exit. Arthur knew that he faced a sudden and total eclipse. The old life had reasserted itself, and in that instant, he knew that it meant nothing to him anymore. It wasn't a life. For days, he had dreaded this moment and tried to think how he would meet it, but it had come upon him too quickly, with an unexpected ferocity, and he found himself staggering for the few words that might make a difference.

"Circumstance is nothing," he said.

She shook her head. "That's not true."

"It doesn't matter a goddamn bit if you don't think it's true. It's a fact. Everyone lives with circumstances. Everyone has reasons. But if you believe that your country is going to war, and you cannot bring yourself to resist your husband's desire to go back there, then it's not a matter of your circumstances. It's a matter of your strength. You have to leave him."

His own words made him afraid.

"Find a wife, Arthur," she said.

He took her face in his hands. He didn't care. He pressed his lips against hers.

"Stop it—" She pushed him back.

"You feel guilty for what happened at the canal, and you feel guilty because you have betrayed your husband. And you think the two are the same thing. But it's not that way—you're wrong. He's betrayed you, and now you're going to let him kill you?"

She wiped her tears away, fury rising. "What do you suggest?"

"Leave. This instant."

She came forward from the shadows, pointing at him, her face twisted in a rage that he had never seen.

"What have you ever done with your life that you throw such a thing at me?" She waited for an answer. "You see my home? My husband? My child? These are *real*. These are hard-won."

"I know——"

"You *can't* know. One cannot get them by wandering around and looking at the monkeys in India. One cannot get them by sleeping with strange women in distant cities. One must die to them. Do you understand me? One must die utterly to them. *For* them."

She tore away from him, back up the stairs. The door of the building closed. He still smelled her, though he stood alone. He still heard her words, the most terrible that anyone had ever spoken to him, the most obliterating, horrific human judgment that had ever been pronounced. He couldn't move. His entire body had begun to shake. The taxi came, honked six times, and went. Arthur set off in the general direction of the bower, past Kotbusser Tor, where he could have caught the subway, on and on, thinking stray thoughts, thinking that he must go to see Frau Herbst, the landlady, first thing in the morning, must get out of Marta's bower, which would be intolerable now.

He wandered through dense stretches of tenement, through dead neighborhoods cut by blue lights. He came to the center of West Berlin and staggered past the remains of the Kaiser Wihelm Memorial Church, a war-smashed stone that had once been a place of worship. He moved through the junkies at the Zoo railroad station, up Hardenbergstrasse to Ernst-Reuther-Platz, then back down the Kudamm, where he poked through the tourist detritus of the Cold War, the cast-off uniforms of disappearing armies, the blue-greens of the East German force that was supposed to have marched against the West in Armaggeddon; the gray, red, and gold of the Soviet host; medals of various kinds, hammered and sickled, the flotsam of an unforeseen, unwieldy disintegration; canteens, watches, mess kits, gunbelts sold out of the back doors of barracks by Russian, Ukrainian, and Kazakh troops desperate for Western currency. He saw hundreds of pieces of the Berlin Wall and thought of George. There were chunks and flecks of whitish gray stone arranged on tables on the street, some in casings of clear plastic, some stamped or painted with the colors of the four Allied powers. The Wall would be sold and sold and sold. Each merchant claimed that the pieces on his table were real, and the pieces at the other tables were fakes, and you could see the fakes with one look. Arthur bought pieces indiscriminately along with a bottle of Berlin Wall homeopathic medicine, newly invented, good against panic and despondency, according to the label. He had beer, then wine, then schnapps.

It was all crap and dust now. He had watched the fall of the Berlin Wall on a television set in Kashmir. Under piles of wool blankets, with a family of twelve, three generations of houseboat owners, proprietors of the houseboat *New Texas,* he had gazed in awe at the blazing screen. The world was changing for the better. First, Communists and capitalists would get along, and then Muslims, Jews, and Christians. It was one of the high points of Arthur's life, watching the fall of the Berlin Wall with that family. But he knew the truth now. The world wouldn't get better. It would sink.

At a kiosk, he bought the latest issue of the *Economist* and read the twelve-page survey of Yugoslavia. Never had a country seemed so tactile. The shape of Yugoslavia was a woman's naked back. Seated at a café on the Kudamm, munching on white chocolate and champagne cream truffles, Arthur read and reread the survey. Each mention of Serbs, Croats, and Bosnians caressed his mind. They weren't peoples. They were words formed in the deep wet of a woman's throat. He dived for them.

That night, he returned to the bower, but he didn't sleep. He lay in the shade of the Black Thing and devised last-ditch strategies. Marta worked around the corner from the old woman's apartment. In the morning, Arthur would rent those rooms. He would not stalk Marta. But he would watch and wait. He would allow himself to be seen, and in time she would come to him, because he was right. She must leave her husband. She feared for her child's safety, and the logic of her fear would prevail.

A T FIRST LIGHT, Arthur threw on a blazer, slacks, and a tie and hurried to Frau Herbst's apartment. The old woman was not happy to see him. She had almost given up on Arthur. But he displayed money, nine hundred marks in cash, and she confessed that she had not yet rented out the rooms in question. At a card table in one corner of a vast central salon, her fingers plucked the diadem cap from a crystal decanter. She dispensed port wine into two glasses and produced a bar of Schogetten chocolate. Above her hovered a wood-carved saint attached to a sunburst, an icon stolen by a German soldier from a Florentine church.

They dickered over price. Rents were climbing in West Berlin. One couldn't get a place in a decent part of town for less than a thousand a month, Frau Herbst's nephew had told her. And how many places would supply coffee and *schrippen* in the morning, and the occasional snifter of Cognac in the evening? On the other hand, Arthur argued, he could find a very nice space in East Berlin for under five hundred marks.

"Not with a telephone connection!" she shrieked.

She had him there. Most cheap apartments in East Berlin didn't have good phones.

"How can you hope to work?" she asked him.

"I'll manage," he said.

She showed him the rooms. They lay on the Apostel-Paulus-Strasse side of the apartment. The main room had a small balcony, large enough for a breakfast table and two chairs, and the balcony looked out on the steeple of the church that Arthur had seen when George first brought him to the square. It had been little more than a week, and yet he felt that he had been in Berlin for years, that he had died there.

"I was forced to move to this location when they Aryanized my late husband's estate in '37," explained Frau Herbst. "A lot of the money was gone, and my friends couldn't support me."

Before, Arthur would have wished for his notebook. The old woman had a tale or two to tell. But he didn't give a damn now. The world of facts burned alive in front of his eyes. They stood together on the balcony and watched a troop of Turkish women in body-length gowns and hooded faces crossing the street with their children and entering the playground on the eastern flank of the church. The children flocked to the swing sets, and the women sat on the railroad-tie rim of a sandbox, speaking among themselves. Frau Herbst peered down with an expression of dismay.

"Those days," she said, "I saw mostly lawyers. One, in particular, a very great man murdered by that swine from Austria." She paused and glanced over at Arthur, as if hoping that he might take a hasty and inordinate interest in her life. But he didn't. "We'll have to trust each other before I get into all that."

Inside the room, which had molded ceilings, and bare walls painted ocher in ages past, lay a bed with a carven mahogany headboard and a mattress pooling in the middle. He could buy a new one, she informed him, if he wanted. The room's last tenant, a construction worker, had fucked the current one into disrepair. She said this without a shred of self-consciousness, as if she had been objecting to the habits of a chain-smoker. In the corner farthest away from the balcony, beneath a dust-crusted portrait of a man in tuxedo, sat a desk, and on the desk, to which she gestured triumphantly, was a green rotary telephone, antiquated and forbidding, a panzer tank in the annals of telecommunication, and yet possibly, Arthur thought, the youngest object in the room.

Frau Herbst noticed his interest. "Still works," she said.

Arthur agreed to seven hundred marks a month, plus seven hundred more as a security deposit. She gave him the keys.

"Promise," she said, as he was standing at the door, "that you will never bring that junkie or her friends into my house."

"I don't know the junkie."

"The Russian does."

"She's Bosnian."

"You abide by my rules!" she cried.

ARTHUR EXCUSED HIMSELF. He made for the entrance of the adjacent building, which housed Marta's travel agency. He passed the tables of the café and the butcher shop. The morning's diners shared baskets of rolls and plates of yellow cheese. He banged on the door of the agency. He could not wait for Marta to come to him. He must confront her. He had to see her.

It was Saturday morning, just after eleven. The place should have been open for business, but the door was locked. Back on the street, he tried to look through the windows. The blinds had been pulled. The butcher Duben came out of his shop, wiping his fingers on a cheesecloth. Marta had told Arthur about their daily encounters.

"You want Frau Mehmedovic?"

Arthur squinted at the man.

"She didn't come today."

In his white smock and smart loafers, the butcher looked like a medical doctor. He had a doctor's demeanor, circumspect and serious. His words had a touch of clinical diagnosis.

"Every day of the week, at exactly the same time, eight o'clock, give or take, she comes walking along here." He indicated the sidewalk, and the exposed bricks of the street, his hand sweeping up to include the church, and beyond it the subway entrance. "But today, for the first time, no." He thought a moment. "First time in two years, perhaps."

"She always comes?"

"Except for Sundays, Frau Mehmedovic always comes, and the day begins. That's how we live."

"What about the green girl?"

The butcher moved back inside his shop and rearranged the corn-fed hens in his display case. Arthur followed him inside.

"Something's wrong," said the butcher. "I hope not, but I think so. Are you responsible?" He placed his hands on the top of the display case. "I'm quite sure it has something to do with you."

"Her husband's back from a trip."

The butcher understood the meaning of this information. His face fell.

"*Duben,* I tell myself. You must help this unhappy woman. But *Duben,* you idiot, she is married. That's what I also tell myself. What you should tell yourself, *mein Herr,* if you have any morals at all. She is quite married." With deliberation, he wiped each of his fingers on a gauze of cheesecloth. "Quite completely married, I believe."

A shopper approached. The bell jingled. There was nothing more to be said. Arthur left the shop and took a seat at the café on the corner, at the table positioned closest to the street, and ordered a coffee. The sky creamed with cloud beyond the steeple of the Apostel Paulus Church. Voices of young girls leapt on the wind. The line of Turkish women processed across the street, the children strung like leaves on a stem between the adults. The line flowed past Arthur and out of sight. Saved the child, he thought, but lost the mother. He put his head in his hands.

TWELVE

IT WAS MY FAULT," she told Tino, sipping a cup of chamomile that he gave her as soon as she walked back into the apartment. "I should have been paying closer attention."

"It could happen to anyone," he replied, remarkably forgiving.

"No," she said. "I might as well have thrown him into the canal myself."

Her words alarmed him, she could see, but he didn't say so. "Don't be ridiculous."

She had dried her tears in the darkness of the stairwell and fought to keep them from coming again.

"I have news," Tino said.

"Do you, Tino?"

"I signed the papers on my restaurant. It's called L'Avventura."

She congratulated him. He held fifty percent ownership, the other half belonging to a partner, Darko Miric, of the Miric family, Croats who owned vineyards in the hills outside Mostar. Tino had gone to school with Darko, and Marta remembered him as a slow, sad, loyal boy and hoped that he had a gift for bookkeeping, because Tino did not. L'Avventura would occupy an old stone building that had long ago belonged to a family of Bosnian metalsmiths. Lately, it had gone to waste as a postcard and souvenir kiosk. The building sat one hundred yards from the Stari Most, Tino's beloved old bridge, one hundred yards from the Neretva. River traffic on the western bank had no choice but to pass it. Tino gave a playfully fiendish grin.

"The aroma of our cooking will trap them," he said.

There was some decent capital. Darko had a $50,000 loan from an uncle in Chicago, and another bundle would come from Mehmedovic relatives in Australia, more than enough to cover the first few months' rent, the various licenses, the hiring of a chef and staff, and the bribing of the tourism office.

Marta fondled the ears of the puppy, which had climbed into her lap, and thought against her will of Arthur Cape. Where had he gone? Was he back at the bower? Could she somehow sneak out and surprise him there? She read the spines of books on the shelves behind her husband's back, her mother's forlorn collection: Thomas Mann's *Buddenbrooks,* Madame de Staël on Germany, Rousseau's *Confessions, The Brothers Karamazov.* Not so long ago, in the days of her happiness, they had been scattered everywhere.

Tino didn't want questions. He would talk through the night. She had no more thoughts on the subject of the restaurant, except, perhaps, to muse on the name L'Avventura, the name of a movie about a woman who disappears on an island and is never seen again. They had seen the movie long ago in Dubrovnik. He had hated it. She had loved it. Now he had named his restaurant after it, and she perceived an obscure warning.

Tino reached for her, and she jumped, spilling tea on the dog, who objected with a shrill whine. Female German shorthairs, Duben the butcher had informed her, tended toward introspection and hysteria, an unfortunate by-product of the process by which they had been bred over the last hundred years. This temperament could be alleviated only by vast amounts of attention. Marta swept the puppy into her arms and held her there, fighting back tears. Tino placed the teacup on the table and put the dog on the floor. Before Marta could get up and fetch a towel, her husband took her hands. He closed the distance between them.

"Will you sit with me awhile?" he asked her.

"What for?" she asked him back.

He began to talk in an unfamiliar way, in a voice of sober, even businesslike conviction. With trepidation, she listened. Tino, it turned out, had been thinking about their many conversations over the last year or so, and it was true, he would finally concede, that Herr Dieterle's travel agency made good money, more money than most small businesses back in Yugolsavia would ever make; she was right about that. But Dieterle's business had an obvious drawback. Marta might feel that she belonged to the travel agency, might even feel indispensable to its success—as she should—but she would never be able to say that the business *belonged* to her. She would never be able to sell the business for ten times the amount that it had cost her to start it. That was never going to happen, because she didn't *own* the business.

She conceded that on this subject, he was right.

He paused a moment in satisfaction. "Thank you," he said.

He went on. Suppose she wanted to open her own business one day. Suppose she wanted her own travel agency. She had talked about it, and he approved. But did it make sense? Did she really want to establish a business in Germany, where she might wait years to become a citizen, to actually vote in elections, on candidates and issues that affected her bottom line every day? Did she really want to do business in a country that dictated her hours, her fees, her rents but didn't allow her to have a say in the political process? Yugoslavia was going to be a democracy now. Wouldn't it be wrong not to give her own country a try, at least, before going second-class in a country that still defined its most basic rights by blood? Think about it, he said. By *blood*. She herself had complained. She was the one who had read the German Basic Law and fumed over the paragraphs on citizenship. She was the one who explained to him that the system was rigged by and for purebred Germans, and against everyone else.

Again, she conceded.

He went on. A return to Mostar did not have to be irreversible. Suppose he was wrong. Suppose the restaurant business stagnated. Suppose tourists no longer wandered inland on day trips but stayed by the sea—he didn't think that it was likely, but for the sake of argument, say that her worst fears came true—they could always go back to Germany. But maybe they would give Australia or Canada a try instead.

"Maybe even the United States," he said.

This was a stumble.

"It's not so easy, Tino," she said. "You know damn well."

Okay, he said, sitting beside her on the chair, so it wouldn't be easy. Nothing was. Their departure from Germany would not have to be final. That was the point.

"And then," he said, "there's the matter of our country."

He started well. He admitted that she had her reasons to worry. She had a point when she mentioned the crazy people in Belgrade. Indeed, there might be trouble. But look at Romania. Look at Czechoslovakia. How long did those troubles last? Weeks? Days? A few *chetniks* with funny ideas were not the end of the world. Tino had run into their father's old pal Mose Silber on the street in Mostar, and thinking of Marta, and her concerns, Tino had specifically asked what the brilliant Jew thought about the future of their country. And Silber had said, Tell her not to be such a pessimist, it is just the way of democracy, where everyone has a say, even the most ridiculous; the country might be worse off morally and aesthetically—it almost certainly would be, the Jew had said, with great books and art replaced by American movies and American pop music—but it would not be dangerous, and for people who knew how to do business, he said, it could well be an opportunity.

"Mose tells people what they want to hear," protested Marta. "He was trying to make you feel good."

Tino's eyes widened. "He did."

She was filled with pity for her husband. But at that moment, she wanted more than anything in the world to leave him.

"I am willing to make a last gesture," he said. He pulled an envelope from the pocket of his coat. "Inside are two plane tickets, one for you, one for Pino. I don't intend to come back here, my love."

She gasped, a hand at her mouth.

"Hear me out," he said. "I can't come back. I must pursue this opportunity. But you and Pino can return to Berlin, and you can follow your dream here. All I ask is that you give mine a try. Come home with me. See what you think, and then make your final decision."

"You can't be serious."

Tino closed his eyes, as if exhausted, and handed over the envelope. Someone had coached him. He had never before in his life spoken with such eloquence. He must have rehearsed for days. The plane tickets were real, open and one-way from Zagreb to Berlin, extraordinary. She didn't believe any of it, and yet she couldn't find the hole. His face, for once, lay open in emotion. The incident on the canal helped his cause immeasurably. He knew that she blamed herself, and he blamed her, too, and this gave him extra strength.

Marta picked up his pack of Drina cigarettes. She hadn't smoked in years. But Arthur's chicken had started an avalanche. She popped one into her mouth, but he didn't act surprised. He lit it.

"You talked to my father?" she inquired.

"Of course."

"And what did he say?"

"What do you think he said?"

She honestly didn't know. Her father had encouraged her to leave Yugoslavia, arguing that with her language skills, she would have a better future in West Germany.

"He wants his daughter to take care of him in his old age."

"He would never say that."

Tino threw up his hands. "How do I know what the hell your father thinks? He despises me."

She laughed. "What about Dubravka?"

"How do I know what Dubravka thinks?"

"You'd better care what Dubravka thinks. Branko takes her to the nicest places in town, so believe me, if she doesn't like your place, you're sunk."

"What are you saying?"

Marta didn't know for sure, but the cigarette tasted good. Mostar, for once, brought back pleasant memories, and gradually, like heat from a bath, a sense of comfortable warmth came over her body. It wasn't pleasure, God knew. She'd had enough of that. Pleasure had almost destroyed her. To her utter relief, she was ready to buckle. She wanted no more fighting. She wanted no more guilt. She was sick of guilt. *Basta.* Something in Tino's words made sense. Something touched her heart. The fear dwindled. She always had those plane tickets. She would damn well use them.

"Let's get out of here," she said.

SHE CALLED DIETERLE and requested a leave. A stricken silence followed. Her boss asked her what was wrong, and she told him that a return to Yugoslavia was under consideration. But even if she decided to stay in Mostar, she told him, she would have to return to Berlin to sort out her legal and business affairs. So nothing was final. She would need a couple of weeks.

Tino made plans for the trip south. He packed most of his belongings into boxes and had them shipped home. The furniture could wait until a final decision was made. Marta began to feel a sickness of elation. She wanted to share a new, secret hope with Arthur. But she buried the instinct. She would do no such thing. To herself, she called the journey a fact-finding mission. She would inspect the kitchen and meet with Tino's business partner. She would help in the choosing of cutlery, crockery, and glassware and help to identify the right bakers and butchers, the right suppliers for wine, cheese, and fish. L'Avventura began to sound to Marta, for the first time, like her own going concern.

One day before departure, she could no longer contain herself. She stole away from Tino for an hour and took the bus to the bower, hoping to find Arthur, but he had gone. She sat on the cot and wept. Then she dried her eyes and locked things up. She would have to find a buyer for the place.

Tino wanted to shower gifts on the people back home—cigarettes, blue jeans, peppermint schnapps, Baileys Irish Cream, two cases of wine, brown bottles of Montepulciano, green bottles of Vernaccia di San Gimignano. Marta warned that they would run over the hundred-dollar limit at the Yugoslav border, but Tino was in a rapturous mood. He would pay the duty. She packed lightly, and he noticed but said nothing. At first, he insisted on bringing all of Pino's clothes and toys, but she objected, and he backed off.

"You're right, of course," he said. "Anyway, whatever he needs, we can find down there."

His words worried her, but it was too late to object. She would keep her part of the bargain. She had to give it a try.

EARLY ON A Wednesday morning, they pulled away from the curb beside the Landwehrkanal. Dawn streamed gold through the streets of West Berlin. It was early, and there were few cars on the road.

After half an hour, heading west and south, they drove through a checkpoint into East Germany. No one wanted their passports. That era had ended. There were men in the checkpoint stalls, and an affectation of meaningful work, but the transit point now had a sullied quality. The imminent disappearance of the state of East Germany had given rise to indolence. The men at the checkpoint looked as if they had already found other jobs.

Marta recalled one memorable day at that very same checkpoint, and wondered if any of these guardians of the integrity of borders had been there in the autumn of 1987. It had been quite a different place then, metal detectors and dogs, the efficiency and tension of a functioning police state. Guards had gone through their luggage. Dogs had sniffed at their clothes. But as soon as Marta mentioned her mother's name, Vesna Bistritza, the man in charge pleaded for forgiveness. He had fawned. He ran inside for a photograph of her mother. It had been hanging on his wall, a still from one of the westerns, and he wanted Marta to autograph it, a ferocious East German border guard acting as silly as a starstruck girl.

Marta wondered about all those East Germans who had ever loved her mother's movies. Where were they now? "The one country where I made it big," the great actress had opined on the day that the East German Parliament voted itself out of existence. She had been in a rage over the telephone, placing a collect call from Crete. "And they have shat it away."

Vesna would be disappointed at the latest turn of events. She had always wanted Marta to find a place of her own out in the world. She had wanted Marta, like her, to leave behind that old, dark land of underground churches, Jewish intrigue, and peasant vice. An indifferent soul waved them through the last stage of the checkpoint. Without interference, they were on their way. Marta broke into tears. She wanted to go back to her apartment, her job, her bower. She wanted Arthur. As soon as they got to Mostar, she would take those tickets and head home, to Berlin.

Tino popped Eros Ramazzotti into the tape deck and sang in Italian for a while. Then he got bored, switched off the music, and asked her, as if he'd been trying to get up his nerve, to tell him again how exactly she had met the American. He sounded suspicious. Marta thought of her sister. Dubravka must have let something slip.

"Marko and George," she replied, wiping her eyes.

He belched out a genuine laugh. *"Those fucking degenerates! I am going to kill those fucking degenerates!"*

He raised a fist back in the direction of the city. She was laughing, too, by the time she got to the part about the apple, laughing with pleasure, with deep glee. Tino put his arm around her, drew her close, and told her that he was proud of his *ragazza*. She tried to enjoy herself.

When they stopped in Nuremberg to see the St. Sebaldus Church, the Dürer house, and the torture museum, Tino bought a pair of Prada heels for her, and a baby soccer jersey for Pino—insignia of Borussia Dortmund, his team. For himself, he bought nothing, not a single bottle of cologne, not a shirt, not a tie. The second night, in Vienna, they walked the puppy along the Ringstrasse. Tino taught the dog to sit and to stay. She obeyed with weary defeat. By the third night, they were in Zagreb, where the mother of an old friend took Pino while Tino and Marta ate grilled fish at a restaurant on Republic Square. Tino was thinking about hiring the chef. The square filled with young Croat nationalists, some of them waving that bizarre flag, the *sahovnica,* the red-and-white checkerboard. The flag had a ghostly beauty in the darkness between the buildings. It did not seem to belong in the present time.

"I don't know why they have to resurrect that thing," Marta complained of the flag. "Why not be more original?"

A young man at a nearby table overheard. He left his chair, walked over to them. "You're Bosnian?"

"I'm Yugoslav."

He spat at the ground on her feet. Tino leapt up.

"Do that to my wife, cocksucker?"

"Fucking Turk cunts don't count as wives."

Tino shoved him, amazed. "Are you crazy? Are you fucking out of your mind? 'Fucking Turk cunt'?"

The other guests in the restaurant began to shout them down.

Waiters came running. The young man dashed away. Tino poured wine down his throat and stared at the checkerboard flag in the darkness of the square. Marta didn't ask him what he thought of this display, and he didn't bother to say. They ate the rest of the meal in complete silence.

T HE NEXT DAY, they reached the Adriatic coast, and Marta took the wheel of the car. The sea glimmered in fens of green, undulating, advancing into the south. She saw the gathering of islands. On and on, the land gobs went, like knees and elbows cocked up in the water, as if great, beautiful men lay out there under the morning sun. Sun stroked the road ahead. Fishing boats crawled back to the coves below, a movement like the descent of feathers through air. Above the road, olive trees straggled down cliffs. Soon enough, there would be pomegranates and grape and kiwi vines. If she rolled down the window, she would smell rosemary, creosote, the brine off the sea, the cool off the hills. This was her country. They had passed the olive line. They had passed into the realm of southern light.

The tourist season had ended, and the road was empty. They had made superb time. In three and a half hours, they reached the exit for Mostar, the small delta of the Neretva, where the river widened as it slid out of the mountains, a cold spark into the warm sea. Marta had never had any illusions about Mostar. It was a country town with an outsized reputation, a poor man's Sarajevo. But she loved the Neretva, the river running through it. It was the one thing in her life that seemed to embody what other people called God. It was more than home, more than the familiar water of her childhood. As a young girl, she had been able to sit for hours on the Stari and stare down into the curve and spill of the river through the high limestone banks. Her brother Esad had drowned in that river, but still she loved it. She loved it even more. When Muslims spoke of Allah, Marta thought Neretva.

She had believed as a child that she could see things down in the waters, the eyes of the *rusalki* that the old Serbian women talked about, the spirits that called to the boys with their flaming eyes. And when the boys dived off the Stari into the water, their dark brown skin glistening, it was like a fable to Marta. They became fish, in her eyes, flickering down into the depths to kiss the spirits before splashing back up into the world, where they never revealed what they had seen, because their lips had been sealed. The car left the sea behind and made its way inland, along the river, up into the dry hills, the bone-white stones.

At the exit for Medjugorje, in Capljina, they ran into traffic. Cars were backed up for miles. A utility truck had hit a mule. The mess would take hours to clean up; blood, hair, and fuel. They switched seats, and Tino turned the car around. It would be better to take the Medjugorje road. Pino woke and began to wail for a meal. The puppy's tongue hung and dripped. Tino slowed down. A car engine gushed steam on the side of the road, and a man in sunglasses ran toward them, waving his arms.

He rapped with a knuckle on the passenger side of the front window. Tino leaned across the front seat and rolled the window down.

"Mostar?" the stranger asked.

Tino recognized him, and they shook hands.

"Back so soon?"

"My wife wanted to see the place. Marta, you remember Mose."

Mose Silber stepped back from the car, removing the sunglasses, revealing kind almond-brown eyes. Until Tino mentioned him, Marta hadn't thought of Mose in years, but now that she was here, back in the hills, she was surprised at how familiar he seemed, how much he belonged to her memories of the city. He had always been a warm, handsome man, one of her father's best friends from school, a lover of her mother's at one time, Marta believed. His manner was expansive. He loved to laugh and tell stories. He was a barely practicing Jew, never dogmatic, more interested in a loud, drunken debate over philosophical principles than in theology. He had been a party member in the same spirit, without taking himself too seriously. Evidently, that affiliation had ended.

With his broad chest and shoulders, his light brown eyes and curly hair, Mose had always seemed exotic to Marta. His mother's family had been around for centuries, ever since coming to Sarajevo from Spain during the Ottoman time, and the old folks in his family could still speak the Sephardic tongue, the Ladino. She also vaguely recalled hearing in school that he was a spy for the Israeli government.

"Osman Lazic's daughter, before my eyes."

"Hello, Mose."

"Climb in," said Tino.

"If it's no bother."

He got into the backseat, and Tino drove on. Marta held Pino, fighting off his attempts to get at her breast. They stopped and bought a bottle of milk, which seemed to do the trick. After a while, she turned around in the front seat and saw that Mose was gazing at her.

"When was the last time?" he asked.

"Years," she said.

He leaned forward in the seat and patted her cheek as if she were still seven.

"You were at university."

"That's a long time ago now."

"It was around the time of that mayonnaise affair."

Marta blushed.

"I did much worse things in my time," he said. "Anyway, as I remember, that was a bit of Isadora's nonsense. She was never a Fascist. But she sure as hell knew how to piss off a Communist government."

"Exactly, and what happened? I had to work on a farm for the summer, and she got to go to Paris."

The mayonnaise affair had been the one and only genuine scandal of Marta's life. At a party in Sarajevo, in her father's apartment, her half-sister Isadora had used an enormous jar of mayonnaise to paint a swastika on a bathroom wall. *Kukasti krst au majonez,* she had called it, hooked cross in mayo, her idea of conceptual art. Someone at the party had ratted to the police, and suddenly everyone was at head-quarters for subversion of the state. Marta's father, a ranking member of the party, had driven up to Sarajevo in a fury, and Marta had spent that summer working like a drudge on her Great-Aunt Zara's farm. Meanwhile, Isadora's father, a famous composer, had congratulated his daughter for taking on the repressive Yugoslav apparatus and sent her promptly off to the Sorbonne to study ethnomusicology. Life in Yugoslavia had never been quite fair.

"You see him much? My father?"

"We meet at the Rondo once in a while. He still believes, your fa-ther." Mose smiled. "It takes a faith of the ages, believe me, and I've lost mine."

He nicked his head at the little boy. His voice lowered to a whisper. "And what's your name?"

"Pino," the boy replied.

"And how old are you, Pino?"

The dark-eyed boy became shy.

"Two," said Marta.

"Osman's grandson is already two. My God. Time flies."

They skirted the edge of Medjugorje and hit the final stretch of road before Mostar.

"Is this business or pleasure?" Mose asked.

"Both," said Tino. "We're starting a restaurant near the Stari. I'm thinking about a Dalmatian cook."

"Your own money?"

"You sound a little doubtful," said Marta, in confusion. Surely Tino had told him about the restaurant.

"Our political horrors, my dear. In a few days, you'll understand."

Tino glanced in Marta's direction, and she realized that she had discovered at least one lie. Tino hadn't spoken to Mose Silber about the political situation in Mostar. That conversation had never taken place.

"How do you see it, Mose?" she asked him.

"The Berlin Wall falls," said the Jew, "and the world changes. What can you do? God kicks everything around. There's a lot of yelling and screaming. People are children, after all. They're selfish. They hate change. And my God, they love to bitch!"

Tino concentrated on the road.

"There are more and more army conscripts around," Mose said. "Lots of boys from Sumadija, for some reason. And all the smart people are leaving, which distresses me."

Marta experienced a chill of deep recognition. Her instincts about the situation in their country had been right, and Tino knew it. He'd known about the soldiers. He must have known, too, that people were leaving. Mose asked if it was okay to light a cigarette, and Marta told him that he would have to roll down the window, which he did. Tino launched into his rote speech about the bridge, and how it would help make money for them. He sounded like a party hack from the old days. "You know that Mostar has more intermarriages than any city in the country of Yugoslavia? That's an absolute fact."

Twilight had come. Marta heard the rushing of winds. They climbed over a bluff topped by a white cross, the transversal touched by a rose-red glow. Someone had died there. "Trust me," Tino went on. "We've always been the best at getting along. We're throwing a party, and everyone cool will be invited!"

"I plan to be." Mose tossed most of the cigarette butt out the window and rolled the window back up.

The Volvo climbed over the mottled back of Mount Hum and rested there a moment. Below, for the first time in years, Marta beheld the valley of the Neretva, the apartment blocks of the city of her youth, their windows blazing in the last red of the western sun. Down below, arching over her invisible river, would be the Stari

Most, Tino's bridge. She could almost see the bridge through the buildings. She could smell ancient stones and hear footsteps in the evening. One look down into the valley, and she could feel the skin of her bare toes against the limestone of the Stari Most, as trusted as the caress of a mother's hand. Her terror faded. It was as if she had never left home.

THIRTEEN

POMEGRANATE BUSHES and kiwi vines enclosed one half of the restaurant L'Avventura. Japanese lanterns floated on gnat clouds. Great night moths bumped against one another, casting shadows, giving everything in the pavilion an aquatic shimmer. Why Tino hadn't bought a place with grapevines, Marta didn't know. Grapes had grown in Mostar since Roman times. Kiwis had been imported from New Zealand sometime in the last twenty years. But Marta kept her reservations to herself.

At the back of the pavilion, beyond the line of pomegranate bushes, the land dropped sheer to a stream that tumbled into the Neretva a few hundred yards from the restaurant. The stream was the Radobolja, and the sound of its running waters echoed through the pavilion, creaks, snaps, and rustles, distant thunder of the river in the gorge. The flagstones were large and polished, and the wicker chairs and tables, arranged around an ancient yew tree rising in the center of the pavilion, suggested one of the nicer holiday resorts on the coast.

The other half of the restaurant included the kitchen, the serving area, and a small bar carved out of an old bellows and forge once used by the metalworking family who had built the place. Like the stone of the bridge, the limestone of the building had worn into a profound softness, cool silk to the touch. She ran her fingers across its surfaces and wondered what Arthur Cape might be doing. There was a lot for a young American to do in West Berlin at night. There were the clubs she read about. Jazz and movies were popular. There were the wild women.

She found herself at the bar. It had been stocked with every kind of imported liquor. Silver fluids shimmered above shot glasses and snifters: loza, of course, and slivovitz for out-of-town visitors, melding into the coppery gleam of Johnny Walker Red and Black, Hennessy, Grand Marnier, Amaro, ranks of Bombay gin, Russian vodka, and Campari. Beneath this assortment ran the Vernaccia di San Gimignano, the Montepulciano, and to one side, making way, like minor nobility for royalty, bottles of *blatina* and *zilavka,* the red and white local wines of Mostar, from the vineyards of Tino's partner's uncle, old Vlado Miric, who had a reputation for superb grapes.

Above the bar, music videos swam like exotic fish across the screen of a television set. Beside the set, in a place of honor, hung a photo of Tino's hero, Marcello Mastroianni, a contentious choice. The Miric family, patriotic Croats, wanted Ante Pavelic up there. They wanted Pavelic and the new Croatian flag, the red-and-white checkerboard of the *sahovnica* that Marta had seen waving in Zagreb. They wanted the flag and the man wreathed in twists of plastic ivy. Old Miric had seen such a display in Osijek and had liked it. Out of the question, Tino had said, and Marta backed him. It would be bad business. Put Pavelic up, and you could forget Serb customers. You could forget the Jews, too. Marshal Tito, maybe, but never Pavelic. He was a killer. He had collected eyeballs in baskets. He was responsible for Jasenovac. These assertions, made by Marta, infuriated the Miric people, who told her that the numbers of the people killed at that camp had been wildly exaggerated, and that anyway she should butt out. In the end, Tino prevailed, and Marcello Mastroianni, rather than Ante Pavelic, was

wreathed in plastic ivy, though, as Marta pointed out, Tino's favorite
actor had not been in the movie *L'Avventura*.

At half past seven, dusk settling on the city, guests started to arrive.
Her father was the first, in the company of Mose Silber. The Jew made
her father look fat, thought Marta. The broad gut of the sensualist,
Osman Lazic, blew out like a sail on the Adriatic. He had too much
chin and precious little neck. He ate plates and plates of fried potatoes
and the little meat cigars called cevapcici for lunch. He drank, and he
smoked, and he bellowed opinions that made his blood pressure rise.
His eyes twinkled, and he moved for a moment, twirling his grandson,
like the dancer that he'd been when her mother fell in love with him.

He could not squeeze Pino enough. And when Pino did his duck
dance, waddling with his elbows out, puckering his lips, her father almost collapsed with laughter. Marta and Tino had been in town a
week, and her father had spent every waking moment in a trance in-
duced by this grandchild. He was astonished at the boy's language ca-
pability and exquisitely proud when Pino spoke German. He rolled
his eyes at Tino's discomfort.

On the afternoon before the party, Tino's parents came to afternoon coffee and insisted on taking Pino home with them. Marta's father had refused to hand over the boy.

"But there is no woman here," Tino's mother had said.

"Take the dog," her father had replied.

"I repeat," she'd said. "There is no woman living here."

"And there never was. Isn't that what you mean? There's no point
in insulting my wife, Comrade Mehmedovic. Nothing you can say behind her back will be worse than what I have already said to her face."

The Great Actress did not come in the first wave of guests. Tino
had invited Marta's entire family, even Vesna Bistritza, and she had
made a promise to come, though Marta knew that her promises
never amounted to much. They indicated outside possibilities.

Tino brought Marta to meet his partner, the scrawny, haunted
Darko Miric. They'd known each other in school, young Miric

reminded her, and Marta said that she remembered. Her husband threw an arm around the taller man's shoulders and seemed to be hanging there for dear life.

Marta took a seat in a wicker chair beside a pomegranate bush and watched a young woman taking drink orders. A worn gray T-shirt strained against her absurdly large breasts, and her blue jeans barely contained her ass, which was hoggish. Her hair tossed about crudely. She was a *fufa* if ever Marta had seen one, and she chatted with Marta's father, who ordered another loza. She seemed to be on very good terms with Tino, who didn't ask for anything. The girl returned with the loza and a bottle of Cognac—Hennessy, her husband's preferred brand.

At Tino's urging, this girl now approached Marta, big, dumb eyes pleased at some mysterious triumph, at the glory of her young body, which had never borne a child, Marta was sure, which had never had to please a man, year in, year out, without thanks, reward, or much love. The *fufa* asked in a way that was far too casual, as if they knew each other, how Marta enjoyed being back in Mostar, and what she would like to drink, the two questions jammed together out of nervousness or laziness or both. Marta got up from the table, brushed past the girl, and almost ran into her half-brother Mato at the entrance to the pavilion. Before she could speak, he threw his arms around her, and she burst into tears on his shoulder.

"So soon the tears," said Mato, amused and concerned in the same moment.

Mato's father, her mother's second husband, the princely aeronautics engineer, Ivo Osterajker, was there, too. A cigarette butt smoldered in one hand, a copy of *Oslobodjenje* dangled from the other. The engineer had gone bald. She got a hug and kiss from him, and then he made for the bar, where he ordered his indispensable Irish whisky and began to complain about his pension.

Marta strolled with her half-brother out of the pavilion and up a stone path to the Stari. They passed beneath the limestone arch of the Halebija Tower and stopped for a moment to gaze at the bridge. In the shadows, it rose like the outline of an ancient burial mound, the limestone a violet hue, its substance transformed into something less solid than stone, as if the Stari, like a mirage, faded at nightfall. For an instant, she doubted the rock beneath her feet. The Stari had been created as a simple piece of functional architecture, a man-made hillock across swift waters, designed by an Ottoman architect and raised by local artisans in the year 1658 to connect trade routes between Ragusa and Istanbul; ninety-nine steps from end to end, with a slight plateau at the top for catching one's breath. One could overstate its beauty, Marta had always thought, but never its presence.

They reached the top of the bridge and watched the deepening of twilight, when the spirits of the river tricked the eye and transformed the entire valley into their bed, steeping the banks, the domes of the mosques, the fingers of the clock towers, the high-rises, the mountain ranges, the sky, everything, in the aquamarine and violet colors of the Neretva, submerging the entire world in a simulation of deluge broken only by the last splinter of fire in the far west. A Yugoslav soldier tossed rocks into the water.

"You're fit," she said to Mato.

He hooked his left arm through her right one. "If you walk over this bridge three times a day after every meal, you'll be fit, too."

"I'll try to remember."

He gave her another squeeze and a kiss on the cheek. "Why the hell did you come back? That cocksucker make you?"

Mato had never liked her husband, and had never tried to conceal his animosity, which, at the moment, she appreciated.

"I'm not allowed to visit?"

She realized that of all her siblings, she had missed Mato the most.

She ran a hand across Mato's bristled head. "So what are you doing these days?"

"Fixing cars. Doing shift work at Soko. Hunting rabbits with Branko on the weekends. What else? Shit here never changes."

Mato leaned on the wall of the Old Bridge, in a pose that she remembered from the lost depths of her life, one elbow down on the parapet, his chin resting on a palm, the other arm crossing underneath. With his soft brown eyes, he stared down into the river. Her mother had those same soft eyes, and so did Pino.

"Do you hear from Mami?" she asked.

"I throw away her postcards. The old man sees them and gets depressed." Mato shook his head and tossed a pebble into the waters. "You?"

"Maybe tonight."

He raised an eyebrow.

"She's coming from Venice. She promised."

Mato laughed, and he was right, of course. He was absolutely right. Her mother had no interest in the city where she'd been a war orphan. And she certainly wouldn't come in the midst of political uncertainty. She had sold her flat in Zagreb and lived in Tel Aviv with an Israeli chopper pilot. From there, she had taken to writing shrill, anti-nationalist invective for Yugoslav newspapers and making herself a despised figure. Croat editorialists had begun to call her a witch.

"What do Catholics believe about adultery, Mato?" Marta asked.

He started to smile, but her look silenced him. "You interested in theology now?" he wanted to know.

"Seriously. What would a Catholic priest say to someone who had cheated on a spouse?'

" 'Go forth, and sin no more,' I guess."

"So it's not so bad?"

He shook a finger and grinned. "I didn't say that."

She absorbed this information. "You're not a Catholic anymore, are you?"

He seemed bemused by the question, as if he had been put to a ridiculous test. "If you're asking me whether I attend mass or go to confession, the answer is never."

"Do you know what happens to Muslims who commit adultery?"

He shrugged. "Who gives a damn?"

"As long as there are four witnesses, the penalty for the woman is death."

"I'm not exactly a scholar, but I don't believe those rules are in practice anywhere in the civilized world. And anyway, you're not a practicing Muslim, so why do you care?"

"So what are you calling yourself these days, if not a Catholic?" she asked him.

He roared for the world to hear. "Yugoslav!"

Then he paused, and his eyes grew deep and sad. "Please tell me you're not going to wear that shit over your head."

Mato's words filled her with anxiety. "I won't," she said. "I'm not. You've completely missed the point."

He sang now in English. *"I don't care about history, 'cause that's not where I want to be."*

"I don't know that song," she said.

"It's the Ramones. They kick ass. Branko introduced me to them."

"Is he still seeing my sister?"

Mato grimaced. "You've got to talk to her. I mean it."

"I'll talk to her."

"He's my friend, but he's changing. This shit in the air is changing him. He's asking me the same questions you are, except that he's serious about it. He wants her to convert to Catholicism."

Marta had her first good laugh of the evening.

Mato didn't seem amused. He looked into her eyes.

"Have your laugh," he said, "then go back to Germany."

THEY RETURNED TO the restaurant, but Mato didn't enter by the gate. He pushed through pomegranate bushes, and Marta saw why. Hanging near the entrance to the pavilion, as if to have a clean line of escape, was his and Marta's half-sister, the Serbian succubus, as she was derisively called by the rest of the family, Isadora Markovic, the illegitimate daughter of her mother and her mother's third husband, Stepan Markovic, otherwise known as Dushan. Mato couldn't abide Isadora. He had been snared in the mayonnaise affair in Sarajevo and had never forgiven his half-sister for it. Unlike Marta, who had been sent home for punishment, Mato had spent a month in a cell in Belgrade. He had been interrogated as a possible Fascist sympathizer for what Isadora had done as a tasteless joke.

Isadora's shining blond tresses fell down the front of a very expensive black leather jacket. At nineteen, she could have been thirty, and the affectation of age flattered her. That had always been her style, acting older than she was, as if she feared youth. During beach vacations years ago, when their mother had gathered the brood, without fathers, under one roof for a week or two, that hair had attracted every boy within a hundred kilometers and made all the girls, except her sister Dubravka, the so-called Circassian, jealous. Marta was the eldest, five years older than Mato, and had missed most of the summertime drama, when Isadora and Dubravka prowled the beaches, devouring boys. Those two still kept in touch, though the Belgrade half-sister had decided that she was an intellectual and did not care for country folk anymore. She modeled for Dior in Paris and talked like a raving Serb nationalist. Her old anti-Communism had become poisonous anti-Yugoslav. Marta considered it all a pose.

The sisters kissed cheeks. Isadora's lips were cold, very French.

"Is Dushan here?" Marta asked.

"He's conducting his new piece tonight in Split." Isadora had always called her father Dushan, his public nickname, as if he were a rock star. Dushan also happened to be the name of the last great ruler of the Serbian Medieval Kingdom, the man who had extended its borders to the shores of the Aegean. The modern incarnation was insufferable.

"Anyway, he won't come to Mostar. He's adamant. He calls it Propagandagrad."

The remark was typically provocative, and Marta couldn't ignore it.

"The Stari is on the Unesco list. All the really cultured people have seen it."

Isadora sneered at the mention of the Old Bridge. "There are a dozen monasteries in Serbia more valuable."

Marta smelled the Parisian scent rising off Isadora. She could see the hint of the label inside the collar of her shirt, could hear the crinkling of the pampered, soaped, scented body within the tooled leather, and wondered, in the proximity of all this wordly sensuality, why on earth her young sister would involve herself in such primitive local politics.

"Dubravka told me that you had become *political*."

Isadora narrowed her eyes. She accepted a glass of sparkling water from a waiter. "I always was political." She drank. "Unlike you."

"I never saw the point."

"Of course you didn't. You're a self-hating Slav woman."

Tino interrupted in earnest. "Dinner is served."

GLASS PLATTERS SLID from the kitchen onto the bar. Delicious odors invaded the pavilion. The pomegranate bushes rustled. The waters rasped. Tino brought grilled squid and trout, roast pig and chicken, cevapcici and kebabs; he brought tomato salad, sliced green peppers, boats of french fries, bowls of kajmak cheese and ajvar, loaves of hot bread, olives, grapes, pistachio nuts. Uscrubbed folk musicians unpacked mandolins and guitars. Tino had wanted his favorite sevdah players at the party, but he lost his preference when he insisted on Marcello Mastroianni. So instead of the Mostarian sound that he loved, he'd had to settle for a pack of ragged, strumming Dalmatians. The food danced off the bar and away to the tables.

The daughters of the Great Actress sat together at the same table. Mato, safely drunk, joined them.

"You should be more grateful," Isadora said in a hurt voice to Marta. "I drove here all the way from Dubrovnik. Dushan was against it, but I came anyway. Only to see you."

Marta saw that she meant it. Isadora had made a real effort. Marta was touched, and she softened. It had been six years, they determined, since the mayonnaise affair, since university, when they had last seen each other. Isadora had not even been at university then. The scandal had occurred during a private party at Dushan's flat in Sarajevo, in the old Ottoman neighborhood of Bascarsija. Isadora had laughed at the police who'd burst into her father's apartment as if breaking up a cell of Nazi terrorists. Everyone who was anyone in Sarajevo had been at that party. It had been one of the great parties in the city's history.

The musicians were feuding over the play list, or money, it seemed. They strummed and stopped and yelled at one another, and strummed again. One of them made a pass at Tino's *fufa,* and Tino took a jab at him. Isadora observed everything.

"That pig," she said, turning her gaze to Marta.

The party became loud. The men tried a wobbly kolo, whirling between the yew tree and the pomegranate bushes, where there was no space. Mose Silber downed loza and toppled backward over a chair. Marta's father sat in the nook of the yew and rocked Pino back and forth, tapping his foot to the music. Pino tried to clap. The puppy quivered beneath her father's chair, a ridiculously unsafe place.

Dubravka arrived, the music stopped, and every eye flashed her way. She paused at the entrance to the pavilion, glanced about her, appreciating the impact of her presence. She wore long earrings, glittering silver, and a tight black miniskirt. Her eyes gave off a mighty blue surge. She had the trademark long legs of the women in the family, and a cleavage visible in the open collar of her blue cotton blouse. Her body announced sex like a cymbal clash, thought Marta, impressed and annoyed at the same time. The pale, light-haired, blue-eyed Circassian women of the north had always been the favorites of the sultan's harem, so Dubravka had always been known as the Circassian. Tonight she lived up to the name.

Behind her, taking off leather gloves, came Branko. His head was shaven, and he wore his sunglasses long after dark. His dark red silk shirt had unbuttoned to his navel; Branko Velakovic, nicknamed Vela, son of a poor family from the hills above Stolac. The couple had come on his new Suzuki motorcycle, bought with proceeds from smuggled cigarettes, Mato said.

Vela had charm, and had never lacked for hard currency, but he didn't have an ounce of class or real education. He had fucked or fought or finagled his way into the good circles, and as Mato's best friend, he had been allowed to come to one of the last of the beach vacations.

Dubravka glided to the table. Behind her, Vela waited his turn to dazzle. Marta did not let him catch her eye. She wouldn't greet a man who hit her sister. Vela gave no hint of giving a damn. He had a way of looking beyond people, toward the hills, as if they were his superiors, and he were responding to internal messages. His forehead was too wide for such tiny eyes and mouth. He wasn't serious. He was nothing, a twisted smile, an affectation of strength. He wasn't worth a hair on Mato's head, though he treated Mato like a sidekick in a western. He certainly didn't deserve Dubravka.

"I like those earrings," said Marta.

Dubravka waited for her sister to show proper respect to her boyfriend. "Branko is the one who gave us the puppy."

"You like her?" he asked in a deceptively shy voice. "She's almost as beautiful as one of you girls."

Marta felt sick to her stomach. "I'm not sure we're keeping it," she said.

"I always remember you on the beach at Lumbarda." He had lowered his voice. "You were the one who would never talk to me."

Mato pulled Vela to the bar, where the photo of Marcello Mastroianni had gone missing. Isadora went to have a look at Pino.

Dubravka sat at the table beside her sister, crossing her legs, jiggling the earrings. She gave Marta an interrogative gaze. Marta blinked.

"You fucked that American boy, didn't you?" Dubravka shook her head in true disbelief, as if a proven fact of human existence had been debunked before her eyes. "You actually followed my advice. Admit it."

Marta got up. The Dalmatians had collapsed in a tuneless heap. Someone cranked the sound of the music video on the television set. It was Madonna, singing "Like a Prayer." Isadora gave the baby back to Marta's father and jumped into the middle of the dance floor, beckoning to Marta and Dubravka.

"We have to dance to this!" Dubravka cried, as if she were sixteen again.

Soon, every woman there, even the *fufa*, had gathered in the middle of the pavilion to move to the beat of that song, which Marta hated. She alone refused to participate.

"Let-the-choirs-sing!"

Tino seemed to know the words by heart. His lips were moving, and his body was swaying a few feet from his *fufa*. He couldn't take his eyes off the girl. Marta understood that he had become a feral, little creature, a rodent. He had not always been so, but he was now, and forever more, in a form of bondage to death and ruin. He feigned tears over their son. He acted like a child who had to be protected from the awful, intolerable world beyond the valley. He had begged, and she had crumbled. But her weakness had passed. Arthur Cape had been right. Tino would get them all killed. He was weak, and she must leave him. She had a man back in Berlin. She had a life. Her arms tightened against her sides. Her entire body balled into a fist. She would take the plane tickets and leave in the morning.

Dubravka's eyes watched her as she moved across the dance floor toward her husband. Marta had made love to another man. She could not pretend innocence. But her husband had made that act inevitable. He had destroyed her faith. He had chewed and gnawed on her affections. He had fucked countless women without shame or hesitation or contrition. One of them offered her body to him on the dance floor beneath the Japanese lanterns, gave him her breasts, turned, and gave him her ass. Marta had to go, but first she had to confront him. He already had another pair of Bosnian hips to bear him a family. He had lied to her about Mose Silber. He had lied to get her down here. Everything was a lie. This business did not belong to her. It was another woman's future.

Her husband smiled down like a god of oils.

"I'm leaving tomorrow," she said.

And she struck him across the face. She walked out of the pavilion and headed up steps toward the bridge. Her husband caught her in the middle of the Stari, almost exactly at the spot where they had met. He grabbed her arm, as if afraid she might jump.

"Give me the tickets," she said.

He reached into his coat pocket and took out the envelope. She took it and knew immediately that something was wrong. She opened the envelope and found a single ticket.

"Where's the other one?" she asked him, attempting to keep her voice down.

Tino lifted it in his fingers and ripped it in two. "I'll give you the apartment. You can't have my son."

"You've become pitiful, Tino."

He placed his fingertips on her cheeks. "Let me tell you something, wife, and I hope you will listen."

For the last time, she did.

"I am what I am, and I've done what I've done. I will have to live with that. But who are you? Look inside. Do you think you have a thousand lives? Do you think you can be a citizen of Berlin and a citizen of Mostar, too? Do you think you can fuck a stranger and remain my wife?" He paused and let her absorb the words. "You can't, my love. There is one life, and this is now yours. You are cast out."

"I'm taking Pino with me," she warned.

Her husband's face ceased to be the one that she had known; it passed out of their years together and into a place of utter cruelty. He caught one of her wrists and drew her close. He put his mouth against her ear.

"Even try," he said, "and they will never find you."

Tino turned away and left her by herself in the brilliant night, on the summit of the Stari, looking down into the suck and rush of the ancient river. She lifted the envelope containing the plane ticket above the waters. Twice, she tried to let go of it. Twice, she expected to watch the envelope ripple away on the stream. But the thing would not fall from her hand.

FOURTEEN

O N THE MORNING OF OCTOBER 2, the day before the Unification of East and West Germany, Arthur received a visit from Eric Hampton.

"We must distinguish, Arthur, between the *pays legal,* if I may prevail upon your French, and the *pays réel.* It's a crucial distinction."

Hampton had taken a seat in the grand salon, and accepted a cup of coffee from Frau Herbst, blooming in gold chiffon. She admired the British gentleman in her parlor, and Arthur could see why. Hampton wore a crisp white shirt tucked into pressed khaki pants. His thin red hair, slightly damp, had been parted on one side and trimmed at the upper curl of his ears. The pocket of his brown wool blazer held a maroon silk handkerchief, and his words had the crisp solidity of his dress, as if the Kempinski laundry service had ironed and starched every syllable the night before.

Arthur didn't speak French, but he thought he understood the general drift. His senior colleague meant by *pays legal* and *pays réel* the difference between the legally constituted country and the so-called real country.

"I follow," he said, feeling flattered. Hampton had taken pains to track Arthur down. He had notified Gavin Morsch, the chief of correspondents, that he would feel bereft if he didn't personally meet his new colleague in Berlin, his very favorite city in Europe. Morsch had given him the address and phone number, but Hampton had not bothered to telephone in advance. He surprised Arthur with the visit, chatting up the landlady before knocking on the rooms of his suite. Arthur had dressed quickly and walked right into a lecture. "Take Berlin. That's simple enough. Two cities, East and West, yes? Until tonight, at midnight, when those two cities *legally* cease to exist, when the governments of those two cities, the Federal Republic of Germany and the German Democratic Republic, children of the Cold War, *legally* vanish, like the two halves of the woman in the old sawing trick, and we are left again with one city. Two into one. That should be clear enough."

"And it very much is," Arthur said.

"But will Berlin become one city in any real sense? What do you think, Arthur?"

Arthur answered with the one piece of relevant erudition at his disposal. "No more than ancient Rome and Heaven could ever merge. One is of this earth, one is a hope and a dream."

"We've read our Augustine. That's a superb start." Hampton took a breath, and grinned as if about to utter a delicious obscenity. "But it's a trick question, and I'm delighted that you didn't try to answer geopolitically. My faith would have been shaken to its roots."

"I'm relieved," Arthur said. "Why is it a trick?"

"Because we both know that only one of the countries will effectively disappear at the stroke of midnight, and that is the Communist one. In the single tick of a clock hand, East Germany's parliament, laws, and ministries, its TV shows, soccer teams, and national industries, its citizens, its very geography, the lines on the earth that once demarcated its existence, will be gone, never to be seen again, except in memory. A child born on October 3 will not, in his or her life,

Arthur, coincide with a single day in the life of this defunct entity, the German Democratic Republic. And yet—and this is my point—the people who live on what was once that territory do not forget. They remember. They will, in fact, continue to live in the invisible city of their memories, the city of blood, the city of cloud, whether the legal authorities like it or not."

Hampton took a deep breath, and Arthur did, too.

"The so-called German Democratic Republic, given forty-one years of grace and not one second more by the archons of geopolitics, will now be history. Everything that once belonged to it, all of its worldly possessions, will fall into the hands of the state on the other side of the border, West Germany, what we know as the Federal Republic of Germany, and its remains will go once and for all, alpha and omega, world without end, amen, into a casket looking suspiciously like a dustbin. And yet East Germany will not be gone. Far from it."

Hampton cast a dire look around the room.

"Far from it," he concluded, feeling, perhaps, that he had made his case.

Arthur thanked him for the debriefing, and he meant it. But he had one question.

"Are you saying that Berlin will never stop being East and West, or is this split between the legal country and the real country, as you put it, only temporary?"

Hampton seemed exceptionally pleased to be taken so seriously. "I'm saying, Arthur—" Frau Herbst listened to Hampton with a spark in her eye, Arthur saw. He was her kind of man, well dressed, well spoken, well connected. Most of all, he was English. He reminded her of a British intelligence officer, she later told Arthur, a man named Plessington, her lover back in the black market days after the war. She refused to leave the room, and he was made slightly nervous. "I'm saying that within every city, there is another city, invisible to the eye, maybe better, maybe worse, than the one we think we know, but in the case of Berlin, that other city will be more visible for a while than in most cases. We will watch it disappear, like a rainbow from a stormy sky. I myself have no doubt you're going to do great things here in Berlin, give it all a fresh eye, but unfortunately, that brings me to the sharp point of this visit. Are you available for work?"

Hampton produced a pack of cigarettes from his shirt pocket and was permitted to smoke, unlike other guests.

"You see, I'd very much like to take one last turn at West Berlin before she goes, Arthur."

"But you don't need my permission."

"Well, but I want your blessing, I suppose. We will be working together quite a lot in the future, and I don't want to get off on the wrong foot."

Arthur said that they hadn't got off on the wrong foot at all, that he considered Hampton an absolute superior, and that he was there to serve, to be commanded.

"You're not chuffed about the hotel room?"

"Not chuffed at all. Just tell me what you want me to do."

Hampton put out his cigarette. "Brilliant. There is something you can do, as a matter of fact, yes. You did a superb job on that police precinct thingy, and you may want to ask your friends in the *polizei* if they know something. I'm told by a reliable source that brownshirt hooligans will be descending on the Unification festivities up around Alexanderplatz, and that the anarcho-syndicalists and Maoists are going to have a go at them. If there is any street fighting, I'd like the magazine to be right in the thick."

"It will be. I promise you that."

Hampton gave Arthur his phone number at the Grand Kempinski and told him to call at six, eight, ten, and twelve midnight with dispatches. After exchanging a few pleasantries about the sons and daughters of the Houses of Windsor and Saxe-Coburg with Frau Herbst, he left, and in his wake, the apartment at Apostel-Paulus-Strasse 40 seemed to sink back into shadow. Frau Herbst retreated into her rooms, and Arthur sat by himself beneath the wing of a stolen Florentine angel, basking in the afterglow of the first unmistakably great foreign correspondent he had ever met. Arthur felt more than admiration for Eric Hampton. It was professional love at first sight. That was a journalist! He had ideas and knew how to articulate them. He spoke French. He was steeped in the past and wise to the present. He loved and knew the world, and he was what Arthur wanted to become.

THE SORROW OF the previous days began to disperse. Arthur bathed and dressed. Work could now begin.

On the street, on his way to the middle of the city, he ran into Duben. After their earlier conversation, Arthur had steered clear of the butcher. He'd wanted no more to do with that Balkan mess.

Duben, polishing his windows, called Arthur over. "You will be sick," he said.

Arthur slid new batteries into his microcassette recorder. He fixed the butcher with his eyes.

"She's been here and gone. This very morning. And you missed her."

Arthur gave a long, solemn shake of the head. The batteries dropped out of the back of the recorder.

"I don't believe you."

"*Doch, doch.* She bought a corn-fed chicken. I have the receipt inside. Would you like to see it?"

Marta had never returned to the travel agency. She hadn't telephoned or attempted to make any other form of contact with Arthur. For one week, once a day, before he finally put the affair behind him, he had rung the bell to her apartment. No one ever answered. Every morning, he had manned his favorite corner of the café between 7:30 A.M. and 9:30 A.M., sipping his way through *milchcaffees,* reading newspapers, watching the entrance to the address of the travel agency, pretending to himself that he was there for reasons of convenience.

Finally, he had summoned his courage and climbed the stairs to her office. The agency had closed on the occasion of German Unity, a note told him, regrets to customers.

Arthur hadn't wanted to know another thing. There had been a momentary plunge into sentiment during his transition from one country to the next. She had been a nurse in an emergency ward, and he had latched onto her face and form, classic Florence Nightingale syndrome. Now that he had recovered, he refused to go back under. "When exactly did she come by?"

"At precisely the usual time." Duben was pointing at the clock above his meat counter. "I sold her one of my hens. But she doesn't eat chicken. Neither does her husband. Who could it be for?"

He hit Arthur with a damning gaze. "She's a vegetarian."

"A mystery," said Arthur. And he turned his back on the man.

HE CAUGHT A BUS up Hauptstrasse, past the battered helmet of the Berlin Philharmonic, beyond the last edges of West Berlin, to the wasteland of Potsdamerplatz. The place seemed to lie far in his past, like an episode from his childhood. Arthur got out at the bus stop, at the brink of desolation. This time, there were other people wandering over the *platz*. They bent to pick up shards of stone or pebbles, mementos of emptiness. He sat on the mound marking the last known resting place of Adolf Hitler and gazed at the distant portal of the Brandenburg Gate, which stood four city blocks or so to the northwest, a mud-brown arch leading from nothing into nothing, and beyond that, rising above the heads of the crimsoning trees in the Tierpark, at the Reichstag. He thought of the famous picture that Marta had mentioned, of the photographer swinging from the parapets of parliament, aiming his lens, through the smoke, at the downfurling flag of the Soviet Empire.

Arthur gazed at the emptiness, and slowly, before his eyes, Potsdamerplatz dissolved. Marta's voice returned. Arthur tried to hear it exactly right, exactly as it had sounded in his ear. Everything that had ever existed here—the grand hotels and gilded cafés, the exquisite chocolate shops and Italian shoe stores, the rail and the roads, the armies of bureaucracies and soldiers, the executions and explosions, the guard towers and tank traps—everything vanished. The future vanished, too, what would eventually rise on the ground where he sat, unnamed, unknown, but imminent, like rain showers advancing on the wind. In Marta's voice, for a moment, Potsdamerplatz belonged to Arthur. And for the rest of his life, he would think of the place in this form, as it now was, in its hour of total emptiness. Marta had come back. But she had broken his heart. He said his last goodbye and left the mound.

THE POLICE AT Schöneberg Precinct had heard Hampton's rumors, too, but they knew nothing for sure about a demonstration. Brownshirt hooligans were expected to gather near the Oranienplatz Park in West Berlin. They would march across the Cold War border just north of the park, then move through East Berlin to Alexanderplatz, where they intended to celebrate the Unification of Germany by smashing windows. This much Arthur gleaned from his sources. It was past noon already. He walked east a kilometer or two and had a look around Alexanderplatz, but didn't see any commotion, so he caught a bus line that took him back south into West Berlin, to a stop near Oranienplatz Park, and, coincidentally, a few blocks north of Marta's apartment.

Against his will, he ended up there. He could not help himself. He rang the buzzer several times. No one answered. He left a note:

"Duben saw you. If you want, meet me at the Brandenburg Gate at midnight."

He spent the rest of the day in a fever, hunting swastikas. He searched the walls of subway stations, the sides of Litfass columns, the gutters of the streets for pamphlets or posters announcing a march. He inquired at Turkish lunch counters, in the bars and cafés of the tougher neighborhoods of Kreuzberg. He looked for groupings of three or more people, asking parties of gay men, Jehovah's witnesses, and some young Norwegian tourists if they were by any chance part of the right-wing demonstration scheduled for that afternoon.

The hour edged on six. He phoned Hampton at the Kempinski. "Nothing so far."

"Keep at it. I'm off to the Intercontinental and won't be back until late, but I'll keep checking messages."

Arthur decided that, as insurance, he should spend the first part of the evening walking back and forth between West Berlin and East Berlin, between Kreuzberg and Alexanderplatz. If anything happened, he would catch wind of it on this route. It was a superb evening, the sun tailing down toward the Rhine and the Atlantic, toward the west. To the east, over Poland, the night seeped in, and a filament of cloud-spun moon could be seen.

Kreuzberg had once ended at the Wall, but the Wall's removal had left open territory on the park's northern side, a strip of earth and grass that flowed around the base of a lone, abandoned East German guard tower. The tower protruded into the evening like a boulder in a river, and a brand new road curved to one side of it, a thoroughfare connecting the two sides of the city.

Across the road from the tower, under its gaze, a colony of squatters had settled. They were *Rollheimer,* anarchists on wheels. They imitated gypsies and moved from place to place in a caravan of cars, buses, trucks, and motorcycles—Enfields, Harleys, Suzukis, a gasping Vespa or two.

If anyone would know about a right-wing political march through this territory, the *Rollheimer* would. Before Arthur could cross the road, a tiny bell chimed twice behind him. He jumped out of the way. A cyclist skimmed out of the shadows. She slammed on brakes and skidded. Beyond her, on the far side of the road, shirtless men in bikini underwear lit a fire in a metal barrel. Children scuttled between tents, beneath lines of wash, cut loose from shaggy mothers, who yelled at goats or tended tomato plants growing out of the body of an East German automobile, a faded pink planter in the form of a car.

"You're living with my great-aunt!" the woman cried. In the twilight, Arthur had not seen the green hair.

"Gaby?"

"What are you doing here? Are you *spying?*"

She walked her bike back toward him.

"Have you seen Marta?" he blurted out.

"Marta?"

"Frau Mehmedovic."

Gaby's eyes threw back sparks.

"*Wahnsinn!*" she hissed, making connections. Insanity! The word unnerved Arthur.

"Have you?"

In an instant, he had credibility with the girl. She walked the bike toward him.

"She decided to take a vacation, so Dieterle told me to piss off for a few days."

The sun sank beyond the camp.

"You two did it," said Gaby. "I picked up that much already."

Arthur changed the subject. "Do you know anything about a right-wing march around here?"

She studied him for a moment and then smiled with genuine warmth. "Want me to ask?"

He was about to follow her across the street, but she put up a hand. "Wait by the guard tower. They don't like American strangers."

At the tower's base, trash shifted in wind. The sides had been graffitoed right to the top, the names of rival Turkish gangs, obscenities, in green-rimmed, dung-like lumps on the eastern flank. When had the East German guards completed their mission? When had the final patrol departed? Yesterday? The tower seemed to have been abandoned in another century.

Gaby returned.

"There's some talk about the Fashos, but we're not part of it. We're going to burn down a department store, I think."

Arthur thanked her and wished her good luck.

"I saw Marta," Gaby said. "She came here looking for me. She gave me money. She's leaving her husband."

"No."

Gaby shrugged. "That's what she told me."

"I don't believe it," he said.

The last day in the life of the German Democratic Republic died in mystery. Marta had left her husband. Like a man resurrected from the dead, Arthur staggered off.

FIFTEEN

ARTHUR MARCHED back and forth between West Berlin and
East Berlin half a dozen times, then gave up on the swastikas.
He wandered for the hell of it. She had that effect on him.
He didn't give a damn anymore about his job and drank a lot of
schapps and beer. He was a reporter. It was a night of profound history. It was the culmination of mighty events, the end of the century.
He grew angry at Hampton for talking him into this interminable
search for brownshirts. His feet burned. The soles of his ostrich-skin
boots had rubbed right down to the nails. When he sat under the
crisp, hot lights of a party tent and tried to take them off, a bouncer
tossed him out of the tent.

Arthur considered the whole thing a bad idea for a party. The German government wanted the Unification of East and West to be an
even more joyous affair than the night of the fall of the Berlin Wall—
within limits, of course. But this would not be like 1989; the event
would have to be stage-managed. A certain anarchic spirit was to be
avoided. Urinating on public monuments was no longer admired,
and the legitimate German authorities were to be respected. But
champagne corks should fly. Bananas and pineapples should be de-

voured. East Germans and West Germans should guzzle, gobble, sing, and dance, and the next morning, with the greatest hangover of the twentieth century, they should set about the difficult task of becoming countrymen.

No one felt quite up to the celebration, though. Arthur interviewed people who were afraid, inebriated, or bored. The party in Berlin was the cigarette before the execution, and no one savored it. He hunted in vain for happiness, for even a fraction of the thrill that must have shuddered through the two Berlins on November 9, 1989, when the world transformed. But the silver-lit tents, the seas of beer foam, never seen in such quantity on that side of town, the gleam of impeccably cleaned streets and walls, the grease-flamed grills, the clumps of people standing quietly around, staring up at the heads of the great institutional buildings, the Arsenal, the German State Opera, the Kaiserdom, the Palace of the Republic—these things whispered of loss and confusion. Arthur could hear it, like human dismay in hospital corridors.

At a booth touting the virtues of Bavarian weisswurst, he flushed down pints of wheat beer and ate veal sausages. He contemplated ditching his notes and going to Marta's apartment. He was disgusted with himself for this spirit of capitulation.

"Goddamn you," he said aloud to himself.

The sausage grillers glanced up.

"Hi," said a woman standing at the bar next to him. "American?"

Arthur was getting very sleepy.

"I'm a journalist."

He didn't have the will power or desire to speak German. Mercifully, she spoke English, too.

"You are covering Unification, like everyone else?"

She had black hair and wore a red skirt. Her eyes had a smart-ass quality. She grinned. She was flirting with him.

"Have a drink with me?" he asked.

"*Nein.*"

Arthur paid his bill and walked out. She followed.

"You forgot this," she said, holding up his notebook.

She pointed at a line of numbers on the cover of the notebook; beneath the numbers was her name: Anna von Hakenberg.

"I do good work for American journalists," she said. "Ask anyone."

She returned to one of the tables in the party tent, and a man put a hand on one of her bare legs. Arthur made for the Brandenburg Gate. It took him most of an hour to plow through the crowds, which had begun to gather around the triple columns of the gate. People were well beyond plastered. They were *blau*. They had been pouring spirits into themselves since noon, chasing beer with vodka, and champagne, and homemade fruit schnapps. The party had gone on too long, and the people were weighed down, crushed halfway to the earth, just trying to stay up, to say that they had been there, to take some sense of accomplishment out of the endurance test of the last half of this longest day. On the western side of the gate, which Arthur had fought like hell to reach, someone had illegally parked a Volkswagen Beetle, but there was no longer any possibility of an exit, and people had begun to vandalize the car, stomping on its hood and trunk as the moment of Unity approached. Premature firecrackers popped. A German flag cascaded down, larger than any flag that Arthur had ever seen, a yellow, black, and red lake of national sentiment that managed to look as dispirited as the people around him.

Midnight came, and the countdown began. *Acht, sieben, sechs.* Arthur had made up his mind to squeeze back out of the crowd, to beat the rush out of the area, when fingers caught him by the shoulder. They caught him with urgency, he thought, as if to rescue him from the sea. He thought for an instant it might be Hampton, come to catch him off guard. Or maybe it was the girl in the red skirt or even a complete stranger.

Marta had been waiting for him since eleven. She had circled within the raving crowd, and her hair had been doused with champagne. Her eyes shone. She showed him the note that he had left at her door.

"You left your husband?" he asked her.

"No," she said.

He accepted this. He was tired beyond words. He'd had as much alcohol as his body could stand. The end of the East German state had come. *Drei, zwei, eins.* Marta took his hands, and her eyes glinted in the darkness. A roar and shriek went up. Silver fire raked the sky. Bells churned; waves of unbroken noise. He took her by the rib cage and kissed her lips.

"Welcome to the new world," she said into his ear.

SIXTEEN

A MAN AND A WOMAN, never quite identifiable in Marta's later memories, wandered the city of Berlin; West across the wasteland into the theoretical East, then out of the East on the U-Bahn line, past stops that had once been checkpoints, into the blessed shopping zones of the West. Marta lost the meaning of compass points. Day after day she discovered the secret links between neighborhoods separated for thirty years, an eternity if one looked at the lifetimes of cats and dogs, but not so long in the end, not even the length of a natural human existence. After three decades, blocks had been reconnected in a day by a single street, a rail line, a strip of abstruse emptiness where ideological empires had once intruded.

The names of the new neighborhoods entranced her; she had never thought of that part of Berlin, over there, the East, as a place of neighborhoods. The consonants glittered hard and bright on her tongue: Prenzlauer Berg, Friedrichshain, Treptow, Mitte, Mahlsdorf, the Scheunenviertel. With Arthur, she peeked into a *hinterhof* or stole a look down a vestibule and shook her head. Buildings were soot-caked and bullet-holed. Tenements had been left to disintegrate. Matter itself had been punished. The dilapidation smacked of Yugoslavia but in the neighborhoods of eastern Berlin, the ugliness verged on beauty, the survival of a city annihilated.

Berlin slurred into rain. November came.

Arthur had a desire to probe things that she would have avoided—Jewish graveyards where tombstones sank under vines or lay cracked on their backs; subway stations hung with plaques commemorating hangings and deportations; public parks that turned out to be mass graves for soldiers. She didn't need lessons in the horrors of the twentieth century; her family supplied that. But Arthur wandered from site to site in a daze, as if realizing for the first time that the atrocities he encountered had all really happened.

She was drawn to the public monuments to socialism. She liked to linger over statues of Lenin and Marx and search out the lesser-known figures, like Ernst Thaelmann, with his upraised chin. She had a fondness for the stone revolutionaries of her girlhood and had been a little sad to find out that most of them would disappear from the city streets, would be carved up and carted off. Not that she had ever had much patience for the university instructors who tried to teach her the tenets of Marxism while trying at the same time to get her into bed, or had ever aspired to do anything but escape from the unwitting sloth of it all, but the stone effigies had become inseparable from summer vacations, family reunions, and school trips, from the life that she had lived in the shadows of the state. They had been lovely, ghastly presences—statues of giant partisans looming over the highway south of Belgrade; Stevan Filipovic, hanged by the Germans, transmuted into rock; the hideous V-shaped thing in Kragujevac, where the Nazis had murdered seven thousand people. The stones had always been there, like dolmens of inscrutable civilizations, but now, in Berlin and everywhere else, the burdens of history had been lifted from the statues. The very mention of them caused embarrassment. History had ended. It had never been. Or so she had read somewhere. Her stone revolutionaries had become hunted men.

"Did you ever believe in Marxism?" Arthur one day asked. They were in Treptower Park, and she was gazing at the forty-foot statue of a Soviet soldier cradling a child in one arm and crushing a swastika with his sword in the other. She was missing her son.

"I never believed. No one I knew did, except my father. He wanted me to join the party so I would do well."

"Did you?"

Tino could never have asked that question, she thought. He knew the answer. He knew most answers, at least superficially.

She shook her head. "After a certain age, I knew exactly what I wanted. I knew which man. I knew which life. I knew which job. And I didn't need the party for any of them. So I never joined."

Marta had never been eager to tell other people what was on her mind. There had been a superb tactical advantage in silence. But Arthur asked question upon question and listened to her answers long into the night. And she talked more than she ever had in her life. His large blue eyes rarely blinked, and his fragile hands usually rested on some part of her body—her knee, her shoulder, her hip. Sometimes, he held her and asked questions that she didn't quite understand.

"Could you ever imagine yourself as a completely different person?"

"How do you mean?"

Arthur's fingers moved up her rib cage. "I mean, could you imagine disappearing in some big American city, like Chicago or Los Angeles, and starting a new job, with a new family, never looking back, cutting all contact with who you had been before? Could you imagine yourself as a new person?"

"No. I cannot imagine it. Can you?"

He sighed. "I used to. I used to want to. Do you think that's wrong?"

"I think it's impossible."

I N THE MEANTIME, as if nothing had changed, she continued to sleep in her apartment on the canal and work at the Adria Travel Agency, saying nothing about her personal affairs to Dieterle. He asked about the trip home, and she told him that she had not come to a final decision yet. It had been a nice trip, nothing more. As if the whole thing revolved around vacation, she asked Dieterle about his stay in a northern Italian spa town.

"I hate myself south of the Alps," he said.

Gaby began to act strange. She spent a lot of time staring at Marta and pestering her with sly comments about her hair or her clothes. She eavesdropped on Marta's phone conversations with Arthur. She asked about living arrangements and the content of her lunches. She was behaving like a little Communist spy.

One day, Marta had enough. During a break, she confronted the girl. "What do you want from me?"

Gaby gave her a mortified blink. "You've done it, haven't you?"

Marta did not try to pretend ignorance. "That's none of your business."

"It isn't, I know. But I wanted you to know that I think you're brave. You're the bravest woman I know."

Marta gave Gaby a long, grim look. "You have no idea what you're talking about. I'm not brave. I'm terrified."

Gaby couldn't understand. She was too young and had no children. To her, Marta had won an abstract victory of some sort. Gaby didn't know the details. She didn't ask for them. She only saw a glorious outline. Marta had left her husband, who was a louse, and taken up with an ambitious American journalist. But this fantasy had made its impact. One day, in late November, the green-haired girl simply didn't show up for work. She never gave official notice, didn't even phone. She left without a whisper. Marta never expected to see her again.

The butcher Duben made daily probes. He asked Marta about the hunting dog. He insisted on seeing the animal as soon as possible to find out whether she had been sold an inferior specimen under the guise of a purebred. He warned obliquely against the wrong kinds of associations and made generally disapproving remarks about Americans.

Arthur became a full-time reporter, and she marveled at his industry. He wrote stories every week about the coming December elections, the state of the eastern Germany economy (worse than anyone had expected; wretched, in fact), the rights of women, the closing of kindergartens, the plight of Soviet soldiers whose bases were closing. Every night, he had interesting stories to tell her, and she wanted to hear them. Now and then, he stayed away for a night on assignment, and she fought down the urge to pack her bags.

DECEMBER BROUGHT SNOW. The two of them moved against the cold, moved from café to *kneipe*, moved every night from the streets to the freezing garden house. They tangled their bodies up in the bower against the flank of the Black Thing, then slept in Arthur's rooms in the Apostel-Paulus-Strasse. She stopped living in her apartment. It became off limits. The mere fact of her past life within the walls of that home would have ruined Berlin, would have summoned up unbearable thoughts of her son, who waited, like her life, for a final answer. She expressed her fears to Arthur, and he told her, If you ever leave me, I will come creeping down the Balkan Peninsula, and I will catch you in the night and put you on my back and bring you north again.

"Pino, too," she said.

"Pino, too."

Her Berlin bank account remained open. Her rent money was transferred at the start of each month. Her utilities were paid. She did not go to the police and deregister—*abmelden,* as it was called. The address of the Familie Mehmedovic continued to exist on the canal. The furniture and photographs, pots and pans, remained in the rooms beside the canal, their silence broken, she imagined, by the occasional ringing of a phone. Her clothes alone migrated to the Apostel-Paulus-Strasse.

She called Mostar and was allowed to speak with her son. They conversed in the native tongue; no more German. Pino cried and said that he missed her, and then he lost his concentration and handed the phone to someone else or left the receiver lying on the floor. Tino's mother lurked, and the phone eventually clicked down, and the hundreds of miles between the two cities crushed the life out of the connection.

Marta began to have nightmares about Pino and dark waters. Those were better than the good dreams, which made her weep. In those dreams, she bathed him or combed his thick wet hair or dressed his body, one piece of clothing at a time, before heading to the bower to pick heavy summer plums. She missed the skein of veins in his chest and the brownish down on his back. She missed the smell of his hair in her mouth and everything else, every word, every sigh, every wail. He would miss her at certain times of the day, she knew; at bedtime, at dinner when he didn't want to eat, when he felt alone or sad or scraped his knee. But at other times, for him, she would cease to exist. If she were to die at that moment, in Arthur's bed, in the middle of the night, another woman would become Pino's mother, the *fufa*. Pino would not remember her face.

Freedom overwhelmed her. On the one hand, she couldn't bear to give it up. On the other, she didn't want it at all. She wanted to throw it back. What was this freedom anyway? Was it the right to be with a man who was not her husband, just like any other free Western woman? She could have done that in Yugoslavia. Was it freedom from her child? This made her sick. Or was it, as Tino thought, merely freedom to be the whore of an American journalist?

She fought to keep Tino out of her mind. She denied his judgments. How could she go back to *his* country? How could she live in a land that would make him feel happy and strong and take almost everything away from her? She thought of the restaurant and shook with rage.

Arthur alone made these thoughts bearable. Marta loved to sleep with Arthur in the decrepit bed in his rented room. Maybe, she thought, because I don't have to pay rent there. I have no obligations and no memories. I am provisional, a guest. This struck her as a distinctly American freedom. No one implied that she should do more, pay more, that she should labor for what she had received. When she cleaned the room, which she did now and then, she did so with an idle, near-sensual lethargy, as if the act had lost any connection to its purpose. She cleaned in order to touch the room in which they slept. Until she went to work, she was a woman without a past.

Frau Herbst disapproved of the arrangements, naturally. She met Marta in the halls and reprimanded her without a word. At ninety, the woman lusted. She stewed over the younger man. One morning, at the breakfast table, she could no longer restrain herself.

"I have done many things in my time. That I admit. But I never shared a bed, as a married woman, with a man who wasn't my husband."

"Except for that lawyer who Aryanized your estate," said Arthur.

"That was wartime."

The charge did not resurface, but the shot had been fired.

M ARTA ATE SWEETS, gained weight, and saved money. She smoked and drank and laughed more than she ever had. They walked through the streets and kissed against trees. Stupid, how happy and young this made her feel. Were people so simple? Out of doors, in the cold, he slid a hand beneath her skirt. They traveled together in rental cars around the edges of the city, and she read from Theodor Fontane's *Wanderings Through the Mark Brandenburg*. " 'Whoever wants to travel in the Mark,' " she read aloud to Arthur, " 'must do so with a love of people and places, without presuppositions. He must have the generosity of heart to find what is good here, instead of nitpicking everything to death.' "

They were driving along the southernmost line of the Berlin Wall, on a road outside the limits of the western city. Marta had driven many times south of West Berlin on the highway between the East German and West German border. But she had never *looked* at the country. It had been irrelevant to her. Now her eyes opened. This limbo of wild grasses was beautiful. It had been East Germany, and beyond that Wall, just there, less than a kilometer away, was Berlin, western Berlin. There wasn't much to see in the zone. It was real-estate-to-be, and soon enough, developers would come and turn it into an American-style shopping center. But from her seat in the car, the land held a riddle that she couldn't solve. It had divided, then unified. A division in the grass had ended. Had it ever really existed?

"I feel like I'm discovering something," she said to Arthur. "Some deep truth about the world."

"It's amazing, isn't it?"

They gazed in wonder at the unremarkable ground. "I don't even know where I am anymore," she said. "I don't even know what country this was."

There were mysteries everywhere. Once, on the edge of a nondescript, moss-scummed lake, Arthur and Marta entered a clearing in the woods and found a perfect circle of pastel cars. The automobiles were East German Trabants and had been left without their tires in a ring in the woods, a mile, at least, from the closest road. The cars came in hues of pink, sky blue, and faded yellow and had none of that quality of biological decomposition that Marta associated with junkyards. There was no metal in sight. The bodies of the Trabants were made of an odd polymer specific to East Germany; when cold, the stuff became brittle and shattered at the slightest impact. When hot, it had a tendency to stink. No one had come up with a way to recycle the skin of the car and turn it to use, so the remnants of Trabants could be found everywhere, littering the roadsides, parked in mud, on narrow shoulders, forsaken. In the clearing in the woods, they had purpose. She had never seen so many Trabants in one place, as if a community of lost vehicles had banded together, traveled far, and found sanctuary, at last, in this remote compound of trees. They made a last stand in the half-light.

In Jüterbog, south of Berlin, Marta and Arthur walked hand in hand into an abandoned Soviet barracks. No one stopped them as they entered the barracks and poked their noses in stalls where tanks had been repaired, as they penetrated high-security buildings that echoed with their footsteps. The generals had gone, and the wind was in charge. A train track ran behind the barracks, and a swath of torn earth indicated the places where men and materiel had been loaded, where the Kazakh and Tatar boys had said farewell to Germany and started the long roll, the two thousand kilometers, home to Moscow. Doors rattled in dead breezes. Arthur rifled drawers for documents. Marta was standing in the brightness outside a mechanic's shop when a child gripped her sleeve. He could not have been more than five, and he was begging, in Russian, for money. She gave him everything that she had, and he darted away. She saw no sign of a mother, no indication of life anywhere else on the grounds, except for a black dog, which appeared out of nowhere, out of the earth itself, and then tore away, just like the boy.

"I saw a Russian boy that turned into a black dog," she told Arthur.

"Let's get out of here, then."

They ran as if the devil barked at their heels.

Love, in the end, might be no more than the attempt to give some-one else a true account of yourself. This thought came to Marta, but she didn't know where to begin. One night, in mid-December, she tried.

"Arthur," she started to say to him in the cot in the bower, "I have to tell you something."

He stopped her with decisive force. "We're going away tomorrow," he said. "Pack light. It's only for the weekend."

She put a hand on his erection and started to move her fingers up

and down, and it seemed to her that she had grasped the knob on a
door to the next life, that if she pulled long enough, she would find
her way into some other place. He kissed her mouth.

"I know what's on your mind," he said. "But trust me. Soon everything will make sense."

"Where are we going?"

"I won't tell."

"Arthur, I want you to tell me where we are going."

"Help," he said.

Perhaps, she thought, in a flight of fantasy, Arthur is taking me to
Yugoslavia. Perhaps he is going to help me rescue Pino.

O N   A   M I D - D E C E M B E R   M O R N I N G ,   well before sunrise, they
took a taxi to Zoo train station. By noon, they had arrived in
Frankfurt, where they changed trains for Munich. The train took an
entire day to get to the southern reaches of Germany. By the time
they arrived in Munich, it was late. The bells in the Marienkirche
tolled the nine o'clock hour. They had dinner in a beer hall and spent
the night in a small *bahnhof* hotel. The next morning, to Marta's hidden disappointment, they boarded a local train to Kaufbeuren, and
she watched as the fortress barrier of the Bavarian Alps approached.
The fields on either side of the track gleamed with new snow. In
Kaufbeuren, they changed trains for an even smaller destination. In
the tiny café of the station, they had a coffee and split a weisswurst,
and she felt something happening to her. This was not a trip to rescue Pino, but she had come south, and she knew suddenly that this
was right. She must go even farther. At noon, they got out of their
last train, and Arthur asked the taxi driver to take them to Neuschwanstein.

She almost burst out laughing. Neuschwanstein! At one point, the
possibility had even occurred to her, but she had dismissed the idea.

Neuschwanstein, the fairy tale castle on every poster in every travel agency in the world, the universal shorthand for a vacation in Germany, the model for the magical castles of Walt Disney. Arthur's eyes twinkled. Ahead of them, looming out of the cloudy white hills, ringed by mountain peaks, were the toy turrets of a childhood paradise. Mad King Ludwig had built his fairy tale castle in the late nineteenth century, the final dead end of the Gothic revival, a Wagnerian sugar pile perched high on a spur of Alpine rock. The castle was not alone. Across the valley sat a second edifice, an orange rococo block on the shore of a silver lake. The village of Neuschwanstein, nestled between the two castles, lay seven kilometers from the Austrian border, and two weeks before Christmas there were no tourists. The tourists came after Christmas, so most of the pensions were closed, but Arthur found lodging across the road from the village's one open restaurant, a cottage almost as small as the garden house in Berlin, but warm, and equipped with fresh linens, a bathtub, a basket of fruit, and a bottle of champagne. Marta became immediately afraid of the room.

Neuschwanstein was very strange. Eyes watched behind windows as Marta and Arthur crunched through the snow. She thought the people who lived year round between these two castles must be cruel and stupid, victims of geography, soured by too much time among works of demented folly.

Night fell, and the mad castles glowed. Turrets on the mountain spur cast an icy azure sheen; over the lake lay an orange gas. Marta and Arthur ate goulash in the restaurant and afterward went for a night walk in the snow. A small voice inside of her asked, What is going to happen now? Deer rushed across the road, a shuffling, muffled mass, visible as a single dark body, antlered, with shining eyes. Arthur stopped her and put a finger to his lips. They held each other and watched the passage of the animals. Then he spoke.

"We have to make up our minds," he said. "I can't pretend anymore. I'm in love with you."

The words howled in her ears. "What are you saying?" she asked him, staring down into the snow.

"If you tell me that you are going to leave your husband, if you promise it, then I will wait. I will be patient. But if you can't even do that, if you think you might have even the slightest inclination to go back to him, then I have to know now. Here. That's only fair."

Marta held him tighter a moment, then began to let go. She imagined a life for herself in a city in Texas, where it would always be warm. They would have a big house full of children, and Yugoslavia would seem as distant as another planet; Germany, too. Pino would speak English and have no memory of his native tongue or her adopted one. He would play baseball and not soccer. He would be like American boys in movies, easy in the world. He would have the American passport, and every vista that it opened for him. Only bad borders would be closed to him. Americans were businesspeople. Women ran big companies. Arthur offered possibilities like jewels. He flung them before her in the snow.

"Okay," she said.

"Okay what?"

There might be happiness in Mostar. She would never be an outsider. She would never have to wonder what the other person was thinking. She would know, in her blood, the deep meaning of all words and expressions. Her mother's path was clear. She had hated the valley, and as soon as she saw a way out, she fled. Marta had never had more sympathy for her mother than she did at this moment. She saw everything and forgave the mess left behind. Had the Great Actress ever had a moment like this one? Had she found herself on the Stari, gazing down, faced with a choice? She had decided against her man, her family, her children, her town. She had decided against the bridge, in favor of the world.

I will *take* my son from Tino, thought Marta. I can. I will.

"I have to think," she stammered out. "Go back to the cottage," she said. "Please."

He didn't speak. He was upset. They didn't kiss. He disappeared, like the Russian boy in Jüterbog, leaving no trace. And she headed in the opposite direction, toward the one bright object in the whole town of Neuschwanstein, a bus. The voices in her head raged. She ran to the side of the vehicle. It wasn't moving yet, but the engine was running, and steam was rising, and the driver was sitting inside a blaze of light, drinking his coffee.

She felt at her waist the traveling belt with her money and passport, and she zipped open the pouch. She climbed into the warmth and light of the German machine, the driver took her money, and in a few minutes, three minutes at the most, the bus motor erupted and the silver object burst into motion. Marta spoke silently to herself as the glow from the blue turrets dwindled away behind her, dwindled into the snow and darkness of the Bavarian Alps. Arthur had asked her to make the choice, and she had.

SEVENTEEN

O N NOVEMBER 1, 1993, not quite three years after his last sighting of Marta Mehmedovic, Arthur Cape read the following letter, carried by the hand of George Markovic from the Hungarian city of Budapest.

To Mr. Arthur Cape, journalist and correspondent—

Please forgive the mistakes and errors in this letter. I have written it in my own language, and my half-sister Isadora has translated for me. If I am lucky, and there is anything divine left in this world, she will find some way to get it to you in Berlin, where, please God, you are still living. You know me. We have met, but it was very brief, one late night in the kitchen of my sister Marta. I am Dubravka.

I have an urgent request, Mr. Cape, offered in despair. Can you save my sister? Three weeks ago, she put me on an aid convoy to the city of Metkovic, where I am now living. Since that time, I have had no word from her, but the shelling on my city increases. I begged her to leave, but she will not. She is willful. She cannot listen. She has no reason to stay in that city, except that her child is buried there.

Please, please, please. I have nothing to offer you, but I am begging. If what they say about the Americans is true, then use every possibility and get my sister out of Mostar.

In hope,

Dubravka Mehmedovic

There was a space, and then this:

P.S. My name is Isadora Markovic, and I am the translator and courier of this letter, which I have given to my alleged relative George Markovic for delivery to you. We have never met, Mr. Cape, and if I am lucky, and if you are lucky, we never will. The fact that you are an American journalist tells me everything I need to know about your moral and professional disposition. We Serbs have come to understand that we are the last Mohicans of Europe, despised by one and by all, and so let me request of you that you lay aside your deep, sick, natural *prejudice, and think of me not as a Serb, though I am proud, beyond your capacity to comprehend, of my great people, of their matriarchal values and their anti-Fascist tendencies. Think of me instead as one of your own people. You, too, are a Mohican, I believe. Marta told me so. So from one Mohican to another, I make this appeal.*

Marta has suffered terrible things in this war. Perhaps you don't know that her husband has left her, and that is the best news. There is much worse to tell. My heart is broken for her. You think——I am certain, I am more than certain——that a Serb cannot have such emotions. You think Serbs kill children with scoped rifles and rape good, decent Muslim women and cannot have hypocritical Western humanist emotions. I will not stoop to defeat your prejudice, but I will say that I love my sister and want her out of that horrible city of the damned. She will never listen to me or anyone else in her family, and in light of current political constellations, no way exists to help.

But you, Mr. Cape, have power to do everything. Power to convince, power to remove. You float on the magic carpet of an American passport. I would call it black magic, except that black magic is good. Your passport is blue magic. Blue like Spanish Fascism. Blue like UN. No matter. Take that power and use it, please, for tasks other than spreading Yugonostalgic lies and propaganda about my

people. Go to Mostar and rescue my sister. Be a Mohican. Not—I repeat—
not *an American.*

One word of advice. Be wary of Dubravka. She has questionable associations.

The letter ended without signature in the middle of the second page. Weak sunshine streamed into Anna's apartment. It was just after nine A.M. on the morning after the Halloween party, and the rain still slithered down panes. The first time Arthur had read the letter, standing in the stairwell, waiting for another cop to question him about George, he had lost his composure. He had fallen to his knees, dropping the fragile papers. Since then, he had gone over it again and again. He had read it so many times that the ink blurred. At last, he gave it to Anna.

She read the first lines and turned away, as if he had presented her with a human limb. She flung the pages away and headed down the corridor to try to sponge pumpkin pie from the carpet in her office.

Anna's cousin Günther made breakfast for them. Hampton had postponed his departure for London. He sat on the floor in the room with the dance floor. Arthur gave him the letter.

"Awful," said Hampton, after reading it. "Poor souls."

Arthur gathered the pages again and reread them once more. He hadn't slept. He could hardly think. After the police had asked their questions, he had stuffed the letter in his pocket and wandered home. In his own quiet space, at the window overlooking the Apostel Paulus Church, he had fallen into a long blackness. The memories welled like blood. He could taste the water of the canal, could see the flight of ducks against the sky. Down in the depths, a pale shape rose to meet him. Arthur had saved the boy. Jesus, he thought, Jesus Christ, how cruel. Death lay within near-death. A dead child existed within the living boy. A childless woman had lived within the loving mother. Destruction erupted from nothing. How had he not seen these things?

He spent the last hours before dawn in a burst of terrible, useless energy, rewriting the Heidegger story from top to bottom. He wrote ten thousand words. He threw whole chunks of Heidegger's philosophy into the pot. "Either the excision of every kind of humanization is held to be possible, and there is something like a standpoint that is free from all standpoints; or human beings are acknowledged as the cornered creatures they are, and we must deny the possibility of any nonhumanizing conception of the world totality." Arthur found lines from Paul Celan's poem about Heidegger's cabin: "Arnika, eye-bright, the draft from the well, with the starred die above it, in the hut . . ." Celan was a Jew who had survived the concentration camps. He had known Heidegger personally, and he committed suicide by throwing himself into the river Seine in Paris. Arthur threw him into the story. But German philosophy could not coexist with American journalism. German philosophy met American journalism, and sentences started to explode. The piece had begun as a one-page story about ties between the most famous German philosopher of the twentieth century and the Nazi Party, and ended as a twelve-page meditation on horror. Arthur sent the story to New York at six A.M. and returned to Anna's apartment.

"I've made a decision," he announced at last.

O FF TO MOSTAR THEN?" Hampton asked him.
"As soon as possible."

"Are you sure it's the wise thing? Perhaps I should go first and make some inquiries."

Arthur shook his head. "Out of the question."

Hampton's face grew wrinkled. "What will you tell New York?"

"Will you lie for me?"

"I could smokescreen for a week. That's easily done. But it's you, Arthur. Are you quite sure you're ready?"

"I just need sleep."

"You must ask yourself two questions," said cousin Günther, who appeared in the room with fresh *schrippen* and sliced yellow cheese. "You must ask yourself: Do you owe this woman a moral debt? That is one, and two, and I must say it softly, do you *love* her? If the answer to either of these questions is yes, then you must forget every other impulse, and you must go."

Hampton gave an irritated squint, but Günther did not yield the opinion. His father was a von Hakenberg caught by the Russians in 1945 and imprisoned for a decade before repatriation back to East Germany. Günther was a moralist and a romantic, a survivor's son who believed in the possibility of redemption. He had done well in the German Democratic Republic. His excellent language skills had landed him a job of privilege as an interpreter for the state translation agency. A candid man with full, red cheeks, sharp blue eyes, and a patch of grayish-brown hair on his large head, he would not admit that his country was a complete failure. In fact, to the horror of Anna's father, he was a devoted socialist who had not wanted to merge with West Germany at all. He did have one sadness, though. He had never met his great love.

Arthur gave him the letter. Günther finished it, handed it back, and shook his head.

"For my part, I do not believe that the child is dead," he said, without any foundation for this belief. "I feel in my bones that it cannot be. Otherwise, why would this letter have found its way to you? The universe is sending a message." He sighed, casting a glance toward the back of the apartment, where his cousin had gone. He offered the cheese plate to Hampton and added, "This George figure has more to say. I am sure."

"We won't be seeing George again," said Arthur.

George had cheated the police. By leaving behind his gun and leaping out a four-story window, he had guaranteed that he would be treated with some delicacy. And he was. He had landed hard on the hood of a police car and injured his leg. Instead of going to jail, he had been taken to the hospital, though the cops would not say where. In the end, the officials in charge of the case did not know for sure how to process George, and Arthur did not help. He shrugged in response to questions. He hadn't seen much. He'd been cowering beneath the table. The Serb claimed that he had been thrown, the police told him with a sneer. George would probably be on the next plane to Budapest. But there was no way to know for sure.

Arthur went to Anna, who crouched over pumpkin pie stains in the back room of the apartment. As soon as he entered, she started to rotate the sponge in circles on the surface of the carpet.

"What do you think I should do, Anna?"

"Go," she said.

The quickness of the answer surprised him.

"Why?"

"Because if you don't, then you will see me as the awful German girl who kept you from doing the right thing. You will hate me."

Guilt was everywhere. It had settled on them like the rain. If Arthur didn't go to Bosnia, Anna would never get over the guilt. He wished that she'd had other reasons. He wished that she'd begged him not to go. An ounce more resistance might have made a difference, might have proven a counterweight to his own feelings.

"It's her child," he said.

Anna stopped sponging. She drew a strand of black hair from her eyes and stared at him.

"If this woman is alive, then we are finished. That much I know."

He put his hands on her shoulders, and they began to tremble. Arthur didn't know what he felt. The letter reached into his mind and terrified him. He had an enduring memory of Marta. He didn't know if it was love. He didn't know if he had ever been in love with her. He'd told her so, and she had left. So love itself was dangerous and strange. He didn't trust love. He wouldn't go to Mostar for that. He would go for justice. His hands were trembling, he saw, not Anna's shoulders.

"I am right," she said.

"I'm not going," he said.

Anna snorted in derision. "Let go of my arms, please. I am trying to remove this pie."

Arthur did as she asked, but he stayed next to her for a long time.

"She's probably dead," he said after a while.

"We shall see."

He looked down at Anna's hand, a miracle of flesh and bone that had caressed him through nights of pain, when none of her efforts to love him had been reciprocated, when each passage of emotion through his mind had been directed away from the woman beside him and toward the one who had tossed him away. The rain outside redoubled its force, drowning Berlin in Baltic waters.

"It's time, Arthur," she said.

BOOK II

DISINTEGRATION

EIGHTEEN

MORNING CAME BLACK to Marta's eyes. She shivered.
There was a long stillness, and she didn't like it. She
looked up. The stars were flickering; they were dying.
Shells tipped out of the western sky, loud as trash into bins. Marta
threw herself down. A rule of survival lived in her skin. If you could
hear the mortars, you were safe. Her fingers wrapped around the
handles of two five-kilo jerrycans containing spring water. For the
first time in hours, she wasn't thirsty, but she craved food. Yesterday,
she had eaten a meal of rice in rainwater.

Mato was late. Hours ago, in utter darkness, he had frightened her
on the floor of her shelter beneath the theater. She had dreamed that
she was under attack by the bugs. He whispered. Shells had fallen on
his point, and men were wounded. The doctors at the hospital had
nothing for him. They were swamped. Some fucking kid lay on an op-
erating table, bleeding to death. No one could be spared to cross the
Stari. Marta had agreed to do what she could. She had limited medical
training. She could stick her hand inside human bodies and pluck out
hot shrapnel. That was about it.

Mato told her to meet him near the Old Bridge, and together they would run across to his point. Since then, an hour had passed.

She peered around limestone bricks. Snipers would wake at dawn. How did her brother propose to cross the bridge in daylight? There it was. Even in the darkness, she could see it. Marta forced herself to think in one direction, turning neither right nor left. She would have to cross the bridge, and the bridge would have to help her do it.

Her husband had always loved the Old Bridge, the Stari Most. He had loved the athletic way it sprang across the Neretva, a leap between rock banks, forty feet up, like a man after a woman, too inflamed to stop, unable to contain himself. That's how Tino liked to think of the span. But Marta did not think something so old could be so horny. She did an automatic calculation. On this cold morning, November 7, 1993—by the Gregorian calendar—the Stari had been standing for four hundred twenty-seven years. Five of those years had overlapped with the life of her son. He had walked on it. He had thrown rocks over the edge. He had said that when he was a big boy, he would dive off of the Stari into the river, like the others. She had told him that he would, when he grew up. Marta wiped her eyes with the back of her hand. She had been forced to come back to Mostar for the sake of that goddamn bridge.

It connected two sides of a town that didn't matter, Marta had said in guided tours long ago, by way of an introduction, a nasty shock to the visitors who had struggled in heaving buses up bad roads from the coast to see this famous work and were always, let's face it, a little disappointed in its size, in its lack of epic grandeur.

Mostar had never been one of the great cities of Europe, Marta would tell the Germans or Italians or British in her semi-official capacity as a tour guide for the municipality; the city had never been a border between states or the capital of a small renowned kingdom. It had never been a Venice or a Salonika or even a Sarajevo. In its day, she had explained in a voice too withering to belong to a young girl— she had been nineteen then, unmarried, disdainful to the point of scorn—in its day, at its best, Mostar had been a trading post, a point on the way between Ragusa and the interior, a road that led eventually to the storied capital of the Ottoman world, Constantinople.

The bridge had spanned a sort of cultural and religious divide. The Catholic church had never penetrated much beyond the eastern bank of the river Neretva, and Islam waned on the western side, but it wasn't a strict line, and no one would have insisted on it or drawn a line of any consequence on the map. You must not think of my city or this bridge as a symbol, she had told the Germans, the Italians, and the British. You should remark on its delicacy, its simple beauty, and pass on. Here, people of all kinds met and vanished. Here, they made business and love. Their children played and disappeared.

"Should *we* disappear?" a British tourist had once tartly inquired.

Marta's attitude had infuriated Tino. The Stari is a world masterpiece, he would insist, a monument to the greatness of our civilization. *Our* civilization? What was our civilization? Marta would ask. Ottoman? Muslim? Turkish? Yugoslav? He never answered the question. *Ours,* he would say; look at it, he would say; look at the stillness and power; look at the way it seems to fly on bird wings between East and West. Five hundred years old, he would say. Not quite, she viciously corrected. And then she remembered that night, infinitely distant, when she had stood on the bridge with Tino, and he had told her, with cold lips, that he was taking her son. She closed her eyes. Tino had been true to his intention, and God knew that he had paid for it.

In the early days of the war, not long after Pino's death, her husband had received a midnight visit from his business partner, Darko Miric, who told him that the restaurant could no longer belong to a Muslim. Tino threw him out. A few days later, other visitors came, and they raped his *fufa* right in front of him. Then they put a knife in her heart.

Marta had seen Tino one last time, in a mass of people on the back of a truck.

"Why stay?" he had wondered, the final question in the great unwinding love affair of their youth.

Her last word had been absolute: "Pino."

A few miles outside of the city, a mortar shell hit the truck, killing everyone on board. The bridge, she thought, gazing westward across the rubble; her husband had moved back for the bridge, and the bridge had taken his life.

WHEN HAD SHE first laid eyes on the Stari Most? Was it in 1974, when her family left Yugoslavia for Germany, that August before their departure, when she had seen her best friend Maja for the last time? Marta had crossed the bridge westward to go to Maja's house in Strelcevina, and Maja had crossed it eastward to come to her parents' place in Luka. They had met at the peak of the arch and said farewell.

Or had it been much earlier? Marta could remember her mother telling her, when she was a young girl of five or six, that she had been carried across the Stari when she was less than a week old. From the hospital to her father's parents' home, she had been conveyed from the eastern bank of the Neretva River to the western bank, with a stop along the way for a suck of milk. The bridge framed Marta's image of her parents before her mother's celebrity and her father's rise through the local ministries, when they would sit for hours in the cafés, perched like birds above the river, drinking coffee, smoking, talking about Artaud, Andric, Brecht, Truffaut, and, of course, Welles (her mother had not yet met the man himself, but she already regarded him as exemplary in his nomadic abandonment of Hollywood). And then there was the bridge's role in her own great love affair.

Tail of a July evening, not too long after Vidovdan, the Stari the color of the dry Herzegovina moon, the cream of the hills infused with the deep rose of fading sun, Marta and Tino had met. Tino had worn a smart gray Italian jacket over a maroon shirt, and until the sun went down, he refused to take off his thick, wide Marcello Mastroianni sunglasses. He called her *bambina* and *ragazza* and said "ciao" when they parted ways. She had loved him, but he had treated her like a starstruck girl. Below them had rushed the violet Neretva, violet out of blue, violet deepening to dimpled black, the bridge losing its cream-pinkish sheen to become as pale as a rumpled white bedsheet. Their hips touched, as they sat side by side on a step near the top of the arch, as they went down the list of lost people they had known in school, the guy who had tried to put his hand down her little sister's shirt at the Kino Partizan during a showing of the Audie Murphy movie *To Hell and Back.* One of his ex-girlfriends, a long-legged Dalmatian who sold cold drinks at the bar on the rocks outside the walls of Dubrovnik, who vanished one August night after diving off a boulder. She swam to Italy, according to legend.

Rock popped two inches from Marta's head, and she flattened herself. The sniper got off two more shots. The shift change had ended. Dawn was coming. Marta scrambled for better cover. She set her back against a remnant of the building that had housed her Uncle Pipa's souvenir business. Water shushed whispery between banks, a sound unchanged, despite war.

She made the mistake of checking the back of her wrist again, as if her husband's Cartier might still be there. But she had sold the watch long ago for a packet of United Nations rice and a bucket of East German laundry detergent, product of the erstwhile Linda *Volkskombinat* in the Pomeranian city of Schwerin, a kind of detergent that she would never, in her previous life, have entertained the notion of using, except perhaps as a novelty. Anyway, she no longer needed a watch to tell the time. She could stick her wet nose in the air, like her dog, and know that it was half past five in the morning, moving toward six. She knew the hour well. Every day, at about this time, Marta woke from bad dreams and wished that she were dead.

. . .

Mato came creeping at last. The southern end of the valley began to rumble with mortar fire. Marta saw that he was alone.

"Shelling Donja Mahala again," he said, and he shook his head. "Why bother?"

"I thought you were bringing someone," Marta said.

"Couldn't find anyone else." Mato handed her a sweater and a scarf. "You must be freezing."

Metal crashed adjacent. Marta bowed her head. Shrapnel came whickering out of the dust and darkness. The shells had landed between the limestone pile and an Ottoman guard tower at the eastern end of the bridge. Everything became quiet again.

"We'll wait another moment, I guess." Mato brushed himself off. "Let those pricks change shifts."

"They already did," Marta told him. She wound the green woolen scarf around her neck and buttoned the black sweater down her chest, covering her mother's worn light blue turtleneck.

"You know what I think of when I see that turtleneck?" Mato asked Marta, his voice trying to be light and pleasant. "I think of Vracar. The day he died. The bitch was in such a state."

Marta looked at her half-brother in the grayness. The Great Actress had received news of the death of Orson Welles on October 10, 1985, a bigger event in the family annals than the death of Marshal Tito a few years earlier. That news had come in Mostar, hadn't it? Or had they learned about Welles on the beach at Lumbarda? Who could remember anymore? But Marta didn't think of Orson Welles when she wore the turtleneck. She thought of the dying man whose blood had spurted across it. She thought of cockroaches in her bed and urine in pools in the corners of her shelter. The shirt was the world. There had never been another one. This had become the indispensable conviction.

She put her hands on her brother's cheeks. He had lost too much weight, like everyone else, and his teeth were falling out, but he was still Mato, still half a brother. She saw a little Pino in his face. She saw a little Pino in everything.

"How's my dog?" Marta asked him.

Mato shook his head. "Don't ask me about that bullshit. You know what I think."

It was a ridiculous question, a question on the brink of madness. Mato wanted to shoot the animal, but he had taken her off Marta's hands while Marta did her civil defense work. The animal had shrunk from dehydration and starvation. She moaned and rattled. Very soon, she would die. And the others in the shelter would be angry at Marta, because she had let the dog live so long. But they had nothing to complain about. No one had had to feed the dog. She had lived on vermin, or maybe she had found a stash of dead bodies. For a while, she grew fat. But in the last few days, for whatever reasons, her forages had ceased, and she was fading again, this time it seemed for good.

"If you were merciful," he said, reading her thoughts, "you would let me do it."

"She can die on her own terms," said Marta. "She doesn't need you for that. Any word from Dubravka?"

"She's safe in Metkovic. As you should be."

They had had this conversation, no point in it. Her brother checked the safety on his AK-47 and cradled the gun in his right arm. With his left, he hoisted one of the battered orange jerrycans. The cans reeked of old gasoline, but the water tasted okay. Fog seeped through the limestone bricks, bringing the stench of dead fires. The shelling of Donja Mahala subsided, and a recorded jeremiad began. A woman's voice could be heard on a loudspeaker, a tape of arguments against the necessity of holding the eastern bank against the western bank. The voice offered safe conduct out of the valley.

Mato slung the gun over his shoulder. He crept through heaped ruins to the road. Marta followed with the other jerrycan. Now and then, Mato threw down his left hand, for balance, and touched the ground, as if making sure that it stayed beneath his feet. Marta watched his feet pick through the rubble, each choice an act of ballet. He wore a stocking cap, but his ears stood out on either side.

They emerged much closer to the bridge. On their right was a parapet that had once marked the eastern base of the Stari. On their left rose the Tara Tower, a bastion of mortar-shocked Ottoman stone. Marta looked at the prospect in dismay. They would have minimum protection. A scaffolding of planks and pipes, covered by blankets, reduced exposure to sniper fire, but between the ruins on the bank and the scaffolding lay ten or so meters of open space. Snipers to the north would have a clear line of fire.

Mato beckoned to her. "I've changed my mind," he whispered. "Go home."

Wind shredded the river mists. Soon, the sun would appear over the lip of the eastern mountains.

"No." To underscore her point, Marta sprang across the road and beat Mato to the tower. They crept along the base of the tower, jerrycans scraping against the limestone. She peered around a corner into the lower valley, where Mount Hum fell hundreds of feet to the Neretva. The current flowed nervously in the shot gold of dawn. In Donja Mahala, at the foot of the mountain, at river's edge, sputtered fires. Planks of smoke drifted on the air. A corpse lay naked on the ground, back turned to them, beside a burning wall.

Marta couldn't tell whether the corpse belonged to a man or woman. She studied the thing as if it might provide a clue to everything that had happened. She had seen so many human beings pass from life to death, and none of them gave the slightest hint of knowledge. She had groped within the chest cavity of one of her father's old friends, hunting for shrapnel between his ribs until his breathing stopped. She had carried stretchers bearing half-naked women, their bodies covered for the sake of insane dignity by old newspapers. In the hospital, she had waded through lakes of blood, blackening crusts of humanity, the stench. She had informed wives that their husbands of four decades were gone, mothers that their babies were not meant for such a fight.

How was it possible that she had not been killed yet? How was it possible that she had not gone to find Pino and her father?

Mato put down the jerrycan and held his sister's hand for a moment. Marta heard the numb call for capitulation emerging again from the opposite bank. Just then, a man's voice screamed back out of the stillness. He seemed to be below them, on the riverbank, and he was calling East to West. Marta could barely understand the words—he might be calling his name, "Zeljko," maybe, a plea, too far away to be comprehended—but the voice sounded familiar, in its dying away, and she felt a pull on her heart.

"Ninety-nine steps," said Mato, "from this tower to the tower on the opposite bank." He pointed. "A distance of twenty-seven meters."

He let these words sink in. "Be sure and look down when you run, or you'll trip over the steps."

Marta nodded. She knew.

Mato made an arch with his right hand. "The Stari humps in the middle, like a camel's back, and you have to be ready for the other side. That's where you fall."

Marta vaguely listened. Mato kept talking.

"Keep left, between the legs of the scaffolding," he said, "and don't waste time getting scared or thinking too much. Just run like hell. Fuck the snipers. They can't hit moving targets."

Marta examined the bridge. War had eaten it. Weeks of mortar fire had chewed the limestone, revealing the ancient skeleton. Black rubber tires dangled like bats from the sides. The scaffolding didn't merit the name—it was just wooden boards on top of a homemade metal cage. Blankets flapped in tatters from tibias of pipe. No sane human would go near it.

Mato winked, kissed her cheek, and charged like a goat up the eastern arch.

· · ·

MARTA DASHED AFTER him into the sunlight. Blankets whipped in the river breeze. She flew across the open ground, her legs feathery. She expected to leave earth and wisp into heaven. She heard a noise and looked up. Snipers were firing. Scaffolding collapsed in her path. Mato kicked pipes aside. Her right foot caught in the metal tangle, but she kept her balance.

Blanket shreds tickled her face. She glanced down. The path beneath her feet looked like the calcified rib of a dead animal, hard, old, and immense. When she looked up again, Mato had vanished over the summit of the bridge. Soon she reached it, too. She perched there, and light flooded her, turning the world black. She felt the slam of her heart inside of her chest and had a moment of dense exhilaration. I am here, she thought, in this place, in my life, in the world, and no other. The Neretva stirred, forty feet down. She drew a deep breath and threw her body down the western slope of the bridge, tripping over the torso of a man, the jerrycan sailing out of her fingers. She thought it was Mato. She started to scream.

"Marta."

The name caught her by surprise. She rolled and tumbled. Her legs hurtled away. The sun came full as a great eye into the world, and Marta lay in the exact center of its gaze. Marta had fallen over the torso, which lay flat against the stone a few feet behind her.

Mato stood inside the arch of the Halebija Tower, at the western end of the bridge, and flailed his arms. But it was fine. By this time, the sniper had aimed. The bullet had left its barrel. Just this morning Marta had been lying in her cot, just like this, waiting for death, wanting nothing, when Pino had walked into the light of the kerosene lamp, unseen by anyone else, had taken her face in his hands, and had pulled her face close. He kissed her lips and put his arms around her neck.

"I'm okay," he said. "You don't have to worry about me anymore."

Marta slid across the paving stones, dragged by an invisible hand. Sun gleamed off her skin, and the sky whistled. Shells landed on the bridge, landed in the scaffolding, and burst wide. Mato tore off her sweater and wrenched away her scarf. He was looking for wounds.

"I'm okay," Marta rasped.

"What the hell happened?" he shouted at her. "You want to die?"

"I tripped."

Mato slumped inside the arch of the tower, catching his breath. "I can protect you from the *ustasha,* sister. They are fucking easy." He pointed a finger at her, and his eye glinted. "But I will be damned if I can protect you from your own shadow."

She had scraped a knee, and it started to hurt.

"What are you talking about?"

"You know damn well."

She shook her head. He got up off the ancient stones, slinging the gun over his shoulder once more, hoisting his jerrycan. The other one was lost.

"Everyone here carries around his own corpse." He offered her a hand, and she took it. "I do. You do. Some of these corpses are very old. They died in bed, surrounded by family, like mine. But some are fresh and very heavy, ready to appear any day now. I'm getting the feeling that yours is one of those. Maybe you want it to be. Is that true?"

She blinked at him, her eyes welling.

"You can save the tears, sister. If I see that corpse of yours one more time, I'm going to slit its throat and dump it in the river. No way it's showing up in Mostar. I am fucking here to tell you."

"You know something about slitting throats, don't you?"

He gave her a cold smile. "You bet I do."

NINETEEN

I N THE CELLAR BENEATH a destroyed apartment building, Marta recited the German articles for her brother, *das, der, die.* He listened and stared at bodies. He had come too late with the water. His men had died, and now they stank.

Their comrades gulped water from the jerrycan. One of them had tied a piece of gingerroot against his arm, but the infection was spreading, red lines crawling out of a pinkish wound. He had a gash, and ginger was supposed to suck out the poison. But it hadn't, and he was suffering, darting glances at Marta every time she opened her mouth.

She paid no attention. German was her salvation. In the shelter beneath the municipal theater, she taught the language to kids. In the dark of the night, she whispered to her dog in German. And when she could, she tried to educate her brother, who promised to get a job in Germany after the war. Mato lifted his head to catch her words while artillery positions in the western range pounded the upper floors of the building.

The word for detergent—*Waschmittel*—took the neutral article. *Das,* as in *das Waschmittel*—Marta was almost sure the word was neutral, ninety percent, but it drove her crazy, ludicrously crazy, because at the back of her brain, a devil existed, a tiny pedant, balding, with glasses and poorly starched pants, a devil who repeated this phrase: "Fluency depends entirely on knowledge of the articles, and knowledge of the articles depends entirely on memorization." God knew that Marta had memorized the articles once, but she was losing her grasp these last few months. She fought article by article for what she had once possessed with ease. The devil in her mind insisted, as if to steal the last hope, that *Waschmittel* took the masculine article, *der,* but how could the German word for detergent possibly take the masculine form?

Men on the floors above screamed for ammo. Marta followed her brother's gaze toward the darkness at the back of the cellar, to the two dead men who were lying beneath newspapers in the far corner of the room. She pitied their bare feet, which she could see. Mato insisted that she take a drink from the communal Cognac bottle.

Someone popped cigarettes from a fresh box of Marlboros, and everyone smoked. The tobacco fumes swirled into the reek of creosote, ginger, and kerosene, into urine, old boiled rice, and the stench of the living.

Marta recited the German articles, and Mato repeated them, taking a swig from a bottle of Hennessy with one hand, a drag off a Marlboro with the other.

"*Die,*" she whispered.

"Dee," he pronounced.

"*Das.*"

Another man joined in.

"Doss." The two men passed the bottle of Hennessy between them.

"*Der.*"

"Durrr."

Their own language did not have articles, no "the," no "a," no "our," nothing tangible to separate things from their contexts, a big mistake, a colossal error. Marta turned down the cigarette but accepted Cognac.

"The articles are implied," muttered the man with the ginger on his arm. He played cards with another man. The lights went out.

"Generator's gone," someone said.

Mato got up and stood in the doorway. He gave orders to the card players.

"Get them out of here," he said, indicating the corpses.

The card players obeyed, but they were sullen. Marta heard them say "*salaam aleikum*" to another man, who approached from a trench on the other side of the stairwell. *Salaam aleikum.* Marta didn't like it. Mostarian men never used that greeting. This wasn't Saudi Arabia.

The bunker went quiet. The bodies were removed.

UP A FLIGHT of broken stairs, soldiers stood watch, and she had an urge to speak with them. She climbed a flight of steps. On the ground floor of the building, light filtered through chinks between sandbags. Fires crackled in the Alekse Santica Street. On the other side of the street, less than a hundred meters away, sat the *ustasha* positions, though they couldn't be seen.

The soldiers raised fragments of mirror above the sandbags and showed her the occasional flash of movement. They used the mirrors to pinpoint the locations of sharpshooters, there and there and there. But she didn't care about the sharpshooters. She wanted to see the rubble of the Rose Hotel.

"There's nothing left of the Rose Hotel," one of the men told her. "Anyway, even if it were standing, you wouldn't be able to see it from here."

"I know," she replied. "My father and my son were inside when they blew it up."

"Cunts," he said. "I'm sorry."

"I'm going over there one day," she told him, "and I'm going to get those bodies. They can shoot me if they want."

The kind soldier gave her hand a pat. "Let me know if you need any help."

She nodded. He nodded. That was enough. She went back down. Behind her, rifle fire snicked.

THE SHELLING BEGAN again, and the basement shuddered. The Stari lay a thousand meters to the south and east of Mato's position. The guns had been striking at it for hours and would not relent.

"Whom do we thank for this?" Mato asked.

He held up the Hennessy bottle.

"Silber," answered one of his men.

"Of course. Where is he now? Any idea?"

Someone else spoke. "Capljina, last I heard. He's negotiating with those Catholic cunts since yesterday."

A voice rose from the shadows in the corner of the cellar where the dead men had been. "You trust the Jew, *Chef*?"

Mato kneaded the lines in his forehead with reddened knuckles. "Why not?" he answered.

The ginger man, still playing cards, spoke up.

"He's a Mossad agent. Israelis used him against Belgrade. Now he's keeping an eye out for mujahideen." The man paused to dispense cards. "His kids live in Israel. Did you know that?"

Marta said, "You're a fool."

The ginger man stopped in the middle of his game and looked right at her. The shelling didn't disturb the dark lines in his face, the derision in his jaw. The cards clicked softly again between his hands.

He said, "All Jews are agents. That's what Jews do. That's what they've been doing for two thousand years, I don't care if they speak French or Turkish or Ladino." The man fixed Marta with his gaze. "That bottle of Hennessy there, for example. That's a Jew masterpiece."

Mato interrupted with scorn. "We don't have enough enemies,

you want to go pissing on the Jews? Are you out of your fucking mind?"

The ginger man pointed at Marta. "What the hell is she doing here, boss? You plan to fuck her?"

Mato aimed the barrel of his gun at the man's forehead. "You be quiet now."

"She's his sister, dumbshit," remarked the voice in the shadows. And everyone laughed.

No one crossed Mato. He had distinguished himself in the early days of the war by chasing Yugoslav army tanks out of his father's neighborhood in Novo Sarajevo. By way of thanks, he had been given a command post close to his father's apartment building, right on the Sarajevo front line, demarcated by the Miljacka River. For one year, he had run special police units out of his bunker, an elementary school. The enemy never breached the Miljacka, and that turned out to be bad news for Mato. His success caught the interest of the Bosnian Defense Forces. They ordered him to enlist. He refused. He would have been asked to fight in cities that he didn't care about. Instead, he skipped town and rode a pack mule over the mountains to Mostar, where he had immediately and gratefully received a unit. His men obeyed him, but they knew his one fragility. He was a Catholic in an army run by Muslims. He might not suffer fools. He might not mind killing people who got in his way, and he never did anything that he didn't want to do. But he could not afford a fight over his sister with his own men.

"As soon as the shelling stops," he told them, "I'm taking her back over the bridge."

Marta fell asleep in dread.

IN HER DREAM, Arthur Cape flew like an angel over the valley of the Neretva, blue wings casting a reflection in moving water, silvery dark against the moon. Arthur Cape was alive somewhere. This fact seemed miraculous. He was alive and might even be in Berlin. When he dreamed, now and then, he dreamed of her, just as she dreamed of him. He swooped low over the valley, down to the waters of the Neretva. The city of Mostar had been divided into East and West—the river had become a wall in the middle of the city, East Mostar and West Mostar, the most depraved joke in the universe. Mostar had become Berlin. Or Berlin had become Mostar. Sneaking like a vampire through the graveyards of Europe, down the rivers, through the mountain ranges, Berlin had come, but not in the form that she had last seen it, not unified, not healed, not free, but in the old disguise, as the city with the split personality, as the twins, driven out of their proper places in the world. Here, in her city, the two compass positions could be given a fixed existence once more. Yes, with enough support, with a good word from the international community, with a little ill will, it could be done. East Berlin and West Berlin would become East Mostar and West Mostar, a very simple process in the end, a displacement of mere hundreds of kilometers, a shifting of bottoms, not some grandiose leap, nothing so difficult as a transatlantic crossing. Arthur Cape understood. He saw. His wings closed behind him, and he plunged into the swift river, staying under for a heartbeat, bursting back out, Pino in his arms. He dwindled to a speck in the high blue sky.

S HE WAS AWAKE. Outside, an entire day had come and gone. A new soldier staggered into their midst. "Gone!" the soldier cried.

"When?" Mato asked.

"An hour ago."

Marta watched her brother's mouth. One dismal word came out of it. "Bullshit."

Marta looked at him, and he returned her gaze. She knew what they were talking about. The Stari had been destroyed.

"We're going," Mato said.

Terror shot through the limbs of Marta's body, as if cockroaches had scuttled up her clothes.

"Move!" shouted Mato.

They dashed across the landing of the stairwell into a trench. Mato lingered an instant. He called to the upper floors of the apartment building, but no answer came. The structure had crumbled; the kind soldier must be dead, thought Marta. Her brother gave her no time to think about it. He entered the trench, and they ran. Bullets sang over their heads, and they dropped, crawling in the mud at the bottom of the trench for what seemed like hours.

At last, they found the place where the path from the Stari entered the Civil Defense earthworks. The unit paused to drink the last of the water. Mato ordered them to lighten their loads for the dash back across the river. The men kept only their guns. He would go with the first group, make sure the bridge was safe, then come back for them. He crept through a hole in the trench. Marta ran after him, and the rest of the unit cursed her and followed. She made a dash for the Stari, but her brother caught her arm.

"It's not there!" he cried. Mortars fell, and the group of them tumbled back into the earthworks.

Mato led them down the side of the bank to the edge of the Radobolja, which flowed into the Neretva. For a moment, they had cover, and the guns on the hills went silent. They would have to split up and make their way back across the river as best they could.

"What happened?" Marta asked her brother, disbelieving. "What's the matter?"

"Nothing's the matter," he said. "Except that this world we're in is a hell."

He ordered most of his men to try to get back across the water, at night, in twos or threes. Marta would stay with him. The men were quiet. They crumpled on the bank and put their heads in their hands. Marta watched the hills. A thing that had existed for hundreds of years had been destroyed, but that was the least of it. Her memory had been destroyed, too. They had taken even her hatred and obliterated it. Mato splashed through the Radobolja to the opposite bank. Up the bank, outlined against the sky, sat half a house. He pointed with his gun at the building.

Marta turned to one of the men. "Look after my dog," she said. "I'll be back in a couple of days."

She waded knee-deep across the Radobolja, and Mato took her arm and hauled her up the side of the far bank into the house, an old Turkish residence. For a moment, the men remained by the stream, staring up at her while they checked their weapons. Morning had come again. Every leaf, every pebble was sharp and clear. Inside the house, peering out the frame of a vanished window, Marta gazed back at the smoke rising where the bridge had been. The valley went still.

"Oh Jesus," said Mato. "Direct hit."

Marta's skin shivered in alarm. He meant to the house, a direct hit to the house. She heard nothing except the river, louder than it had ever been, but she saw her brother's mouth open wide in a scream, and his eyes grow dark as they beheld the explosion. She felt her own feet disappear into the depths, her own hands reaching up for the man swooping down, and she thought, in the second before unconsciousness, I am coming, my love.

TWENTY

ARTHUR SAT in the domestic terminal of Zagreb International Airport, legs crossed, the first light of dawn kindling trees across the road. He shared the empty, gleaming space with a detachment of United Nations troops waiting for transport to one of the safe havens. The men were Belgians and very young. They had stacked their pale blue helmets on their packs, which lay in ordered rows on the newly mopped floor of the zone approaching the departures lounge. There were three lines of helmeted packs, ten or so in each line. The helmets were violet blue in the dimness of the terminal.

A blue age, George had said, subterranean homesick blue, an infectious idea; Arthur had turned thirty-three in September, and that was a blue age of its own. Where had the three years between thirty and thirty-three gone? He had memories of trips from one end of Germany to the other, but they came in the form of a hotel room, the same one, over and over again, whether he was in Wiesbaden, Arnstadt, Zittau, or Lörrach. When people told him that he had an interesting job, he nodded until they backed off. Interesting implied interested, and Arthur had not been interested in anything in a very long time. He had put one foot in front of the other. That had been his level of interest.

The Belgians suppressed yawns and eyed the concession stands, which hadn't opened. Arthur tried to eavesdrop on the men, but they spoke French, and he couldn't understand. He wondered where they were bound; not for Mostar, he knew. Spaniards had responsibility for Mostar. For half an hour, until the dawn flight to Split, Arthur observed the men and their helmets, which glimmered now in lighter shades, in pewter, as new sunlight made its way into the recesses of the terminal. The men did not seem gloomy. They ate chocolate bars and smiled at the women unlocking registers at the Croatian Airlines ticket counter.

He thought guiltily of Anna. Every so often, for as long as he had known her, she had asked him an irritating question. "But are you happy, Arthur?"

She was one of those people who organized her life around the achievement of the regular pleasures. Small joys recurred in Anna's life—friends, projects, meals, parties. She was German, and she had her national shame, but she had figured out how to negotiate her way around it and into a mundane but real happiness. She was a superb woman and would make another man very happy. But Arthur had to be honest. His Blue Age had descended in Bavaria three years ago, when Marta abandoned him, and since then, he could never have answered Anna's question in the affirmative. Anna couldn't change the fact. The world had acquired a stain.

War spread. Masses of refugees moved across the earth; they crossed seas and continents to reach the eastern borders of Western Europe, where German boys burned them alive in their beds. Love had passed away. The ecstasy of regeneration had failed. And the Blue Age had come, like a spell of winter on the earth. Though he would never have admitted it to a fellow journalist, Arthur could not easily separate world developments from personal misery.

The Belgians departed in a chaotic jumble, and Arthur's plane began to board. An hour later, he was in Split, on the Adriatic Coast, where he began the long drive south.

T HE SEA GREW in his dashboard. The stone points of islands cut luminous waters.

Dubravka's letter lay folded inside his wallet, or rather the letter from Dubravka translated and annotated by Isadora. Arthur didn't need to read it anymore. He knew its contents like a Bible verse from his youth. But from a practical standpoint, one short paragraph gnawed at him.

One word of advice. Be wary of Dubravka. She has questionable associations.

Marta's sister had come out of Mostar alive. She was a refugee in Metkovic. The plan should be simple. He would go to Metkovic and find Dubravka, and she would lead him to Marta. But then there were these lines, written by Isadora. The lines complicated matters. If Dubravka had questionable associations, whatever that meant, could she be trusted? Did Isadora mean to imply that Dubravka had her own reasons for luring Arthur down south? Was Marta actually in Mostar?

The questions opened doorways to even deeper, greater mysteries, to the deepest and greatest of them all. Why was Arthur going to Mostar? Hampton had asked him point-blank, and Arthur had been self-righteously dishonest. "Only a monster wouldn't go."

"Rubbish," his friend had replied. "That's utter rubbish."

"You may be right. I'm sure you are."

Hampton recoiled. "Can you honestly tell me that you're in love with this woman?"

Arthur resented the question. Out of deference to rank, he would never have asked Hampton such a thing. Did he *love* her?

In the last week, he had become a reporter again. He had requested every last bit of information on Mostar from the *Sense* magazine library: travel guides, scholarly histories, Fibys reports routed out of the State Department, analyses from Kroll and Jane's, stacks of wire stories. At a picnic table overlooking a windswept Dalmatian shingle, Arthur ate french fries and read the numbers of the last Mostar census. According to the census, a third of the inhabitants of Mostar were Muslim, a third were Catholic Croats. Most of the rest were Serbs, a three-way split that had turned into a three-way war. The Serbs had launched the first attack, then the Muslims and Croats had turned on each other.

Or rather, the Croats had trapped fifty thousand Muslim men, women, and children on the eastern bank of the Neretva River and had been trying for the last six months to dislodge them or starve them or shatter them with mortar shells. If Marta was alive, she would be one of the fifty thousand. She would be living like a rat in cellars, drinking boiled river water, getting barely enough food from week to week to stay alive. Arthur stared at his potatoes as if they were nails. Had he been in love? It seemed important to be able to answer this question, one way or the other. Anna believed that he was. Hampton thought that he wasn't—otherwise, once the war started, why hadn't Arthur done more to find out about Marta? Love created a logic. In Hampton's opinion, Arthur hadn't displayed it.

Sun shot through cracks in low-gathering cloud, and the sea burned aquamarine.

"I never associated her with the war," Arthur had told his colleague.

"How can that possibly be, if you don't mind my asking?"

"My mind is not your mind. It has its own logic."

"There are two kinds of people, Arthur, those who believe that there are two kinds of people, and those who do not. I am in the latter category. So I try not to simplify things. Yet you still haven't answered my question. Are you in love?"

Marta had never written him. For months after Neuschwanstein, Arthur had expected a letter. None ever came. She had been ashamed of their affair, or angry with him for violating some implicit, unspoken principle, or she had been scared. Maybe she had come to loathe him. It was like a country-western song. She went for a walk and never came back. She left her things at the foot of the bed and made the last bus to Kaufbeuren.

If you ever leave me, Arthur had once said to Marta, in a moment of heedless romanticism, I will creep down the Balkan Peninsula, and I will catch you and put you on my back and bring you north again. But he hadn't. He had not even tried. He had felt like an utter fool, a rube. If she had wanted him to give chase, she would have given him half a chance. She had not, and he refused to go with fists swinging into her world, into some small dusty city in Yugoslavia. Later, when the war broke out, he hadn't tried to find out whether she was safe. She hadn't tried, so he hadn't tried.

At the time, he had considered himself wise. Now he knew the truth. He had made the greatest mistake of his life, a mortal error. He had not been in love, perhaps. But he had been ready. And he still was.

FARTHER DOWN the coastal road, he found the driveway of a de-stroyed house. He parked and watched the darkening of the sea through exposed joists. Sunset crimsoned the waters.

He knew at least one thing. He would make good on his promise. He would take her back to Berlin. But then what?

Up until the arrival of the letter, he could recall each line of Marta's face. She had come to him often in his dreams. After the let-ter, as if offended, her memory had vanished. He could put pieces of her face together—the blond hair, the ponytail, the green eyes, her lips. But it was a composite. The letter about Marta had erased the memory of Marta. This made him think a shaming thought. He did not really want to die for the sake of this woman, no matter what she had once meant to him. And he had no idea what he would do with her if he ever got her back to Berlin. Was he happy? Was he in love? The questions could not be answered.

He fell asleep in the car, under stars, in the driveway of the destroyed house.

The next morning, he struck out for Metkovic, which left the sea, veering inland under a bridge. Right there, at the ramp, a river cut through mountains and poured into the Adriatic. It had to be the Neretva, Marta's river, which flowed through her city on its way to this delta. He stopped the car and stood on the bank. Marta had described it to him as a mountain river, flowing fast through a gorge, but here it was wide and slow. The wind chopped its waters. The Neretva river existed. Here it was. Marta was close.

IN THE MIDDLE of the city of Metkovic, Arthur encountered a military checkpoint. Men stood beside wooden planks and sandbags, wearing unconvincing uniforms. Their green fatigues had an offhand feel. One wore a bandanna, another a beret, the last a backwards baseball cap. A checkerboard flag flapped between sandbags. Arthur produced the blue-rimmed UN Protection Force identity card, but the man in the baseball cap shook his finger.

"*Dobro,*" Arthur replied, his one confident word in Serbo-Croatian.

He began to reach for the wallet in his pants pocket, but the guns quivered, and he raised his hands instead.

"*Dobro,*" he repeated several times.

"No *dobro!*" the man in the baseball cap piped up. "No fucking *dobro.*"

"What do you want?" Arthur asked him.

The officer gestured for Arthur to get out of the vehicle. Arthur weighed the request. Journalists died at roadblocks. They also made a living out of telling thugs to go to hell. The man in the baseball cap reached inside the car and unlocked the door. He went through Arthur's wallet and fished out German marks. He searched clothing and his computer bag, which, to his visible disappointment, didn't contain a computer. Arthur glanced across the street. On the far side of a traffic circle, in the saddle of a faded white UN armored person-

nel carrier, sat a soldier in a blue helmet. He glanced with bored eyes
in Arthur's direction. The helmet became a purple shadow in the
fading western sun. Just beyond the soldier sat a two-story hotel.

A woman in a surprisingly smart red satin blouse and black pants
came with hip swings of importance down the steps of the hotel. She
had the officiousness of an airline hostess. As she crossed the traffic
circle, her ass, at last, drew the eyes of the United Nations soldier. She
clicked in high heels across the asphalt to the checkpoint and spoke
bad German, asking Arthur if he had a visa for something called the
Republic of Herzeg-Bosna. No, he told her. He had the UNPROFOR accreditation. She shook her head. A silver cross glittered between her
breasts.

"Do you have one hundred German marks?"

"I had a lot more." Arthur indicated the men, who now ignored
him. "Ask them."

She had a pleasant chat in her own tongue with the men, tossing
them packs of Marlboros, then motioned for Arthur to come along,
and he reluctantly followed. The man in the backwards baseball cap
hopped into Arthur's rental car, put the car into drive, and spun away.

"Where do I report a stolen vehicle?" Arthur asked.

"Did you know that it is illegal to bring Croatian rental car into Republic of Herzeg-Bosna?" she asked him.

"Republic of what?"

Another checkerboard flag hung from the second floor of the
hotel, just like the one at the checkpoint, red-and-white checkerboard, rimmed with dark blue, like a coat of arms. The checkerboard
snapped and boiled in wind above his head.

"I'm looking for Mostarian refugees," Arthur told his escort.

She went behind the registration desk of the hotel. The building
had clearly been expropriated for the Republic.

"You cannot be here without proper accreditation. You must go
back to Zagreb."

"I won't."

"In addition to accreditation pass from army of Herzeg-Bosna, you also need pass from the Information Office of the Croatian Defense Ministry. Do you have?"

Arthur pulled out Dubravka's letter and told the woman that the letter in his hands had been sent to him weeks ago from Metkovic. It concerned a woman named Marta Mehmedovic, who was trapped in Mostar. He had come to bring this woman out. Apparently, the representative of the Republic could read English. She took the letter, and Arthur noticed again the cross on her chest. A memory of the East Berlin airport came to him. Here he was at another border and in grave need. He was weaker now than he had been in those days. He had fallen somehow. Maybe he had betrayed the God of the cross and been punished. Maybe he should have become a devout Christian on the instant of his salvation by the customs official. That would have been the grateful thing. But he had not. He had proceeded to get involved with a married woman. Still, he dug into his wallet.

"I see your cross." He slapped his sister's pocket cross onto the wood of the counter. "I am a Christian, too," he said. "Like you."

The woman's dark eyes fixed on him in hard points.

"No, you are not a Christian like me."

"Because I don't believe that Jesus Christ is the son of God?"

She almost smiled. "That could be one reason."

"But doesn't that cross stand for something more? Doesn't it stand for compassion and humanity? Doesn't it hold you to certain universal obligations?"

She returned the letter. "I have closet full of these," she said. "My family was butchered in Slavonia. My father is dead. Many people die. Many Croats. Many Muslims. More Croats, I can tell you." She paused. "So you have letter. So you have cross. So what?"

Arthur felt betrayed. He buried the cross back in his wallet, and in that moment, he felt the woman take compassion on him. She fingered her silver cross between her fingers and pondered.

"Just to show you that I am a real Christian," she said, and she beckoned him to a street sloping up the hill beside the hotel. "Café Raj. Up there. Ask for General Vela. He's a Mostarian. Maybe he can help you. I don't know." She shrugged. "*Auf wiedersehen.* Bye-bye."

A RTHUR FOUND the Café Raj. Under the sign, men in black leather jackets reclined in white plastic chairs, black boots on tabletops, shot glasses flashing. Within one jacket, Arthur glimpsed a pistol. Its owner stared at Arthur's Justins.

"I'm looking for General Vela."

The man hitched a thumb at the door to the bar. Inside the Raj, under a garlanded sketch of a man in epaulettes, Arthur took a seat.

"*Pivo?*" asked a barmaid. "You want a beer?"

"I'm looking for General Vela," he said.

"Have a beer," insisted the barmaid. "On the house."

Arthur accepted the beer. It came, and it was ice cold, and he drank it down. He asked where he could find refugees from Mostar, but the barmaid shrugged. Men began to play a game of darts. Arthur drank alone and waited. The barmaid watched the door.

Night came to Metkovic, the crowd in the Café Raj grew, and the chief patron of the Raj appeared, looming over Arthur. He was dressed, like the others, in black boots, but he wore purple sweat pants and a red bandanna around his throat. His forehead was wide and white under an extreme crew cut. He flipped off his shades and revealed eyes too small for such a big skull, pink from lack of sleep.

"What can I do for you?" he asked in good American English.

He took a stool at the bar beside Arthur. Big men in lederhosen took their places on either side of him and held their hands behind their backs. One of them wore a T-shirt advertising the Hard Rock Café, Zagreb. The other had the Iron Cross tattooed on his left bicep. They were blond, like Arthur, but with bodybuilder physiques and square jaws. Arthur took some satisfaction in noting that he was taller than this man.

"You're General Vela?"

"Are you an American journalist?"

"Yes, but I'm here on private business. I'm looking for a refugee from Mostar."

Vela smiled. "Lots of them. Did you have a beer?"

"I saw blue helmets out there. Would they know how to help me?"

Vela shook his head and offered his hand. "I'm the man. I'm Branko."

"Arthur."

"You sure you don't want another beer, Arthur?"

Arthur put his hand over the top of his glass.

"I lived for two years in Jackson Heights, in Queens. New York City. What's your newspaper?"

Arthur reached into his wallet and pulled out his sister's pocket cross. As if it were another press credential, he handed the cross to Vela, who stared down at the symbol in mute confusion. He looked up at Arthur with a confused smile. "I don't understand."

"A token of the seriousness of my business," said Arthur.

"I'm afraid I have to correct you," said Vela in a pleasant voice, displaying Arthur's cross like a visual aid in a lecture. "It's not money. And it's not a gun. So it's not a token of seriousness. But I'll accept it anyway. I know religious people who would like it."

Vela tucked the cross into his shirt pocket, and Arthur produced the letter. Vela seemed intrigued. He motioned for the men in lederhosen to step away, and he unfolded the letter. He pointed to Dubravka's signature. "I know this woman," he said with faint annoyance. "But I had no idea that she had written you a letter." Vela sucked in his cheeks. "How do you know her?"

Arthur paused before answering. "I met her sister in Berlin."

Vela's eyes glittered. His interest was piqued. "An American in Berlin. I believe I've heard about you."

"I'd be surprised."

The wide white forehead furrowed, and the man seemed genuinely touched by something. He leaned forward on the stool and ran a hand over his almost shaved skull. He clasped his hands together.

"I know this Marta Mehmedovic. Her husband had a restaurant near the Stari Most. The Old Bridge. The restaurant was called L'Avventura, after an Italian movie, though I never understood why. They always had good Italian wine, and the squid was outstanding." He kissed the tips of his fingers. "The Italian restaurants in New York City, where I lived, they all have Croatian chefs making seppia, but the restaurants call themselves Venetian, because no one in New York has heard of Croatia. But this Mehmedovic restaurant served it very nicely. They had a photograph of Marcello Mastroianni above the bar."

Vela frowned as he looked down. His voice might have come from rock. "He died, I believe, and the restaurant burned to the ground."

"Is his wife alive?" Arthur asked.

Vela shrugged. He finished his beer and wiped his lips. "You have UNPROFOR credentials?"

Arthur handed the card over.

"I'll see what I can do."

R AIN FELL for three days on Metkovic. The streets ran like rivers. Arthur slept in a room in the hotel and walked every morning up to the Raj for news. Every night, he walked home, disappointed and wet. The denizens of the café greeted him with familiarity. The barmaid seemed to take special pity on him and tried to engage him in conversations in German. She fed him cevapcici and tried to find out what he liked to watch on television. Sport? *Kino?* News?

Long past midnight, on the fourth day, Vela returned. At three in the morning, lights came on in Arthur's room, and Vela stood at the foot of the bed, glaring down.

"I don't have good news," he said. "You better get dressed."

He tossed the United Nations press credential on the blanket and left the room just as quickly and silently as he had entered. There were no bodyguards this time. The pension creaked with night noise. Arthur grabbed a T-shirt and jeans from his computer bag and put his contact lenses in his eyes. Vela came back.

"I don't want too many questions," he said. "She's still in shock."

For a second, Arthur didn't know whom Vela meant. Then Dubravka entered the room, and he was stunned speechless. Vela offered her a seat on the bed, and she took it. She was no longer the girl Arthur had seen in Berlin. That girl had been a blue-eyed beauty, with long thick brown hair and perfect pale skin. This girl was no longer a girl. She had been starving. She had been sick. She was still sick. Sores speckled her face and hands, and her teeth had become a jagged brown. She had the mouth of an animal. Arthur leaned back against the thin wall of the hotel room, and the wall shook. He began to understand. Marta would look like this, too, or worse. He had to prepare himself. He owed her that much. What were skin and bones anyway? The eyes would not have changed. Arthur remembered them, violet in the darkness, shot with green in the bright light of day. Like Dubravka's eyes, they left wisps of darkness in the air where they settled. They were sad, comforting, immense eyes. Arthur reached for her hand, and she gave it to him. She wore silver earrings and a coat of golden brown animal fur. A gloss gleamed red on her lips, and her sores had a crimson blush. She shook with a cough. Vela put a hand on her elbow. They were lovers.

"George delivered the letter to me last week," Arthur said. "I came as fast as I could."

Dubravka replied in Serbo-Croatian, and after a few seconds of silence, in which Arthur's heart began to pound in his ears, Vela interpreted. "You're too late," he said.

"What?"

Dubravka answered, Vela echoing, "She's dead."

The words cut. He could feel himself losing balance. Vela watched him and waited. Arthur put a hand on the headboard of the bed. "How?"

"She was killed in a mortar attack."

"When?"

"One week ago."

The tears began to spill from his eyes. "Jesus," he stammered. He sought to regain his composure. "Are you sure?"

Dubravka got up and came to Arthur. She was crying, too, black tears sliding down her cheeks. Vela looked away. Words wheezed out of Dubravka's chest, and she waited for him to interpret.

"She went to the front line to tend wounded soldiers, and a mortar hit their position. A lot of soldiers saw it. There's no doubt."

Dubravka went on, waiting for Vela's echo every few seconds.

"My sister never forgot you. She told me once that you were the only man who ever listened to a word she said. She thought of you a lot and often wondered if you were still in Berlin. But she told me she couldn't contact you after what she'd done." Dubravka paused again. "She never told me what that was. Can you?"

Arthur put his hands to his face. Dubravka continued. "A few weeks ago, she made me get on an aid convoy. She told me that she would follow me out as soon as she got a chance, but I knew that she wouldn't. After her son was killed, Marta refused to leave. She wanted to die. Now she has."

"When did Pino die?" whispered Arthur.

Dubravka spoke in a soft voice, as if in respect for the dead. "Last May."

Arthur took Dubravka in his arms, and they wept together. Vela left the room. When he came back, he placed a bundle on the floor at Arthur's feet, a heavy thing wrapped in old towels, and for one clear instant of horror, Arthur thought that Dubravka had brought him Marta's remains.

"This," said Dubravka, Vela her echo, "is the last member of the family."

Vela pulled aside the blankets and revealed a darkish clump of shattered creation that did not appear to breathe and did not appear to move. Dubravka bowed her head and went silent for a long time, a period of minutes or hours in which everything in the room, in Metkovic, up and down the Balkan Peninsula, seemed to stop. In that long space, Arthur grasped the shape of the universe. He grasped the exact magnitude of everything that he had done since the winter of 1990 in Berlin. He was in love. How sad, how terrible; he was in love, and she was dead. She had moved into utter darkness. What remained? A dog in a blanket. The animal had minutes to live. A blank space awaited it. A blank space awaited Arthur. Everything would go dark. The earth would vanish. Time would give out. Life would fail. No one would remember. The world was a wolf, and it had eaten her. It had eaten her son and her brother. She had no more thoughts in her head, no touch in her fingers, no more love to give. She had no memory. Arthur could still want Marta. He could even be jealous. He could want vengeance or desire her body or entertain philosophical and religious speculations about her whereabouts. But Marta's position had changed for the last time. She would not shift or move one more inch in the universe. She was gone.

"You want her?" asked Dubravka, Vela echoing.

The dog looked dead, but if she lived, Arthur wanted her. Arthur would fight the engines of Hell for her.

He folded the blankets over the body and hoisted the animal up. Their business was finished. He wanted to leave. He would walk back to Germany, if necessary.

"Your car's out front," said Vela. "No one will bother you anymore."

Arthur grabbed the computer bag off the floor and stumbled toward the threshold of the room. He thought of Dubravka and turned. He wanted to apologize, to express gratitude or remorse or affection, to offer to take her back to Berlin, where she would be safe. He would do anything she asked. He would take any risk.

"Dubravka," he said, "I'm so sorry . . ."

She had taken his place on the bed and drawn the fur coat tight around her body. Arthur saw an emotion of tenderness on Vela's face, and she returned the expression. He spoke to Dubravka in their tongue. But Dubravka did not answer. Vela repeated his words, leaning over her. She put her hands beneath her head and gazed up at Arthur a moment. The gaze lasted an eternity.

"Goodbye," she said.

She closed her eyes.

TWENTY-ONE

H E TRIED TO FEED the dog portions of rice and venison, leftovers from the buffet of a hotel in Split, but she would eat nothing, at first. She couldn't hear, he was sure—blood clotted her ears—but she sensed his presence, acknowledging him with a growl when he drew near. It looked as if someone had fired a gun into her face. Her nose and mouth had congealed into a dark mass. The rims of her eyelids had crusted over. Beneath these scabs, the moistness of an eyeball glimmered.

In a hotel room in Rijeka, her tongue broke free of her mouth and lapped sideways into a glass bowl. After a few tries, scattering food across the floor, she pulled off a morsel or two. Long after the last of the food was gone, she licked the innards of the bowl. She whined for water, then vomited what she drank. Her ass bled. Arthur theorized that she must have been near the impact site of a mortar shell. It had blown out her eardrums and damaged her muzzle, but he could find no evidence of shrapnel in her body.

He drove during the day, arriving at hotels long after dark, leaving long before dawn, avoiding other people as much as possible. Night after night, he carried the animal upstairs and then, with a few hours' sleep, back down, loading her into the backseat of the car, heading north. He stopped so she could defecate, but she had no leverage. She hobbled about, attempted a crap, managed streams of blood and urine, and retreated back into the car as if into a cave. If he touched her, she snarled and tried to bite. Once, she almost got him. She reeked of rotten meat and maggots and heat. For a day, she seemed to improve, but after Rijeka, she quickly deteriorated.

Three days after leaving Metkovic, Arthur strode into the lobby of the Hotel Esplanade in Zagreb, the dog folded deep in towels and thrown over one shoulder. She had started whining and shivering. Arthur dropped his credit card on the counter and asked if he could make a long-distance phone call. The clerk took down the number and indicated a wooden stall across from the registration desk. Arthur squeezed into the stall and waited. The phone rang, and he picked up.

"Hello?" It was his sister Philippa, an ocean of time zones away, seven or eight hours behind him.

"It's me," he said.

"Arthur?"

A spasm of emotion hit him. The dog was bleeding on his shirt.

"This is beyond me," he said.

"What is beyond you? Where are you?"

"I'm in the city of Zagreb. In the country of Croatia. And I need help."

He heard an intake of breath. Philippa lived in Dallas, Texas, on the far side of the moon.

"I have no fucking idea what I'm going to do with this animal!" he cried.

He hung up the phone, shoved out of the stall, and requested the nearest veterinary hospital. The impress of the card was taken. An address for a vet was found. A porter took the key and his computer bag, and Arthur set out for the animal hospital, five minutes away, according to the concierge.

He barged into a reception area devoid of humanity. A radio played somewhere. Arthur smelled rubbing alcohol and wet animal fur and heard the paws of things rattling in cages. Knocking twice on the door leading into the recesses of the office, and receiving no answer, he lost his patience. He went inside. A man in a white smock flicked a cigarette into a sink and stared at the blood on Arthur's shirt.

Arthur spoke in German. "Are you the vet?"

The doctor, if that's what he was, didn't reply. Hair hid most of his face. He'd been up to something when Arthur entered. He had just put an object into a drawer. Arthur placed the bundle on the floor and unwrapped blankets.

The doctor pointed an accusatory finger at the floor. "Get it out of here."

"*It* is a dog."

"I don't care if it's the pope. I said get it out of here."

"She's been in Mostar."

"Mostar?"

Arthur nodded.

"Dear Christ," the doctor said.

"Can you help me?"

The vet opened his coat and pulled out a pistol. He aimed at the dog. "My special remedy," he said.

Arthur scooped up the animal and ran out. He had a last idea. He followed tram lines up chilly streets. Zagreb rose on a slope, mounting slowly, with the help of steps, to the institutional core of the ancient Habsburg city. He heard familiar words in his mind, two of them, not quite intelligible. He had never been told their precise meaning, but he knew that the words denoted a place. Marta had gone to this place with her mother. She had gone there to pray, and when she did her breathing exercises she thought of this place, and the memory brought her peace. Arthur climbed stone steps against mountain wind. The words, the name of the place, played at the tip of his tongue, but it would not come. He moved at great speed against muffled people.

At last, he found it. There was no sign. He had not asked, and no one had shown him the way. But he knew. He walked down an incline, through an archway into shadow, and he knew. This was it. He had expected something different. In his imagination, the place had been longer or larger. Within seconds, he passed through it and back into the evening.

Kamenita Vrata. Marta had spoken the name once or twice. When she closed her eyes to do her breathing exercises, she imagined a place called the Kamenita Vrata, no more than a way station, a transit point between two sections of the city of Zagreb, a hinge in a door, no more, but within it teemed spirits that Marta had trusted.

The Kamenita Vrata was a tunnel. On one side of the tunnel lay a massive slab of old city wall. On the other, there was a hollow containing pews. People sat in the pews and prayed, old women, scarved and hardened. They bent forward on their knees and murmured under the hiss and snap of beeswax candles.

Across from the pews, on the other side of the walkway, embedded like a gem in the old city wall, was an icon of the Virgin Mary. Arthur began to understand why he had come. He lowered the dog to the pavement in front of the icon. The Virgin was barely recognizable. The details of her face could not be seen. She receded into black depths. People stopped and crossed themselves or lit a candle or stood close to the walls, reading words. There were hundreds of words embedded in the wall, the same words over and over. *Hvala ti, majka.* Thank you, Mother. People read, touched, and kissed the words. Arthur would thank her, too, if she saved this dog.

Just then, as if by sorcery, a man appeared in the face of the wall and almost stepped on the dog. Arthur staggered back, reaching for emptiness to catch his fall. Metal keys dangled from a hand. But it hadn't been magic, Arthur saw. The man had stepped out of a wooden door buried in an alcove in the stone wall, and within seconds, he began to speak a Roman Catholic liturgy in Latin. Arthur pushed his way through old women. He made his way to the farthest corner of a pew, pressed his hands together, and prayed.

He had not spoken to God in many years. He had not communicated with his own particular deity, Jesus Christ, since high school.

"Save her," he said. "I implore you."

In high school, during the most fanatical phase of his religious life, Arthur had prayed to Jesus Christ for something that he no longer understood. He had asked for help in rejecting the world. That's what he remembered. In the beginning, before he understood the terms of Presbyterianism, he had prayed for girls. He had sent up a hope that girls would agree to go with him to dances or that they would like him enough to return his phone calls or let him touch their bodies. Later, a youth leader in a baseball cap and Dallas Cowboys practice jersey had informed Arthur that God was not a vending machine. He must not ask for anything concrete. He must ask for the exact opposite, in fact. He embraced this idea and yearned to be free of the desire to care about anything on earth. *Consider the lilies, how they grow; they toil not, neither do they spin, and yet I say unto you that Solomon in all his glory was not arrayed like one of these.* Arthur had learned how to pray with the lightness of a child.

"Save the dog." He repeated the words again and again. After his disillusion, Arthur had considered faith either an excuse for bloodshed or a protection against fear. Now, for the first time in his life, he saw it as a means simply to live. If he could just believe in this one possibility, that God could save the dog, then he could also continue to breathe.

The priest reentered the wall. The crowd dissolved. Around midnight, Arthur lit a candle and said a thank-you. He wrapped the dog in her blankets again, hoisted her over his shoulder, and stumbled on tired legs back down the hill to his bed.

TWENTY-TWO

MARTA NEVER HEARD the explosion. There had been nothing to hear. The force of the blast knocked her into the protection of a slab of old, leaning limestone, its fall prevented by even bigger slabs. The rest of the building came down, and she lay a long time in the dark, until Mato pulled her out.

For days, she lay in a trench on the western bank of the Neretva. Her ears rang. Her eyes would not open. Her muscles and bones implied knives. The cold wind spun down out of the hills and gave her spasms like a woman in childbirth. She called for her son.

The passage over the river did not open again for many days, but at last Civil Defense managed a pontoon bridge across the Neretva, and Mato himself carried her to the eastern bank. That was two weeks after the mortar attack on the house. Two weeks later, Marta came out of her delirium long enough to comprehend that she had been believed dead. Word had spread. The residents of the shelter beneath the Municipal Theater told her that someone had taken the dog, which had been near death. That had been in mid-December.

February came, and winter dwindled. Armies began to prepare for spring offensives. A mortar shell fell upon the market in Sarajevo, killing sixty-nine people, and the world beyond the borders of Marta's country came suddenly alive. Snows thawed, river waters swelled. American jets screamed across silver skies. The air began to smell of cherry blossom and of the corpses beneath collapsed buildings. Cockroaches crept out of hiding.

THE WARRING ARMIES on either side of the Neretva called a cease-fire, and the guns in the western hills became still. The snipers paused. Men began fishing in the river again, and the inhabitants of East Mostar began for the first time in months to walk free under the sun. One evening, feeling steady on her legs, Marta stepped out of the basement of the Municipal Theater and inhaled the peace. It was March of the year 1994.

Mato escorted her down a street called the Brace Fejica. As a hero of the Civil Defense, Mato had received his choice of shelters, a Croat bakery with half a roof and two dry rooms, and he wanted to share it with Marta.

Every few meters, she needed a rest. They sat for a moment on a sandbag. Sunlight glanced off the hills and coursed through the valley, darkening the branches of the pomegranate trees behind the Karadjoz Bey Mosque, sharpening the lines of Arabic on the tombstones in the cemetery grass.

Neither spoke. Marta didn't have much need of words anymore. Language had become pure again. If one needed bread, one asked for bread. If one wanted a blanket, one asked for a blanket. The rest had become useless.

Mato looked sharp in his baggy camouflage pants and dark green T-shirt. He required nothing on this earth. Sunglasses rode on the top of his shaved head and caught shards of the day. His legs slid like swords into the upper rims of heavy brown boots, and the boots were spotless. Mato had a boy who shined them.

"Cease-fire won't hold," he said at last.

"Be a little optimistic."

"You be."

Marta smiled. "You look well," she said.

But she didn't know anymore what her own words meant. Did looking well mean being well?

Mato rubbed one of his biceps. "I heard something," he said.

Judging by the look on his face, Marta didn't want to know about it.

"A Mostar girl turned up in Metkovic a few months ago and started seeing Branko Velakovic. She's a Muslim. Civil Defense people here think she's some kind of a spy."

"Doesn't mean it's Dubravka."

"Of course it's Dubravka."

They continued up the hill, past a woman baking loaves over a fire. Marta saw a sack of meal, half emptied, and wondered how the woman had come by it. Mato would know. Around them, as the day waned, other fires kindled. Mostar became an open kitchen. Smoke wrinkled the air above the ruins. Across the Neretva, church bells chimed, and the sound touched Marta's heart, coming like a voice from the past, a fleeting memory of the Apostel Paulus Church at lunch hour, one ring, coming through the windows of the Adria Travel Agency. She felt an unwanted emotion. Church bells now belonged to the western enemy. She must think of herself as two people—Marta of Berlin, and Marta of Bosnia; Marta Before War, and Marta After War. There could be no union between the two, not anymore.

Mato scrutinized the hills. Marta bought a loaf of bread.

He asked her a question. "You know the difference between the war in Sarajevo and the war here?"

She shook her head. She knew very little about the war in Sarajevo.

"Most of the soldiers on the ridges above Sarajevo are strangers. They don't know who the hell they're killing, and they don't want to know."

They were climbing steps now, and Marta wanted another rest before they crossed the Avenue Marshala Tita. They found the sill of a shattered window.

"Here there are no strangers. Here *everything* is local. Do you see? That's why the cease-fire won't hold. Everyone here knows everything. They know who did what, and who is responsible. So they won't fucking stop until they're all fucking dead."

Marta was surprised at how many cars moved on the Marshala Tita. For a time, in Mostar, automobiles had ceased to exist. The technology of the combustion engine had been all but lost.

"You know I'm right," said Mato. "Will you rest until the bastard who killed your son is in his grave?"

Marta knew the name of the man who had driven the explosives into the hotel where her father and son had been hiding; he was a civil engineer who used to dive from the Old Bridge into the Neretva. He had gone to university with Mato's father. One of these days, she would find the home address, which would not be difficult, and tell the man to his face what he had done. If someone killed him first, she would be sorry. If he was killed afterward, she would have no problem. Marta was not alone in her knowledge and her desire. Lots of people could say with absolute precision who had come in the morning, who had come in the evening, who had arrived at noon. Neighbors and colleagues had shot husbands and fathers in the streets. They had penetrated wives with knives and cocks, and mocked the names of the dead. They had forced the sole survivors of executed families across the river, shooting into the backs of people whose lives and minds they had already destroyed.

Pino Mehmedovic had last been seen on May 8, 1993, ten months in the past—that's how she thought of it, though months no longer functioned for her as a unit of time. His moment on earth had come and gone so quickly, and yet his life bloomed in her mind like an entire fragrant age of humankind, like one of those periods predating human life, the Triassic, the Cambrian, the Precambrian, when mar-

velous creatures walked the world in unimaginable glory. She saw
steam rising from baths, meals on bright-painted plates, herself reading stories, her voice a thundering love. It seemed that she could recall every word of every book that she had ever read to him. Such an
endless, beautiful epoch, yet his obliteration had taken only an instant. The mystery had become total. She did not understand. She
never would.

Her family had been forced out of the house at gunpoint. Thanks
to Branko, the women had not been molested, but that had been his
one and only benediction. Marta and her father ran, her father carrying Pino. Dubravka had stayed behind, screaming at her lover, accus-
ing him, as if he didn't hold her life in his hands. Marta and her father
had made it to a hotel near the Bulevar, but in the lobby her father
ordered Marta to go back and get her sister, who still had not come.
He would take care of Pino. They would be safe in the hotel. The
building belonged to a Croat and represented a substantial invest-
ment. Her father knew how Croats worked. They loved money more
than anything in the world. Marta resisted. Her father pleaded. His
words became terrible. He raved. All of his guilt about his neglected
younger daughter rose like a bile. Why didn't she care more about
Dubravka? What the hell was wrong with her? Had she inherited her
mother's lizard indifference? The city was exploding, Pino was crying,
her father was bellowing, and her sister was missing. And that was it.
She had gone, and they had waited in the lobby with dozens of others. She had seen the truck. She may have even waved toward the
driver in some atavistic urge toward neighborliness, waved to him
just moments before he drove the vehicle, a Czechoslovak-made
military transport, into the parking lot in the front of the hotel, before he parked the truck, turned off the ignition, and scrambled out
for dear life. She shut her eyes in rage.

"Say the cease-fire holds," said Mato. "You know who's going to
run this place?"

"The United Nations."

He gave her a look of complete disbelief. "Fuck, Marta. Listen to me."

"I am listening."

"This will be Branko's city."

Mato paused and deliberated his next words. He seemed to have a very specific purpose. "The United Nations says that there are two kinds of people left in this valley. Catholics and Muslims. But the United Nations doesn't know shit. There are only two kinds of people, ever, anywhere, at any given moment, in this world: those who have slit the throat of another human being and those who haven't. Branko is in the first category. You are in the second."

"So?"

"So the people in the first category are the ones who rule the world."

At last, they crossed the Marshala Tita into the municipal park, which had become a cemetery. People relaxed beside homemade wooden oblongs, smoking, staring at the names and the years, white numbers on green backgrounds, 1992, 1993, 1994. They laid cherry blossoms on the mounds and glanced in anxiety at the hills to the west. Marta knelt before a grave bearing the names of her son and her father. No one was in the grave.

"I've given some thought to being a good Muslim," she said.

Mato groaned. "You? Do *hijab?*"

She patted the bare earth at the base of the oblong. Around it, she had arranged a ring of evenly sized white rubble stones, but they seemed to have shifted wildly since her last visit. She hadn't been able to come in months, not since the destruction of the Stari.

"Did you ever know my Great-Aunt Zara?" she asked Mato.

Mato shook his head.

"My father's aunt. She was a peasant woman, and she embarrassed the family, but he used her well. Whenever we got into trouble, he sent us straight to Zara. I had to go live with her during the summer after the mayonnaise incident. He wanted me to get in touch with some deeper moral truths, he told me."

"Fucking hypocrite. Like all of them."

Marta had begun to think a lot about her Great-Aunt Zara, who had lived with her illiterate husband in a village on a hill outside Stolac, raising tobacco, grapes, and almonds out of the parched ground. Zara had taught Marta everything she knew about Islam, which was little to nothing. Unlike the home of Marta's childhood, the smelly, crowded little farmhouse had a Koran, and in the evenings, after work, Marta had listened to Zara read suras aloud. She had found them beautiful but remembered nothing specific. At her great-uncle's insistence, she had worn a headscarf, like her aunt. Five times a day, they had fallen on prayer mats and prayed toward Mecca. With her aunt, she had crossed her arms over her chest and put her head to the floor as well. They had not kept halal; it was just too difficult. But they fasted on Ramadan and rarely ate swine. Once a week, on Fridays, the old man made his way to a mosque in Mostar. Zara never went. It never seemed to matter to her. She knew the imam personally, but she also knew the local priests and participated in the village Easter celebrations, and she consulted a *kaladzije,* an old woman who lived in a tenement in Stolac and claimed to be in touch with spirits. Zara never spoke of Mohammed but talked quite a bit about something called the Srednja Zemlja, the Middle Field, which could have been an allotment of land just beyond her own property line, a place where demons exercised powers over human beings, especially over women.

The sun left the valley, but light remained, a golden sash. Mato took off his sunglasses, and she saw that he was exhausted. In his night face, emerging in the municipal park like a moon among the grave markers, she saw tracks of deep violence, visible as scars. His eyes had sunk into their sockets. His gentleness had gone, too. Death had a vigorous life in his body. The muscles tightened in his neck as he became angry. In the dusk, people peered at him.

"But then I think," she said, repointing the stones in the ring around the empty grave, mollifying him, "that if I did become a good Muslim,

Pino wouldn't recognize me. We never had a Koran in the house. Did you know that? We had Tolstoy. We had Shakespeare. We had Krleza. We may even have had a Holy Bible somewhere. But no Koran. I would have been embarrassed. Did you ever read the Bible?"

"Fuck no."

Getting up, she dusted off her knees. "I used to be a *business*woman."

Mato's irritation burst out. "Let me tell you something. I met a Franciscan who was driving a truck for Catholic Relief, and he told me that it was my duty as a Christian to stay in Sarajevo and raise my children Catholic. You know what I told him?"

He was making her smile again. "I can imagine what you told him."

Mato raised his fingertips in two points.

"I said fuck you, brother. I'm going to America with my Serb Orthodox wife and I'm never looking back."

Marta had finished cleaning up the grave. She planted a kiss on the earth, and they left the park, heading south, in the rough direction of the Stari. Mato bought a cup of coffee from her Uncle Pipa, who had taken no time at all to open a café in the ruins of his shop. The café consisted of dolmen-like stones, employed as seats, and it had a view of the western bank of the Neretva. Lights twinkled on the opposite side.

"They have electricity," said Marta.

The river could be heard, singing through the gorge. Brother and sister ambled up the slope of the street to the remains of the bridge. She gave him a piece of bread to chew. Down below, the water had lost its shape.

"I'm thinking of the night of Tino's party," Mato said.

"We stood right about there." Marta pointed into the air. She could see the stone sweeping up and away from her. She could see the form of the bridge like a shadow dissolving into darkness. Kids sat on the edge of the ruin.

"I'm getting out," Mato said.

His woman was a Serb and feared for her life—and for his life. Mato had kept the relationship hidden from almost everyone.

"She says that the army is going to force me to enlist again," Mato said. "That they're going to force me to die fighting her people. She says it's going to happen any day now."

"Listen to her, then."

Friends would sneak him out. Only his wife would know, and she would tell his father, who would take it hard. The princely engineer had survived the entire war on the sixteenth floor of a building in Novo Sarajevo.

"You can come," he said.

"To America?"

"Why not?"

Off to the north, under stars, Marta heard the beginnings of a call to prayer, the first shock of a human voice against silence, the twisting, coiling human voice. She could not ever remember hearing that sound in her valley before. It struck her as beautiful and strange.

"I knew an American once," she said. "I liked him."

"So."

"So kiss America for me, Mato."

The next day, snipers shot two men fishing in the Neretva. The day after that, her brother vanished.

TWENTY-THREE

O N A F R I D A Y E V E N I N G in early April, as men wandered home from mosques, a faded white United Nations jeep rolled up in front of the collapsed Croat bakery in the Brace Fejica. Marta sat outside, on the street, contemplating two large, damp sandbags and counting buttons. The driver of the jeep was Mose Silber, dressed, as usual, in tweed jacket and white shirt. He'd slept in the clothes, by the look of it. His cheeks had shrunk a bit. Marta wanted to drag the sandbags from one side of the street to the other, but first she had to pay for them. She dropped twenty buttons into the hand of a child, the son of a neighbor who did a good barter business. She would use one sandbag as a table; the other would plug a hole.

"Have you seen the Germans?" cried Mose, leaping out of the jeep.

Marta shook her head; no sign of them yet. Rumors were spreading, though. German aid workers had begun to appear in dark blue trucks. Marta stood back from the sandbags, assessing, and realized that she had paid too many buttons. It had taken her a week to find them, too.

Mose handed her his jacket. "Where do you want them?"

She pointed inside the bakery. "Isn't it the Sabbath?" she asked.

Mose stacked one sandbag on top of the other and began to shove both across the ground. He groaned. His eyes bulged, and his face turned red. Like everyone else's, his diet had suffered, and he was weaker than he wanted to admit. She directed him to a narrow path through the broken façade.

"Nice place," he called from inside.

The bakery had excellent qualities. Half of its roof remained intact, so with a fire, Marta could stay reasonably dry. Unlike the basement of the Municipal Theater, it got fresh air and rarely stank. And it was too small to accommodate anyone else. Cockroaches were still a problem, though. She joined him inside.

"Now a bit of talk," said Mose, rubbing his hands together.

Marta lit a candle and placed it on top of her new dinner table, the smaller of the two sandbags. She had become an insatiable trader. On any given day, she handled candles, smashed furniture, locker doors, and car hoods for protection against sniper fire; metal cots, bullet-riddled pots, broken bottle glass, needles, rice, grease. Sandbags, exchanged for the buttons and the last of her tub of East German laundry soap, could be used as all-purpose furniture; shrapnel had a thousand uses, could be plate, bowl, or spoon; combs made forks; glass cut like a knife. The hollow shell of a television set made a cupboard for her silverware. Objects passed through her hands, fulfilled their purposes, and moved on. Behind the sandbag, she had her bedding, a pile of German blankets, stitched in Korea. Above the bed, there had been a bread oven, which now served as a repository for her four items of clothing. She had a metal pipe for protection.

She offered Mose tea, and they talked about the Germans. She had seen men and women in blue jeans walking the Brace Fejica, pointing at rubble, gesturing at places where homes and businesses had been, offering a second chance with their sense of confidence, their utter freedom of movement. She had seen a head of hennaed red hair and known the nationality right away. Only German women used that rinse. But she hadn't spoken to the people, hadn't wanted to accost them. In truth, they had scared her a little, even though she understood their presence. The European Union would be assuming temporary control of the city. Its bureaucrats would administrate, organize, and rebuild, and Germans, the strongest, biggest, most efficient Europeans, would be deeply involved. She had heard that a German might actually be put in charge of the city, a rumor too strange to be true.

"I hate to admit it," said Mose, "but I'm happy to see those Germans."

"I'm surprised to learn that."

"But you feel the same way, of course." Mose gave Marta a rueful smile.

The Germans had an oddly hallowed place in the saga of their extinguished country; the German invasion in April 1941 had been the beginning of the state of their youth, of Communist Yugoslavia, the government spitting in the face of Hitler, tearing up a newly signed treaty, people dancing in the streets, national pride reborn. Then the German planes razed Belgrade. King Peter flew away in a British plane, and the war began, the great crusade against Fascism memorialized in her mother's movies. After Fascism lay in ruins, Nazi Germany ceased to be an enemy. It became the bloody womb of the Revolution. How many divisions of Nazi troops had it taken to subdue Marshal Tito and his Partisans? Twenty-one divisions? Hadn't the Partisans, by holding down so many German divisions, forced Hitler to delay his Russian offensive, thus guaranteeing the German defeat? Hadn't Tito been the one true hero of the Second World War?

But Marta had always had her own private German history. The sound of the language, the *words,* had always touched her mind like sunshine. One must admit the possibility, she thought, that peoples, like people, can change. And the Germans had changed, she believed. This had been her mother's belief, too, though of course the Great Actress was biased. She had made a career out of exploiting the desperate Wild West fantasies of Saxons and Pomeranians.

When she was fifteen, Marta met a West German boy who rode and fixed motorcycles. He came with his family to the beach at Lumbarda every year, and for two years, they went together. Horst liked "Purple Haze," James Dean, and Harley Davidson and didn't give a damn about Rilke, Beethoven, or Nietzsche, which Marta's mother held against him. Marta had meals with Horst's family, and they treated her like one of their own. They complimented her German, asked her questions about her parents and her home, and let her spend the night as if she were their son's fiancée. Horst's father had lost a leg in the battle of the Ardennes Forest, but he had made his own prosthetic, and ended up with a job in a bank and a life to be envied. His family even vacationed on the Dalmatian Coast. This biography made a lasting impression on her. A man loses his leg and wins a life. That was Germany! The spiritual opposite of her own dead and buried country!

"Do you still keep in touch with anyone in Berlin?" asked Mose.

"Why?" she asked.

He shrugged. But he seemed to know something. His eyes sparkled with knowledge. Had he seen Arthur Cape? She forced herself not to ask such a ludicrous question. Arthur Cape must be far away by now, in some other life that she could not fathom, entering the offices of other strangers in São Paulo or Beijing or New York City, getting hit by other kinds of apples. The memory of their meeting still made her smile.

"Take a ride with me," said Mose.

THEY STOPPED AT a warehouse, and Mose honked. The long, rectangular building hadn't suffered much damage. A slender woman slipped through the doors of the building, and Marta knew immediately that she was a German. Everything about her seemed familiar. She had short blond hair and dark blue eyes. Her arms were lithe and strong. Mose climbed out of the driver's seat and hurried

into the warehouse. The woman took his place in the jeep and regarded Marta, one hand on the steering wheel.

"Gaby!" cried Marta in wonder. German words fluttered into her
mouth. "What in God's name are you doing here?"

"I'm here for you," Gaby replied.

"*Mein Gott,*" said Marta, her entire body trembling with the fact of
this angelic presence. The girl had meat on her bones.

"I owed you," Gaby said. "When you came back to Berlin that
time—when you tried—something changed in me. I saw what you
were trying to do. I saw that you were . . ." She stammered a moment. "You were changing your life. So I left Berlin. I borrowed some
money from my crazy aunt, and I went to Africa. And that's how I
met these people. They rebuild destroyed cities. We do, I mean. They
helped me to find you. So did Herr Silber."

Gaby began to sob. "Marta, I'm so sorry about your son."

Marta had nothing to say about this. She waited.

Gaby wiped her eyes and changed the subject. "Do you remember
that American journalist?"

"Do you mean Arthur Cape?"

"*Right.* Arthur."

"We were lovers," said Marta. She had never put it that way before,
as a matter of incontestable fact. The words didn't feel wrong. They
didn't feel superfluous. Gaby nodded without surprise. A breeze ruffled them, and a memory came to mind, like a gift: Arthur and she
drinking port wine with Gaby's aunt, Frau Herbst, nibbling the Schogetten chocolate that the old woman liked to serve in Tiffany bowls;
sitting in the caverns between her vast snake-encoiled credenzas and
her sunburst Florentine saint while she told them war stories, Arthur
leaning against Marta, his ear in her hair. The old woman had told
them a story about the last days of the Battle of Berlin, when she flew
the Union Jack to keep British bombers from dropping their payloads
on her head. A German pilot saw Frau Herbst's Union Jack and put a
bomb through her roof. The explosion destroyed the parlor where

they sat, and Marta remembered delight at the thought, the idea of the two of them, she and Arthur, sitting in midair together in a place that no longer existed. Past and present merged. You'd never know, Marta had told the old woman, that the parlor had been destroyed. The old woman told Marta that she looked so radiant she must be in love.

"How is your aunt?" Marta asked.

Gaby grimaced, and a bit of her old wicked self emerged. "She still hates me. Are you hungry?"

Marta was. They got out of the jeep and entered the factory by swinging open a heavy metal door. Marta smelled traces of cool tobacco. The warehouse had stored tobacco leaves. Mose beckoned to them from the far side of a hall full of parked forklifts. Beside the forklifts, in rows along the walls, were pallets laden with lumber, panels of glass, and mortar. The place swam with the good odors of work: wood, oiled machinery, and benzine. Before they could enter another door, which lay between two forklifts, Mose put a hand on Marta's shoulder.

"I had to be discreet."

Inside the room, reading a movie magazine, sat the Circassian herself, her sister Dubravka. She had one fat, black eye.

MOSE EXPLAINED EVERYTHING in an apologetic voice. He had removed Dubravka from a predicament. That's how he put it. He had paid bribes and run a roadblock. No one else could have done it. One remaining bridge connected the eastern and western banks of the Neretva, and only Mose, Jew and noncombatant, could cross without hindrance. He carried mail and medicines. He passed messages. He was Mostar's one last universal postman. Both sides of the city respected him. Both used him. And he had been glad to help.

Marta did not thank him. "Why in the name of God did you bring her back here?"

"I heard that you were alive," her sister said. "And I knew that you wouldn't come to see me."

Marta's anger burst. "You could have started a new life. You were safe—" But she stopped then. Her sister's face would not allow her to continue. "Did Branko do that to you?"

Dubravka's face dipped to one side, and Marta saw another token of violence, a bruise running down the right cheek to the chin. Mose gave Marta a look. Her sister had never been safe.

"We had a fight," said Dubravka, her voice flat. "He wanted me to convert. He told me he was tired of sleeping with a Muslim."

Gaby spoke up. "Dinner's ready."

She and Mose left the room.

DUBRAVKA OPENED the movie magazine again, but she wasn't reading. Her stillness hardened. At last, Marta sat beside her. She hated to admit the fact. She was overjoyed to see her sister. The sight of her long hair brought tears to her eyes, but she refrained from touching it.

"I'm sorry. I didn't mean to sound so upset."

"I deliberately provoked him," Dubravka said. "You know how I can be. It's partly my fault."

Marta swallowed. "How did you provoke him?"

"I told him that he better stop hitting me or I would tell all his secrets."

Fear prickled in Marta's chest. "What secrets?"

"Things he's done. Places where he's done them. I bet no one knows more than I do."

Dubravka closed the magazine and looked at Marta through her decent eye. The other one glistened in a slit of dark flesh. The swine had not merely hit her with the back of his hand. He had used the butt of a gun.

"Mato told me that you went back to him, but I wouldn't believe it."

Dubravka reached out and took one of her hands. "You think love cares about war?"

"I don't even know what that means."

Dubravka nodded. "But you should." She was weak. She should have been eating well, but her arms seemed as thin as they had during the fighting. She reached into her pants pocket and pulled out a small yellow square, a piece of plastic bent in two, Marta saw.

"I stole it from Branko," Dubravka said.

"I don't want anything of his."

"It's not his."

With reluctance, Marta took the object, a laminated yellow card of some kind, and unfolded it. She looked up at her sister. She felt a secret insult, an inexplicable attack by her sister.

"What does this mean?"

Within the laminate lay a cross, and beside the cross were words in English. Marta shook her head. Her sister must be forgiven. She had never quite lived in the world as it existed. She occupied a middle field, where fog obscured everything but desire and fear.

"Has this war made any impression on you at all?" Marta asked her sister. Her hands shook, and she tried to tear the plastic in two. She tried and failed. "Why would you give me this thing? It's the symbol of our torture and horror and rape. Do you think that there is a cross on my son's grave?"

Dubravka's good eye widened.

"Oh God no!" she cried. "It doesn't mean that. It's not religious at all. It's your American. He gave it to Branko for some reason."

"Arthur?" Marta was even more confused. "This belongs to Arthur Cape?"

"I saw him in Metkovic," explained Dubravka. "I wrote him a letter and told him to get you out of Mostar, and he came."

The plastic containing the cross had become warm in Marta's hands.

"But I told him you were dead, so he went back to Berlin."

"You told him I was dead?" Marta felt a weakness in her body, as if she might fall.

Dubravka folded her arms around her sister, and for the first time in weeks, Marta rested in the comfort of family.

THE SMELL OF DINNER made its way into the room, and they followed it. They found seats on a bench at one end of a long wooden table, surrounded by other members of Gaby's technical-aid team: carpenters and plumbers, roofers and tilers, clerks and drivers—young men and women who had volunteered to rebuild Mostar, to clear away mountains of rubble, refit roofs, reimplant glass in windows. They smiled at their guests, as if they had no opinion on any subject at hand. Some of the team helped local women bring food and plates to the table.

It was a German *Abendbrot,* a ritual that had once been part of Marta's daily existence. There were spreadwursts in bright red wrappings, mettwurst, leberwurst, edelwurst; tiny triangular cheeses in silver wrappings, tubs of butter and dickmilch; plates of meat, bologna, salami, parma ham; baskets of black and brown bread. Marta admired these wonders but kept her hands in her lap and stared at the darkness gathering among the forklifts. She fought her rage and her confusion. That swine Branko had hit her sister again. And then he had let her come back to Mostar to die. Arthur had come and gone, bearing, of all things, of all horrific tokens, a cross.

The members of the team spooned Dr. Oetker yogurt and muesli into their mouths. They pointed Camel cigarettes at steam rising from Jakobs Kröne coffee, as if they sat in a student mensa in Berlin, as if none of the things before them had ever vanished from the face of the earth. Marta smelled chamomile tea, and the scent became a taunt. She closed her eyes.

Individual members of the team began to rise. Forklifts hummed back into motion. Nightfall did not put a stop to the work. Through open doors came pine planks, red ceramic tile, window frames. Truck engines revved. Mose spoke in hushed tones with Dubravka. Gaby shooed everyone else away from Marta and offered to give a guided tour, and Marta nodded, though she wanted to go home and crawl into her bed. The team wasn't functioning at capacity yet, Gaby said. They lacked the raw materials. Fighting had destroyed the local construction businesses, so the wood had to come all the way from Hungary.

"By the way," said Gaby, "you'll never guess who I'm using now as a middleman for my timber. George Markovic!"

Marta barely heard the name. Gaby steered Marta back toward the dinner table and handed her a stack of papers. Marta didn't ask her what the papers signified. Gaby pointed out the sections requiring information and signature.

"You can start tomorrow, if you want."

Marta thought that she must be lost in a dream. Old friends appeared. Lovers hovered. Her sister had returned. German wurst and salaried work landed in front of her.

"I need to go home now, Gaby," she said.

M OSE DROVE MARTA and Dubravka back to the bakery. He looked at them with perplexity. He's well rid of us, thought Marta.

The sisters got out, and the jeep sped away. Marta led the way into the bakery, stumbling over the sandbag before she could find and light a candle. Dubravka took one look at the place and sighed. She could have gone to Zagreb. She could have found a man in any city in Europe. But she came back here, thought Marta, and now she understands the depth of her error. Marta gave her a United Nations blanket and gestured to her pallet beneath the bread oven. They would have to share a bed for the first time since girlhood. She offered tea. Dubravka curled up in the blankets, and before long, she snored. Marta was glad for the peace and quiet, glad not to have to share the silence. I'm a mean old *strega,* she thought.

She ate cold rice with Dr. Oetker whole-wheat bread and marmalade, gifts from Gaby. She washed down her meal guiltily with a cup of the tea and gave some bread to the family that had moved into the remains of the sweetshop next door. They were pitifully grateful.

By the light of the candle beside her mattress, for the first time in years, Marta performed what she remembered of her breathing exercises. Rain rasped at the gash in the roof above, a brief valley storm. She concentrated on the exercise, wishing that she had learned proper yoga, but she'd never gotten that far in the Ayurveda class at Schöneberg Community College. There had never been time. The effort gave her a respite. The storm inside dwindled.

She crossed her legs and exhaled a long stream of air, a snake length of damp. She inhaled smoke, benzine fumes, and river fog, and thought of the Kamenita Vrata. An hour passed. She slowed her breathing, and her head became heavy. She heard distant shouts and the sobs of a woman who seemed to be giving birth. Nothing shook her concentration. She followed a trail. Her breath came and went like the river, and as the night deepened, she attained a rhythm with it. The Neretva spilled into her senses. She smelled and felt and tasted the river. In the middle of this trance, which felt like a triumph of the utmost clarity, her sister's voice intruded.

"I forgot to tell you something."

Marta opened her eyes. In candlelight, draped in blankets, Dubravka leaned against the sandbag.

"I gave your dog to the American. I didn't know what else to do."

Marta continued her breathing exercises, inhaling, exhaling. She closed her eyes, and a sweet blackness bloomed inside of her. God is great, she thought. Arthur Cape had her dog.

TWENTY-FOUR

A RTHUR NEVER SAID a word to anyone about his encounter
with Dubravka. When friends asked about his new dog, he
said that she was a stray. He had found her near death in a
destroyed village in the Balkans and nursed her back to health. Not
even Anna knew the truth about the animal. If she had suspicions,
she never let on. She never again spoke of the letter, or George
Markovic, or Marta Mehmedovic. If Arthur even hinted at these subjects, fear lit her eyes.

Arthur tried to change his life. He became a vegetarian, living on
buttermilk, wine, celery sticks, and hard rolls, a diet manufactured in
his darkest nightmares. He attempted and failed at breathing exercises. He worked hard to come up with new stories. He slept poorly.

The world became strange. Bizarre phenomena occurred. Several
of his paychecks, Express-Mailed by *Sense,* ended up in the hands of
the Bosnian refugees on the ground floor of his building. He didn't
know how it happened. The same delivery service had been bringing
the checks for months. The couriers knew where he lived. And yet
the checks landed with the Bosnians. Late at night, the refugees
slipped the mail under Frau Herbst's door.

The phone stopped ringing. No one from the magazine phoned late at night with a quick assignment. His last effort had not gone over well. Hampton sent desperate e-mails. "Ten thousand words on Heidegger! Are you mad?"

Arthur tried to make amends. He took a train to Budapest to work up a pitch about post–Cold War depression, hoping to leave his nightmare life behind for a few days. He did a few interviews but lost his train of thought. The nightmare followed him. He purchased a double cheeseburger and french fries in a newly opened American fast-food chain. Bag in hand, he went to see an American movie in the original English-language version with subtitles. The movie started, but it wasn't the one that had been advertised in the newspaper. He watched a seven-hour, black-and-white Hungarian film without subtitles, bells tolling, dogs scavenging, leaves blowing, wind sighing, children murdering cats and drinking rat poison. The cheeseburger dropped to his feet. Afterward, he refused to get into a taxi. He roamed the streets of Budapest, but couldn't get back to his hotel. He didn't know the city at all. When he came, at last, to a familiar public square, a tall man in a T-shirt screamed at him through a megaphone, saying, in English, accompanied by a Hungarian interpreter, "Plato is *dead,* Voltaire is *dead,* Karl Marx is *dead* . . ."

Some time later, Arthur ended up in his bed, stripped of his clothes. He didn't know how he had gotten there. Terrified at what was happening to him, he called his sister.

"I'm coming to Berlin as soon as possible," she said. "Late July. Can you hang in there?"

That was a month away, but he said that he could.

THE HEAT WAVE began after Seven Sleepers in late June, ocean swells of high temperature enveloping the city. Berliners had no air conditioning, so at night they fled their apartments and camped in cafés on the streets, drinking *pils,* arguing politics, listening to the

World Cup wrap-up on the radio through hours unruffled by breezes. After dark, the dog would start to pant and whine, and Arthur would take her water bowl into the bathroom and refill it. Thanks to the war, according to her German veterinarian, she had become a psychogenic water drinker, meaning that she had a psychological need to drink more water than her body actually needed—a condition perhaps related to a period of profound thirst, the vet had speculated, though not necessarily. Then again, who could blame her for being a psychogenic water drinker in this heat? Arthur's left index finger traced the declivity running between the two lobes of the dog's skull. Her nostrils sniffed up into his hand. He couldn't remember her name, but it didn't matter. She was the one consoling force in his life. He preferred spending time with her to the company of other human beings, and she seemed to like him as well. She was a noble animal, and Arthur felt that their souls communed.

Meanwhile, he waited to be fired. Word would come any day. He had sent ideas to the various section editors, proposals about every aspect of German and Central European life, but Gavin Morsch's last message, dated early May, warned him to stop badgering his editors with trivia. He had to find stories with larger relevance to Americans. Hampton stopped e-mailing, but he sent warnings by regular mail. Foreign coverage was dissolving, eight to six to four pages per week. Coverage of the world would be totally erased, and Europe would be the first to go. The editors of *Sense* hated Europe, and they despised the Balkans. A secret memorandum was in circulation, Hampton said, in which the publisher of *Sense* revealed that he had always loathed continental coverage, except for a few sentimental favorites—swastikas, Communist spies, French actresses, German hygiene, and the comedy of Italian government. Now was the time to bury the rest in an unmarked grave. "Nothing but freelancers, as far as the eye can see," wrote Hampton. "Termination of the Berlin, London, and Paris bureaus. Liquidation! I never thought that I would see this day come. The Americans are turning their backs on the world, as if they bloody can!"

It wasn't paranoia. Hampton was right. Arthur could feel it. The ground had given way. The American occupation of conquered Germany had come to an end. The bases were closing. Commissaries were shutting down, no more Oreos for dollars in Berlin, surely a sign of doom. And with the retreat of the troops came a kind of relief. One needn't worry so much about the world anymore. It could take care of itself. No more dominoes would fall, except, inevitably, in the American direction. No more wars would need to be fought. History had ended, and with it, coverage. The stock market was on a rebound, though.

"The star chambers are meeting," Hampton concluded his most recent letter. "Both of our names are on the list."

A s PROMISED, Arthur's sister Philippa arrived in late July. She stepped out of her taxi at the corner of Apostel-Paulus and Akkazien. Arthur, Anna, and Günther applauded. They had been waiting for an hour at the curbside café. Arthur had been telling stories about Philippa, preparing his friends for his Texan sister, who spoke no German and knew little or nothing about Europe. They seemed indifferent. But as soon as Philippa smiled, Günther melted. He knocked over his chair in an attempt to reach her luggage.

Back in Texas, Philippa had never had much success with men. She was deemed too formidable in her opinions. Her religious commitment and her barbed sense of humor scared potential suitors. Günther saw none of this. He had never met a Texas girl, and this one hit him like one of the fabled comets. She stood six foot three with thick blond hair to her shoulders, bluebonnet eyes, and a tan. She was as big as her brother in her shoulders and hips. Günther declared a picnic. Before anyone could object, he was off and running to the gourmet Italian shop in search of treats.

Arthur made rudimentary introductions. "This is Anna."

"Girlfriend," said Anna.

"Sister," said Philippa. She wrinkled her nose.

Anna actually smiled. She gave Arthur a skeptical sideways glance. "You made her sound like a barbarian."

"Typical," said Philippa.

Günther returned with a basket full of food and drink, cream-hued Appenine mountain cheeses, prosciutto, peaches from Aix, Sicilian tomatoes smelling of sunlight, everything illuminated by bottles of prosecco, pale green glass reflecting the brilliance.

"Frau Herbst!" cried Arthur.

Dressed like an iris in willowy yellows, the old woman and her new Irish chauffeur Pat were just headed out for a day of shopping.

"This is my sister, Frau Herbst."

Philippa put on her best East Texas shine. Without consulting anyone, Günther invited Frau Herbst to come on the picnic, and she immediately accepted. She insisted that Pat drive everyone, and the chauffeur's mournful sigh made no difference.

"Somebody should ask Philippa if she wants to go on a picnic," said Anna.

"I love a picnic," she said, like the polite Southerner she was.

Günther told Pat to drive to Park Babelsberg. The grounds had once belonged to Prussian royalty, and later to the Communist state of East Germany, when it had been his mother's favorite spot for picnicking. Now it was just one more piece of united Germany, a lawn of green, neither East nor West.

They parked in a lot in the woods. Günther led the way down a gravel path. Arthur gave his arm to Frau Herbst. Anna and Philippa chatted and ambled. The chauffeur took the rear, gathering sticks along the way to throw to the dog.

A castle loomed ahead. Günther pointed to turrets rising above the heads of chestnuts. The grounds of the castle fell gently to the shore of the Wannsee Lake, still and blue at that hour of the day.

Anna laid the picnic on turf a few feet from the water. Günther asked Philippa to admire the view. Half a kilometer away, right in front of them, between two banks, a road ran over a bridge.

Günther pointed at the span.

"The Glienecke Bridge. You know what it was once used for?"

"No idea."

"Trading spies. That was East. And that was West. And the two powers would exchange their prisoners across the bridge."

"That's fascinating, Günther."

"Now you know what is it used for?"

She shrugged.

"Nothing. And that is very beautiful. Like you."

Philippa blushed. Günther became bashful and hurried back to geopolitics.

"Sometimes I wonder what it all meant, the division of the city," he said. "If you walk around it now, it's beginning to feel normal, the two cities into one, as if the one city is growing up like weeds, you know, through cracks. Maybe it was always there, and we just couldn't see it."

"Couldn't see what?"

"The one city within the two cities. It was always there, a healed Berlin. No wall. No tanks. No guns. It had to be, yes? But it was trapped inside, this other city. Like a bug in a cocoon."

Arthur listened and thought of Hampton—cities revolving within cities, constantly arising and collapsing, the healthy giving way to the sick, the sick returning to health. And the people were like the cities, containing their own deaths, and within their deaths, other lives, unexpected, as shocking as the fact of mortality. Things looked fixed, but they never stopped moving.

THE CHAUFFEUR SHUCKED his coat and hurled sticks for the dog. Arthur skipped a stone across the water, and Anna made a face at him. She looked wonderfully well, he thought. All of a sudden, he was feeling better. What had changed? Was it his sister? The dog chased sticks into the water. Anna arranged the food in pleasing ways. Arthur stuck prosecco bottles in the mud for chilling. Frau Herbst propped herself up on pillows beneath a bright yellow beach umbrella.

"Why are the historic buildings of Berlin so ugly?" she asked. "I would be happy if that Bulgarian would wrap all of them and take them away."

"He's had enough problems trying to wrap just the one!" snapped Anna.

She was sensitive on the subject of Bulgarians and wrapped buildings. Her new job at a respected Berlin public relations firm involved promoting the idea of a highly touted, very controversial, and very time-consuming art project, the wrapping of the German Reichstag. Parliament had voted to allow a Bulgarian artist to cover every inch of the historic building in a polypropylene fabric.

Frau Herbst looked exasperated. "Can you explain something to me? Why does he have to be Bulgarian?"

Anna went red in the cheeks, but she practiced an admirable restraint. She laid plates, sorted napkins, discovering that Günther had neglected to bring adequate silverware. The clouds dissolved, and the sky became a silver slant, the brightness of the edge of a knife. Anna gave up. She pulled off her jeans and T-shirt and waded into the water after the dog, who whined and wheezed in her pursuit of sticks.

"You'd never know, would you?" Günther had a hand on Philippa's elbow, and she didn't seem to mind. "You really wouldn't, Philippa. This animal has been through so much. You should have seen her when Arthur brought her home from the Balkans. Disgusting. Death incarnated."

Philippa grinned at him. "What do you do for a living, Günther?"

"My problem is that I don't care for Berliners anymore," Frau Herbst moaned from beneath her umbrella. She spoke loudly, for the benefit of others. "They are vulgar, pitiful people. They have turned my Kempinski into a whorehouse."

Anna reappeared like a water nymph, breasts and hips dripping the waters of the Wannsee.

Arthur had one of those moments of utter clarity, when memory came to him in an undiluted state, like water in a mountain stream. He remembered his first night with Anna. After Marta left him, he had found Anna's phone number and called. Her boyfriend was out of town, and they went dancing till dawn at a club called Tresor. Afterward, he peeled off her wet T-shirt, and they made love in her kitchen, early spring rain thumping against the windowpanes. Even now, on a bright summer day, he could hear the sound of that rain.

Philippa grabbed Arthur by the hand. "I haven't even been here a day, and already people are taking off their clothes in public. No wonder you're getting overwrought, Arthur."

Günther sensed a tremor of excitement in the air and blushed like a schoolboy. Anna put on her clothes and started to organize the picnic in earnest. Arthur strolled down the bank with Philippa, and they had their first real chance to talk.

His sister put her arms around him and gave him a helpful squeeze. "Now what's all this about?" she asked him. "What's gotten into the great adventurer?"

Arthur spoke for the first time, to anyone, about Marta's death.

"My God, Arthur. Does Anna know?"

"I don't want her to."

She gave him a hug. "Life finally caught up with you, I guess."

"With a vengeance. I don't know what to do with myself."

She patted him on the cheek. "Stay cool, little brother. That's the trick now."

THEY RETURNED to the picnic. The prosciutto and peaches were already gone, thanks to Pat and Günther, but the alcohol hadn't been touched. The heat of the day intensified. Prosecco bottles came sucking out of the mud, one after another, until every last drop had disappeared. Tongues started to fly. Günther lapsed into a slurred Denglish, every other word in Anglo-Saxon or Deutsch. The chauffeur snored. Arthur became drunk and sunburned and told everyone the story of his pocket cross and the customs agent at the East Berlin airport. Most of the people at the picnic had never heard the story before. Even the dog seemed to be listening.

"Can I see it, Arthur?" his sister asked.

Arthur emptied the wallet. A faint breeze scattered business cards, receipts, and cash across the grass, and Arthur snatched at them. Then he stopped and put a hand to his head. The business cards fluttered. The dog sniffed a yellow receipt. Arthur knew where it was.

"Shit," he said aloud. Vela had the cross. He'd kept it.

The chauffeur slept on, but the pleasing torpor of the afternoon had shattered, as if a shot had been fired. Unspoken names lay on the air. Arthur grew nauseous and stumbled to the edge of the lake. His sister put her hands on his shoulders, and he vomited into the Wannsee. Anna crossed her arms, watching with new suspicion.

TWENTY-FIVE

AT LAST, Arthur received a story assignment. The eastern German state of Thuringia would open the subterranean city of the Mittelwerk to a few select visitors. He was among them. The city, once the hub of Hitler's V-2 rocket program, lay beneath a mountain, on the edge of a potash mine. No civilian had been inside since 1945.

Herr Werder of the Thuringian Culture Ministry, a blunt-shouldered, round-cheeked man with real candor in his face, parked his golf cart beside a curtain of black industrial rubber. Behind the rubber lay a pair of rusting metal doors attached by hinges to living rock. Arthur and Philippa exchanged glances. She had begged to come. Herr Werder handed out heavy-duty, rectangular flashlights and asked his guests, as a precaution, to shine their beams.

"In here"—Herr Werder gestured with his keys at the black rubber curtain—"is an entire city." He waited for Arthur to translate the sentence for Philippa. "But work in this city stopped in 1945, and in 1947, when the Russians dynamited the entrances, everything fell into darkness. There is no electricity, and no light. There are slave laborers buried in the walls. Please be respectful."

"I'm having second thoughts," whispered Philippa.

"Too late," Arthur whispered back.

"There are forty-seven discreet chambers in the Mittelwerk," explained Herr Werder, "and as many as seventy-five rockets in varying phases of decay and disrepair. We will see only a few."

He unlocked the metal doors embedded in the rock of the mountain and clicked on his flashlight. Arthur saw, at his feet, beer cans and crumpled cigarette packs.

"This part was a smoking area for the miners," said the guide.

The doors closed behind them, and the electric light blinked out. The flashlight beams thinned into nothingness. We have left time behind, thought Arthur. We have slipped through a crack in the chronology. They began to walk behind Herr Werder, their feet crunching on shattered rock. Arthur heard Herr Werder's breath, pulsing ahead, almost embarrassing in its intimacy, Philippa's from behind, in biological rhythm. They marched through a series of darknesses. They crunched on rock. Arthur began to feel space expanding around him, thistles of cold air here and there. The Mittelwerk seemed empty, but undead. There was life in the darkness, a tension in the stillness, like the great live silence of the Rio Grande gorge. He kept his flashlight on the ground in front of him, as Herr Werder had instructed.

After a long journey, their guide raised his beam. "Hall Twenty-four," he said.

Philippa gasped. They had walked to the edge of a vast wrecked laboratory. Entrails of equipment littered the floor: rusting, dumped file-cabinet drawers, heating coils, tortured cable, spilled pipe. There were chairs and tables, dollies and pullies. Public address speakers drooped like stalactites from the ceilings, wide arches receding in the dusk. Herr Werder picked through crap at his feet. Arthur reached down and picked up a damp, flat, blackened tongue of material. The darkness wanted to tell him something.

Herr Werder shone a light on the object in his hand.

"Shoe," he said.

"Lord," said Philippa. "How horrible."

Herr Werder studied something else on the ground.

"Cup." He lifted a dented metal drinking cup.

"You know what's funny about this place?" Arthur felt as if he were talking to himself. "It feels as if it's as ancient as the mountain, but it's younger than our grandfathers. It reminds me of something, but I can't think what."

"It reminds me of hell," said Philippa.

"Feels like the back entrance," said Arthur.

Herr Werder wanted to show them Twenty-one. "If you like Twenty-four," he said, "you will be amazed by Twenty-one."

They crunched down a slope and through a passage with a low ceiling. Arthur began to feel the weight of the earth bearing down on him. He banged his head.

"Over here." Herr Werder was beckoning. The ceiling rose again. Their guide pointed his beam down. At his feet glowed a pool of malachite green, as if a giant eye had opened in the ground.

"See down there," said Herr Werder. Within the eye, submerged at a depth of some feet, lay the silvery remains of a rocket thruster, a round metal ring lying beneath a line of glistening scum, in a mouth in the earth. Arthur knelt over the pool, his nose a few inches from the water's surface. He could not take his eyes away. He was looking down through time into the uttermost end of things. He knew it. From the beginning of his life, he had yearned to see into the secret heart of the world, and here it was. In the thruster of the rocket, manufactured half a century ago to destroy the cities of Great Britain, Arthur saw History and Time and Death, the living presence of these things unified and abandoned in the darkness, where no one else could discover or comprehend them. The complexity of existence collapsed into a single bright point. He could see Marta down there. He could see her city, its life and death; and their city, Berlin. His thoughts became clear. The waters held a message. There was not one city. There were not two. The cities of man were infinite, blooming, burning, collapsing, dying.

Herr Werder pointed again with his beam. Philippa took Arthur by the collar and turned him away from the pool, which dissolved into darkness as quickly as it had emerged. Ahead rose the fuselage and nose of a toppled V-2 rocket, sunk to its midriff in water, unapproachable but intact. Had a wartime shock knocked the rocket to one side? Had long years of settling done it? Had the water? Herr Werder didn't know. To Arthur, the rocket seemed to have been waiting decades for this moment, to convey itself—its message—to him, lying beneath his mind like the city beneath the mountain.

"I want to get the hell out of here," said Philippa.

BACK AT THE HOTEL, in the city of Nordhausen, Arthur ordered potatoes and sauerkraut. His sister had the Thuringian sausages.

"Can you imagine dying in a place like that?" Philippa asked him.

Arthur shook his head. He didn't want to think about it. He didn't particularly want to write about it.

Philippa put down her fork and took a swallow of beer. "What's the matter with you? You haven't said a word since the mountain. It's creeping me out."

Arthur stared out the window of the restaurant into the windows of a war-destroyed, reconstructed medieval German *rathaus.*

"That kind of thing shakes my faith, I have to admit," she said. "Not the thing itself, but what it suggests. I admit it. You wonder about the existence of God when you see a thing like that."

Arthur said, "Maybe I'm going to die soon."

Philippa wrinkled her brow and looked at him with growing concern. She had collected a few specimens of mountain gypsum for their geologist father. The specimens sat on the top of the table beside the platter of sausages.

Arthur put his elbows on the table and clasped his hands over his meal, which sat untouched.

"I am no longer afraid of death, Philippa."

She had started to cut one of her potatoes open, but his words stopped her. She put down her utensils.

"It only came to me down there," he said, "when there was nothing in the world between me and the absolute darkness of history."

Her eyes narrowed, and she paid attention, as if her sole purpose for coming to Germany had been to extract this confession.

"Something is happening to me," said Arthur.

She crossed her arms. The restaurant was closing. The *wirt* wanted them out. He slapped his washcloth against the top of the bar. Nine chimes rang in the belfry of the *rathaus* across the street, announcing the coming of closing time in a destitute place. The *wirt* opened the door of the restaurant and gestured with a hand at the brown coal evening, as if the interior of the mountain had flushed into the sky.

Arthur loved his sister, but she would never understand. He had crossed over the divide. He didn't know exactly how. He didn't know why. But somewhere in the mountain, Arthur had entered History. His sister stood on the opposite side of an impassable gulf, outside of time, apart from the past. She lived in an eternal Dallas, where the future was everything, and yesterday was nothing. It was a blessed realm, thought Arthur, that place where his sister sat, though he had never known it until now. It was a blessed state to live outside of history. She was beloved of God.

TWENTY-SIX

DUBRAVKA BURST into Marta's cubicle at the technical-aid office and began to scream. Her clothes had been torn, and her arms were bleeding. She broke into sobs. Something had happened, but Dubravka wouldn't say what. For a time, Marta held her, stroking her hair.

"Tell me, *draga*."

"Fuckers!" Dubravka sobbed in rage. "It's just motherfucking bread!"

Marta should have known better. Dubravka's second trip to the western bank of the Neretva had gone badly.

"Tell me what happened," she murmured into her sister's ear.

THE FIRST TRIP across the river had been such a success. Her sister had crossed the new bridge with a minimal shopping list and no real destination in mind. Once on the western side, she stayed on one or two main streets, strolling in idle curiosity. Not much could have gone wrong under those circumstances. Dubravka even purchased two or three of the items on Marta's list.

That was a test, and she had passed. But the second trip had been more important. The shopping list had been longer and had been written with a specific set of concerns in mind. Marta hadn't outlined those concerns, in order to avoid scaring her sister, but she made it clear that her shopping list must be the priority this time. The list called for basic supplies—candles, batteries, salt, sleeping bags—and she wanted quantities of them. Nothing on the list was incidental or superfluous. The goods could only be obtained in western shops, and so Dubravka would have to go once more over the river.

Dubravka asked why they needed so much of each item.

"Just in case."

Dubravka caught it. "In case of what?"

Marta hadn't wanted to answer. She wouldn't answer. But she had her reasons, a small bright flare at the edge of her consciousness, and Gaby, away in Budapest, hondling for construction materials, could not calm the anxiety. It haunted her in snatches of urgent, overheard conversation, in the nervousness of men loitering on the street, in exchanges of gunfire at night over the river. People were leaving the city, or they were disappearing from the streets, huddling back in their basements. Rumors spread. The new European Administrator of Mostar would be assassinated as soon as he set foot in Mostar. The western bank had new supplies of weapons and money. War would return, and this time, Europe would abandon East Mostar to its fate.

Marta refused to ignore the warning signs. She needed supplies. A makeshift metal bridge had replaced the Stari, and two hundred and fifty people per day had permission to cross it: women, children, and Mose. That was the rule. Some days, more were allowed. Other days, no one passed. The bridge was the one existing transit point between East and West, the single point of unification. One had to organize well for the crossing of it. One had to have a precise intention: where to go, what to do, and very important, when to be finished. Darkness on the western bank was to be avoided at all costs.

Marta had seen right away that her sister could not keep focus. Dubravka would waste time. She'd meet old boyfriends and insult their girlfriends. She'd see something in a window and go in the shop and try it on—they had new plate glass windows over there, Dubravka had reported in envy and awe after the last visit West. Under the best of circumstances, she would return with half of the list.

"Why don't you go with me?" Dubravka had reasonably asked.

"I work."

Marta had taken a job as interpreter for Gaby's reconstruction team, and she gave herself to it completely, leaving the bakery at dawn, returning long after dusk. The European Administrator would arrive soon, any day now, and the team had to have its house in order.

"I'm sorry, but that's how it is."

Thinking back, stroking her sister's hair, breathing words of comfort into her ear, Marta realized that she should have gone. Gaby would have given her the time. I was wrong, thought Marta, and a coward. But she had her reasons for staying on the eastern bank of the Neretva.

IN TRUTH, she was obsessed with crossing the river. She had been thinking about it for weeks, ever since the beginning of the cease-fire.

She had a plan. On her first trip to the West, she would not go shopping. She would not buy a single thing. She would head straight for West Mostar police headquarters. The authorities would be annoyed. But she would dress in Dubravka's one pair of nice stockings, her one pair of decent coral earrings and one fine blue dress, and she would address the police as if the war had never happened, as if one single injustice had been committed and nothing more but that injustice was howling and huge and would have to be set right. She would go right to the duty officer in charge and demand to know when the rubble of Alekse Santica 14 would be cleared so that she could retrieve her son and her father. They had been under the rocks for more than a year. It was irresponsible and barbaric. Would they allow their own loved ones to languish in this way? She was a mother. They had mothers. The mere thought of the conversation filled Marta with such rage that she had to stop whatever she was doing and bow her head. So she stayed on her side of the river and waited for the coming of the European Administrator.

I T   H A D   B E E N about bread. Rather than go to the bakery that the old Muslim women liked to use, the least hostile of the West Mostar bakeries, Dubravka had gone to her favorite, a place on the far side of the Café Rondo.

It had been a pleasant walk. She had been alone for most of it. Eyes watched her from behind windows, but that was to be expected. She passed the beautiful old linden trees with their roots gentling like molten wax into the pavement. On their trunks, she read the black-framed Catholic death notices, recognizing names and feeling, against her will, sorry for those people and their families. She even had the impulse, quickly stifled, to call on the bereaved and express her sorrow.

She came to the bakery and waited in line. From the first, she could tell that the people had known, more or less, who she was, what she was. She heard their thoughts in the silence of the shop. They didn't understand why she had to do business on their side of the river. *Their* side. Couldn't Muslims bake their own bread? Hadn't the international community supplied them with enough flour to bake bread for the entire valley?

Dubravka stepped up to the counter and asked, in a humble, unassuming tone, for *hljeb*.

The word for bread had always been *hljeb*, yes? No matter where one lived in the city, when one wanted bread one asked for *hljeb*. The shopgirl looked at her as if she had asked for shit. The baker had been working in the back. Now he stepped out, and Dubravka had the impulse to turn and run. But she held her ground.

Again, she asked for *hljeb*. This time the baker spoke. She had been coming to him for years. He knew her by sight. But his eyes became flints.

Kruh, he said. The word is *kruh.*

I say *hljeb,* she replied.

But we don't use that word anymore. That is your word. We sell *kruh.*

And here, Dubravka admitted, she made her mistake. She should have behaved better than those people. She should have taken her money and walked away. But the shop girl and the other customers had enjoyed her humiliation. They had made her look ignorant, or worse, crazy for using a mere word. They had made her feel filthy and stupid for the first time in all of the months of the war. Not even the bombardment had been able to do that, and Dubravka wanted revenge. The words pushed at her mouth, and she wanted to say them. Did they know who her friends were? Did they know that she had once been with the man that they all revered?

If *Branko* knew what you were doing here, she blurted out, *he* would torch the place.

The baker came out from behind the counter. You're threatening me, slut?

He took her by the elbow and led her to the door of his business. She jerked her elbow away, shaking in rage.

When he finds out, she screamed at the baker, you are a dead man.

"Oh Dubravka." Marta put her head into her hands. "Oh my God."

Dubravka ran. Never had she moved so fast. She tripped over a root and skinned her knees. The baker had come out. She could see him behind her, fat and red. He was speaking with a cop who happened to be passing by. He was telling the cop and pointing.

She got to her feet. She tore the death notices from the trees. How had she ever felt compassion for these animals? It was *hljeb*. It had always been *hljeb*.

Then she saw it, the silver Mercedes van sitting in front of the building that had once been the Café Rondo. The silver Mercedes van with the tinted black windows had been parked there all along, and she knew that Branko was inside, in the front seat, and that he had watched her go down the street to the bakery and was watching her even now as she staggered for dear life back to her side of the river. Branko Velakovic, General Vela, the *Jefe*, Vanisher, Angel of Death, her ex-boyfriend.

Marta had heard enough. It was bad. It could not have been worse, in fact.

Someone over there would now focus on the name of Mehmedovic, on the sisters. *Idiot,* she wanted to say, how in God's name could you stand there and invoke his name, of all names, when you know that he would be more inclined to put a bullet in your brain than help you? But she kept her thoughts to herself. Her sister needed to drink something. She needed to lie down and sleep. *Hljeb* was the word for bread. She shouldn't worry. She had been right. The baker had been wrong.

THE NEXT MORNING, Dubravka left the shelter early, and Marta had the place to herself. She heard the noise of the crackling fire in the sweetshop next door. A family of refugees from Stolac had moved into the space. One of the daughters was pregnant. A husband was missing. The mother scavenged, sewed, cooked. Her father and his two sons prayed five times a day, and when the father went for coffee in the evenings, his progeny peered at Dubravka and Marta through the cracked stones, brown-eyed boys in white skullcaps. The mother of the family had noticed Marta without a headscarf and had offered one, her sister's, no longer of use, green and pink, with a lotus-flower motif on the trim. Marta took it out of politeness and put it away.

On her way to work, Marta passed a homemade mosque in a shelter. A stereo system played the muezzin's call to prayer. Men bowed eastward onto mats, touching their heads to the ground. They washed their heads and feet in buckets of river water. These men knew something, she thought. They were praying for a reason. There would be another war.

In the office, forklifts hummed. Marta had a tea and waited for Gaby, who was supposed to return any moment from Budapest.

Gaby came. She had met with George Markovic, and he had asked about Marta.

"He has some news, but he wouldn't tell me. He was being cagy."

"This makes me nervous. What news could it be?"

"Who knows? He was pretty mysterious. I wouldn't give it too much thought."

But Marta did. The cross inside the plastic hung on a string around her neck, and she wondered if the news might have something to do with it. George knew Arthur. George had introduced her to Arthur.

"How is George?" she asked, hoping to glean more information.

"He wears a suit and a tie."

Marta laughed. "I don't believe you."

"It's true. So help me God."

"Does he ever mention Berlin?"

Gaby picked up a can of Coca-Cola, her eyes sparkling.

"Not to me."

B REAK CAME, and the team assembled at the dining table with the benches. Gaby made a surprise announcement. Everyone could have the rest of the day off. Around noon, the European Administrator would arrive. He would take a symbolic stroll across the

makeshift bridge over the remains of the Stari. She invited everyone
to come along.

"He's a German we can all be proud of," she concluded. "He makes
me proud, and I hate Germans."

A German was going to run Mostar, a western German and former
mayor of Berlin! For the first time in years, she would be living in a city
run by people who knew what they were doing. She would be in the
care of rational human beings, and the insane Balkan business would be
settled. She would go to this man, Hans Kreischler was his name, and
she would speak to him in his language, and within days, if not hours,
the trucks would rumble into the Alekse Santica street, and her son
would be restored to her.

She hid her face from the others. These wild thoughts of hope
filled her mind, and she was ashamed.

On their way to the bridge, Gaby explained how the new government would work. Kreischler would rule Mostar by decree, like a
pasha. He would sit with absolute power in his headquarters at a
hotel on the western side of the river, the Hotel Ero, right up against
the Demilitarized Zone, and the mayors of the two sides of the city
would come to him, and together they would go down the list of the
things that had to be done. Kreischler would say that they must bring
electricity back to the eastern side of the city, and there would be
some haggling, some horse trading, the Bosnian way, but it would be
done. He would say that they must reinstate the running-water supply, and it would be done. No one would be allowed to leave the table
in anger. Everyone had to talk. They would talk, smoke, and talk
some more. If someone misbehaved, Kreischler would know about it
immediately.

Under him, there would be an administration chosen from across
Western Europe—from France, the Netherlands, Ireland, Great Britain,
Sweden, Denmark, Italy, Spain. Engineers would rebuild the bridges.
Reconstruction teams would rebuild the town. There would be doc-
tors. There would be cops. Of course the cops would not be allowed

to carry firearms and would not have the authority to arrest anyone, but they would be a symbol of a unified city police force until the two sides came up with their own.

"Think of Mostar as Noah's Ark," Gaby said. "The rest of Bosnia sinks, and we float."

At last, Kreischler came, moving with a sly smile before and above the two mayors of Mostar, and Marta was surprised to see how big he was, over six feet tall, with a wonderful overhanging belly, like her father's, the belly of a man who enjoyed life. But he wasn't soft. How could he be? He had run West Berlin in the 1970s, when it was a hard city, a city of students, draft dodgers, occupation soldiers, and criminals. As he came forward, passing her, she saw him absorbing everything. She saw his will beyond the lenses of his glasses, and, she thought, he saw her.

Hassan, they came to call him in the days that followed. Though a few of the Fascists on the other side gave him the Hitler salute, and talked like Nazis about the German rescue, awaited since the days of Ante Pavelic, Marta perceived the truth. Hans Kreischler was Europe. And Europe would not be defeated.

O NE AUGUST NIGHT, Mose Silber paid a visit to Marta. They had tea and talked about old times, but he had a purpose, as usual.

"Dubravka has been visiting West Mostar quite a bit," he said. "Do you know why?"

"You're mistaken." Marta shook her head. "She's terrified of West Mostar."

"I don't think so."

Marta could not hide her astonishment. "Are you sure?"

Dubravka's trips had been noticed by security details on both sides of the river. Unlike other women, she didn't carry groceries or letters or belongings. And every day, she went to a certain club owned and operated by the friends of Branko Velakovic. During her visits to this club, a familiar silver van usually made an appearance, and both the van and Dubravka stayed for hours.

"I assumed that you knew," Mose said. "That's why I'm here."

"I haven't seen her in a while," said Marta. "She's up before me, and back after I go to sleep. Now I know why."

Mose stared at Marta with unblinking eyes, and she thought about something. Dubravka knew Branko's secrets, what he had done, where he had done it, or so she said. Marta shuddered.

"Let me talk to her," she said.

T HE NEXT EVENING, when her sister turned up it was long after midnight. Marta confronted her. "You're going to get yourself killed," she said.

"You mean Branko." Dubravka slipped out of pink drawstring pants and a powder blue tank top. The clothes looked new. She pulled off pink socks and new sneakers. Her hair, uncut, swung past her ass. No other woman in East Mostar looked so nice. She had been cosseted and caressed as a refugee. Someone had made sure that her cuts and bruises mended and her belly never growled. Vela, thought Marta. He had given her shelter and then wanted her to pay for it.

"We're trying to be friends," she said, shivering, pulling on a warm T-shirt for sleeping.

Marta caught her sister by the arm. "You could get us both killed. You could start another war."

"That's a bit much." Dubravka reached for the string around Marta's neck, the piece of plastic dangling from it. "Look at your lovely piece of jewelry." She lifted the string until the cross appeared. "Better not let your Muslim neighbors see. They'll plant you in the ground and throw rocks at your head."

Marta jerked the string from her sister's fingers and let the card drop back down against her chest.

"It has no religious meaning at all."

"So you have your *amour fou,* and I have mine. What's the difference?"

Dubravka gathered blankets around her. Marta sat on the sandbag and tried to speak without anger to her sister. It took an effort. "Make me understand."

Dubravka lowered her eyes, musing. "Did you know that Branko's father committed suicide when he was eight years old?"

Marta recoiled. She hadn't known but found she didn't care. Not every child of a suicide chose massacre as a form of recovery. Most didn't. But she didn't say it. She listened.

"He had to take care of his raving, drunken mother, who despised him. They were poor. You have this idea about him, but he's really very brave—"

"He's a murderer."

"He is the only person on earth who ever truly loved me."

"If you believe that," Marta told her sister, "then you are damned."

Dubravka's face hardened. She stared back defiantly. "Happy with your new German friend?"

"*My* friend?"

"He favors Muslims," said Dubravka. "That's what everyone says."

"You are a Muslim."

Dubravka leaned forward, and her voice faded to a dry scratch. "I know something."

"What do you know?"

"Something about Branko," she said.

"What is it, Dubravka? You better tell me."

Her sister became grim. For the first time, the magnitude of her situation seemed to occur to her. "He's going to get rid of the German."

Marta put a hand over her sister's mouth. She blew out the candles in the bakery.

"We're going to the police," she whispered.

TWENTY-SEVEN

THE EUROPEANS BUILT a new bridge across the Neretva, and they called this bridge the Pioneer. It was the first of the city's seven spans to be rebuilt, and Hans Kreischler presided over the christening. He stood at the top of the river's steep bank, above the rush of waters, and announced the start of a new era in the life of the city. No one tried to kill him. It was mid-September.

Late on the night of the christening, Marta sat at a table for six in the restaurant of the Hotel Ero, interpreting a conversation between Kreischler and the mayor of East Mostar. She had landed the job at the last minute, and nervousness made her throat itch.

Seven people sat at the table, five men and two women, and the men were arguing about travel plans. The words flew fast. Her responsibility was the East Mostar mayor, and he did not speak a great deal. Across the table sat the mayor of West Mostar and his interpreter, a Croat woman about ten years older than Marta, who had dressed as if she'd been invited to a Viennese cocktail party. She had introduced herself by telling everyone at the table that when she visited Chicago, U.S.A., she stayed with the vice president of Sears Roebuck. She had vacationed on Lake Michigan with the vice president of Sears Roebuck. No one had asked the woman to identify Sears Roebuck, and Marta had felt stupid for not knowing what it was, but she did not pretend, and the woman had sniffed out her ignorance and now sneered.

The East Mostar mayor spoke, and Marta's tonsils tickled. "No one can decide but you, Hassan, but, *bitte sehr,* here is my opinion."

Kreischler's eyes gleamed in pouches beyond his spectacles. He smoked a thin brown stub of cigarette, the end of which pointed up from his lower lip toward his nostrils.

"You must not go to Sarajevo tomorrow."

Marta scribbled his words on a notepad on the table in front of her. The mayor of East Mostar stopped and waited. She cleared her throat. German jumped out of her mouth. With every word she improved, but she would have liked more time to hone her skill—her one undeniable skill—before performing in front of this particular audience. She used the words on the notepad, a flawed technique, similar to delivering a speech with the script in one's hands. As she gained confidence, she lifted her eyes and plugged into Kreischler with her full concentration, and he received her words, she believed, as if they had come straight from the mouth of the East Mostar mayor.

"No helicopter?" Kreischler asked.

"We are not going to get a helicopter. That is clear. UNPROFOR says we are a priority, but *bitte sehr,* Hassan. This is a fiction."

Kreischler nodded. He took the glasses off his face and rubbed his heavy-lidded eyes.

"What else?'

"The Igman road is too great a risk. This we know. The Serbs will not grant you passage on such short notice, and they are fully capable of firing on you if you defy them. Mr. Izetbegovic must understand. We cannot put you in danger. We cannot afford to put this"—the East Mostar mayor gestured at the room with his hands, but meant the nebulous presence of power—"*this* at risk."

Kreischler raised a hand, as if to dampen an unseemly compliment. The mayor came to an abrupt stop and nodded to Marta. She indicated to everyone that he was finished. Scorn played on the lips of her West Mostar counterpart. Or perhaps she had applied too much lipstick.

"Nothing to add," she said. "We wouldn't dream of telling you what to do, and anyway, you wouldn't listen."

It was not clear whether the West Mostar mayor had meant his comments in this way. Kreischler thanked the East Mostar mayor for his advice. He turned to Marta.

"You are an excellent interpreter, *gnädige Frau*. What is your name?"

"Marta Mehmedovic."

"My compliments on your German, Frau Mehmedovic. Outstanding. Really."

The East Mostar mayor looked at his watch and begged to be excused. Kreischler shook his hand.

"But if Frau Mehmedovic can stay a while longer, I would be grateful," the German said, "in case Ms. Ruzic cares to take a break at some point."

Marta tried not to blush. She was proud of herself. That evening, the regular interpreter had called in sick, and the Administrator's offices had scrambled in search of a replacement. It was not uncommon. Such emergencies cropped up, but Marta had never before been called. This time, she got lucky. Gaby had been at the Ero, and when she overheard the discussion about the sick interpreter, she offered Marta without hesitation.

"I'll sit in the bar," Marta informed the press flack for the Administration, a Russian lent to Kreischler by the United Nations.

The bar looked desolate, a surprise to Marta. According to Dubravka, people flocked to the Hotel Ero. The hotel restaurant was an Italian café transplanted from Rome. But on this particular evening most of the tables were empty. The EU policemen and their girlfriends had gone home. There were a couple of men who might have been journalists, and Marta saw a lone European monitor, one of the white-uniformed *sladoledari,* the ice cream men, as they were called. Over a glass of port, he perused a topographical map. The ice cream men supposedly monitored the fighting and the peace, like referees of a British sport, but the exact nature of their work puzzled Marta. One of them, a man named Murray, had a reputation for making delicious paella. Another had just been reported missing in the karst. Between these two pieces of information lay the mystery of their actual role.

She ordered Orangina. The headwaiter counted rolls of hard currency. His subordinate joylessly accommodated Marta's request. The bottle of Orangina smacked down hard on the Formica tabletop. She pulled a stack of old German and English magazines out of her purse. Gaby had gathered them from visitors to her program and on her travels through Western European airports. On the cover of *Stern,* for a story on the ozone layer, a naked blond Aryan girl stood in a field of sunflowers, her fair skin baking in the perilous ultraviolet; no signs of irradiation, thought Marta, unless you counted the bright red nipples. At the bottom of the stack, she came across a copy of *Sense.* She stopped a moment, touching the wrinkled cover. It was the face of a man in a coat and tie. Had Gaby known? Excitement stung Marta's brain. She leafed through the pages, scanning for the byline, and there it was— Arthur J. Cape—beneath the headline "Ghosts Alive Beneath Rocket Mountain." She read, "Officially, the tour took three hours, but the clocks stopped as soon as we entered Kohnstein mountain. The light died. The words failed. Only the rockets seemed to breathe."

In the restaurant, the silence deepened. Marta finished the article and looked through the front windows for signs of life. Two United Nations jeeps had been out front. Now they were gone. Dim, almost out of sight, sat an armored personnel carrier. She had seen it earlier, on her way into the Ero, a machine with the personality of an abused zoo animal, chipped, scored, dented, and dumb. Marta couldn't see the helmet of its driver.

She craned her neck around. The journalists were leaving. The ice cream man folded his map. Something was wrong. The tables and chairs of the Ero restaurant shivered. For an instant, she thought that she might be getting faint. She saw a look of terror on the face of the headwaiter, and her instincts flared. She threw herself to the floor.

UN troops thundered for the back of the hotel, toward the offices of the European Administration. Other men bounded out of shadows, Croat police in gray dress and black jackboots; they had been invisible before. A handful of European cops showed up, their hair mussed, as if they had just crawled out of someone else's bed.

The shivering of the tables had stopped. Marta rose and ran to the table where Kreischler had been. She found the butts of smoldering cigarettes. Fear grew in her mind. All of a sudden, she did not want to be on this side of the river after dark. She had no idea who would escort her home. No one paid any attention to her, though more and more people were entering the Ero. There were no obvious signs of an attack, no fire or broken glass or broken masonry, but an attack had occurred. She was sure.

She found a spot in a chair between potted ferns. Eventually, late into the night, a Spanish soldier told her the news. Kreischler's rooms on the second floor of the hotel had been destroyed. A rocket launcher had fired grenades through his windows. Since then, Kreischler had not been seen. She thanked the soldier, and he went on his way. She heard wild rumors. European staff would be evacuated. Tanks had been seen on western roads.

She fell asleep in the chair between the ferns and dreamed of Arthur Cape, lost beneath dark, haunted mountains.

In the morning, Mose took her home in his jeep. He was dressed in his usual tweed coat, a rumpled mass over white shirt and blue jeans. He did not bother with pleasantries.

"Your sister is in terrible danger," he told her. "Did you know that?"

Marta knew. After going to the police, Marta and Dubravka had parted ways. It had been over a month ago. "The cops told me that she would be protected."

He gave her an odd sideways glance. "That was before."

She hesitated to speak. Her words always had consequences. He pulled into the parking lot of the train station, where they could talk without being overheard. Men loitered in the ruins. After going to the East Mostar police, Dubravka had been sequestered. She had been given bodyguards, and her whereabouts lay beyond a wall of deep secrecy. Branko's spies had been in East Mostar, asking questions. The great General Vela was nervous. He had moved too fast to get rid of the German.

"What is it exactly that the police know?" Marta asked.

Mose's eyes gleamed with doubt, but he relented. He put a hand on Marta's shoulder and spoke into her ear. "Your sister eavesdropped on a meeting." The veins at his temples coiled out. "They thought she was asleep. The door was cracked. She puts Branko in the assassination attempt. She's identified four other men at the meeting."

Marta understood with a chill that her sister's life would be worth nothing now. Branko Velakovic had been officially designated a war criminal. His paramilitaries stood accused of massacre before and after the cease-fire. There were extensive charges of rape and theft. His men had blown up mosques and burned entire villages. There were numbers of witnesses, all of whom had referred to Branko as General Vela, but they had not stepped forward. They were afraid for their lives. Dubravka alone had given information. She alone had been brave or stupid or vain enough to name Vela. He had insulted her once too often, and then she'd discovered her conscience.

"She will die if she persists," said Mose.

For a moment, Marta studied her father's friend. She wondered if he really operated alone, beyond the fences of the warring camps, as it appeared, or if he perhaps took orders from a higher authority. Both sides accused him of selling out, of working to obscure ends for the Israelis, the Germans, even the Americans. She had never believed these rumors. She thought there was a much simpler explanation for his extreme behavior, for his relentless shuttling between the guns: Mose had lost his mind. She had seen the progression. The initial attack by the Serbs had made him angry, and he had fought like a regular soldier. But the second slaughter, the butchery of one half of the city by the other, had cut his soul in two. His family had gone to Israel. His friends had been executed. But he had stayed, moving here and there, gathering pieces up, gathering pieces of himself, as if they were shards of the one city, as if he could reconstruct Mostar within himself, and then return it to the valley of the Neretva intact. But it was the ambition of a madman. Anyone could see that Mostar would never be one city again. The ax of God had split it asunder. Mose didn't care. Mose no longer had rational convictions. He barely had a name. But he was a Jew, and the valley had saved his people long ago, when the last scourge had come, and now he would save the valley. He tended it like a garden or like his own grave. He would never leave.

"Give me your blessing," said Mose, "and I will get your sister out of here."

"She will never agree."

"I can convince her."

"No, Mose, you can't. She's doing this to spit in his eye. What's the use if she's not here to enjoy it. It's not my place to give a blessing."

The following week, four men were arrested for the attempt on Hans Kreischler's life. All came from West Mostar. All were known associates of Branko Velakovic's. Each had been named by Dubravka Mehmedovic.

I N   T H E   A U T U M N, on an October evening, Marta decided to go for a walk. She didn't speak. The night was bright. A round gold moon steamed above the mountain rims. Juniper and rosemary scented the air. Beyond a line of broken buildings, the river spluttered. She came to a mosque, the Karadjoz Bey, and knew that it wasn't an accident. This was her destination. She lingered awhile in the courtyard, beside the dry fountain, then went around one side and found her way into the graveyard. The mountain guns had tried to wipe out the Karadjoz Bey. They had decapitated its minaret and cleaved its dome. But the war had ended, and here it stood.

Marta put a leg over a wall and climbed into the graveyard. In the autumn, in Mostar, the pomegranates ripen on the branches. Most of the fruit had been picked, but one or two globes would still be hanging, hidden in the tall rank grass, shielded by the turbaned stones of the exemplary citizens of the Ottoman Empire. Her feet broke sticks, and an invisible creature stirred. She became stealthy, as if hunting.

A child was staring at her through the bars of the graveyard, a boy of five or six. He tipped his head at a pomegranate. There, to her right, hung one, tied off at the top. She pointed. The boy nodded and smiled. She reached into twigs and spiderwebs. No one had disturbed this corner of the cemetery in a while. Her fingers locked around the hard shell of the fruit. She gave a clean jerk, and the pomegranate snapped off the branch. The boy, who had watched with wide excited eyes, put his hands together. She passed it to him through the bars, her body leaning against the cool metal of the fence. The boy wandered away. No one else was there. She stayed in the high grass between graves and placed her arms across her chest. She knelt. The act caught her by surprise. She faced east and gazed at the moon. Her sister lived. The Administrator survived. The peace endured. There was reason for hope. There was reason to believe. And Marta discovered, to her shock, that she did. She remembered a line from a sura in the Koran, recited by her Great-Aunt Zara, "*Surely the god-fearing shall dwell amid gardens and a river, in a sure abode, in the presence of a King Omnipotent.*"

TWENTY-EIGHT

O N CHRISTMAS DAY, at two in the morning, Arthur Cape sat in the International Press Café in western Berlin and waited for George Markovic to appear. Across the street, rain beat on the trestles of the Zoo train station, sweeping trash and humanity into abysses beyond the light. Bright red Christmas bulbs darkened the café. A handful of people occupied tables in the dimness. The place ran twenty-four hours a day, seven days a week, and in Berlin, at that hour, on the very birthday of Christ, it was the last refuge of whores, criminals, and junkies.

The phone had rung in Arthur's rooms, and he had known somehow, even then, who might be calling.

"Bro."

"George?"

"Got to meet me."

"Goddamn, man. What time is it?"

"You got the dog?"

"George Markovic?"

"International Press Café. Zoo station. One hour. Sophie B. Hawkins A-side on the jukebox."

So Sophie B. Hawkins had been on the jukebox for an hour. Arthur had selected the song, "Damn, I Wish I Was Your Lover," so many times that the waitress had asked him not to play it again.

Anna had known. "Don't go," she'd said.

"It's George."

She gathered the blankets around her body. "I don't care. What could he possibly have to say to you?"

"He must think it's important."

"So what?"

With Anna's help, he had almost closed the door for good on Marta Mehmedovic. He had tried to accept her death as an accomplished fact. One day, he thought, with time, she would become a normal memory; never a happy one, perhaps, but that was all right. Anna wanted him to leave Frau Herbst's rented apartments and live with her. She did not talk about marriage. She was still opposed to all of that bourgeois *unsinn*. But she would consider having a child with him. Arthur had no good arguments against this proposition. Another man would have leapt. But he hadn't. He had waited.

He put another coin in the jukebox. He did not feel that he had a choice. He wasn't sure if George had meant Sophie B. Hawkins as a signal between them, but he didn't want to take the chance that his old acquaintance would take umbrage and back out of the meeting. George could have but one reason to reach him.

"If you go," said Anna, "I'm finished with you."

"Oh come on."

He couldn't see her eyes in the darkness. "No, Arthur. I am done with this Bosnian nightmare. I am sick of it coming back into my life."

Arthur felt the rise of a dark rage. "You're talking about a corpse, Anna."

"But this corpse won't die. She won't get out of my house."

One of the men in the café got up from his table with effort and limped toward Arthur. He was drunk and sick, thought Arthur. The brown walking cane and business suit could not conceal that he was homeless. Arthur dug a twenty-mark bill from his pocket. The man had gaunt cheeks and very little hair. A widow's peak thrust down toward his eyebrows. A French white shirt sagged beneath a silk tie, and his slacks needed a hem, as if he had shrunk since buying them. Brown eyes bulged out of hollowed sockets.

"Christ!" cried Arthur.

"Don't even know me?"

Arthur gaped. "George?"

George's breath smelled of pea soup, not alcohol. "Wasting disease of Asians. No cure. I said to my Hungarian physician, When did I go to Asia? And he says, George, I give you address of a very good doctor in the United States of America, and very good luck to you, but in my opinion, you are finished in six months."

Arthur felt a kind of terror. Once again, George had appeared like a ghost. "You've been sitting there the whole time? Why?"

"Can't be too careful anymore. My name is on lists. Not just police. Russians. Chechens. Business is getting ugly. I'm sorry, but I must watch you a little bit, make sure you don't try to fuck me."

The waitress approached and asked George in a deferential voice if he wanted anything else. George sent her away with a request for *mineralwasser*. He leaned his cane against the wall and took a stool.

"I'm sorry for not recognizing you," stammered Arthur. "I was thinking of the last time we met—"

"I was fat boy then."

"Your leg still bothers you?"

George put both hands on his right knee. "I jumped four stories and broke it. Cop broke a collarbone. This will never heal, I think."

There had been an operation. He reached down toward the floor, pulled off a shoe, and showed Arthur the star-shaped scar on his calf.

"So what exactly is your business now? You never explained."

"Herrend china. Romanian oil. Midgets. That's main source of income."

"Midgets?"

"I manage midgets. Yes." George shrugged and accepted the glass of *mineralwasser*. "I broker a very good midget to owner of bar in Osijek. This fellow dances and sings very nice. I make good money from midgets in former Soviet Union, for sure. They are beloved entertainers." Then, without a break, having downed his drink, he added, "I also broker construction materials for rebuilding Balkan cities. And I sell a few guns. And that's why I'm here."

"Why are you here exactly, George?"

George took a long breath. "You better be ready for what I am about to say. You will not like it. You will call me a liar."

Arthur knew before George got the words out of his mouth. "She's alive, isn't she?"

BOOK III

THE TWO CITIES

TWENTY-NINE

A city must be obliterated before it can be divided in two.

Thus began Arthur Cape's final story proposal for *Sense* magazine, written and submitted on New Year's Eve, 1994, one day before he drove south toward Mostar on the Adriatic Coast road.

Human beings do not build cities to be divided in two. Urban planners do not project forward to the day when a city will split and harden into two discrete mathematical halves. This is not how it works. So cities must first be destroyed.

In the twentieth century, two examples come to mind, one of them at the very center of the world, the other wholly obscure. The city of Berlin, destroyed in 1945, divided officially into East and West Berlin in 1961. The Bosnian city of Mostar, torn apart in the past two years, is in the process now of splitting into East and West Mostar. One slight historical fact disturbs me so much that I cannot get it out of my head—the two cities have a date in common. On November 9, 1989, the Berlin Wall fell, ending the division between East and West. On that same date, four years later, November 9, 1993, the Mostar bridge collapsed, cutting the heart out of the middle of the city. But more on this unsettling coincidence later.

Mostar is my story, so let's start there. According to my source, a businessman with many years experience in the Balkans, with intimate knowledge of the city, Mostar may officially be at peace, but it is actually at war. After its cease-fire, this meaningless little city in Herzegovina might have been expected to recede into quiet shadows. The people there might have been expected to go back to their lives. But they have not. Maybe because they are utter savages, as an editor at Sense *recently remarked to me, maybe because they occupy the very edge of Europe, like bird's nests in a Cornwall cliff, maybe because they are nothing more than a misnomer of Europe. One way or another, they haven't seen fit to compromise, and Mostar stands once again on the brink of bloodshed.*

But as I've said, it's wrong to speak of Mostar in the singular. There is no longer one Mostar, according to my source. Instead, we have East Mostar, which is Muslim, or Bosniak, as they like to call themselves, and West Mostar, which is Croat and Catholic. In between lies a strip of annihilation, a demilitarized zone, which is a lawless jungle of ruins and belongs to neither side but keeps the two peoples safely separate, and a river, the Neretva, which residents see in quasi-mystical terms.

Another interesting detail: the man in charge of the two cities is German. I won't bother to comment on the historic baggage Germans carry in this part of the world, but you may imagine that it isn't happy. But for whatever reason, the Europeans have seen fit to place a German in charge of this fragment of the Bosnian morass, and this German, Hans Kreischler, a former mayor of West Berlin, theoretically runs the two cities from a base in a small Mediterranean vacation hotel known as the Ero.

I say theoretically because this man is in serious trouble, though neither the bureaucrats in Brussels nor most residents in Mostar know just how bad things have become. Kreischler maintains the appearance of authority, but he has lost any semblance of it. The two cities live under a reign of mafias, and these mafias are fully prepared to go to war again. Weapons flow into the valley. My source should know. He sells them. One spark, my source says, and there will be a cataclysm. You rightly ask: What the hell happened to the cease-fire?

In September, someone tried and failed to assassinate the German. In October, the German struck back, arresting several members of the West Mostar mafia. In

November, the head of the West Mostar mafia, a man by the name of Velakovic, known in the valley as General Vela, demanded the release of these men, and the German refused. Now he, and his staff, are virtual prisoners in the valley, and if there is a fight, no matter who wins, he and his people will be killed. This is a certainty, my source tells me. (I should add a personal note here. Under odd circumstances, I had actual dealings with Velakovic. To be specific, he gave me a dog. Though he is reputed to be a monster, he has a personable side, and I fully believe that I can obtain an interview with him. I also believe that I might have sources close to Kreischler, but that's another story.)

Finally, you put the obvious question: Why the hell should we care about any of this? We hate the Bosnian story. We have always hated the Bosnian story. We don't give a shit whether they all kill each other. We would be happy never to hear another word about these little people and their little squabbles.

Very well put. Do you mind if I give a rather long and philosophical answer to your very serious questions?

I believe that these two cities have a meaning that goes far beyond this valley. I believe that they have a universal significance, in fact, that we must urgently unravel before we (by we, of course, I mean the entire human race) manage to exterminate ourselves. I owe an obvious debt here to our excellent colleague Eric Hampton, whose recent manifesto I cosigned, you may remember.

Hampton speaks of the two cities in a metaphorical, even an allegorical sense. He does not mean East Berlin or West Berlin, East Mostar or West Mostar. In the largest sense, I believe, he is speaking in the language of Saint Augustine. He means the City of God, the ideal city, the city of our hopes and dreams and aspirations, the city of our peace and contentment, and the City of Man, the real city of our flesh and blood and bone, of our torment and disappointment and death, the real city that we are always trying to escape. These two cities are forever at war on this earth, and we are responsible for this horrific fact.

But I'm talking as if cities were real things, like people or animals. Are they? Do cities, for instance, have self-knowledge?

Right now, you are scowling. You are making phone calls to the Human Resources Department. You are thinking about deleting this file. But wait, this is a difficult question to answer in the journalistic context, but not absurd and not impossible. Most cities don't have self-knowledge, as you probably guessed, but a few do. What am I trying to say? Just as dogs don't know that they are creatures called dogs, and salmon don't know that they are named after an Englishman named Salmon, most cities don't know what we call them. They don't even know that they are cities; or, at the very least, borrowing Hampton's terminology, the real city, the city of flesh and blood, does not know. That is the sadness. The real, living, tormented city does not know itself until it has been wiped from the face of the earth then torn in two. At that point, knowledge, like a sword, descends.

The sadness of this city is that it only comes to know itself once it has died. Mostar didn't know that it was Mostar, a place where generations had come and gone, in an intermingling of skin, stone, blood, and bone, until Mostar perished. This is not a form of knowledge that anyone, man or woman, should ever desire. It is the equivalent of understanding the meaning of legs once they have been amputated. When this knowledge descends on a city, the streets themselves understand. It comes in the smell of the rain in the trees. It can't be escaped. And it is a vision of hell.

Destruction doesn't bring this knowledge. Plenty of cities have been destroyed and rebuilt, and go on their way, believing that their essence has been salvaged, even when their buildings and people have not. No, it's destruction followed by division. That's the key. The division of a city is a form of living death experienced by only a few places on this earth. Mostar and Berlin are such cities. They are like people. They know that they can cease to exist. They can cease to be. It is a form of wisdom to be avoided at all costs.

But it's what we already know, every man and woman, and so we should have been able to avoid making these cities in our own image. But we've failed somehow, and the cities, all of them, are beginning to divide. That is why I am so filled with terror. It is why I am going to Mostar. The two cities are a distant vision of something else. They are calling to me, telling me that this division is like a virus. It should have stopped in Berlin. It should have been stamped out. But it wasn't. Another city caught it, and now it occurs to me that all cities will. Remember that unsettling date? November 9? It is a secret code connecting Berlin and Mostar to the rest of the cities of the earth. It is the event horizon. This is not mere geopolitics. Why on earth should an insignificant Mediterranean backwater like Mostar be divided into East and West? It makes no sense unless something more vast and mysterious, more irrational and malevolent than human power is at stake. When we divide ourselves, we are practicing insanity. When we divide ourselves, we are eating ourselves. It is our endless Augustinian sickness, the City of God against the City of Flesh. No division ever heals. No division ever lasts. We force our-selves into the mold of eternity, then we fail and tear ourselves apart. We die of our wounds and are born again into the same effort. We are boxed in transit be-tween two great points never reached, East and West, wrecked by God on the in-terchange between the horizons. That's my story. Interested?

New Year's Day, 1995, and the Dalmatian Coast had shuttered up. Wind tore sheets off the Adriatic. Waves sprang over highway em-bankments, whipping the windshield of Arthur's rented Opel, splat-tering the glass with salt and sand. In the backseat, the dog wouldn't sit. She stood on all fours, wobbling and whining, staring out first one window, then another. It was cruel to bring her back to Mostar, even inhuman, but she had escaped death, and Arthur needed her luck. And if this turned out to be one more of George's horrific goose chases, then he would need her company.

He had sent the labyrinthine story proposal to Eric Hampton and left a message on his answering machine, a goodbye of sorts. He re-vealed everything that hadn't been in the proposal. Marta Mehme-dovic was rumored to be alive, and if she was, he would get her out. The story proposal was his way of letting the magazine know how he felt about things, like a last will and testament. He had used these words on the answering machine, and he regretted them now. Hampton would get worried.

One way or another, Arthur hoped that his colleague would ap-preciate the sentiments in the proposal. He knew that it would come as a surprise to everyone but Hampton, but he had needed to say his piece. Arthur's star was rising again. The story about the V-2 rockets had restored his prestige. It had been picked up by broadcast news and radio. Gavin Morsch, the chief of correspondents, had begun to call Arthur once more, and his name was uttered again at Monday-morning meetings. The business editor considered him a star, even praising a story about machine tools, saying that it was the kind of thing that should be the bread and butter of the magazine: short, tight, and sound. No one joked about Heidegger anymore. But these improvements no longer mattered. As soon as Arthur heard about Marta, he lost interest in everything else. It was as if the entire world had died.

This wasn't strictly true. Arthur continued to care about a few other things, and one of them was Hampton's situation, which his proposal might well have made worse, though he hoped not. Arthur had wanted his colleague to have at least one more ally in his war against the masthead of *Sense* magazine. Hampton had not merely complained. He had lunched with the publisher and demanded that the entire executive editorial staff, including Morsch, be fired. He had tried to instigate a coup d'état, in effect. He believed that the editors were disgracing the magazine. *Sense* had become a laughingstock among serious journalists. Of course, the editors were not alone in the crime. In the name of profits, the accountants were squeezing world coverage. They were forcing the editors to withdraw from the very world that America had won. Morsch and his ilk no longer pretended to be interested in Bosnia. They had turned their backs on Africa. China would be next. Hampton resisted like a freedom fighter. He wrote an open manifesto to the staff, calling for a referendum on the future of the magazine. During the Cold War, America had been a beacon to the world, the manifesto said. American journalists had carried the light of this beacon into every corner of the earth. They had been exemplary. Now that the Cold War was over, they couldn't simply withdraw. The world was not a football game. The lights must be kept on.

That manifesto did not affect world coverage at the magazine, but it did mark the beginning of the end for the senior European editor. The veteran of two decades could no longer get his stories into the magazine. He became persona non grata, though no one had yet found the courage to strip him of his title or get rid of him altogether. Morsch told Arthur to stay out of it. Just after Christmas, he'd told Arthur to ignore Hampton and focus on his work, like everyone else. Arthur agreed to take this under advisement, then he put his signature at the bottom of the circulating copy of the manifesto and wrote his story proposal. It was the holidays, and he hadn't had a chance to speak with Morsch or anyone else since.

Arthur left the coastal road and reached Metkovic, trailing trucks through the center of the city. In Metkovic, he stopped for a sandwich and bought a gun. George had given him the name of a man who sold "decent old Czech stuff for okay prices." Arthur decided on a pistol manufactured in 1977, the year before he graduated from high school. It was just a precaution, George had said.

There were two ways into Mostar, by highway or back roads. The highway followed the line of the Neretva River. The back roads crossed the Neretva at Capljina and reached Mostar over the pilgrimage site of Medjugorje. It was impossible to say which of the two roads would be open. There were always troubles. Arthur would have to improvise.

He tried the highway first but came to a United Nations checkpoint. The road had closed, no explanations given. The Medjugorje road remained open, however. Arthur turned around and headed back. By the time he reached Capljina, the sun was setting westward. Medjugorje lay thirty miles away, according to a sign. He crossed the river and headed into dusty country. The land flattened. There were homes, half-new, half-shattered; shining white crosses wreathed in plastic flowers, fluttering with red-and-white *sahovnicas,* erected on rises of land that suggested burial mounds. He passed through a town called Citluq. Men drank watchfully in front of cars and cafés. Cats flickered in sunset glow. The dog murmured her growls.

The eastern sky darkened. The land rolled up and away until snow-capped mountains emerged. Three jagged peaks bit the sky; a fourth, farther east, resembled a molar, an immense, slow chewer of time. Did Mostar lie below those mountains? They seemed infinitely remote, like dreams of space. Their peaks flushed pink. No way he could make them before dark.

He came to another UN checkpoint, a forlorn way station, a few barrels, loose strings of razor wire, sandbags, and stones, a maintenance hut the size of an outhouse. Trouble had been there in recent days. Men in ragged uniforms hovered on the sides of the road. They had some official capacity, cradling machine guns, but didn't wear the UN helmets or bear the insignia. Arthur was reassured anyway. Conducting the actual business were the usual blue-bereted UN soldiers. The road slid into a corridor of sandbags, razor wire, and cinderblock. A bar had to be lifted manually by one of the UN troops.

"Any problems?" Arthur asked.

The soldier did not smile. "Always."

He waved the car through, and Arthur descended a switchback on a cliff face. The guardrails had been ripped away. Shipwrecks of mountain lay ahead, but the molar, the one landmark that Arthur had hoped to follow, had vanished. The road rose again, and the car reached a gap in the cliffs. He drove through the gap, over a hump, and into a valley. At the bottom of the valley lay the city of Mostar.

Arthur put on the brakes and gazed down. He didn't know what he had expected. The city in his mind would never be found on a map or on this earth. It had long ago taken the shape of Marta Mehmedovic. But here, before him, was an actual place called Mostar, and people lived in it. Arthur couldn't see the Neretva River. He had read in German newspapers that the river divided West Mostar and East Mostar, but it was hard to tell the difference from this perspective. Up high, it looked like a lot of places in Europe, gloomy skyscrapers, sprawl of gray development.

He put the car into gear. Abandoned bunkers yawned on the left. The sign for Mostar loomed out of the dusk on his right. The word itself had been crossed out and replaced with a black, spray-painted graffito: *Hrvatska.* Croatia.

ARTHUR CAME to a wide avenue and turned down a lane toward a sign indicating his destination, the Hotel Ero. Dark had fallen, and there weren't many lights, but he found one more sign and came to the hotel. At the Ero, he parked behind a UN jeep. Winds came shrieking out of the eastern sky. The dog followed him, cowering in the onslaught of gusts. Arthur could not quite believe his eyes. Even in the darkness, he saw such devastation as he had never seen before in his life. It lay in almost every direction. The hotel had been spared— it didn't seem to have a scratch.

Arthur found a stick, and the dog leapt after it. The wood clicked in her teeth, but she didn't land at first. The winds held her. For an instant, she flew, and Arthur had the thought, a stoic one, that the winds would carry her into the sky in a final upward trajectory. She came down a few feet away and scuttled back for another toss. He heard the doors of the hotel swinging open.

"Good Lord, you are slow," said a familiar voice. "I beat you here by a full day."

Arthur wheeled around. Eric Hampton, turtlenecked and grinning, lit his cigarette and flung the match into wind.

THIRTY

ARTHUR SURPRISED HIMSELF. He was overjoyed. His fear and loneliness diminished. They shook hands.

"You knew I would come?" Hampton asked.

"I had no idea that you would come, but I'm glad."

Hampton looked as he always did—smooth and trim. Here, in a destroyed place, surrounded by the ghosts of violence, he appeared ready for a five-course meal in the finest restaurant in Paris.

"You look like you've had a long drive, Arthur." Hampton indicated a road beside the Ero. "Care to stretch your legs?"

Arthur glanced around.

"Is it safe?"

"Safer than the drive you just made." Hampton pointed with his cigarette hand to a line of rubble that lay one hundred fifty feet or so to the east, beyond the eastern end of the hotel. "That's the DMZ."

Arthur thought he saw movement in the ruins. "Who's in there?"

Hampton shrugged. "No one really says. The Bosniaks own it technically, but I can never get a straight answer on the subject from the European Administration. For all I know, there may be Afghani warlords in there."

Hampton put a hand on Arthur's elbow and steered him toward the western end of the hotel. "We're going this way."

Arthur had been looking forward to a hot meal and a glass of wine. But he couldn't say no to Hampton. The man would remain his superior, no matter what happened, sitting like a benevolent journalist-king over the European realm. It was a comforting thought somehow. They came to the western corner of the Ero and turned into a wide, broken thoroughfare. As they walked around the corner, Hampton pointed to a blackened area on the second floor.

"Former quarters of the EU Administrator. In September, some local gangsters tried to assassinate him."

"I know," said Arthur, thinking of that long night in the shabby Berlin café, where George had told him everything, ad nauseam. "It was Vela."

Hampton gave him a searching look. "What on earth are you up to, Arthur, if you don't mind my asking? Something foolish, I'm certain. Do you know that your story proposal read to me like a suicide note? But I'm not surprised. When it comes to this woman, you tend to lose your sense of proportion."

"Is that really why you came, Eric? Your concern for me?"

Hampton conceded the fact. He paused, head trembling a bit. "Yes, among other reasons. I'm the only one capable of reading between the lines, aren't I?"

They passed into regions of rat and shadow. Westward stretched emptiness where buildings had stood; to the left, eastward, a city block lay half tumbled. Sandbags protruded from windows. Graffiti unscrolled in black curls, names of American heavy-metal bands.

"Besides, I wanted to tell you myself, Arthur."

"Tell me what?"

"That I'd been sacked." Hampton seemed mortified, for an instant, by his own words. "You are my last friend at *Sense,* Arthur. My own fault really, but I don't regret it. There's a principle involved. But I've worked at the magazine for virtually my entire professional life, so I wanted to give account of myself to someone I trusted, who might understand, and I'm afraid that's you."

Arthur's throat tightened. "I'm so sorry, Eric. Were they pricks about it?"

They started walking again.

"Morsch left a message on my answering machine. He said, and I quote, 'You're out.' He didn't mention it to you?"

"He told me nothing."

A UN jeep rumbled at snail speed through potholes in the street. Headlights picked up the peregrinations of the dog, sniffing her way from bullet hole to bomb crater. The jeep came to a still, crunching stop. A horn honked, the dog skipped onto the sidewalk. The vehicle trundled on, its red lights receding, the night returning to black, deeper than ever.

"Morsch did offer me a job in Washington, D.C., which I handily rejected. They had me marked down as a senior State Department correspondent or some such thing, but I didn't see the point. If you aren't out in the world, then you can't cover the world. You can't bloody see it from Foggy Bottom. I can't anyway. These Washington creatures seem to think that they have telescopes for eyes."

Arthur nodded his assent. "I think my days are numbered, too."

"The proposal, you mean?"

"Yes."

"It's your life. I wouldn't have sent the damn thing. It makes Heidegger look like the Pentagon papers. "Why, Arthur?" His question echoed in the desolation. "Morsch has been full of compliments about you lately. Why did you write it?"

"I think I'm going a little crazy. Maybe I'm in love with a dead woman. Maybe I've always been a little off. I don't know. But it's clear to me that those people in New York are assholes and idiots, and I didn't want to play their game anymore. Besides"—Arthur sighed—"I'm not sure I'm capable of journalism anymore. I don't trust my eyes so much."

"You never did."

"Thanks, Eric. Then it's decided."

For a moment, there were lights—the Western European police station, Hampton told him. Off to the right sat a single wood-shingled house, badly damaged, followed by a row of shops. Beyond the shops, alone and bizarre, loomed an incomprehensible shape, a sleeping giant of the mountains.

"What in hell is that?" Arthur asked.

"That is the Hit Department Store."

"The Hit?"

"The name applies in more ways than one. The authority of the European Administration ends approximately there. Everything else in the West belongs to Vela."

"Jesus."

"A bloody mess," Hampton said. "Imagine the depths of stupidity and barbarity that allowed such a thing to happen. And it will be an open wound for years. East and West will have nothing to do with each other."

"Déjà vu," said Arthur. "You know that essay of mine borrowed a lot from your thinking. It was all about the two cities."

Hampton chuckled. "So I saw. They'll be very cross."

"The *cité réel* and the *cité ideal,*" said Arthur. "You remember?"

The dog sniffed at their feet. Hampton tossed a rock. "Are you trying to provoke me?"

Beyond the humped back of the Hit Department Store, soldiers occupied a checkpoint. Arthur saw the points of cigarettes, tiny bits of fire.

"Anyway, I'm taken with your theory," his colleague said. "There is only one city, one true city, the model for all cities, and we're looking at it."

THEY ENTERED the Hotel Ero, and Arthur experienced a wave of human heat. Bodies bumped in flight. Waiters in white jackets and black bow ties hurtled between tables. Fresh hard currencies fluttered. Bare-shouldered girls peeled fifty-dollar bills off wads of cash, yelling at boys in black leather jackets, whose Ray-Bans blazed. Soldiers in blue berets and bureaucrats in white uniforms cut veal with gleaming knives. They roared in laughter over espressos, port, and whisky; there were photojournalists bumming smokes, aid workers picking up women, mercenaries comparing sidearms, and another category of people whom Arthur could not identify, elderly men and women in what appeared to be bathrobes dodging the waiters, who paid no attention to them.

Hampton indicated a spot near the bar, caught a waiter's attention, and claimed it. At an adjacent table, a woman suckled an infant. Her companion, a very large Scandinavian, drank shots.

"I'll be sitting there," said Hampton. "Give me the dog. You check in."

Arthur approached the registration desk. The woman wore a transparent yellow blouse over a black bra.

"You have a reservation?" she asked.

"No."

She handed him a chocolate egg wrapped in purple foil. "In Medjugorje are many fine hotels."

"I'm not going to drive back to Medjugorje tonight."

"Go and have a drink then. I cannot help you."

Arthur took the chocolate egg and her advice. He went to find Hampton. Glasses of whisky came.

The correspondent lifted one in a toast. "I'm going to get very drunk," he said. He brought the whisky to his lips and took a sip. He wiped the moisture off his upper lip. "I ought to tell you one more thing. I am not officially fired until the end of January. Morsch did me that favor. So I'm also in Mostar to do my last story. You gave me the idea in your message."

Arthur sat, bewildered. "You were my alibi. If you're down here on a story, what's my excuse?"

Eric finished one whisky and waved for another. "Sorry about that.

But you won't begrudge me, under the circumstances, I feel sure. They're going to give you my job, Morsch says."

"I won't accept it."

"Of course you will." He downed his second glass. "Anyway, I'm doing the Mostar story and you're not. I insist. It's the last time that I bigfoot you. Ever."

Arthur did what he had never done before. He reached out and patted his colleague on the shoulder. "Okay. Since you're doing the story, why don't you tell me what's going on here."

"First, drink up."

Arthur threw back his first glass, Hampton his third. He spoke. "Muslims have four men on the eastern side of the DMZ, charged with an attempt on the life of the German who's running the place. They've got a witness who can connect the men to Vela, and in the meantime, things are getting rather tense."

"Meaning?"

Hampton caught a waiter. He ordered two schnitzels. "Meaning violence."

George had told Arthur some of this, and more. But Arthur kept it to himself. "It seems quiet outside."

"It's always quiet until it's not. That's the first rule of war reporting, Arthur."

"Where's the dog?" asked Arthur.

Hampton gestured toward the next table, which was empty. She was trying to find a comfortable position, circling like a snake around the table's single leg.

"So now you know my details," Hampton said. "What about yours? What's the plan?"

Arthur had his second whisky. He was starting to feel a heaviness in his head. "Find Marta and get the hell out."

"And you're sure she's alive this time?"

Arthur shook his head. "I'm sure of nothing."

The dog would not rest. She whined and stuck her head in Arthur's lap. He shooed her away, and she scrambled under the table, finally resting her head beside the wheels of the baby carriage at the next table. The suckling mother put her infant back in the carriage and was having an adult chat with her Scandinavian, an imported Western European cop. Schnitzel and french fries came. The waiter brought more whiskies. Arthur knocked back his drink and ordered another. He had not been seriously drunk since the picnic in July. Hampton's news, his own fears, the city's tension—it all made him want more alcohol.

Hampton snorted. "Magazine is dying anyway. Ad pages down. Passaround numbers low. Cover sales, too. Meltdown."

The dog growled, a low hum like the sound of bees. When she got nervous, in his experience, she became unpredictable, even mean. At those times, she seemed to relive her war experience. The woman with the baby gave her a fretful glance.

"Do you know how long I've been with *Sense* magazine, Arthur?"

"Twenty-three years."

"Twenty-three years. An entire career."

"You're the greatest journalist I know."

"Do you know how long it took them to sack me?"

Arthur shook his head.

"Less than a *minute*."

Before Arthur could offer another empty condolence, Hampton hurled the schnitzel away. Unintentionally, he hit the woman at the next table, and the face of the Scandinavian cop turned bright red. The cop stood up so fast that his chair fell over. Hampton got up, too, and began to shout obscenities. The cop towered over him by at least half a foot. The baby began to scream.

A vast sorrow came over Arthur. The Scandinavian had Hampton in a headlock. Sorrow became rage, and Arthur charged the cop, going for his face.

"Stop," said a quiet female voice behind him.

THIRTY-ONE

MARTA MEHMEDOVIC fought yawns. Hassan had been studying documents for hours, poring over plans for an electrical plant. Vela had threatened to blow it up, and the German wondered how easy it would be to do this. Every ten minutes or so, he asked Marta to step forward and interpret something. Engineers came and went. Cigarette smoke filled the room. At last Hassan said, "I'm ready for my chicken piri piri."

She volunteered, as usual, to get it. His secretary got the word and phoned the kitchen. Chicken piri piri was no local dish. Hans Kreischler had vacationed for much of his life in the Algarve, in Portugal, where the dish was a staple, and his favorite; the Ero chef had learned how to make a passable version, and now the dish had become one of its specialties, Chicken Hassan.

Marta took the elevator down to the first-floor lobby, braced herself, as she always did, to walk into the bar, waved at the registration-desk hostesses, and entered. She looked down all the way to the bar, avoiding the glances of the thugs and scorpions who did their business there. Everyone knew her. There had been attempted bribes and assorted threats. She reached the bar and nodded at the bartender, who knew her.

"Five minutes," he said, pouring a glass of mineral water for her.

She turned around, and a dog jumped at her. She let out an involuntary shriek. The tongue lashed at her face, and the stub tail spun. And then she knew. This was her dog.

"Ilse?" she cried. Marta's heart began to race. She looked up.

"Whose dog is this?" she asked the bartender.

He pointed at a table three feet from the counter. "The drunks'," he said.

One of them had his back turned. The other rose before her eyes and shouted in English at one of the Western European policemen, a Dane, as she remembered. The argument turned into a fight, not unusual in the Ero bar.

"Him!" the waiter cried, grabbing her arm, almost leading her to the table. She saw whom he meant, but the man wasn't familiar. Just then, his companion leapt out of his chair, and Marta gasped as she saw the face. It was Arthur.

"Stop," she said softly, but he didn't hear.

The Dane put a fist in Arthur's jaw and sent him tumbling through tables to the floor.

Marta yelled now, " 'Stop!' I said."

She told him that the Administrator would ship him right back to Denmark if he lifted another finger. She called for help from the waiter and tried to wake Arthur. The other man sighed in annoyance. "Oh for God's sake," he said.

Arthur did not make entrances well. This was now an established fact. The first time she ever laid eyes on him, he had to be helped off the ground. Marta wetted a napkin and wiped the blood from Arthur's nose. She gave the Dane another look, and his girlfriend glared back. Waiters straightened tables and chairs. The usual rhythm of the Ero resumed, but patrons of the bar observed Marta with cold eyes. The story would get around. Her name would be mentioned everywhere, and her sister's name, too. Her fear returned. She must get back upstairs as quickly as possible.

"Eric Hampton," said the Brit, Arthur's friend, the man who had originally picked the fight. He stood in front of her, offering his hand. She nodded, and he leaned forward, supporting himself on the back of a chair.

"You know Arthur," he said.

"Years ago in Berlin."

They both looked down at the subject of their conversation, who had not regained consciousness.

"Then you must be Marta."

"That's right."

He offered a hand. "I'm Eric Hampton. I've heard quite a bit about you from our friend here."

She felt herself blushing. This was a ridiculous situation. "Can you help me get him out of this bar?"

Hampton looked sheepish. He was having a hard time keeping his balance. "Of course."

Waiters came and gave a hand. The six of them moved Arthur to a loveseat across from the reception desk. As they passed, people at the tables craned their necks to look at the big, comatose American, heaved forward by men half his size, and they laughed. Marta wondered if anyone in the room, besides Hampton, knew of her connection to this man. They couldn't possibly.

"You're a journalist," she said, at last, when they had propped Arthur up with pillows.

After a moment, Hampton nodded. "I've seen you with Kreischler. You're his interpreter? Yes?"

"German language."

"Your English is excellent."

"It's crap, I'm afraid. Others are much better."

Hampton laughed. "May I bring up a delicate subject?"

Marta hesitated to give him permission. Time had not stopped.

The crisis upstairs had not passed. Kreischler would be asking why she hadn't returned with his dinner. Hampton watched with curiosity as she retied the scarf under her chin, the lotus-trimmed square of cloth given to her by her neighbor. Marta didn't cover all of her hair, as other women did, as Sister Farida did, but she took comfort from the feel of the scarf around her head. She accepted its protection. She knew that Arthur would be surprised to see her this way. He might find her amusing or ugly. He might not even recognize her. But she wouldn't take it off.

"What's Hans Kreischler going to do about his prisoners?"

"They're not *his* prisoners." She cast a look around the room. Already, waiters and others were watching her conversation with the journalist.

"Whose are they, then?"

"I cannot say anything. I hope you understand."

"Too visible."

"Far too visible."

"Shall we get Arthur to a room?"

She nodded. "I'll have to be clever. No vacancies right now."

On her way to the elevators, she stopped to look at Arthur, a sleeping blond giant on a scrap of furniture. There were no wings in evidence. His face looked drawn, but he was well fed. Some girl was keeping him, she thought, and hoped that she was nice. His hair had grown too long, and she would advise him to cut it, though God knew it was none of her business. How real he looked! What would he think of her? At the very least, she should find a mirror. Maybe she would take off the scarf after all.

Hampton caught up with her. "Just tell me. Is Kreischler going to be evacuated?"

Marta became angry at the suggestion. "He will never run from these criminals."

"But he's out of his mind. Vela will shoot him in plain sight. Surely he knows that."

The elevator doors closed, and she didn't have time to tell him the rest. The Spanish battalion in Medjugorje had been summoned. A rescue operation would mobilize the following day.

MARTA FOUND a storage closet and went back down for Arthur. With Hampton's help, she got him into the elevator, where his eyes fluttered open for a quick moment.

"Oh my God," he stammered. "You?"

He wasn't shy. He touched her cheeks, her forehead. She experienced his fingers as if they were flames around her face. They stopped as quickly as they'd begun. His eyes closed again, and his arms drooped. He hadn't seemed to notice the scarf.

On the fifth floor, Marta led Arthur out of the elevator and to the storage room at the end of a corridor. Within were stacks of fax rolls, and several tiers of boxes containing pens, paper clips, scissors, and tape. She had cleared a place among the boxes, and Hampton laid Arthur on his coat on the floor. The dog curled into a ball next to Arthur's body. The sight of them together gave her a shudder. If she shut the storage room door, would they disappear forever?

"You have to go back downstairs now," she told Hampton.

"I thought as much." He gave her a tired smile. "You two are going to have an interesting conversation."

Arthur's eyes opened and closed. On a shelf in one of the offices, Marta found a battered light blue UN helmet. She filled the bottom with water for the dog and returned to the storage closet. She left the helmet wobbling on the floor and went to fetch blankets and something to eat. She realized she must have a mirror. She could not go back to him until she had seen herself. But mirrors were hard to find in the Ero. She searched every bathroom on the floor, every one except for the bathroom belonging to Hans Kreischler. He would have a mirror, he alone. The rest had been stolen. She gave up and went back to looking for food. She found English tea biscuits, and fed them to Ilse. Marta spread the blankets over Arthur. They had been stripped from beds and used as curtains to make separate work spaces, but no one cared about privacy at the moment. She was kneeling on the floor, straightening out the wrinkles, when hands took her by the waist and kissed the back of her neck. She tried to hide her face. Her teeth had gone bad. Her skin was awful. Arthur bent over her, his knees on the floor, his chest arched over her back. His hands moved up to her rib cage, holding her steady as he gave the back of her neck another kiss, and another. He pulled away the scarf. She let go of the blankets and turned to face him, reaching with her right hand for the door, which had slightly cracked, and shutting it. She reached for his face, touched his nose, his golden eyebrows, the coarse mess of his hair. She took hold of his skull and stared into the blackness for the longest time, at the artifact of his presence within inches of her body. She gazed back into memories of a place and time that had ceased to exist. She could not recall anything specific, but she felt that in this room the heart of a dead universe had come back to life. Their time together had not been an accident. It had not been a mistake or a joke or a disaster. It had not been meant to humble or discredit or destroy her. She kissed him on his cracked lips. And he kissed her back, and touched her cheeks and lips, and held her body as if he would never let go of it again.

SOME TIME LATER, they lay together, clothes rumpled, unbuttoned, a mess, and Arthur rubbed his fingers over the face of the pocket cross. He was breathing slowly. She wished that she could have had a chance to look at herself in the mirror. She wished that it hadn't happened so quickly. But there it was. She hadn't thought. She had acted. There could be no question of apologies or regrets. She couldn't see Arthur's face in the darkness, but she thought that he might be smiling.

"I've been wearing it around my neck for months," she said.

"I'm flattered."

"It reminded me of you. That's all."

He ran a finger through her hair. "And Jesus is one of the prophets of Islam, right?"

"Yes," she replied, "Jesus is one of the prophets. Are you religious now?"

He kissed her again. "About you."

A KNOCK CAME on the storage room door. Marta put on her clothes and retied the scarf around her head. Kreischler had been asking for her. Through the windows of the fifth-floor offices, sunlight streamed. People stared at her with horror in their eyes. Before she entered Hassan's office, she got the bad news. Vela had issued an ultimatum. Either turn over the men in the East Mostar jail or he would burn down the hotel and everyone in it. Marta found Kreischler in his office, smoking a cigarette, having his morning cup of coffee.

"*Liebe* Frau Mehmedovic," he said, "are you well?"

"Of course, Herr Kreischler. Forgive me for disappearing last night. I had urgent personal business."

He waved away her words. A Mozart symphony played on the wireless radio.

"I merely wanted to discuss something with you," he said. "It's the matter of your sister."

"My sister."

"Yes," he said, gesturing at a chair. "I'm afraid we have a problem."

THIRTY-TWO

MARTA SUDDENLY HAD a bad feeling. She had never let her boss down. She had never missed a day of work, never been late to a meeting, never once left uncompleted a task that he had assigned. She was grateful to have a job that so many others wanted.

In Mostar, hundreds of beautiful women had language skills, and most of them were ten years younger than Marta. None of them spoke Deutsch quite as well as she did, but dozens could manage. The work did not require literary mastery. One did not need to know Goethe to work for Hassan, but the job did demand a certain linguistic finesse. Kreischler spoke at different speeds, in varying tones, with a constantly shifting sense of theatrics. People saw him as plainspoken and uncomplicated, but Marta had never believed these qualities to be the whole man, and her work with him confirmed it. The German could be blunt, even mean. He could play the *Volksmensch*, spinning yarns, employing obscure proverbs that had the whiff of mendacity. He told filthy jokes one minute, turned broody and philosophical the next, then finished the day as a manically obsessed businessman who found one small discrepancy between his books and wallet and could not rest until the mystery clarified. Late at night, when the pace of work overtook him, he would slump in his chair and reminisce about his childhood in Berlin, his memories of the firebombing of the city, which had never left him. One vision, in particular, haunted him: He had seen one of his teachers swallowed whole by a bubble of molten asphalt.

Berlin's destruction had prepared him for Mostar, he had told Marta. That's why he believed himself to be the man for the job. Everything in his life had prepared him to come to this destroyed place, to bring hope from the German people, who had committed and endured their own horrors. He spoke to her, Berliner to Berliner, in those moments.

"You are a survivor, like me," he once told her. "I can see it in your eyes and hear it in your voice."

Kreischler's burdens lay on her, too. A twenty-year-old equipped with verbs and nouns might handle the demands of a press conference, but she could never comprehend the gravity of the general situation, could never appreciate the near-inexpressible weight of history on every single word uttered by the German in residence at the Hotel Ero. Marta alone could do that. On the other hand, in honest reflection, she had to admit that the most important qualification for the job had nothing to do with language skills. The German had to like you. Before she got the job, this fact had made Marta despair. Hassan had to want to be around you, and who could manufacture such a relationship? Who could make that happen, with even the most steadfast will?

One evening, as she was waiting to perform her duties in the Ero, the decisive moment occurred. She had been summoned to a meeting and kept waiting for hours. Hassan's personal secretary, a woman imported like herring from Hamburg, had struck up a conversation.

"Forgive me for asking, but you are the daughter of Vesna Bistritza, *nicht?*"

Marta gave a startled nod.

"Do you know, I loved *Chitto Harjo* so much. I saw it so many years ago, my God, it must be more than a decade."

The Great Actress had deplored the movie, Marta remembered. She had tried to get it pulled from distribution. *Chitto Harjo* had a badly cut nude scene, showing breasts saggier than cinema could tolerate, even East German cinema, and the worst dialogue, according to her mother, that she had ever been forced to utter.

"That one wasn't seen by a lot of people."

The woman gazed at Marta as if she were the actress herself, stepped out of the Crazy Snake wars and into her office in this godforsaken place.

"You remind me of your mother."

"Do I?"

"Certainly you do."

"That's funny. She always played the dark type."

"It's the strength in your face, I think. The look of the squaw."

"*Ah ja.* That's understandable. I live like a squaw now."

The secretary had given a pained grin. "I only saw the movie once, of course, but it made a great impression on me. I especially liked the bread-baking scenes. So authentic. It made me want to learn everything that I could about squaw bread. Hobby-like. And I saw all of the other movies."

Kreischler's secretary asked if the Great Actress had made it through the war, and Marta said that she lived in Tel Aviv and no longer acted in the movies. The demise of both East Germany and Yugoslavia had put an effective end to her film career. These indiscretions with an adoring fan would have unfuriated her mother, and the thought gave Marta pleasure.

"Your German is exquisite," said the secretary. "You should work for us more often."

And now, Marta thought, standing before the man, he knows about my sister, and everything will come crashing down. I have let him down.

"I apologize for my absence."

"Please don't mention it again," he said.

He took off his glasses and rubbed his eyes. "Frau Mehmedovic," he said at last, "the time has come to be honest with each other."

He sat back in the chair and pressed his palms together. Behind him, on the wall, hung a color-coded map of the population concentrations in the Mostar canton. The secretary brought him another coffee and said, "Good morning, Frau Mehmedovic. Would you like something?"

Marta asked for a coffee. After the woman left, Kreischler said, "Have I ever asked you a single word about your sister's role in this affair?"

"Of course not."

He cleared his throat. "Have I ever insisted that you wear your clothes a certain way or remove that scarf or do anything one way or another that did not bear upon your work here? Has your personal life ever been an issue here in our work?"

She shook her head. "Of course not."

He gave a rueful sigh. "I am afraid that's about to change."

Marta's heart sank, though she didn't quite know why. He paused a moment, thinking. She was used to it. She could imagine what he might say. Ever since the arrest of the assassins, bitterness had grown in Mostar. There was talk of progress, all the time, dawn to dusk, but it had become impossible to act. One needed cooperation between East and West. One needed good faith. But it didn't exist. There had been agreements at the highest levels between Croats and Muslims. There had been handshakes in Washington, D.C., the removal of guns, and the crossing of borders. A thing called the Memorandum of Understanding existed. This document hadn't been a ruse. It hadn't been a sham, like so many other agreements. The people of Mostar had promised to understand one another. They had agreed to a higher form of understanding. But there was no understanding.

Marta had been in the room when Kreischler received the first communication from Branko Velakovic. The men in the East Mostar jail had been imprisoned long enough, almost four months. The Administration must either produce the witness, hand her over to be questioned by the legitimate West Mostar authorities, or Kreischler must release the men. She had interpreted the exchange but had said nothing to Kreischler about Dubravka's role as the witness. It didn't matter, she reasoned. Besides, she had been too scared.

The East Mostar chief of police was a decent and courageous man. He did not scare easily. He had prefaced his comments to Kreischler by promising a fight, if it came to that. But he felt compelled to tell the Administrator that was there another view in the matter. According to Vela, the men in the East Mostar jail were innocent. Their arrest had been political. The Muslim girl who had identified the men was a prostitute and a spy. Furthermore, the men in the jail were important. They had family and friends who would not suffer this treatment gladly. Certain names did not need to be mentioned. The police chief had been warned. East Mostar had twenty-four hours. If it didn't release the men or hand over the witness, the consequences would be dire. West Mostar would do whatever was necessary to get back its people. Marta had translated the conversation between the chief and Hassan had word for word, and still she had said nothing. When Hassan had asked it if might be possible to turn over the witness for questioning, she stiffened.

"They'd kill her," said the chief of police.

Now Kreischler put a direct question to Marta. "Where is she now? Your sister?"

"Mose Silber knows. I don't."

"That's the truth, Frau Mehmedovic?"

"Everything that I have ever told you is the truth, Herr Kreischler. I've never lied."

He called for his aides. Several people entered, all of them speaking at once. The Spanish battalion had been alerted. Troops were on the move, but no one could say when they would arrive. Word of the developing situation had reached the international wire services.

Kreischler focused again on Marta. "I have to know one thing."

She nodded. "Anything."

"This isn't some personal act of revenge by your sister against an old boyfriend? You can assure me of that?"

"She has her reasons to want revenge, believe me," said Marta.

"I don't doubt it," replied Hassan. "That's not the point."

"What is the point, if I can ask?"

Hassan gazed at her with forbearance. "The point, my dear, is that I am putting my office in jeopardy in the name of evidence given by your sister. So I must believe in her, as I believe in you."

Marta defended Dubravka as if fighting for herself. "I can assure you. There was a romantic relationship with Branko Velakovic. That's true. But my sister stepped forward because of her conscience. No other reason. She knows everything."

Kreischler finished polishing his glasses. He raised his hand, and the room went silent. He put the glasses back on his face.

"We release nobody," he said. Everyone applauded, then a hard silence fell.

THIRTY-THREE

AT DAYBREAK, a mob set fire to Arthur's rented Opel. He gazed out the front window of the Ero and thought of the pistol he'd bought in Metkovic. It was in his computer bag. Surely this was the moment for its use. He'd go for the smiling one with the porcine face. Or if he was quick, he'd make it two, the pig and the scrawny old guy in the cowboy hat and camouflage shirt. He would take out the Czech-made pistol and watch the high spirits slide out of their eyes. Their dearest thoughts of love and home would fly through the backs of their skulls. And why not? Why shouldn't they receive a summary judgment? Thanks to those two men, who had laughed as they'd poured the gasoline through the passenger windows, he had lost his means of getting Marta out of Mostar.

There would be other ways, perhaps, but they would be infinitely more difficult. A small voice in his head tried to be wise. It was in the nature of things for his car to be torched, the voice told him. Or more to the point, it was in the nature of things during wartime for things to become more difficult. And this was wartime. Or had he not grasped this fact quite yet? Officially, a memorandum had been signed. Officially, the bureaucracies had taken charge. But the valley was at war.

Black clouds welled out of the Opel's windows. The car had been put into neutral and rolled down the hill to the ruins of the DMZ and set alight. It had happened in a matter of minutes. In the night, the official vehicles had been moved. His alone had remained in the parking lot in front of the Ero. At first light, the mob had come swelling into the space in front of the Ero. The first thing they noticed, it seemed, was Arthur's Opel. They smashed the windows first and tried to hotwire it, but the engine wouldn't turn. They attempted to flip the car over to no avail. There were a few men, at first, then dozens, then hundreds. They shouted slogans as they marched in circles. Pistols gleamed in shoulder holsters. Rifles hid in long coats.

"Did the car have Croatian plates?" Hampton asked.

"Who gives a damn?"

"Usually, they don't destroy cars belonging to their own ethnic square." Hampton was counting men. "I make them about three hundred plus."

"What do you think they'll do?"

"Storm the hotel, I should think."

The hotel was garrisoned. West Mostar gendarmes had been stationed on the first floor. At the moment, those men were enjoying Marlboro cigarettes in the bar. The Western European police force had small arms at its disposal, but trainee cops from Antwerp and Dublin had no experience of pitched battle. This left a smattering of UN troops.

"If I were you," Hampton said, "I would find Marta."

Arthur lingered a moment, unsure of himself, unsure of anything that was happening. He threw his arms around Hampton.

"Thank you for everything," he said to the startled man.

A RTHUR RUSHED to the storage closet, hoping to find Marta, but she wasn't there. The dog had vanished, too. He went back to the guards, and they directed him to the fourth floor, where the animal had been placed in the custody of French Eurocops who called her Lulu and tossed her a crumpled coffee cup. The dog bounced off the floor like a fawn in a meadow.

The cops seemed unfazed, but others wore an air of resignation, sitting around the hotel's single satellite phone, gloomy as cave dwellers huddled around the last fire. Some sat on floors, staring at postered walls, smoking through a final pack of cigarettes, reading back issues of the newspapers of the great cities of the continent, *Le Monde,* the *Frankfurter Allgemeine Zeitung, Corriere Della Sera,* dailies printed months ago. Their eyes were red slits. They looked at the gun in Arthur's waist and became even more concerned with their lot.

Arthur couldn't get a straight answer about Marta. She had been there five minutes ago. She hadn't been seen in a while. She was with Kreischler, and her location must be kept secret. Finally, after a mild explosion of temper, he obtained what seemed like a plausible destination. She had accompanied the German to the other side of the hotel, to the eastern flank of the building, where the old-age pensioners lived. To reach those floors, Arthur would have to cross the lobby and go behind the elevators.

First, he moved down the corridors of the western end of the hotel. He didn't want to cross the lobby, a journey that seemed Saharan in its prospect, and find that he had been deceived. He would cover every last inch of the western side. He would grasp its exact parameters. There must be back rooms. There must be places to hide. The Ero was smaller than it looked. He reached the ends of corridors quickly. He tried handles on doors, and some of them opened; a few were empty. In one, he found the distant aftertaste of a Mediterranean vacation, two narrow beds, side by side, a shower that was no more than a hose and a drain, a proper toilet, and in one drawer of a chest, a wrinkled, sand-peppered German-language map of the Dalmatian Coast. Other rooms were still occupied. He stumbled on people hugging in tears, making love, and doing crossword puzzles, and one man who had packed his valise and waited for further announcements like a traveler awaiting a train.

He identified every exit in the hotel. One was up front, in the police headquarters, and useless. It fed right into Kolodvorska, where the mob had massed. Behind the hotel, in a recess, lay a dining pavilion. Once, there had been a service exit leading into Alekse Santica Street, but this street had become a part of the DMZ, and the exit was now blocked with sandbags and concrete.

Arthur passed the bar and entered the mysterious eastern wing of the hotel. The elevators didn't work, so he sprang up steps in the darkened stairwell. He rounded a corner and ran smack into a gathering of ancient men and women in robes and pajamas. He spoke to them in German, and they understood him and were desperate to ask questions. They wanted to know what was happening, and he told them. Then he asked them who they were, and their stories washed over him. They all lived in the hotel. The armies let them stay. They had lost their homes and their families. They had nowhere else to go and didn't ask for much. They lived on a front line and could have died at any minute if the guns on the eastern or western hills made the decision to end their tenancy, but it didn't matter to them. Death held no surprises.

They were Yugoslavs. They had fought the Germans. They had loved Tito. They were Croats, Muslims, Serbs, Jews, and Italians. Who cared? The eldest worked their lower jaws with difficulty, raised bone-thin fingers, clutched his arms, touched his hair. They had been born with Habsburg identity cards, but the First World War had ended all that, had ended Franz Josef, whom they'd adored, even though he'd failed so miserably—the Great War, the war of 1914, Gavrilo Princip, the assassination. Yes, Arthur said, trying to keep up, the First World War. They became subjects of another country, the Kingdom of the Serbs, Croats, and Slovenes. They became Communists, every one of them, Communist Yugoslavs, and that was all right, even if Tito had made big mistakes, and he had, indeed, made enormous mistakes, but his children had done much worse. Look what they had done to Mostar. Look at it, a disgrace. Their hands and heads shook. Some of them dropped their old heads into their hands, and the tears came.

"Where is Kreischler?" Arthur asked them.

"Gone!" they shouted in unison.

THIRTY-FOUR

H E WAS IN A DREAM in which the two of them meandered through the Christkindlmarkt in Nuremberg. At first, they walked together, but later, as the night deepened and widened and the people in the stalls became indistinct, as they shrugged and told him that he had already asked, and that they had answered countless times, he found himself alone. He had lost her somehow. They had been holding hands without speaking, under snowfall, never stopping long at a particular stall, never long enough to sample the *Rauchbier* or the *rostbratwürstchen,* never long enough to watch the pigeon tell their future by picking a number from a wooden slot or to purchase a box of Russiche Brot or have a conversation with any of the merchants. They walked and walked, but the market never ended, and Arthur began to fall asleep, and her hand slipped out of his fingers, and her blond head bobbed away in the direction of the St. Sebaldus Church. He thought that he would catch her, but every time he reached her, she turned out to be some other woman. The night grew cold, and the stalls winked out, one by one, like stars, until he was wandering in the darkness, crunching snow, understanding, at last, that he was lost under an endless alien sky and would never see Marta again.

She woke him in the storage room.

"Where have you been?" he asked.

"East Mostar," she told him. "Everything's going to be fine. Vela backed down."

Arthur barely heard these words, unbuttoning her shirt, tearing the scarf off her head. She accepted him in the darkness, her body forking around his waist, her fingers in his mouth, his fingers in her vagina, the wetness and warmth of her body telling him everything.

UNDER BLANKETS, between stacks of paper and boxes of paper clips, they talked about everything that had happened between them in Germany.

"Did you despise me?" she asked.

He thought about this question. He put his hand on her hip, on that animal moment in her body when the upper flesh slid like a river current into the lower, and he held on to it, feeling how thin she was for the first time, feeling a sinew of the war.

More than anything, he didn't want to speak one more pointless word. There had been too many. He kissed her on the lips. "I had an inkling that you would leave me."

"I was a coward," she whispered.

He took her by the shoulders and kissed her mouth. "What I felt for you, at first, was a simple blackness. I went back to Berlin, and I could feel this blackness in my head. It was like my own hand coiled into a fist in my head. And every day that passed, as I didn't get a letter, as I didn't get a phone call, my fist tightened. What had I done to deserve such treatment?"

He kissed her again and again, so she would stop crying. He didn't hate her. He had never hated her.

"You do hate me," she said.

"No. It was worse. You became mythology. Because, you know, when humans meet gods, they are changed. You had appeared as a woman, but you acted like divinity. You acted with the impunity and the indifference of divinity. You absconded, like divinity."

"You forced me," she said.

He kissed her again. "I know, and now and then the truth occurred to me."

She listened with hurt in her eyes. "Did it never occur to you that I was in as much pain as you were?"

He drew a breath. "I knew so little about you."

She nodded. "I know. Me too."

"You had to be a thing. That was the only way that I could explain it all to myself. To me, the suffering in my head outweighed everything. But I never hated you."

"Thank God you say that."

He kissed her again. "I loved you. I loved your talk. I loved the way you moved. I loved your breathing exercises and your German. I loved it all so much that I had no idea what to do. And that's the answer to your question. I never hated you. But I wasn't ready for you."

"I know exactly what you mean," she said.

HE SWALLOWED. He had his own question. "Did you, even for a single instant, consider leaving your husband for me?"

Marta pulled away from him and wrapped herself in one of the blankets that lay beneath their bodies. He interpreted this move as a retreat. His talk had brought her unease. But she tried to answer. "I didn't run at first," she said. "At first, my thoughts were rational."

"You're the most rational person I have ever known."

She shook her head. "Let me say this thing another way."

He put a hand inside the blanket. "I'm cold," he said.

"Come inside, then. You mustn't be cold."

They nestled within the blankets.

"This person you are asking this question to is no longer here," she said. "Do you understand, Arthur?"

"You're here. I can feel you."

"No. *I* am here. But Marta Mehmedovic, this woman, she has gone."

She paused, her fingers in his hair.

"This name, for instance. Mehmedovic. It's the name of my man. You know? Mehmedovic. He is murdered in the year 1993. With him, he takes his name. My name. He takes the whole meaning of this name. I keep it, yes, but it is no more the name of the woman that you knew. That woman was his wife. That woman was attached by name to a man who is now forever gone."

"Okay . . ."

She became cross with herself. "First thing. I'm sorry for my English."

"Speak in German, then."

"No. Your language is English, and when we speak, you and me, we speak in English, and maybe one day, maybe, you learn my language. No more German between us, Arthur."

He nodded in the darkness.

"That woman in Neuschwanstein was also a mother. You have not asked me about my son. Why?"

Arthur's body registered the shock of the question. His fingers stopped in mid-caress. It all came back. His grief began to make him shake.

"He is dead, Arthur. I can say now. My boy is dead."

She began to weep, too, as she had never done in his presence, the tears pouring out of her eyes, onto Arthur's arms and legs, tossing out of her with a force that she would not be able to contain by herself. He gripped her body and brought her to his chest and held her tight.

"I have not much more left in me," she said.

"*Dobro,*" he said.

This word, pronounced "dough-bro," made her laugh.

"Oh, you remember the one word that I taught you. Very good. That is beginning."

"I do listen," he said.

She wiped her eyes with the blanket.

"I did consider to stay with you, but—I must tell you this—it was not possible then. I wasn't strong enough."

"Are you strong enough now?"

She sat up in the darkness. He tried to kiss her, but she stopped him.

"What are you saying, Arthur?"

He saw that she'd had no idea why he had come. No one had bothered to tell her. He hesitated a moment. Once he said it, there would be no taking it back. She was breathing a few inches away from him. Her precious heart beat. She was alive. She had been dead, and now she lived. How many men were ever given such a chance?

"I'm taking you out of here," he said. "Now."

She put fingers to his lips, without speaking, but he could feel in the tremor of her touch that she had turned him down again.

THIRTY-FIVE

A T DAWN, the Spanish battalion reached the Ero. Marta sat at her desk two doors down from the Administrator, having a cup of chamomile and sorting through a stack of recent Bosnian, Croatian, and Serbian newspapers that had been dropped on her desk. It was amazing how quickly the normal routine reasserted itself. The paper delivery, which had stopped for a week, now resumed.

Arthur lay asleep in the storage room, where she had left him with the snoring dog. In her desk drawer, wrapped in a newspaper, was his gun. She had found it that morning among his things and had not, at first, believed her eyes. Arthur Cape had no business with a gun. What in the world had he planned to do with it? Protect her? If that was his intention, he would have been better off with a flak jacket, which he didn't possess.

She took the gun out and had another look. The weapon smelled of rust and the palms of human beings. She was sure that it was a dud. She put it back in the drawer. If Arthur asked, she would tell him that guns were forbidden to civilians in the Ero; his had been confiscated and would not be returned.

She waited impatiently for Hassan. She craved news. But Kreischler had been in a meeting for hours with his closest aides. Both of the mayors were in there, too. Surely he needed her help. But when she'd wandered down the corridor to see if he had made a request, the secretary turned her away with a resolution lacking in its usual politeness. No one had yet asked Marta about her tie to the American journalist, not even Hassan, who would have good reason to worry about a relationship between his chief interpreter and a member of the press. She had been meaning to bring the matter up, had, in fact, wanted to use this quiet morning to explain her dilemma to him, to ask his advice, but there was no admittance.

She had returned to her desk when Gaby appeared. "Where's Arthur Cape?" she asked.

Down the hall, the satellite phone rang. Hassan's secretary picked it up.

"You know about him, Gaby?"

"Where's his car?"

"They destroyed it."

Gaby put her hands to her forehead. "*Verdammt!*"

Marta began to feel uneasy. "Why are you so upset?"

"They came for Dubravka last night." Gaby's eyes blazed in her pale face. "She only got away by sheer luck."

"Is she all right?"

Gaby lowered her voice. "She won't be for long. You have to get her out of here now."

Marta became irritated at her tone. "Mostar does not belong to Branko Velakovic. Hassan proved it."

"Is that what you think?"

"I know it."

Gaby did a double take, as if Marta had spoken nonsense. "Kreischler gave Vela what he wanted. That's how he lifted the siege. He handed over the men. Surely you knew that."

Marta had not been admitted to the final round of negotiation, and now she knew why. Gaby kept talking, making things worse.

"Vela knows who ratted him out. He knows without question that the witness is Dubravka."

Marta thought that she would be sick. "Hassan would never allow that."

"He had no choice."

"But if he let the men go—?"

"He traded. There's a difference."

"Traded for what?"

"For himself."

The contents of Marta's stomach, mostly tea, spilled onto the desk.

"You have to leave Mostar this very minute. Do you understand?"

"Where's my sister?"

"European police headquarters. She's safe there for the moment. Vela won't dare attack in broad daylight, but he won't wait long. He can't afford it."

The siege had not ended, then. The victory was a lie.

"You go to Kreischler now," said Gaby.

"I won't have anything more to do with him."

Gaby snatched her by a wrist. "You will ask for an official letter, which you can take across the checkpoints and all the way into Germany. It must be on his letterhead, and it must state that you are on urgent official business for him. He knows everything, and he's prepared to help."

"I won't, Gaby."

"Then I will."

Gaby burst into Kreischler's office. The personal secretary came running after her. Kreischler wiped the lenses of his glasses.

"Please forgive me," said Gaby, "but this cannot wait."

Hassan blinked at Marta.

"*Ach ja.* I have it right here."

He didn't ask his colleagues to leave the room. They took a moment to sip coffee and enjoy someone else's trouble. The mayors and
the French bridge engineer watched her without curiosity. They
seemed to know everything. Marta hung a moment in suspension, as
if tied by two threads to opposing poles. She wanted to express her
rage at his decision. She wanted to tell Hassan to his face that she considered it a betrayal. In the same instant, she wanted to express regret
for having interrupted the meeting, an unthinkable lapse. She wanted
to say to him that he had sentenced her sister to death with his exchange, and that she understood the situation, that every person in
Mostar lived in a state of risk. Everyone had been given a chance to re-
sign and go home. No one had left, not even Hassan, whom these
same men had once tried to kill. One should not complain to him, of
all people. The German rifled through a mass of documents on his
desk, outriders flying off the sides. He held up a single piece of paper.

"We will miss you, Frau Mehmedovic. I will miss you. But I'm
afraid that you have to go now."

Marta concentrated the whole of her feeling into a single sentence.
"My son is buried under a building in Alekse Santica 14, and I cannot
leave him."

Gaby took the letter from him.

He put the glasses back on his eyes.

"I will do what I can about your son," he said.

Gaby had already told him what should go into the letter, and it
was there. The mayors of East and West Mostar and the French bridge
engineer observed with the dispassion of stone lions, guarding in official gloom the approaches to her city. Hassan reached for Marta's
hand. She stumbled backward out of the room.

THIRTY-SIX

THERE WAS A PLAN. Gaby had snagged a UNHCR jeep, and
Arthur must drive it. Gaby had wanted to drive, but she was
Marta's well-known friend. If she left the city, her way would
certainly be watched. Arthur, on the other hand, was a stranger, just
one more Westerner. He would drive across the Pioneer Bridge in the
middle of the city and head out of East Mostar to the UN checkpoint
on the highway. Gaby didn't know how many kilometers to the
checkpoint. Maybe twenty, she said. It didn't matter. Mose Silber
would meet them at the checkpoint and escort them the rest of the
way to Dubrovnik, where they could catch a chartered plane to
Frankfurt.

Marta and Gaby sat in the bar of the Ero. At a nearby table, Arthur
spoke with Hampton, and Marta heard every word. Arthur was asking Hampton to come, but the Brit declined. He was smart. He didn't
want to leave the city with the sitting ducks. Marta couldn't blame
him. Gaby made nervous chat. There wouldn't be time to stop at
Marta's shelter and pick up belongings. Marta would have to make a
list, and Gaby could mail her things later. But Marta had no list. She
had no precious possessions, nothing to pack or bring. She would

now become the perfect refugee, nothing to her name but the clothes on her back.

"How did you know Arthur Cape was here?" she asked Gaby. "I never told you."

"Hassan told me."

"You're lying." Marta observed Arthur out of the corner of her eye. "You cooked this up with George Markovic."

Gaby stared a long time without answering. Marta could see the connections now. Mose Silber was in it, too.

In the end, Gaby shrugged her shoulders. "Your name is on the death list, too, Marta. It's not just Dubravka."

"That death list is nothing new. Why didn't you get us out of here months ago?"

Her friend looked at her with incredulity. "What a pain in the ass you are, Marta!"

Marta smacked her hand down on the table. "I'm not going till you answer my questions!"

Gaby blurted it out. "Hassan needed you! He needed someone with your knowledge of Mostar and your language skills. Someone he could trust. But things have changed now. Your sister has made you a liability."

Marta felt a constriction in her throat. She had worshiped the man.

Gaby said, "Kreischler has no credibility now in West Mostar." She peered through the front windows of the hotel. "And as long as you are in his office, someone who has actively cooperated with East Mostar police against Vela, he will have none. It's that simple."

Marta got up. She couldn't listen to this anymore. Hassan had his realpolitik. She had what was left of her life. She sat beside Arthur, hooking an arm through one of his. Hampton had a wry smile on his lips. "I don't imagine you *slept.*"

"Don't embarrass me, Eric," said Arthur. "Are you coming or not?"

Hampton gave Marta a sad smile. "On the contrary, I mean to stay.

The official lie about Mostar has been exposed. Warlords control the city. Kreischler is a prisoner. The EU mission is a sham."

"*Sense* will never publish it."

Hampton laughed. "Of course not, Arthur. They don't give a damn. Now, listen. I've got something to say to you."

"Oh Christ."

Hampton laughed. "I came half a continent to say goodbye to you, so you're damn well going to listen."

Arthur crossed his arms and waited.

"Please don't take this the wrong way, but I've never really considered you a journalist."

"So you've told me."

Marta interrupted. "Of course he's a journalist. What are you talking about?"

Hampton's eyebrows went up. "It's no insult, my dear. It's a fact. He knows it himself. He always ran his facts through some deeply subjective machine that I never understood but always enjoyed. I'm the one who got you hired, Arthur. Did you know that?"

Arthur said that he hadn't known.

"I've never regretted it either. But what I want to say is this. It might be time for you to learn the bloody trade."

Arthur grinned. "No, Eric. I'm getting out, too."

This announcement pained the older man, Marta saw.

"No, that's just it. I forbid it. This is not an art. It's not a profession. It's a trade. You learn it. You master it. And you hold it. And it's something quite precious. America is leaving us, Arthur. She is disappearing. I don't know why, but it's not my mission to save her. It may well be yours. You have the passport. That's part of your job, though I don't think you know it."

Arthur's face had gone red. His eyes were shining. "You're the best," he said.

Hampton resisted the emotion. "That's not necessary, is it?" He looked around him, surveying the hangovers in the Ero bar.

"Twenty-three years as a correspondent. The entire world really. And Mostar is where it ends. Total irrelevance. Two cities at the edge of nowhere. I believe this is where I have been heading all my life. Don't you?"

A dark blue sedan pulled up outside, and the three of them went to meet it. Gaby followed behind. Day burned high in the mountains. The valley sank in shadow. Arthur left her side and went to inspect the remains of his Opel, baked to a dusty black, a potato left too long in a campfire. Marta called him back, and his name bounced among the destroyed buildings of the DMZ lying in abandonment just beyond the scorched front fender of his car. Within the ruins, nothing stirred. Two birds, distant black specks, circled the eastern peaks. She was glad to have Arthur's gun. Tucked inside her woolen coat, it made her feel more secure, almost as good as Arthur's pocket cross hanging around her neck, or her headscarf, which she retied behind her neck.

The dog caught a few last sticks, then leapt with a bark into the backseat of the jeep.

Dubravka got out of the back of the sedan. A member of the Spanish battalion in a light blue beret guided her by the elbow to the jeep. She wore a hooded blue sweatshirt and gray sweatpants. The soldier helped her into the back of the jeep, and she sat beside the dog, gazing westward. She removed her hood, and Marta saw that she had shaved off her gorgeous mane, every last strand. Their eyes met, and the truth passed between them. Together, they were fleeing death. Marta went to her.

"They made me wear this crap," said Dubravka in a cracked, exhausted voice. She looked as if she hadn't slept in weeks.

She remained a beauty, Marta thought, something more ancient now apparent, a quality never glimpsed before. The almond shape of her face, the perfection of that form, recalled faces on mosaics that Marta had seen in the Roman buildings of the coast, in the chapel in

Diocletian's palace in Split. She might have been a princess of Trebizond, bride to a sultan.

Arthur belted himself into the driver's seat, and Marta slid into the back with her sister. Gaby covered their laps with blankets. "Hide beneath these once you hit the highway. It'll be safer."

Hampton reached up and shook Arthur's hand. Gaby spoke to the Spanish officer in the beret, asking one last time for an assurance that the road would be safe. Marta watched the man nod his head, but a certain quality in his neck and back, a deficit of confidence in the pitch of the shoulders, made her wonder if anyone in the city, at any given point, could offer more than a prayer to those who traveled the roads without armor.

She caressed her dog's silken ears. Arthur turned around in his seat and took her hand.

"It's not so far," he said.

Marta touched his cheek. "Drive fast, please."

Arthur kissed the knuckles of her hand. He put one hand on the steering wheel and another on the stick. He fired the engine. Gaby pulled reflecting shades over her eyes. Dubravka laid her head against her sister's shoulder.

"Next stop Akkazienstrasse," said Arthur. He popped the clutch, and the jeep shot forward, squealing around the side of the hotel, hitting Kolodvorska at a dead run. Tree branches shook in the wind. Light rose in the eastern sky.

THIRTY-SEVEN

H E REACHED THE CHECKPOINT beside the Hit Department Store and braked. To his right, rising beyond the Hit, were the slopes of West Mostar, Vela's country. UN troops waved him through. He wheeled the jeep around the checkpoint and drove east down the slope toward the river, past a mosque of eggshell white. The minaret had broken and toppled headfirst into the earth. The road ended at the Pioneer Bridge, and on the far side of the bridge lay East Mostar, the way out. Arthur eased the jeep up the ramp.

"Arthur." In the rearview, Marta's eyes darted to the left. Three armed men had stepped from the ruins of the DMZ. All wore green fatigues. One had shaved, one had a beard, and one wore a scarf over the lower half of his face and stayed in the shadows.

Arthur fished the Administrator's letter from a pocket. Before he could hand it over, the man with the beard said in English, waving a finger, "No passage today. Turn around, please."

Arthur said, "Orders of the European Administration. You want to see my papers or just step aside? I'm in a hurry."

He gunned the engine. The foremost of the men put his hand on the rim of the driver-side door. There was a lassitude about the gesture, a show of easy informality. He took the letter and tried to read it.

"German," he said in English. "I don't read German."

"It says to let us pass."

"Bad times in Mostar, brother. No passage across the bridge today. I am sorry."

He handed the letter back to Arthur, who replied, "If you don't let us pass, there will be trouble for you."

Arthur displayed his press credentials. The first man snapped his fingers, demanding identification from everyone. Arthur lifted the UN-PROFOR necklace from around his neck and rummaged in his coat for a passport. He watched Marta in the rearview mirror. She showed her EU Administration credentials. The men became impatient. Marta explained in Bosnian that her sister had no credentials. They were citizens of East Mostar. The men consulted, and the one wearing the scarf pointed at Marta's throat.

He asked about the string around her neck. She deflected the question. She said a name; her half-brother, thought Arthur, the one who had emigrated to America. Did they know him? Arthur could almost understand her words. We are in this together, she might have been saying. We have suffered and endured on the same side. Why bother us? Why not let us go on our way? There's our city right over there, just across the water. Two of the men seemed to agree. The beardless one flipped through the credentials in his hands, passed them to his bearded companion, who nodded. These two men waited for the approval of the third. He stepped forward, and when he spoke, it was in English.

"I know who you are," he said. "The two whores. The daughters of Baba Yaga. That one fucked Vela until he threw her out." He aimed the barrel of his gun at Dubravka. "And that one is fucking this Americano. One of Hassan's girls told me she wears a cross around her neck." He shifted the barrel of the run to Marta. "Let's have a look."

Marta refused. The man's dark eyes burned in crevices and seams of brown. He called out an order in his own language, this time in impatience, and the younger man pointed at Marta's throat. She plucked the laminated yellow card out of her shirt.

"A cross," the younger man said. "So what, Mamdo? She's a Mostarian. Doesn't mean anything."

"It's everything." He leveled his weapon at them. "This is not Mostar anymore. This is East Mostar, and we don't wear crosses here."

It was an odd moment for Arthur to understand finally something about an object that had been in his life for as long as he could remember. He had always been around crosses. They had been in churches, on walls, in the Bibles in hotels, on the bumpers of station wagons. He had taken them for granted. When the cross had saved his ass at the East German airport, he had begun to believe that it might have secret powers. In Mostar, though, he saw something else. A cross was a credential. Show it at one border, and the guns lowered. Show it at the next, and they began to blaze. If the men with guns didn't love Jesus, you were dead.

Arthur put the jeep into reverse and slammed its back fender into a wall. The men unslung their Kalashnikovs. He jammed down the clutch, wrenched the steering wheel left, ducked, and hurled the machine forward, right at them. They shrieked and sprang away. The jeep spun back up the slope.

Arthur caught Marta's eyes in the rearview mirror. She was staring at him, speaking without a word. They had two choices now. They could go back to the hotel or they could take their chances on the western roads, Vela's roads. Arthur waited. Marta nodded. There was no going back. Nothing was safe. Arthur honked, blew past the checkpoint beside the Hit Department Store, and headed for the western ridge.

THIRTY-EIGHT

MARTA HELD Dubravka's head in her lap. She placed her hands upon the edges of the hood in which Dubravka hid, and made an effort to believe, for one moment, that she could delve by touch into the interior darkness of her sister's mind. Failing that, she wished for what was gone. She wished to caress her sister's long hair as she had done so many times when Dubravka was little, when she cried at some minuscule disappointment or hurt, or when she was older and sulked over a boy, or during the war, when the bombardment eradicated thought and feeling. In those terrible moments, as if summoning a genie, Marta had run her fingers down the lush, ambivalent trails of her sister's hair and felt the existence of greater, deeper things than mortar shells. But the hair had gone and could no longer summon rapture.

The jeep thumped up the back streets of the western city. Marta studied the left half of her sister's jostled face. What had really happened to Dubravka the night before? She had said nothing. Marta did not think that she ever would. It had been a near thing. She had come close enough to death to be paralyzed by it. The jeep began its ascent to the notch beside Mount Hum. Mostar faded behind, perhaps for the last time in this life, thought Marta. But she had no desire to look back. When she died, she would climb no higher than this ridgeline. There would be no heaven of the prophets. She would come back here, to her little brother, her child, and her father, to the city on the river, another fraught, amazed ghost. The afterlife was a closet, where the dead hung in endless rows.

A truck cranked backward into the road, and Arthur hit the brakes, throwing them forward. The truck stalled. The engine rumbled in the morning air. The driver seemed to study them in his side mirror. Then he got into gear and left the road, heading up the side of Hum with a load of gravel. Arthur popped the clutch of the jeep and pitched it forward down the slope. The city was gone.

They reached the bottom of a dip in the road and started back up a long incline. Arthur shifted twice, and the vehicle sped up. At the top of the incline, they struck a plain. Rock coiled out of the northern hills to the right-hand side of the road, a natural gateway to the flatland. A red-and-white checkerboard symbol had been splashed onto a boulder at the spit end of the spur, painted in slapdash beside a black-stenciled pair of letters, U and N.

To the left of the road, southward, the land lurched down into cliffs. The checkpoint could be seen ahead in the distance, detritus on an arid shelf. Blue berets moved in large numbers between the maintenance hut and the roadblock.

"Thank God," said Arthur. "They must have heard about us."

Marta spoke into her sister's ear. "Blue everywhere," she said.

"Something's wrong," replied Dubravka. "No one should be there. Tell him to turn around now."

Marta blinked in the expanse of light. "What are you talking about? I can see the soldiers myself."

Dubravka pulled the hem of her hood back from her eyes. She sat up. "This is an undisputed road! There's no reason for so many soldiers. Turn around, Arthur!"

The wind blasted her words away. Arthur's head twitched, as if he vaguely heard a voice, but it was too late. The road sloped down into a slight depression and hit a thread of asphalt between sandbags and barbed wire. Arthur pushed the jeep, bouncing through potholes, slowing at the last minute. He dodged a barrier of rocks, zigzagging around, and stopped at a white bar manned by the soldiers. Two dozen or so men milled, glancing at the jeep from the corners of their eyes. Dubravka shook her head. Marta's fear began to rise. On her one visit to this checkpoint, with Hassan, there had been an armored personnel carrier situated across the road from the hut, and the uniforms of the men had been neat, their boots slick and polished. Southward, she saw a curl of dust.

One by one, the sentries began to toss their berets into the sky, onto the ground, away into the breezes. For an instant, the sight was beautiful, light blue birds on the wing in a wasteland.

"Run the bar!" cried Marta.

Blood thrummed in her ears. She could feel the pulses in her hands, at her thighs. She could feel the life inside her.

The dog thought that the hats were a game. She yelped, sprang over the door, out of the car.

Arthur turned in the seat. Their eyes met. He took her hand and seemed to be on the verge of speaking. Gravel crackled at the western end of the checkpoint, and a silver Mercedes van with blue-tinted windows came around a spur of rock. Arthur let go of Marta's hand and reached for his computer bag, where, she knew, he expected to find his gun.

The men kicked the berets in the dust. A group of them huddled around the dog, caressing her back and ears. One stuck his rifle into the car and told Arthur to lift his hands, which Arthur did. Marta decided that she would beg. She would suck their cocks, if that's what they wanted. White Renault trucks skidded into the sand beds beside the checkpoint. Others blocked the road behind the jeep. One man brandished a scoped rifle, as if hunting boar. The silver Mercedes van grumbled toward them over ribbed and creviced asphalt.

Arthur told bad lies. "A convoy is coming here from Medjugorje. Spanish battalion. We were in radio contact."

Someone snickered. A few men gave nervous glances toward the East. "Spanish Battalion is protecting Mostar, dumbshit," said one of them.

"You are interfering with a mission sanctioned by the European Administration," said Arthur, reaching again for the letter. Marta knew it was pointless. They had never been meant to leave the city.

"Fuck all Turk-loving German cunts," she heard someone say.

The silver van stopped at their front fender, on the opposite side of the roadblock. The men lowered their weapons and cleared out of the way. The van's engine idled for a few seconds, then went dead. The side of the vehicle opened with a bang. A hand could be seen, a boot. Branko Velakovic emerged in a cowboy glide, dust slithering in breezes behind him.

Arthur stopped talking. Marta saw that Branko had retained every bit of the wretchedness of the boy she had known, the hungry desperado who chased girls from good families, in search of a home. He had adopted the title of General since then, and though he didn't wear stars or stripes or anything else that might have conferred genuine rank, he carried himself like a man festooned in medals. He always had. In Branko, son of the suicide, there had always been a pretender to thrones. He made his way around the roadblock to the line of sandbags at the immediate left of the jeep. Behind him, his men threw rocks at the maintenance hut. The stone clanked against metal. The dog whined.

Branko ignored Arthur and Dubravka and spoke to Marta first. "I see you," he said, "and I think of the beach at Lumbarda. Do you know that? I have a very vivid memory."

Marta shook her head. "I don't see you at all. You're less than a shadow."

"Seems like so many summers to me, but it was probably just one or two, right? You were definitely there. Hot little bikini."

Vela took off his sunglasses, revealing small, bitter eyes that Marta could not recall ever having seen before.

"It was beautiful there, man." He shook his head. "You people knew how to live. I remember at night you would pull mattresses outside on the porch, and we'd sit and watch the fishing boats and the islands in the sunset. And in the house, didn't your mother have some beautiful movie posters?"

Marta nodded. She did.

"I remember that western. *Play Me the Song of Death.*"

Branko turned his attention to Arthur. "You know, my man, you're a crazy fucker. You even brought back that motherfucking dog!"

Arthur had told Marta of their meeting. Branko seemed genuinely angry to see him again. He seemed insulted.

"It's my choice what I do," said Arthur.

"Mine, too, fucker."

Marta thought of something her brother had once said: two kinds of people—those who have slit a throat with their own hands, those who have not. Vela was no general. He was a murderer. The Memorandum of Understanding meant nothing to him. He ran a hand across his shaven head.

A gun cracked, a second, then echo.

"My men are shooting that bitch of a dog," said Branko. "The Lord gives, and the Lord takes. *Basta.*"

"Mato would be disgusted with you," said Marta.

"Fuck him. He's a dickless American now."

At last, Branko's eyes fell on Dubravka. Until that moment, he'd ignored her, but now he was looking, his face tightening in rage, growing red. He turned his head away and spat in the dust. Marta clutched her sister's arm. Whatever happened, they would not be separated. Marta looked up and saw that Arthur had used that one moment of distraction to search the computer bag in the passenger seat.

"All of you," said Branko. "Get out of the jeep and get into that hut."

Marta understood the options before her, and she chose the one that rose in her throat. She spat in Branko's face. His lips quivered like snakes, but his eyes didn't close. He wiped her spittle with his sleeve.

"My mother always said you were the best of them. You were the catch, she said. You would go out and be something. But she was wrong, the old drunken slit. You're going to end up a dead whore in the road, just like your sister."

Vela nicked his head at his men, and they gathered out of the dust. Gasoline fumes were on the wind. The engines in the white Renault trucks boomed into life. Branko gripped Marta by the hair and wrenched her in a single movement out of the jeep. Her left arm snagged in barbed wire. Her knees landed on top of a sandbag. He ripped the scarf away from her head, reached into her coat, found the gun, and jammed the point of it into her ear. She was pressed against his side, and she could smell him. She could smell his breath and the stench of his humiliation. The sky was blue and endless. She gazed straight up into it and thought of her son.

"You defile this land," Branko said.

She sank her teeth into his wrist, tore her left arm away from the wire, blood spurting down her fingers. She put her hands on the side of the jeep and tried to lift herself off the sandbag. She must get back to her sister. She must get back inside the jeep, and Arthur must drive away. Blood was everywhere. The jeep was not moving. She reached for Dubravka, but her sister had disappeared. She had crawled out of the jeep and was tumbling into the dust at the roadside. She removed her hood, and the crowd of men moaned. She was walking through them, over them, across the berets on the ground, to Branko, who backed away from the sandbags and stared at the vision of her bald skull, staggered by the sight, as if beholding a ghost. He didn't move. She shoved past the men with rifles. The sandbags were too much for her, so she walked back down the alley between them, a dozen yards, to the point where the wire and the sandbags ended, past the first of the white trucks. She was not timid. She knew exactly where she was going. Marta slumped on the top of the sandbag and watched her sister put one foot in front of the other, coming closer now, on the sand bed beside the road, alongside the wire, level with the jeep. Dubravka put both of her hands around the stock of the gun in Branko's hand. She made him lower the gun, kissing the backs of his hands, showering his knuckles with her kisses. Slowly, his grip loosened. Dubravka took the gun away from him and came to Marta on the sandbag and spoke into her ear. The murmuring was soft, like an endearment.

"This is my gift," she said. "Accept it."

Marta wanted to touch her hair, but it was gone, the lobe of her skull, smooth and clean, the skin of an infant, moving away from her. Right before Dubravka got into the silver van, Vela's hand on the nape of her neck, she peered back at Marta, and in the spot where she had been, after the van had gone, Marta believed that she saw two smears of darkness on the air, a scorching of the emptiness, wisping away. Marta screamed her sister's name, the word echoing away into the hills. The dog sniffed the blood on her arms. She felt the void, and she was teetering, losing herself in the rising darkness of the morning. Arthur caught her just as she fell.

EPILOGUE

THAT JUNE, in Berlin, George Markovic turned up again.

"You moved," he said, standing in the corridor of a Kreuz-berg apartment building. Arthur hardened himself.

"I didn't think you'd be able to find us."

George looked perplexed.

"No more adventures," Arthur bluntly said. "I'm sorry. That's how it is."

"You blame me for these troubles?"

Arthur shook his head. "No. Of course not. But it would be better if you left us alone for a while."

"You sound angry," said George.

"It's not that I'm not grateful to you, George. I am. But I'm also nervous."

George put his hands in the pockets of a Levi jacket. He had gained some weight back, but his clothes no longer announced a man of power. The blue jean jacket and the shirt came from the Gap. Arthur couldn't shut the door in his face, and George wouldn't leave. He seemed to study the matter with sympathy.

"I am hard on your nerves, bro?"

"We've spent the last five months in a state of shock," Arthur tried to explain. "You have to understand."

George gave a sigh and a smile. "Okay. I won't stay long."

Marta called from inside the apartment. "We need to go, Arthur. Who is it?"

They had been on their way to pick up Frau Herbst. At ninety-four, the woman still insisted on rigid punctuality. She had asked Arthur to escort her to see the Wrapped Reichstag, and though he no longer lived in her rooms, though Marta and he had moved into their own place, he had agreed to escort the old woman. Anna's Bulgarian artist, Christo, had wrapped the entire building in cloth, and for more than a year, ever since the German parliament had approved the project, the old woman had been complaining about the lunacy of it. How stupid! What a waste of money! A colossal waste, in fact—typical Berlin sensibility run amok. Now, more than anything, she wanted to see it.

Marta came to the door, tying the scarf around her head.

"Oh Lord," she said.

GEORGE HAD NEWS from Mostar. He said this, and Marta's heart began to pound. She didn't wait to hear it. She needed a moment. She hurried into the kitchen quadrant of the studio, ostensibly to brew a batch of Bosnian coffee. It would be her sister. They had found her somewhere. Marta had done enough crying. Those emotions felt like physical wounds, and she could no longer allow them. If she wanted to live, she had to stop grieving for Dubravka. It was like bleeding to death, and she had already lost too much blood. She put water into a saucepan and ignited a flame.

The two men made small talk. "How's Budapest?" Arthur tersely asked.

"Budapest is dead for an honest man. Only Russians now."

"I'm sorry, George."

"You are not alone. I am sorry, too."

Marta ground the beans herself with a hand-hammered metal grinder. She had been looking forward to their excursion. Gray skies had cleared, and the sun sparkled in the trees. She had woken with a sense of fragile comfort.

"What will you do now?" Arthur asked.

"Cosmetician schools in Transylvania."

"Do you know cosmetics?"

George rolled his eyes at the question. Arthur didn't ask him why he had come to Berlin, and Marta was glad. That conversation belonged to her, and when she was ready, she would have it. The dog sniffed at coffee grounds spilled on the floor. She didn't have time to clean them up.

"You look very pretty," George called from the other half of the room. "Is that a new dress?"

"Arthur bought it for me. It matches the scarf."

George's eyes darted away.

"Arthur doesn't like it much either, but he's more polite than you, George."

George shrugged. "What's new?"

The coffee was ready. She dumped the grinds into a metal canister and poured the boiled water on top of them. The soft brown scum rose to the top of the canister. She put everything on a tray and brought it into the room.

"I'm going to go," said Arthur.

Marta was grateful. He had listened enough. He had held her through countless awful nights, when she didn't have the strength to bear everything alone. But now she could. She wanted to.

"I'll meet you," she said to Arthur.

ARTHUR TIED the laces of his nice pair of shoes. Frau Herbst had asked him to dress nicely for this excursion. He should think of their visit to the Reichstag, she advised, as a gallery opening or an opera premier. Marta had put on her new green cotton frock. Until George's arrival, she had been as radiant as the approaching summer. The sadness never left her eyes, of course. The Great Actress had called from Tel Aviv and congratulated her daughter on getting out of hell alive. Marta had agreed with her mother for once. She was out of hell, alive. But hell would be there for the rest of her life. Now and then, if she was lucky, the memory might grow dim.

Arthur checked the clock. He would be late for the old woman. He had a faint tremor of unease. As a reporter, he had hated to be late. He had always arrived early for interviews. Now, for the time being, the interviews had stopped, but he retained the anxiety about coming late to them.

Arthur had left *Sense*. His magazine had been the home of Eric Hampton, and without him it was fatally diminished. Morsch had been furious. He had blamed Hampton for poisoning Arthur against the magazine.

But the chief of correspondents had also said, "After that last thing you wrote, it's probably for the best. What the hell was that anyway? Did anyone request an anniversary piece?"

"I took the initiative."

"Well," Morsch said, sulking, "it wasn't really journalism."

"Well," Arthur said, "according to Hampton, I wasn't really a journalist."

In May, five and a half years after it began, his staff job expired. The benefits lapsed. The checks stopped coming.

Arthur straightened his tie. He was hesitant to go. "You're going to be okay?" he asked Marta.

"I'm going to be fine." Marta and Arthur spoke English together. It had become their language. With every day, she communicated less in German. She still loved Berlin. She loved the German way of life. But the language, her attachment to it, had become inseparable from things that could no longer be loved.

Arthur would have given the world to know Marta's mind at that instant. He wanted to imagine her thoughts exactly, to feel what she felt in her silence, to give himself a share of her sudden joy or endless sorrow or shame or hope. She'd said more than once after their return, in a tentative voice, that one had to admit the possibility of good fortune in this life, too. Wasn't that true? She had asked him the question, and he had told her what he believed. That it was true. In his life, good fortune had come. In most lives, it came, sooner or later, just like evil fortune.

She told him to go without her to the Reichstag. He shouldn't disappoint Frau Herbst, and she needed to be alone with her cousin George. She kissed Arthur on the lips, warm and reassuring. He thought of Bavaria. He remembered trudging through the snowfields below the castle of Mad King Ludwig, the most pathetic hours of his life, returning home by himself, to a Berlin of rain and sleet. But she kissed him twice more on the lips and said that she loved him. She said that she would bring the dog.

Is it Dubravka, George?"

George gave his head the smallest of shakes, not Dubravka. There had been no word from her or about her. "I can sit?"

Marta pulled out a chair for him. George brought news from Hans Kreischler, whom he had met through Gaby, and who now used him from time to time on unofficial errands in the Balkans. George's alleged blood tie to Marta had been his key selling point, he admitted.

"What's the news, George?"

George swallowed. "I don't know exactly what this means," he said. "I'm almost afraid to tell you."

A wild fear rose in her. George put a hand on one of hers. The rubble had at last been cleared from Alekse Santica 14, and beneath it, as expected, the work crew found her father and the bodies of ten others who had died in the explosion. They had excavated every last corner of the ruin. Kreischler himself had overseen the job, and when they reported their findings, he became impatient. He had told them to look again. There had to be a child, he insisted, but they had scoured the basement and found no one else. No other human being had been with Marta's father, who was badly decomposed. There was no doubt in anyone's mind. Osman Lazic had not died with his grandson.

Marta could see a patch of sky out the window of the studio apartment. She felt herself flying into it.

"He could be alive," George said.

God is great, she thought.

ARTHUR STOOD with Frau Herbst in front of the billowing shape of the Reichstag, in front of its outline, and Frau Herbst told him about the night that another Bulgarian, a man named Dimitrov, had set fire to it. Bulgarians had a thing about the Reichstag, she guessed. She had been thirty-three years old then, and a good-looking woman. She was fucking lots of different men, she told him, never mind her husband. One of them was a lawyer who insisted that Dimitrov started the fire, and she had never ceased to believe that Dimitrov had done the job. Later, it came out that it was a show trial. Dimitrov was a Communist. The Nazis had needed a scapegoat. But she'd never liked the look of that Dimitrov, an anarchist and an arsonist, a Bulgarian. She had been in a taxi, and the radio said that the building was on fire. Her husband, the Jewish gambler, had been away in Zurich, and she had been in the taxi with one of her gigolos. The gigolo had wanted to go see the burning, but she didn't care to. They were on their way to a party at the Hardenbergs'. That was her memory. Or had she been in Zurich? Now she couldn't precisely remember. Had the man in the car been her husband? The Reichstag burst her memory open. The years after that had been good and bad. She had won the concession for her Italian shoe store—though, of course, she revealed to Arthur, the concession came in 1939, one year after the previous owner, a Jew, had been kicked out, one year after the Kristallnacht pogrom. The story got worse and worse.

"What is that stuff?" Frau Herbst asked him, touching the material. Arm in arm, they had strolled up to the Reichstag, which was hidden from their eyes by a rough silvery cloth.

"Aluminum-coated polypropylene, I'm told."

"Is it flammable?"

She had a world-historical twinkle in her eye. They strolled away from the building, through crowds, turning around every so often to see how the building changed from distance to distance. At that hour of the early afternoon, the wrapping took on a bluish hue, one shade deeper than the color of the clear Berlin sky, the approximate tint, he thought, of United Nations helmets on the floor of the Zagreb Airport before dawn. People gathered in masses on the long lawn before the building. There were clowns and buskers and bursts of light from hundreds of popping cameras. Carts sold wurst and *pommes frites.* People picnicked, dozed in the grass, mesmerized by the thing, talking dreamily about it, venturing close to touch the fabric as if it were the hide of a unicorn. The farther away Arthur and the old woman walked from the Reichstag, the more mysterious and beautiful the wrapping became. The folds rippled in the breeze. The blue of the grand tarp caught tints of green from the trees and altered in hue when the day grew dark—or bright—by even the slightest fraction. The tarp could be heard, the whipping of vast folds, the tugging of the polypropylene away from the stone of the object beneath. The four horns of the Reichstag reared in masque.

Arthur gazed a long time at the passing away of momentary hues and colors in the Reichstag depths. What was this work of art meant to suggest? A mirror? A present? A bomb in a package, he thought, left on the floor of an airline terminal. He began searching the crowd for Marta, wondering how much time would elapse before he panicked. He had a brief, fanciful notion that Christo should wrap Mostar.

He should place an entire destroyed city inside one of his packages. What would people do? Would they slaughter one another to the last man? Or would they join forces and tear themselves out?

He asked Frau Herbst what she thought the building symbolized.

"Bulgarian impudence!"

The tarp whipped in breezes. The day drifted westward, darkening. The blue of the cloth deepened, catching the first tint of sunset.

Anna and her cousin Günther happened by. The moment began in awkwardness, but Anna had renounced Arthur and knew how to convey this renunciation in every word and gesture. Günther asked after Philippa, and Arthur gave him the news. She had been accepted into the seminary. She had met a man who wanted to move to the Bering Strait.

"Very cold," he said with a rueful smile. "Berlin weather is much better."

"So what does it mean, Anna? This thing?"

Anna turned to him. "Mean?"

"Aren't I allowed to ask?"

"What does a city *mean,* Arthur?"

He didn't want to get into a fight.

"What is underneath that tarp?" she asked him.

Frau Herbst blew out a sigh of scorn. "The goddamned Reichstag! What else?"

"Are you sure it's the Reichstag in there, you old bitch?" Anna cried. "Maybe Christo has made the building vanish. Have you looked beneath the tarpaulin? How do you know that the Reichstag will still be there when it lifts? Maybe something else is in there, waiting to get out. Maybe when it gets out, it will eat us all alive!" She addressed a last word to Arthur. "At the very least, I hope that it eats you."

She strode away, trailed by an apologetic Günther. Arthur became sad. He had not behaved well toward Anna. He had not behaved well toward anyone until he brought Marta back from Mostar. That was the end of the Blue Age, the beginning of something new, Year One,

Stunde Null. The prospect made him nervous. The more he gazed at the Reichstag, the more he saw Anna's threat. The thing was not docile. It was hungry. It was a bomb, stuffed with imaginary cities, like nails and glass, waiting to be detonated. Any second, it would burst. It would shatter through the admiring crowd, cutting down flesh with a shrapnel of towers, bridges, graveyards, and homes.

The sun was dying. The cloth turned golden red, kicking and squirming and trembling in the wind. The tension was excruciating. The tarp flapped like a vast bird.

MARTA FOUND ARTHUR in the last of the dusk. The dog leapt after her. She told him what George had said.

"I want to leave tomorrow," she said.

"Back to Mostar?"

"Yes."

Arthur was afraid, but her eyes couldn't be denied. A small homeless boy was wandering the back roads of hell. Alive or dead, he must be found. The dog rolled in the grass. The old woman snored. A moon rose over Berlin. The cloth of the Reichstag went silver in the twilight, and the city sank into its folds, in a river of shadow. The city seemed to crouch around them in the darkness. Marta put her arms around Arthur.

"All right," he said. "In the morning, we'll head back south."

CHRONOLOGY

1914   Habsburg Archduke Franz Ferdinand is assassinated by a Bosnian Serb radical, Gavrilo Princip, in Sarajevo, an event that leads indirectly to the beginning of the First World War.

1918   The founding of the Kingdom of Serbs, Croats, and Slovenes, a state carved out of the collapsing Austro-Hungarian and Ottoman empires. This will become the first Yugoslavia, a highly unstable creation, like many of the countries created after World War I.

1918   End of World War I. Treaty of Versailles, which officially recognizes the new Yugoslav state and penalizes Germany heavily for its involvement in the war.

1929   The Kingdom of Serbs, Croats, and Slovenes officially becomes Yugoslavia.

1933   Adolf Hitler comes to power in Germany.

1939   Germany invades Poland, and World War II begins.

1941   Yugoslav government signs a pact with Hitler and is immediately overthrown. Nazis bomb Belgrade, and the Germans invade and occupy Yugoslavia. Birth of Croatian Fascist puppet state, which begins to murder Serbs and Jews. Birth of the Partisan resistance movement, Communist cadres under Josip Broz, also known as Tito, and the Serbian royalist resistance movement. Under the occupation, these three entities fight a civil war against one another.

1944   Belgrade is liberated by Soviet Red Army Yugoslav Partisans under Tito.

1945   End of World War II. Germany and its capital, Berlin, are occupied by the Allied Powers, split between the Soviet Union on one side and Britain, France, and the United States on the other. This divide will eventually solidify during the Cold War.

1948   Tito breaks with Stalin, marking the start of a unique geopolitical path for the Yugoslav Communist state.

1961   Construction of the Berlin Wall, making two separate cities: East Berlin and West Berlin.

1980   Death of Tito.

1985   Mikhail Gorbachev becomes the leader of the Soviet Union.

1987   Rise of Slobodan Milosevic, a former Communist apparatchik who uses inflamed Serbian nationalism to vault to power. He becomes the driving engine of the disintegration of Yugoslavia.

1989   November 9: Fall of the Berlin Wall.
       November-December: Collapse of Communist governments throughout Eastern Europe.

1990   Unification of East and West Germany on October 3.

1991   June: Croatia and Slovenia declare their independence from Yugoslavia. The Slovenes fight a brief war with the Yugoslav army, but the Serbian government of Milosevic allows them to leave the union.
       July: The war with Croatia begins.
       December: Germany decides to unilaterally recognize Slovenia and Croatia as independent states.

1992   January: Cease-fire in Croatia.
       March: Fighting breaks out in Bosnia.
       April: United States and European Union recognize the independence of Slovenia, Croatia, and Bosnia.
       May: Serbs begin the siege of Sarajevo. War breaks out in Mostar between Serbs on one side, Bosnian Muslims and Croats on the other. Muslims and Croats go to war. Fighting breaks out in Mostar.

1993   November 9: Croat gunners destroy the Old Bridge.

1994   February: End of Muslim-Croat war. A mortar shell hits a market in Sarajevo, killing sixty-eight people. Cease-fire in Mostar.
       March: Muslims and Croats agree to form a federation. Peace ostensibly comes to Mostar.
       July: European Administration takes over Mostar.

1995   Serbs overrun the city of Srebrenica, formerly declared a safe haven by the United Nations.

August: NATO begins to bombard the Serb armies.

December: The signing of the Dayton Peace Agreement marks the end of the Bosnian War.

ACKNOWLEDGMENTS

Thanks to my superb editor Cindy Spiegel, who believed in this book before it was even written and gave immeasurable help along the way; to Susan Petersen Kennedy, for believing in the work; to my agent and friend Gordon Kato; to Chris Knutsen, for his efforts; and to Jessica Firger; to Debra, for everything, for room, patience, intelligence, for the love to let me loose with my imagination; Joe, who had to do without his dad on many a Saturday and Sunday; and long-suffering Ruby, who finally gets her due; to my parents, who never failed to ask me how it was going; to Tolbert and Sharilyn, for giving me Taos, and my sister Molly, for giving me confidence; to Mark and Reba, tireless supporters; to my dear friend Goran Brajdic, who guided me in thought and judgment as I wrote about his destroyed homeland; to Svetlana Brajdic and Maja Brajdic, and the Green family, who introduced me to them; to Sanja Kazazic, Richard Medic, and Zoran Mandelbaum for their invaluable insights into the life and death of the city of Mostar; to Stephen Long and Meliha Nametak-Long; to Ivan and Mira Brajdic, Zoran and Jadranka Mitic, and Sveto Markotic; to Sanja Mahac; and so many other citizens of the former Yugoslavia who gave of their time, hospitality, and insight; to Hans

Koschnik, for an interview long ago; to my aunts Margaret Helen, Virginia, Dian, and Genene; to Jennifer Breheny, for her editorial brilliance; to James Hynes, for comments and conversations on everything from Balkan wars to Buffy the Vampire Slayer; to Anthony Schneider; to Amanda Davis, who heard me complain about this book countless times and always listened with her wry smile—I miss her so much; to Scott and Sofia Karambis; to Morley Safer and Steven Reiner, who gave me gainful employment; to Doug Wright, for years of friendship and a second life on the stage; to Murphy Martin, who always believed; to Lesley Israel; to Adrienne Nassau; to Gilles Pequeux; to Christian Caryl, for giving us a home in Berlin; to John Tagliabue and Robin Knight, constant inspirations; to Michael Klipstein, Melissa Drier and Erwin Leber, Lise Schmitz, Jan-Peter Boening, Margarete Winter, Martina Rellin and Stefan Pucks, Katie Hafner, Andreas Meier, Joe and Iwona Trenkner, *die Familie* Homola, and all of those other Berliners who inspired this book. Thanks as well to Jeff Schneider at Vassar and Tony Abbott and Scott Denham at Davidson for giving me the chance to read early drafts of the book in public. Finally, like a lot of people who care about this part of the world, I am indebted to the writings of Timothy Garton Ash.

John Marks, author of *The Wall*, is a producer at CBS for *60 Minutes* and a former reporter for *U.S. News & World Report*, for which he was also Berlin bureau chief. He has written for the *New York Times* and the *Wall Street Journal*, among other publications, and holds an MFA from the Writers' Workshop at the University of Iowa. Marks lives in Brooklyn, New York.